The Guernsey G

Mary Wood was born in Maidstone, Kent, and brought up in Claybrooke, Leicestershire. Born one of fifteen children to a middle-class mother and an East End barrow boy, Mary's family were poor but rich in love. This encouraged her to develop a natural empathy with the less fortunate and a fascination with social history. In 1989 Mary was inspired to pen her first novel and she is now a full-time novelist.

Mary welcomes interaction with readers and invites you to subscribe to her website where you can contact her, receive regular newsletters and follow links to meet her on Facebook and Twitter: www.authormarywood.com

BY MARY WOOD

The Breckton series

To Catch a Dream
An Unbreakable Bond
Tomorrow Brings Sorrow
Time Passes Time

The Generation War saga

All I Have to Give
In Their Mother's Footsteps

The Girls Who Went to War series

The Forgotten Daughter
The Abandoned Daughter
The Wronged Daughter
The Brave Daughters

The Jam Factory series

The Jam Factory Girls
Secrets of the Jam Factory Girls
The Jam Factory Girls Fight Back

The Orphanage Girls series

The Orphanage Girls
The Orphanage Girls Reunited
The Orphanage Girls Come Home

The Guernsey Girls series

The Guernsey Girls
The Guernsey Girls Go to War
The Guernsey Girls Find Peace

Stand-alone novels

Proud of You
Brighter Days Ahead
The Street Orphans

The Guernsey Girls Find Peace

Mary Wood

PAN BOOKS

First published 2024 by Pan Books
an imprint of Pan Macmillan
The Smithson, 6 Briset Street, London EC1M 5NR
EU representative: Macmillan Publishers Ireland Ltd, 1st Floor,
The Liffey Trust Centre, 117–126 Sheriff Street Upper,
Dublin 1, D01 YC43
Associated companies throughout the world
www.panmacmillan.com

ISBN 978-1-0350-3684-4

1 3 5 7 9 8 6 4 2

A CIP catalogue record for this book is available from the British Library.

Typeset by Palimpsest Book Production Ltd, Falkirk, Stirlingshire
Printed and bound by CPI Group (UK) Ltd, Croydon, CR0 4YY

Visit **www.panmacmillan.com** to read more about all our books
and to buy them. You will also find features, author interviews and
news of any author events, and you can sign up for e-newsletters
so that you're always first to hear about our new releases.

For my dear friend Valerie Clifton.
By my side for twenty-five years. Love you x

PART ONE

A Time For Change

Chapter One

Olivia

February 1941

Olivia's bruised body ached, but the pain couldn't match her broken heart. Cradled in her friend Annie's arms, Olivia felt safe for the first time in months.

'We can do this, Olivia. We can.'

Annie said these words over and over, but still Olivia wept. How could they ever get over losing their loved ones?

'Olivia, we must open our hearts to our new life. Karl will be waiting for yer. He needs to see a smiling mummy return to him. When he sees the photo of you and Hendrick in his bedroom, he kisses you both goodnight and says, "Smiley Mummy".'

'Oh, Annie, you never told me that before.'

'We had so little time to say anything in our calls, luv, we could only pass the coded messages. But oh, Olivia, we have a lot to tell each other. Not today, though. We must make today a happy day for you and for little Karl.'

Olivia nodded. She knew in her heart that it would be a happy day, but she wondered if her beloved Karl would even recognize her?

The last time they'd been together was not long after his

second birthday in May last year, just before she'd had to return to Guernsey for what was meant to be two weeks to help in her father's bank but turned out to be nine months of living hell, when Germany invaded her beloved island and she'd been unable to leave.

Now, she wasn't returning to London as the vibrant young woman she'd been. Her shoulder-length hair no longer shone with health but hung limp and lifeless. Her dark eyes were sunken and still showed the signs of bruising caused by her German captors during her imprisonment and brutal rape.

Olivia shuddered as the memory of what had happened inside the rotten, foul-smelling cell came back to her. She closed her eyes tightly, trying to dispel the disgusting scene of the hateful Gunter, and German soldier after German soldier violating her body . . .

Spittle came to her mouth, and she wanted to splatter Gunter's face with it. A Nazi through and through, Gunter had betrayed her husband Hendrick, his former childhood friend.

But later that night Stefan, another of Hendrick's friends, had rescued her.

Although a German soldier too, Stefan hated the Nazi regime. And while serving on the Isle of Guernsey he had fallen in love with Olivia's dear friend Daphne.

Never had she felt more relieved than when Stefan took her to a remote beach and she saw Daphne waiting with Guernsey's port master, Bertie, who was set to smuggle all three of them off the island.

Annie held her closer as if she sensed her thoughts were giving her pain, and in a gentle voice told her, 'Nearly there, luv. Nearly home.'

Home was a three-storey dwelling in Bethnal Green, in

4

the east of London, arranged into four flats which Annie had inherited after the death of her sister Janey. There were so many memories for them etched into every brick in every wall of the house that Olivia wondered if these would chisel away at any effort they made to carve a new life there.

Would she, Annie and Daphne ever find peace? How could they with the war still raging?

What must it be like for Daphne, seeing London for the first time as she stared out of the car windows – not at the busy vibrant city that Olivia had known, but the bomb-weary one with broken, smouldering buildings?

And how her heart must hurt as she thought of Stefan taken prisoner the moment they had landed in England.

And would Bertie settle here?

He'd brought them safely to the mainland and now he sat in the front seat of Annie's police sergeant's car. As a seafaring man who'd only ever known life in Guernsey, would he be able to make a life here?

Olivia thought about how their life would now include Beth, Annie's little niece, and Ian, an East End lad who Annie had rescued when his home had been bombed and his family killed.

Olivia had to believe everything would come right in the end, that their hearts would heal from the pain of those they'd lost. And as they did, maybe they would become a new family.

Bertie would have his son, Joe, to help him. Joe had got away from Guernsey weeks ago with Henry, a Guernsey soldier who had been in hiding until Joe could get him to safety.

With some trepidation Olivia asked, 'Annie, what happened to Joe and Henry? Did they make it to England and find you?'

Bertie turned to look at Annie. 'I'd hardly dared to ask, Annie. Is me Joe with you?'

'No, Bertie, he made it safely, but when recovered, he signed up and joined the army. Henry had to report back to his regiment and Joe volunteered for the same unit. They're stationed together, somewhere in the Far East.'

Bertie dropped his head for a moment, but then looked up, pride shining from his face for his son. 'Then we're sure to win this bloody war! They'll kill every rotten German they come across!'

Olivia felt a smile play on her lips as she thought that this was the spirit she must hook on to.

Bertie grinned at her. 'That's the way, Olivia. I saw your determined look of old flash across your face. You keep remembering what your Hendrick is doing to that end too. And with the four of them – my Joe, Annie's Ricky, your Hendrick and Henry – all fighting for the same thing, it will happen.'

'You know about Hendrick?' Annie looked astonished.

Olivia, who'd sat up straight now, told her, 'Yes, I told Bertie on the boat coming over how Hendrick, although vilified by the Guernsey people for being a German and work- ing for the German government as a translator and interpreter, had really been on our side. The secrets he passed to me to pass on to you were a massive help to the British government in deciding strategies.'

Annie's police sergeant, who'd driven Annie down to Southampton to collect them, spoke for the first time. 'I don't think you should be talking about that, girls. Remember we are at war and walls, and even cars, have ears.'

'Sorry, Sarge, you're right.' Annie turned to Olivia. 'We must maintain the secrecy of what we and Hendrick did. If we fall into talking about it loosely, we may trip up and increase the danger that Hendrick is in.'

'Yes, of course. Sorry, love. Neither Bertie nor Daphne will say anything.'

Daphne nodded her affirmation. Her face showed the grief she felt at being separated from Stefan. She'd been devastated when he was arrested as she'd imagined the British would treat him as a hero for rescuing them all from Guernsey, not take him as a prisoner of war.

Annie saying, 'Look, we're here! Oh, Olivia, Loes is at the door with the kids!' changed the atmosphere as they all looked out of the window.

There, in the arms of his lovely Nanny Loes, a young Dutch girl who'd come to work for them in Guernsey but who had stayed here in London when Olivia returned to the island, was her little Karl. Only he was bigger than she remembered him. He was no longer a baby, but a little boy who had Hendrick's features, with the same unruly fair hair and deep blue eyes.

As soon as the car stopped Olivia jumped out and ran towards them, her face fixed with a bright smile.

Loes bent and set Karl down on the path, telling him, 'Go to Mummy, Karl, run!'

Then he was in her arms and part of her world came right as he clung to her before pulling back and looking at her with a quizzical look. 'Mummy?'

'Yes, my darling, it's me. I'm home, my darling boy.'

'Mummy not leave?'

'No, never, ever again.' But as she said the words a strange feeling came over her. She shook it off as she called out, 'Come here, Loes. Oh, Loes, thank you.'

And then she clung to Loes as best she could as Karl

turned in her arms and put a chubby arm around Loes's neck too.

'Loes, Nanny.'

'She is, my darling, and now you have Mummy too.'

'Mummy and Nanny.'

'Yes, yes. Oh, Karl, I love you.'

'Daddy?'

'Daddy will be home one day.'

'Nanny says Daddy will stop the bombs.'

'He will, but it will take time, my little one.'

A laughing Annie prompted them forward. 'Let's all go in then, eh? Come on, Karl, mate, let Mummy get inside.'

Loes turned at Annie's words and went into her arms. 'It's good you are back, Annie; the walls will quieten now.'

Olivia pursed her lips and knitted her eyebrows together in a quizzical frown.

It was Loes who enlightened her after greeting Daphne and Bertie, both of whom she knew well from her life on the island of Guernsey before war fully broke out. 'It's just that Annie is the rock that holds us all together, Olivia. Without her, my nightmares return.'

As Olivia went to reply, an unruly-looking dog came bounding out of the house barking his head off, but he quietened when an adorable boy of around ten years of age appeared and reprimanded it.

'Ruffles, behave! These are family, mate.'

'You're Ian, I take it? Pleased to meet you, love.'

'What happened to your face?'

'Oh, these bruises are my war wounds.' Olivia managed to laugh and marvelled that Karl hadn't said anything, though he had traced his fingers over her face.

'You're a hero . . . Annie told me.'

'Ian, let us all get in, luv,' Annie put in. 'And where did Ruffles come from?'

Loes explained. 'He found his way back to the farm after bolting when the bomb exploded, and then seemed to be pining that much that Mr West, the man who told me he is acting as farm manager, thought he would be better with Ian. And so he found us through the solicitor and rang me. I told him it would be fine to bring him, thinking it would be good for the children, especially Ian.'

'Oh, that's wonderful . . . Oh, Ruffles, you mongrel! It's good to see yer, mate.'

The scruffy-looking dog wagged his tail.

Olivia had listened to this conversation with increasing pain. They were talking about the farm in Kent that had been owned by Rose, another dear friend, where everyone had been staying for a Christmas break and where so many of their loved ones had died. Thank God her little Karl, Annie, Loes and Beth had survived.

'Right, Annie,' her sergeant was now saying. 'You get everyone sorted and have a rest as I don't want you to report to the station until you're good and ready.'

'Thanks, Sarge.'

'Well now.' The sergeant put his cap back a bit further on his head and scratched the few strands of hair he had left. 'Olivia, I haven't told you yet as it all seemed too soon, but I must now. I informed the War Office that I was picking you up, and they told me to tell you that you're to report there in the next few days. They want to talk to you about Guernsey and, well, they may have a few more questions for you.'

Olivia nodded. She'd expected this. After all, she was still considered to be an agent of theirs. 'I will, just as soon as I feel ready.'

'Don't leave it too many days, they can get impatient. They haven't the time to give understanding, only to do all they can to stop Hitler, and you could be part of that. Not that I know how, but you may have some missing threads of knowledge that they don't have.'

'I promise. I will go tomorrow or the next day.'

The sergeant took a piece of paper from his top pocket. 'This is your contact and who you must report to. Read it and then burn it.'

Olivia sighed as she took the paper. It seemed her world of espionage was set to continue.

'I'll be off now, Annie. I'll see everything's in order at the station and then get back home for a rest.'

'Ta for everything, Sarge. I couldn't have managed without yer.'

'I'm always 'ere for you, Annie, luv. Now you take care, and the rest of you too. You 'ave an 'ealing process to go through.'

It felt reassuring to hear the cockney accent. Annie used to speak in the same way, but gradually she had dropped most of it and begun to sound her aitches, probably due to the influence of Lucy, Annie's contact at the War Office.

Inside, the house looked almost the same as Olivia remembered, except she saw that the stairs leading to the cellar, which had been converted to a flat since she'd left, were covered with linoleum rather than being bare stone.

Annie saying that she would put the kettle on brought Cissy to mind. Dear Cissy would have given her such a hug and been a great comfort to her. She could hear her saying in her northern accent, 'Eeh, lass, you're home.'

But was she? Would any place ever be home again?

'Mummy?'

Looking down into Karl's upturned face, Olivia smiled. *Yes, this is home. My darling son has made it his, and so will I.* This idea was reinforced when Beth looked at her tentatively with her big brown eyes. 'Aunty Annie says you'll be aunty to me too.'

'I will, little one,' she told Beth.

'But me mum is still me mum.'

'Always, darling.'

'Me mum's with the angels.'

'Yes, she's smiling down on you.'

'She's with Angie and Angie's with the angels.'

'Angie?'

Loes cut in. 'Yes, your mum is with Angie. Now, let Aunty Olivia sit down, dear.'

'Aunty Olivee can sit next to me.'

Olivia smiled. But then a loud protest took her attention. 'No! Mummy sit with me!'

'Now, now, Karl, you can sit one side and Beth the other.'

'My mummy!'

Beth's bottom lip trembled. Annie scooped her up. 'Now, little one, we've to help all our guests to settle, haven't we? Say hello to Daphne. Daphne looks after Aunty Olivia. And this is Bertie. Bertie is a boatman who brought Aunty Olivia and Daphne back home to us.'

Beth dropped her head in shyness.

Bertie grinned at her, his twinkly blue eyes showing love and friendship. His hand stroked his long grey beard. 'I'm grateful to be here with you, Beth, and Karl, and your Aunty Annie, and Aunty Olivee as you called her. I think we'll get along just fine. Though you'll have to take me to where there's water, as I'm used to being surrounded by the sea.'

Beth grinned back at him and put out her hand to touch

his beard. 'The canal's over there.' She pointed towards the window.

'That'll do fine.' Bertie raised his eyes to Annie. 'I brought me stash with me, Annie, so maybe I'll be able to buy a canal boat? I made a good bit of money by turning a blind eye to antics that went on in the middle of the night with them as wanted to smuggle. And blind eyes come at a price.' Bertie winked.

Annie laughed and Olivia felt glad to see the first real smile since Stefan had been taken away curl Daphne's lips.

'Drink your tea and then we'll have to sort things out as to where we're all going to sleep.'

A silence fell.

Ian saved the day by acting with an emotional maturity much older than his appearance suggested. 'Come on, everyone, Ruffles wants a walk. I'm taking him to the canal, and you can all come.'

'The canal, is it? Well, I'm game for that,' Bertie said, and before long there was just herself, Daphne and Annie.

Olivia glanced at her dear friend. 'Well, I'm back, Annie.'

'You are, luv, and yer have Daphne here too. Together with Loes and Bertie, we're strong and can face anything. Remember that.'

Olivia felt for the first time that Annie was right. They could begin a new life, but she would never stop hoping that her old life with her beloved Hendrick would one day be given back to her. And that they could be a family with little Karl, something they'd never experienced for longer than a few days.

Chapter Two

Annie

Annie didn't feel as strong as her words, but she remembered those of the housekeeper of Wallington Manor, the home of Olivia's aunt and uncle, where she'd worked as a maid and where she and Olivia had become unlikely friends: 'Busy hands and busy minds don't leave time to pine.'

Well, she could apply that logic to not having time to sink into despair.

'Right, as Bertie said, it's up to us to sort out the sleeping arrangements. Olivia, what if you share Janey's flat on the top floor with me?'

Olivia nodded.

'We'd be a help to each other if we stay close and there's plenty of room up there. We could get the sarge and one of the old-time coppers to help Bertie change the double bed for two singles for us. Karl and Ian shared a room after Ian arrived and Loes has an adjoining room to that, with Beth taking the third bedroom. Though Loes has been coming into my bed at nights.'

Olivia interrupted. 'No, don't change the double bed. I'd rather sleep with you, Annie.'

Annie smiled. 'I'm glad you said that, Olivia. I've gained comfort from Loes doing that.'

Daphne surprised them then, just as Annie was about to say that she could sleep in what used to be Cissy's flat, when she asked, 'Is there room for another bed in with Loes? Only Loes and I got on well when we were in service together in Olivia's father's house . . . That's if Loes won't mind sharing.'

Annie nodded. 'There is and that's a good idea, as Loes won't feel lonely then. We'll sort it all out.'

Daphne looked relieved. Annie understood. None of them wanted to be alone during the night hours. 'And so that leaves Bertie. He could have Cissy's old flat then. It's all ready, everywhere is. I changed all the beds in the whole house as soon as I got home from the farm – made everything as fresh as I could.'

As she said this, Annie saw Olivia look around Mum's living room where they sat discussing her plans and, as if answering an unspoken thought, Annie said, 'Me mum's still here, Olivia, I can feel her presence.'

'Yes, and it's lovely to do so. I love this room. Vera is in its very fabric, smiling away from her wheelchair. Or sitting at the table playing cards with Cissy, or playing the piano . . . Oh, Annie.'

Annie sat down beside her on the brown sofa that now sagged a little and took hold of Olivia's hand. Daphne squashed in on the other side of her. For the umpteenth time, Annie repeated, 'We can do this. We can.'

It was Daphne who said, 'We can, Annie, we can. If we stand together, we can.'

Feeling the pressure of Olivia's and Daphne's hands on hers steadied Annie. No matter how many times she said they could cope, she didn't really feel she could. But she was making herself do so. Making herself function normally and trying to see the future as a new challenge – one that would be so different from the past.

It seemed to steady Olivia too, as for the first time she made a plan for the future. 'You're right, Daphne, and as soon as I can I'll go to see Daddy's solicitor and find out how I stand financially, as we'll all need to contribute to helping run our new home.'

Daphne chipped in then. 'And I'll have to find a job as I need to help pay our way too.'

'Yes, we all have a lot to do before we can go forward. I've to sort out Lilly's, my late mother-in-law's, house too.'

A silence fell over them.

Olivia broke it as she said in a gentle voice, 'Tell us all that happened, to Lilly, and . . . dear Cissy, and everyone, Annie. It may be good to get it off your chest, love.'

'I'll try.'

As she told of the awful tragedy of the stray bomb hitting the farm and how she'd lost her sister Janey and so many of her family and friends in the resulting fire, and of Jimmy, her brother-in-law, being shot while his regiment was engaged in battle, but surviving and returning home a deranged man, of him murdering Angie, the youngest of his and Janey's children and sister to Beth, and how he was now in a secure prison for life, Annie shuddered at memories she'd tried hard to suppress.

'Oh, God! Dear Annie, how you and Loes have managed to carry on is a miracle. You are so brave. But you know, I never really liked Jimmy, nor did I trust him, not after he cheated on you with Janey when you and he were engaged to be married.'

'Oh, I long ago forgave him and Janey all of that, luv. In

the end, it did me a favour as it brought Ricky into me life. Janey, however, didn't deserve all that happened, nor to die as she did.' Annie's heart dropped in her chest. The world she'd tried to make right was revisiting her. She gasped at the impact of the pain of never seeing her sister again, but then more hurt and anguish piled on top.

'And – and for me Ricky to be in that awful place tears at me heart.' Once more she drew in a deep breath as a familiar pain shot through her.

Olivia's hand came onto her back. 'You've been through so much, Annie. We all have. But now, you must remember what you always told Janey. That she was to cry her pain out of her body and not to store it and allow it to drive her mad as it did in the beginning. You're right, we can get through it all, but only by talking to each other about everything and weeping out the pain it has given us.'

As she said this, Olivia let out a huge sob.

Annie turned to take her into her arms as tears streamed down her own face. As they clung to one another, Daphne's arms came around them both. She didn't speak, but gently held them.

At last, they calmed. Olivia's head lay on Annie's shoulders and Annie, feeling strangely lighter and once more able to cope, rested her head on Olivia's.

'We needed that, Annie.' Olivia sniffed and wiped her eyes before asking, 'So, you said in all of that that you know where Ricky is?'

'Yes. The Red Cross informed me that he's a POW in Stalag XX1-D, in Poznań, Poland . . . I have a locket. Look. Rose, Jimmy's mum, gave it to me not long before she died. She said to keep Ricky's notes in it – he wrote to me on scraps of paper . . . I keep them close to me heart.'

16

'It's beautiful. And real silver, and so big. Just look at the filigree on the front . . . No, don't open it. Save that for another time. We're coming to a calm place now, and that will set us off again. Are you all right, Daphne?'

'I am. I feel the pain you're both going through and it makes my troubles seem nothing. I just hope me mum's all right.'

'Let's hope she got over to the Isle of Sark to be with her relatives.'

'It's the not knowing. But yes, Olivia, I do have that hope.'

Sniffling, Annie decided that getting on with everything that needed doing was the best policy. She untangled herself and stood up. 'Right. We'll make this flat of Mum's the place we can all congregate. We'll have another sofa brought up from the basement and turn Mum's bedroom into a playroom for the kids as we'll need Mum's bed upstairs for you, Daphne.'

Now she was making plans again, Annie could feel her strength coming back. 'You know, thinking about it, that's the only bed we need to move if you're going to sleep with me, Olivia. I reckon we could do that ourselves, girls, and not bother the sarge today.'

The next half an hour was full of giggles as Annie found the huge spanner that was used to dismantle the bed and they set about the task of stripping it down.

The frame and headboard were no problem – they each took pieces of it up until it was all in place and put together – but when it came to moving the horsehair mattress, they found it had a mind of its own. It sagged in the middle as they tried to manoeuvre it through the door and up the stairs, and almost had them tumbling down, before pinning Olivia to the wall.

For a moment they could do nothing as they collapsed in laughter, until Olivia begged them to release her.

Finally, they had it in place and were making it up for Daphne.

When all was accomplished, Annie felt exhausted, but her spirits had lifted, and she could see the others felt better too.

'Well, I could do with a bath after that!'

Olivia was pouring with sweat.

'Now yer know what it feels like to be a maid, Olivia,' Annie told her. 'You're one of us, for sure!'

For a moment Annie could have bitten the words back. Olivia looked hurt by them, but then a smile appeared on her face, which broke into a giggle. 'Friend of maids and one of them . . . I'm honoured.'

Annie was left wondering where such words had come from as Olivia had never treated her, or Daphne, like they were her maids. Despite Olivia taking it so well, she was upset with herself.

With the three of them busying themselves with getting a meal ready, Annie gradually forgot about it as they peeled potatoes, chopped carrots and sliced onions. These they added to the tin of sliced spam that Annie had found in the cupboard.

'I see Loes managed to get a loaf of bread, but there's no fresh meat on the cold slab, so that must have eluded her. You need to be strong when out shopping as the women elbow the weaker ones out of the queue. Though why they do I don't know as, like all East Enders, they share what they have anyway. They just can't bear not getting any of whatever's going.'

'It was the same in Guernsey. If ever there was a queue for food, it was rarely an orderly one,' Daphne put in.

'It's a big part of my work as a copper, keeping order. I hate it. It's like we're making things more difficult for everyone by policing them so rigidly . . . You know, the last time I saw my Ricky, I was trying to get cardboard to help the folk around the poorer end to black out their windows. Since then, the sarge has ordered a more softly, softly approach and that seems to be working.'

'Annie, will there be an air raid tonight?'

Daphne's voice sounded afraid.

The same had been on Annie's mind as they'd moved the beds and made things ready. She hadn't the heart to tell them both then that most nights were spent in the air-raid shelter, but now seemed the time to broach the subject.

'There could well be, luv. But don't worry, once we have the hash simmering away, I'll take you to the shelter to show you how comfy it is. We only go down once the sirens sound now, whereas Mum . . . well, all of them, used to sleep down there all night every night.'

Soon they had a hash of sorts bubbling away. Annie transferred it to a large casserole dish and put it into the oven. 'There, that'll be ready for our tea . . . dinner tonight.'

Saying this, Annie realized how she'd slipped back into calling the evening meal her tea, when she knew that Olivia would only think of it as dinner.

Both Olivia and Daphne were amazed by the shelter that Janey had had put into the garden. Annie told them, 'The bunks are all ready for us. I've put clean sheets on them too. I had to go into Cissy's stock of linen and what Loes brought from the apartment, so you'll recognize most of it, Olivia.'

19

Olivia didn't look too sure as she glanced around the dome-shaped shelter at the bunk beds lining each wall and the chamber pots all shining clean and stacked up in the corner.

'We bring flasks of hot tea down and when Mum . . . well, Mum used to set us off singing, making it a jolly old time. Oh, and we've an oil stove that keeps us warm.'

'I never realized it was this big!'

'Some of them aren't, Daphne, but Janey insisted we should all be comfortable down here. Well, them, mainly, as I always worked nights.'

'You won't now, will you, Annie?'

'I may have to, Olivia. But don't worry, you'll all be together. Even the little ones, either in the flat or down here. You'll be a comfort for one another.'

Olivia didn't look convinced and Annie thought how damaged and broken they all were.

'What about if we need the loo, Annie?' Daphne eyed the chamber pots. 'I mean, with Bertie in here as well.'

'That curtained-off area gives a bit of privacy, but it's needs must and believe me, as bombs are going off around you, your modesty is the least of your concerns.' Annie didn't tell them that she'd never slept down here with a man present but she knew she must reassure them – a task that was tearing at her heart as her own demons visited her, giving her pictures of her lost ones snuggling down in the bunk beds. Their laughter echoing off the walls, their voices singing out the old-time music hall songs, their spirit never dampened, though their fear was always visible in their eyes.

'Look, me darlin's, I know this is all new to yer as after the initial air raid that hailed the invasion of your island, you haven't experienced a bombing raid, but there's no alternative.

Many have shunned the shelters and been blown out of their beds and to kingdom come. None of us want that. We've suffered enough . . . What I'm trying to say is, please find the courage to take this as normal. Do it in a cheerful way so as not to upset the kids, and make the most of it . . . Olivia, this is where your singing could come in. You could make it a fun adventure getting us all singing . . . Please, girls . . .'

Olivia responded. She turned towards Annie. 'Well, I think it's a wonderful venue – the acoustics may not be good, but hey ho, we'll sing Hitler off the map just as my choir tried to do back in Guernsey!'

Daphne giggled. 'I'm looking forward to it now. It'll be like when we were young children and camped in the garden – scary, but a great adventure!'

Annie relaxed and smiled. 'That's the spirit. The kind of attitude that has got Londoners through so far. And, like them, nothing can daunt us Guernsey Girls!'

They all giggled, then Daphne, who hadn't heard the expression which had been used as a code name for Annie's and Olivia's message passing, said, 'I love that! As that is what we are, including you, Annie, as you love the island and are loved by its people.'

'Ta, luv. I do have a deep affinity with Guernsey and the folk of the island and one day we'll all go back there, I promise . . . Listen, I thought I heard the door go, someone has returned. We'd better go up else they'll think we've abandoned them.'

Over dinner, Annie told the others of the plans they'd put in place and the drill for the air-raid shelter.

Loes smiled broadly at Daphne. 'I like the idea of us being in the same room. We will look after one another.'

Daphne grinned back as she nodded her agreement while chewing away on a mouthful of the delicious hash. But Bertie wasn't sure about it all.

'Would I be better in the basement flat, Annie, rather than the one across the hall? I mean, I know that sounds presumptuous, but I reckon I'd be safe down there from any air raids and it'll mean you ladies can keep your dignity, and I can have me own home with my own front door.'

Annie caught Olivia's expression, willing her to say yes. And it did seem to be a good solution to Annie too. She couldn't think why she hadn't thought about it. If the house took a direct hit, Bertie would be safe in the foundations of the house.

'Yes, that's a great idea, Bertie. Though you'll be welcome in the shelter if ever you want to go down.'

'And any of you are welcome to keep me company . . . Annie, I can't thank you enough for offering me a home until I can get back to me own home in Guernsey. I'll try not to be any trouble and will contribute a rent for my flat and look after meself. I've done that for a long time and can carry on doing so. I won't be a burden to you, love.'

'You could never be that, Bertie. But I want yer to be as happy as yer can be in the circumstances, and to live yer life how you want to. I know yer ain't used to having womenfolk around, so none of us will bother yer, but we will be here for yer, love.'

Bertie nodded. His eyes filled with tears.

All four girls hugged him. Daphne went further. 'You've always been a father figure on the island, Bertie. At times scaring the lives out of us, but mostly showing us kindness as we grew up. It'll be good to know you're living close to us.'

Bertie got out a grubby-looking hankie, but then, he'd

had no chance to wash anything and hadn't clean ones to use. He dabbed his eyes.

Annie thought it time to lighten things up. 'Right, let me, as your landlord, show you your new flat. Loes will have to move her things out for you.'

'Oh, I can do that quickly, Annie. I don't have a lot . . . And I too need to thank you. You have cared for me and got me through some of the worst times.'

Once more, Annie found herself being hugged. She had to swallow hard. Ever since losing so many of her loved ones, when shown love, she wanted to cry.

'Well, everyone, that's us all sorted, and only using two of the flats available to us.' She giggled. 'I might let the other two out and become a property tycoon!'

They all looked nonplussed. 'Ha, I'm only having yer on – trying to lift the moment. I won't be doing that . . . well, not for money. But there are so many homeless now, it does seem wrong to have rooms and not offer them.'

Although they all agreed, Annie could see they were a little afraid that she might do it. She understood. Damaged as they were, they weren't ready to accept others into their lives. They still needed to cling on tightly to those they had. She gave a wry smile. They even wanted to sleep within feet of each other!

But she didn't mind. If that was what it took to help them all to heal, being a bit crushed for space was a small price to pay.

'Right, there's pots to wash and kids to get to bed and then clothes and the basement to sort out. Let's busy ourselves, me darlin's.'

There were giggles now as they scurried to complete a task each. Loes opted for getting the little ones settled, and encouraging Ian to have his wash and don his pyjamas, while the rest of them went down the cellar steps with Bertie.

Bertie clasped his hands together as he looked around. His smile showed his appreciation, as did his low whistle. 'It's huge! Three bedrooms, a large living room and a kitchen, all to myself!'

'Well, it runs the length and breadth of the whole house, love. The only thing is that we'll need one of those sofas up in me mum's old flat, and that you have to climb the stairs into the backyard where you'll find the lav, and a tin bath hanging on the wall next to it, which is easily dragged down here.'

'It's perfect, and I don't mind either of them things happening. It's a lot lighter than I thought as well. Thanks again, Annie.'

'You're welcome. I owe yer a debt, mate, for bringing Olivia and Daphne safely to me. You took a massive risk and could have been shot.' Knowing this was emotive, Annie quickly went on to say, 'Right, first thing is to pull out the trunk of clothes that Loes brought with her from your father's flat, Olivia. It's in the small bedroom. Then we can sort out some clothes for you all.'

When at last they left Bertie to his home, making sure he had everything he needed to make himself a drink and some supper if he wanted to, Annie managed to find enough cocoa powder to make the four of them a drink.

'It looks a bit like ditch water as we ain't got much milk, but it's hot and comforting.'

They sat in silence for a while, in what Annie would always think of as Janey's flat. Before the war, the view from this third storey was beautiful at night with lights twinkling in the

24

water of the canal and the sky peppered with stars. With the blackouts, there was nothing to look at.

But then, with the fire crackling in the grate and just having the lamp on, it was cosy. The chatter was relaxed and, Annie thought, happy too. She hadn't thought that word would ever feature in her life again, but yes, there was a happiness in the room as anxieties and heartache had been shelved for a while and the four of them were bravely facing the future.

Chapter Three

Olivia

They hadn't been in bed long when the siren blasted the air. Olivia sat bolt upright, threw the covers back and dashed towards the children's bedroom.

'Blimey, slow down, luv.'

Olivia could tell that Annie was trying to sound reassuring as she continued, 'The last thing you need to do is to frighten the kids. We've plenty of time. The siren goes off when the Luftwaffe are spotted coming towards us and that can be half an hour away. Make it a game for them. A sort of midnight camping in the garden, as Daphne likened it to.'

With her heart pounding and memories of her only experience of a bombing raid vivid in her mind, Olivia tried to steady herself as she recalled scenes of devastation at her beloved St Peter Port. The burning tomato lorries, the bodies, the fires – they all screamed at her and increased her fear.

'Olivia, it's all right, luv. We'll be safe. Go and get the children and grab one of their story books too. I'll see if—'

Whatever Annie was going to say went into an almighty blast that shook the house. Their bedroom door flung open. Daphne and Loes appeared, their faces a mask of terror.

26

Annie jumped out of bed and took charge. 'Loes, you've done this a dozen or more times. Come on, help Olivia to get the children. Daphne, grab something warm for everyone to put on. I'll go and get a kettle full of water. We have cocoa and tea in the shelter. Hurry!'

Everyone followed Annie's direction and before they knew it, they were braving the outside world. A world that to Olivia seemed to be one sheet of flames that lit up the sky as if it was daylight.

The droning noise of many aircraft assaulted her ears. But then she heard a different sound as a whining, failing engine came nearer and nearer.

Olivia looked up into the skies. An aeroplane was tumbling from the sky towards them.

Screams around her hastened her footsteps.

Annie's voice penetrated the uproar. 'Everyone, hold on to each other in a line and follow me. We must get into the shelter. Hurry!'

When they were all inside Annie pulled the blackout curtain across the door, leaving them in what felt like a black hole. The children whimpered. Ian's voice soothed. 'Nothing to worry over, Annie'll soon 'ave a light in 'ere.'

As if to order, Annie struck a match and lit the oil lamp hanging from the ceiling. Olivia released the breath she'd held and her stomach muscles unknotted as the dome they were in suddenly felt like a haven to her.

Until the crash that sounded nearby.

'That was over the canal.'

As Annie said this, she dimmed the lamp and made for the door. 'I'll be back in a moment. No one come out, I just need to see if the pilot needs help.'

'I'll come, Annie. If he's German, I can talk to him.'

Annie didn't protest.

Outside was like stepping into a burning hell. Olivia glanced at the house, saw it was intact, and inwardly sighed with relief. But across the road a house fire lit the night air, and the tail of a German aircraft was sticking up from the canal.

When they reached it and Olivia gazed down, she marvelled at how the canal, sparkling with the light of the many fires around it, carried on rippling its way around the German plane.

'I'll check the house first, Olivia. Our own are more important.'

Seeing a huddle of people, Annie went over to them. Olivia heard her shout, 'Is everyone out?'

'Yes, luv. We were making for our shelter, but the back wall collapsed, and we couldn't get to it. We thought out 'ere in the road would be our best option. We can spy the buggers, and what they're up to from 'ere.'

'Make yer way over to our shelter, Ron. Take everyone, you'll all fit in. Not to sleep, but you'll get a seat on the bed. Tell the girls in there that I sent yer.'

'Ta, Annie. Yer ain't on-duty, are yer?'

'No, but once a copper, always a copper, so I had to come out and see if I was needed. I'm going to see if that pilot made it. If he did, I might bring him to the shelter. But don't worry, he's just another human following orders. If he needs help, we must give it.'

'Yer right. 'E's someone's son, no doubt, so we'll care for 'im for his mum and dad.'

'That's the spirit, Ron.'

Olivia smiled at Ron, obviously, by his age, the granddad of the brood he stood with, but she hadn't expected any kindness towards any of Hendrick's fellow men. It gave her hope for Stefan in the POW camp, and Hendrick, if ever he made it to England too.

Making their way down to the towpath was easy as the fires lit their way. Listening for the sound of anyone calling out was not so, as the noise around them hadn't lessened.

To Olivia, it was horrific, and she wondered about the resilience of the people who lived here. People like Ron, comforting his family and talking to Annie as if they were in the middle of any ordinary night, and yet his house was burning down in front of him.

Taking courage from Annie, Olivia did as she was directed and carefully trod the reeds, calling out in German, '*Ist jemand da?*' – Is there anyone there?

A movement near to her feet made her jump, then a hand grabbed her ankle. She stiffened with fear, calling out, 'Annie, help me!'

'*Ich werde dir nichts tun. Hilf mir!*'

In German, Olivia told him, 'We will help you, but you must throw any weapons you have into the water!'

His reply, understood by Olivia, was, 'No, you take my gun. It will keep you safe.'

Annie had made her way to them. 'Is he hurt badly?'

The pilot told Olivia his legs didn't seem to want to work.

'Tell him that I am a police officer, and it is my duty to inform him that he is now a prisoner of war. As such he will be treated well. And tell him that I need him to hand over any weapon and then I will call for an ambulance for him.'

With this done, Annie pulled out her two-way radio and spoke into it. Within seconds someone answered. Olivia heard Annie tell them of the German pilot.

'Right, that's done. You can tell him that help's on its way, and that we'll stay with him until it arrives.'

It wasn't long before the sound of ringing bells vied with the explosions and aeroplanes ducking and diving overhead.

When the stretcher bearers were in sight, the pilot grabbed Olivia's hand. His whispered, 'Come with me,' held the fear of a child facing the darkness.

When Olivia told Annie what his plea was, Annie shook her head. 'It won't be allowed, luv. Tell him there will be interpreters at the hospital and that he mustn't be afraid, he will be treated according to his rank.'

Olivia thought of their own prisoners of war and the stories Hendrick had told her of near starvation. This pilot was lucky. His war was over.

The bunker seemed packed to the rafters as Ron, his daughter, who Annie introduced as Rita, and her three children, Freddie, Mike and Philip, were sat on the edge of one of the beds.

All six children, including her little Karl, had terror in their eyes.

Annie turned to her usual fallback cure. 'I'll get the kettle boiling. We've cocoa for all, but the kids can have a mug each first as we haven't many mugs.'

Loes put in, 'And there's still some of those oat biscuits that I baked and put into a tin the last time we were down here. Do you remember, Karl?'

'I do!' Beth piped up. 'I liked them, Loes!'

They all grinned at Beth, who seemed the only youngster not fazed by all that was going on.

When the children had drunk their cocoa, cooled by adding cold water from a huge jug Annie had brought in with her, Olivia could see their eyes getting heavy.

30

'Right, who's for a story?'

To cries of 'Me! Me!', Olivia scooped up Karl and sat in the place he'd occupied, hugging him to her. With the gesture her heart stopped racing and she felt in charge of her fear. The other children snuggled up around her.

She began to read from *Farmer Boy* by Laura Ingalls Wilder and by the time she reached the line *Down a long road through the woods, a little boy trudged to school* . . . Karl and Beth were asleep, Karl with his head on her shoulder and Beth resting her head on her lap. Olivia closed her eyes and allowed the joy of this to seep through her.

'Tell us some more, miss.'

This eager request came from Freddie, who Olivia had learned was the youngest of Rita's family and the same age as Ian. His freckled face melted her heart. When he lowered his head a little, golden curls fell around his face.

'I will, but let us get these little ones tucked up, shall we?'

Loes helped with this.

Soon all the youngsters were sleeping and tucked up in a top-and-tail fashion in the largest of the beds.

Ron looked over at Annie. 'What facilities 'ave yer got in 'ere, Annie? Only Rita's in need of the lav.'

With this, Olivia realized how much she needed to pee too. Feeling hot inside at the thought of what she must do, and seeing how it didn't seem to worry these folk, once more brought home to her that for all she'd suffered, it was nothing to what these Londoners had been put through. Taking a deep breath, she said, 'I'll come behind the curtain with you, Rita. I can't hold it much longer.' And though dying inside with embarrassment, she made herself do what had to be done.

* * *

Olivia was no longer the rich girl, the cossetted daughter of her wonderful father, but still she had far more than most.

Once tucked up in bed, Olivia thought about her aunt and uncle, of Wallington Manor in Cornwall. How she wished she knew how they were. She hadn't seen them since 1936, when they'd visited her and Annie in the hospital after the tragic train crash. And the last letter from them was just before the German invasion of Guernsey. She didn't even know if they were still alive!

Sleep eluded her as her thoughts went to Hendrick. Had he made it to Switzerland where he'd told her in that last fateful message he would make for? Was he safe?

If only she could hear from him.

Her heart ached for news, and her body ached for his touch. Just to be held in his arms.

Turning over for the umpteenth time, a hand found hers. She knew it was Annie. Had she lain awake worrying about her Ricky?

Squeezing Annie's hand, she hoped it sent a message that she understood.

The next morning, it became apparent that Ron and Rita couldn't return to their family home. There was nothing left of the large house but gaping holes, twisted, blackened beams and smouldering ashes.

Olivia held Rita as she broke down in tears. Ron shook his head. 'We ain't much for going to one of them hostels, Annie. I don't know what we're goin' to do.'

'I have two flats empty here, Ron. Me mum's and Cissy's.'

'Yer mean yer'd let one of them to us, girl?'

'Of course I would. I think Cissy's would be best. It

has two bedrooms . . . Oh, this is Bertie that I told you about . . .'

Bertie had come up the stairs. 'Is everyone all right? That was some air raid. Had me shaking in me shoes.'

'We are . . . well, alive anyway,' Annie told him and then introduced her neighbours, telling him what had happened to them. 'They lost everything . . . I've offered them the flat that I offered you, Bertie.'

Ron piped up, 'And we'll very gratefully take it, Annie. Ta, girl . . . Pleased to meet yer, Bertie. I 'eard last night 'ow yer saved Annie's mates.'

Bertie smiled. 'Well, it's down to us all to do our bit . . . I'm pleased to meet you too, but sorry the circumstances are such. If you need any help, let me know . . . Oh, and if you don't want to be huddled in the shelter with the ladies, Ron, you're welcome to keep a bedroom in me flat. It's safe down there.'

'Ta, I'll see what Rita 'as to say about that when we can 'ave a chat. At the moment, we've a lot to sort out, and would be glad of yer 'elp to see whether we can salvage anything before the scavengers move in. And I reckon a visit to the Red Cross is on the agenda too, then we need to get some shopping in.'

Bertie shook his head. 'The salvage I can help with, but I don't know where to start with your other problems. Mind, I'm going to look at buying a motor today, so I'll be more help to you then.'

Olivia smiled. She could see the two men were going to get on and thought that would be lovely for Bertie, who had faced the prospect of a houseful of women.

Annie, as always, took charge, taking these thoughts from her as she said, 'Right, I'm sure everything will be sorted.

Now, let me show you the flat.' The keys she took from a hook on the wall of the hall, where they were all kept, rattled in the silence that had fallen.

As the door opened, Olivia could almost feel Cissy's presence. Cissy had so loved her little home. Much of the furniture had come from Olivia's father's flat and seeing this and having Cissy so vivid in her mind struck pain into Olivia's heart.

How she even functioned with so much grief weighing her down Olivia didn't know. She only knew that as long as Annie could do it, she would too.

It was later that day when Ron and his family and Bertie were engaged in bringing what they could save from Ron and Rita's home, which didn't look much, that Olivia decided to start to get her own affairs in order and go to see her father's solicitor.

She was glad of Annie saying she would come along too.

'I've to drop into the police station first, Olivia. Then I can drive us out west to see your solicitor.'

When they reached the police station in Stepney, Annie said, 'Come in with me, luv. The sarge'll be pleased to see yer again.'

'Pleased' didn't describe the sergeant as he bawled at Annie to come into his office the moment he caught sight of her.

Annie glanced at Olivia with a look that told of her trepidation.

'You need to come in too, Olivia. I have a very serious matter to take up with you both.' The sergeant's face looked as grim as he sounded.

As soon as his office door shut behind them, he said, 'Right, Annie. You're in trouble, girl!'

'But—'

'Sit down, both of you.'

With her stomach churning as different scenarios occurred to Olivia for why the sergeant could be so angry, she took the seat he offered, and looked around her. There didn't seem to be any privacy for the sergeant or anyone as this was a corner of the office that his officers worked in. Nor was there much natural light. Three of the partition walls had glass around the top half and the window to the outside looked out at another wall.

'I have to tell you, Annie, that you are in danger of being arrested for possibly sheltering an enemy. A very serious offence.'

Olivia's heart dropped. Annie looked aghast and, like her, obviously hadn't a clue what was going on.

'I think you referred to her as Loes? How long has she resided with you? Why wasn't her presence reported to me? Annie, I'm shocked by this. You're one of my best officers. What on earth possessed you, girl?'

'Loes isn't an enemy!'

'That ain't for you to decide, Annie. You – all of us – must report all foreign nationals for assessment immediately.' Turning to Olivia, he said, 'And you will be culpable in this if proven, but in the meantime, you must report to the War Office this afternoon, Olivia . . . And you too, Annie. I've been ringing your phone all morning to tell you of this new arrangement, Annie . . . Now, I'll send Betty around to your house to pick up Loes.'

'No, Sarge, please. Let me and Olivia bring her in to you . . . Please, Sarge . . . And, I'm sorry. Truly sorry. But the

Netherlands have been neutral; they didn't want to be occupied and fought valiantly not to be. But just because they lost that doesn't make them the enemy. Besides, Loes has lived in Guernsey for the past four years. She is Jewish and knows nothing of what has happened to her family. Her imagination gives her nightmares. And their fate, whatever it is, would have been hers had she not left the Netherlands and gone to work for Olivia!'

'All these things are mitigating circumstances, Annie, but did you know that Loes's father is German?'

Olivia heard Annie's gasp. It matched her own. She had no idea of this. How could Loes not have told her?

'And what I say to you, Annie, is that as upholders of the law, our job is to follow it to the letter and ensure it is being followed by others.'

'But I always have! Those in Britain from the Netherlands weren't on the list of aliens to be reported, Sarge. I knew nothing of the nationality of Loes's father . . . What will happen to her, Sarge?'

He let out a sigh and shuffled some papers on his desk.

'Her being a Jew makes her vulnerable in more ways than one. And it is more likely to lead to her being sent to a camp . . . Now, don't look like that! This wouldn't be decided on the basis of her being a Jew, but for her own safety. It would put her out of reach of the clutches of those who would exploit her position – her own father, even, who we now know is collaborating with the Nazis.'

Olivia's blood ran cold. Would her Hendrick be classed as having done this? Would his work as an interpreter and translator for the Nazis make him an enemy, even though he used his position to transmit vital information to help

Britain? And what of Loes? Why hadn't she mentioned her father once war broke out?

But then she remembered that the information that came to her about Loes from the agency who'd supplied her was that she'd been brought up by her mother alone. No mention of her father.

'May I say something?' she now asked.

'Yes. And I hope it's something that can be of help.' For the first time, the sergeant looked kindly.

'I don't think Loes knows her father.' Olivia related what had been written about Loes by the agency and how there was no mention of her father. 'At the time I assumed he must have died when she was very young, but it wasn't my business, nor did it have any bearing on whether she was suitable for the position of nanny, so I didn't ask questions about it and it was never mentioned.'

'Do you still have a copy of what you were told? It would help your and Annie's case if you can prove that you had no idea about Loes's German connections. Especially as it was the agency who passed the information to the authorities. They supplied their original interview paper. Loes had listed her father as German. Though she did state that she hadn't lived with him since being a five-year-old. They said that they only rediscovered her information when your payments to them stopped coming. They understood the reason, of course, but it prompted them to open a new file on Loes so that they could claim back payments in the future.'

'I haven't got a copy of what they told me about Loes, all my papers are still in Guernsey, but the agency must have. Surely, they would have kept all correspondence between us? I can assure you it didn't contain anything like this.'

'Yes, I imagine they will have. They seem very efficient. They probably didn't think it relevant at the time. It would greatly help your case, and Annie's, if we can show that you didn't know and if Loes will state that she hadn't told you . . . This is why I must insist that I send Betty to bring Loes in. If I allow you both to do that, it could compromise your position as it could be argued that you begged her to say that she'd never told you.'

Olivia could see this. She looked over at Annie and saw the fear in her eyes. She understood the seriousness of their situation and that Annie would be torn by the sergeant's last statement between her loyalty to Loes and her need to protect their position. But she also knew that she had to show Annie she was on her side and in agreement. 'Annie, the sergeant is right.'

That simple statement visibly relaxed Annie.

'I agree, Olivia, but what will Loes think of us? It feels like we are betraying her.'

It was the sergeant who answered. 'I will have Betty tell her the reason why I would not let you bring her in yourself, Annie.'

'Ta, Sarge. Will we be able to see her?'

'Only in my presence with Betty attending too. I'll just go and have a word with Betty now.'

When he'd left the office Annie reached out. Olivia took her hand.

'Betty's a good sort and a great police officer, Olivia. She can be a bit short with people, but she's my friend and knows how much I think of Loes. She'll treat her with kindness, I'm sure of that.'

Olivia could only nod. She found her whole body was trembling. First Stefan and now Loes. What would be the fate of her beloved Hendrick if he made it to England? Somehow, she must stop him. *If only he would contact me! But then, he doesn't know that I have escaped Guernsey.* Taking a deep breath, she clung on to Annie's hand as if it was a lifesaver. *Please, God, help us.*

Chapter Four

Annie

Although the sergeant's office was familiar to Annie, at this moment it felt alien, as if she no longer belonged there as a policewoman because now she was an accused.

The mess the sergeant's desk was always in, and the way the picture of the King always hung at a slight angle, weren't part and parcel of her everyday – not today, for now they seemed as if she'd never seen them before.

But despite her own feelings of fear, the anxiety she knew Olivia was experiencing made Annie pull herself up. She must stay strong. 'It'll be all right, Olivia. We didn't know. Loes will tell them that.'

Brave words, but her own mind was in turmoil. Shielding anyone considered to be an enemy of the state was a very serious offence. Would they be believed when they said they didn't know?

'But why didn't she tell us? Tell me?'

'She probably never thought it relevant.'

'But it was relevant after war broke out!'

'Yes, and by then Loes had witnessed what you went through over Hendrick being German, and may have thought that would increase if your nanny was found to be half German too! I'm sure she wouldn't have realized the danger she was putting us in.'

'No. You're right. Loes often spoke of her mum and sister. She feared for them. And I never questioned her as to her father. I accepted that she was brought up by her mother and would tell me what happened to her father if she wanted to. I've never been one to pry but, oh, I wish I had asked her now.'

'What would yer have done, luv? What *could* yer have done? I reckon it's best yer didn't know. You'd never have given her up to the authorities.'

'Would you have, Annie?'

'Yes. I would have talked to Loes about her and my position and asked her to declare herself as having links to the enemy. Yer see, there's different categories given to foreign nationals from alien states. They range from "A" – being high risk and having to be interned – to "C" – being low risk and allowed to continue to live in the community. I reckon Loes would be a low C. Though I can't see it being looked on favourably now, as she didn't declare her status.'

'Oh, Annie. What can we do?'

'I'll speak to me sergeant when he comes back. He'll tell us our and Loes's position. Try not to worry. I'm sure we'll be believed. Though that copy of what yer were told by the agency will be vital. As will Loes swearing she never told us.'

The door opening stopped further speculation.

'Right, when Loes is brought in, she won't see you both but be taken straight to the cells to await the War Office investigation and interview. I've told Betty to tell her how this came to light and that you both have been informed but

41

won't be allowed to contact her until she has been seen by the officials.'

'She will be all right, won't she, Sarge? I mean, Loes ain't a risk to the state, is she?'

The sergeant's eyebrows rose and his lips clamped together.

'Think about it, Annie. If her family in the Netherlands are detained in a camp where we understand Jews are taken once their country is invaded by the Nazis, then those who need information could blackmail Loes by saying that doing as they ask will keep her family safe and threaten consequences if she doesn't play ball.'

'But . . .'

Olivia's movement next to her stopped Annie going further. Olivia was staring in disbelief at the sergeant.

'There are no "buts", Annie. We are at war . . . Our enemies are capable of anything in their quest to conquer us. Now, I want you to go straight to the War Office. Have you got your car, Annie?'

Annie nodded, renewed fear clutching at her stomach muscles. The War Office seemed like the enemy. Their decisions could determine her and Olivia's future.

Once outside, Olivia's arm came around her. 'I'm scared, Annie.'

'I know. I feel the same. It's like our world's been turned upside down yet again. When will it all end?'

'Shall we go home first and make sure Daphne's all right with the kids and let all the others know what's happening?'

'No, Olivia, luv, I don't think that's a good idea . . . I'm thinking as a cop now. We may compromise our situation even further. Let's do as the sarge says and go straight to the War Office.'

* * *

42

Annie parked her car a couple of streets away. 'We'll walk the rest of the way, Olivia, as I doubt that we'd get a car through security . . . It's going to be difficult enough as it is as your papers haven't come through yet.'

'No. I thought this visit would be about that, not what we're facing.'

'Well, you've got your contact, and we have been summoned, so we'll give our names and see what happens.'

They had turned into Horse Guards Avenue and there before them on the corner of Whitehall was the imposing and yet beautiful building that housed the War Office. The white stone of its structure seemed to gleam in the rays of the low winter sun. Its dome looked almost majestic against the background of the pale sky, which held menacing white clouds, telling of a snowstorm ahead.

Being shown into the main entrance further played havoc with Annie's jangled stomach. She wanted to be sick, but took a deep breath, wishing that she was in uniform as then she was full of confidence.

Her sense of insignificance increased as they stood in the echoey hall, with its magnificent staircase of marble seeming to go in all directions.

A door to the side opened. 'Mrs Kraus and Mrs Stanley?'

Olivia's name was spoken in a derogatory tone. Annie felt her almost crumble by her side. Incensed, Annie stood up straight and with a proud, but dismissive tone replied, 'WPC Stanley, sir.'

'Oh?'

The small man dressed in pinstripes and with a shock of blond hair eyed her up and down. 'Yes. I see now. Come this way.'

They were shown into an office that was crammed with

furniture: a huge desk that looked centuries old, a bookcase that held fat files and two high-backed green leather chairs. Behind the desk sat a strikingly handsome man in his thirties with dark hair, a black moustache and wearing brown pinstripes. His blue eyes were like steel.

'Sit down.'

As he said this, he waved a hand at the man who had announced them.

'So. We're faced with a set of extraordinary circumstances. Two of our field agents accused of harbouring the enemy. One even married to the enemy!'

Annie felt Olivia stiffen. 'I beg to differ. I am married to a very courageous man who has helped Britain's cause immensely at great risk to himself!'

'Quite right. I was being flippant. But at least it got you to use your tongue. Neither of you are on trial here. We are grateful for the risks you took, especially you, Olivia . . . May I call you that?'

Olivia nodded as she visibly relaxed.

'Though this latest is a very serious matter and we need to address it. We're not looking to do so by criminalizing you. Your work has been very valuable to us, and we need that to continue.'

Olivia further shocked Annie then as she said, 'I will give any further help I can, but not unless I have your assurance that my husband will be safe if he makes it to this country.'

'He is safe. He is in Switzerland, and it's arranged that he will stay there. He knows where you are.'

Olivia gasped. Annie reached for her hand and felt Olivia's grab hers tightly. 'Can I visit him?'

'No.'

'Contact him?'

'No.'

'But—'

'Your services are needed. We cannot compromise your position. But more of that in a moment.' He turned his gaze on Annie. Her blood ran cold. There seemed nothing human about him. His answers to Olivia had been abrupt, providing no explanation, leaving Olivia floundering but not objecting.

'Now you, Officer, are in a different position. You have been housing an alien. A potential threat to this country.'

Annie took her courage from Olivia. 'I knew nothing of Loes's parentage. We never really talked about her and her life. I did what anyone would do. She's me friend's nanny. She was stranded here. I took her in. She became a friend and nanny to me sister's little girl too. That's all there was to it. There was no suggestion that I was shielding her. And I don't see what threat she poses.'

'I believe you, but it will need proving. You see, Loes's father is collaborating with the Germans. There is intelligence that he informs on, and he helps to round up fellow Jews. It is believed that he even betrayed his ex-wife and his other daughter. The assumption is that he knew where Loes was. And that the Germans on Guernsey would have told of her no longer being there. They would find out from locals where she went – staff of your father's household in particular, Olivia.'

Olivia seemed to sag and Annie squeezed her hand.

The man, who hadn't introduced himself but who they assumed was Brinston – the name Olivia had been given – softened his tone. 'I'm sorry about all you have been through, Olivia, and you too, Annie. My hope is that you both now do all you can to beat the Germans. You have so far been admirable in all you have done.'

Olivia's 'thank you' was almost a whisper. Annie couldn't speak, only incline her head.

'Back to Loes's position . . . The fear is that she could be used. That under threat of her family being harmed, she may be forced to work undercover for the Germans.'

Annie couldn't believe timid Loes could ever do anything like that, but then, if her family was threatened, she would find the strength. Any of them would.

'Now, it's our belief that her family have already come to harm, but we can't be sure. A lot is coming out about the treatment of the Jews, which we can't verify, and so cannot make public. For Loes's own safety, we will intern her.'

'No!'

'I'm sorry, Olivia, we have no choice.'

'But where? Will she be all right? Can I visit her?'

'She will of course be cared for . . . I mean, she won't be given any special treatment, but we will try to house her near to London . . . As far as visiting . . . well, there's something I need to speak to you about. We want you to consent to work as an agent for us . . . To join Agent Lucy.'

Annie knew her mouth had opened, but she couldn't utter a word . . . Olivia to go to France! No! She needed her. How would she get through it all without her?

Before either of them had time to speak, Brinston turned to Annie. 'And though you cannot go to France because of the language barrier and, I dare say, having no knowledge of that country so not being able to fit in as a local, you cannot visit Loes either. It will put you in danger. We don't know how many traitors are working in this country. But each one will know of and try to get at Loes. That's why it's imperative that we get her away as we cannot risk these people getting at those who knew her to force them to do

46

their dirty work. You will join the air force and be sent to Lincoln, Annie. There you will work in observation – a vital role, plotting and on outlook duties.'

'No! I – I can't! I have the kids to think of!'

Annie glanced at Olivia. Her face had drained of colour, but her voice was strong as she asked, 'Do we have a choice?'

'No. We must protect you. But what we are sending you to do, Olivia, we had on the cards anyway, before this came to light over Loes. You are an excellent candidate. Your knowledge of languages, your background in Guernsey . . . Being so near to France, many of your customs are the same as the French. And then there's your intelligence and knowledge of the German people, especially the military.'

'I have requests, though. Can I express them?'

'Go ahead.'

'I want to know that my son and the other children are safe. What you are planning seems to show complete disregard to them and their welfare. I want them to be taken to the countryside with Daphne, and for Annie to be nearby so that she can get home frequently to be with them.'

Brinston was quiet for a moment.

When he spoke, he said, 'I will investigate that possibility.'

'I couldn't give myself to what you are asking without this assurance. I haven't been with my son for a year. All that kept me going during that time was knowing that he was with Annie and Loes. Now to have to leave him again, I need to know that he will still have Annie.'

Finding ideas coming to her now, Annie asked, 'Couldn't I remain a police officer, but be stationed elsewhere? Most rural areas have a police house allocated to their force. Couldn't that be found for me so that I could remain living with the children?'

'These are scenarios we hadn't looked at. The most important consideration has been getting you away from London, and yet using your skills. I will give this some thought and attention.'

'When will all of this happen?' Olivia asked.

'You will be allowed three days, Olivia, but in that time, you will report to sixty-six Baker Street every afternoon at three thirty for briefings. This will begin tomorrow.'

'But I have my father's affairs to put in order.'

'You must instruct his solicitor to do that for you. We know he uses a London firm.'

They knew everything about her and Olivia, Annie thought, but then, they had been classed as agents for a long time now even if her own involvement had only been through Lucy.

She so wanted to ask how Lucy was. They'd become good friends, but something told her that she mustn't. And in any case, her mind was full of what had already been discussed, and with pleading with God to make it possible that she was allowed to work as a policewoman in a rural area and have what were now her only family – the children – with her. And, of course, the lovely Daphne, who was quickly becoming like family too.

After documents were signed by Olivia and herself, one of which being the Official Secrets Act, and being told the implications of breaching them, Annie and Olivia left the stuffiness of the office.

Once outside, they clung together in a hug. It came to Annie to say, 'We can do this.' But she didn't, as right now she was unsure they could.

They went immediately to Olivia's father's solicitor's office. Neither of them felt like carrying out this duty, but knew they had no choice.

Not half an hour later, it was shocking to Annie to sit with Olivia as she learned just how depleted her father's estate was.

The solicitor, an older gentleman with an air of being a man of the world, showed them into his office, a room full of huge, thick books. They lined the walls and stood in piles on the floor, and two had to be cleared from each chair to allow them to sit down.

Once they were seated, the solicitor shook his head. 'I haven't good news for you, I'm afraid, Olivia, but the investments lost with the collapse of your father's bank were colossal. And this is despite his efforts to inform every investor of how the land lay with the Germans requisitioning everything he owned, as many left their money in accounts with him. His assets over here – the apartment blocks and other property – barely covered it. There is a small amount of his personal cash in banks here, and I am looking into Swiss accounts he had, but . . . Well, I'm not sure how to tell you this next news. Your father always promised me he would talk to you about it, but I wonder if he did. Do you know anything about Mrs Davies?'

Olivia looked puzzled.

'I thought not . . . I'm afraid that your father has also left a legacy to someone else apart from you and your son, Karl. This means that effectively his estate is to be split three ways, leaving you very little.'

Annie saw the blood drain from Olivia's face once more.

'Someone else? But who?'

The solicitor cleared his throat.

Sensing there was a shock in store for Olivia, Annie found her hand and squeezed it. None of the tension she felt in Olivia eased. If anything, it increased.

'Mrs Davies lives in a house owned by your father in Wrexham . . . I'm sorry, I can see that all of this has come as a surprise to you. But many years ago, your father and Mrs Davies had an affair . . .' Again, the solicitor coughed.

Olivia's hand tightened and her nails dug painfully into Annie's skin, but Annie bore it, knowing she was all Olivia had to hang on to as this shocking tale unfolded.

'It was after he lost your mother. Mrs Davies had also lost her husband. They met at a function here in London . . . She was one of the waitresses at the do. He told me that they were both lonely and just drifted together in the beginning, seeking solace. However, after a time they did find a deep love for one another and though Mrs Davies – Rosemary – wouldn't leave Wales, your father visited her every time he came to the mainland. She will be very upset to hear of his death and the manner in which he died.'

Olivia didn't comment. After a while, she asked, 'And this lady shares equally with me and my son whatever assets Father left?'

'Not equally. But there is a legacy left to her along with a proviso on where she lives. The house goes to you, but Mrs Davies keeps it as her home for as long as she wants it – rent-free.'

Olivia remained stone-faced as she asked, 'Just how much has my father left?'

Annie held her breath, not wanting her dear friend to be penniless. Not after all she was used to having.

'Mrs Davies was left a legacy of one hundred pounds. So with what your father's estate is worth now, that is a sizeable chunk. There was a further two hundred pounds to be put into trust for your son – a clause added when your child was born . . . The balance of the estate after these are paid then comes to you. Your largest asset will be Mrs Davies' house, which is worth an estimated five hundred pounds. After that, you have investments, which I am afraid are almost valueless, and two hundred pounds – very little when you think in normal circumstances without the collapse you would have been looking at thousands plus valuable property portfolios.'

Olivia's head dropped, but then she lifted it in a defiant gesture. 'My father had no choice in the loss of his business. The collapse was down to the invasion alone, something the mainland government did nothing to prevent. Father was an excellent businessman and built up an empire with his investment bank and property portfolio. It is just a pity that he had to tie them together to try to survive. Please may I have details of how I can access my money and the address of the house Mrs Davies lives in? Is Wrexham far from London?'

'At least five hours' drive, I think . . . Your father often went by train to Elsmere and from there he told me he got a cab to Kingsmill Road, Wrexham, but that usually took him three to four hours. But he enjoyed train journeys and said he arrived relaxed rather than exhausted . . . Olivia, I really am truly sorry. I liked and admired your father. The circumstances of his death are horrendous, and must have greatly affected you, my dear. I will do all I can to make everything regarding your father's estate as pain free as possible and, as your father's trustee, I will oversee the sale of the properties. I will try to cover the debts and have a surplus that would add to your legacy. But I cannot promise that.'

Olivia's 'thank you' was humbler than her outburst had been, which had shown Annie just how the Guernsey people viewed the government in relation to all that had happened to their lives, and she didn't blame them. She'd loved the island and its people when she'd lived a while with Olivia – such happy days. And, like Olivia, to know they were left unprotected made her angry too. Olivia had lost so much.

Outside, Olivia looked close to tears, but she held her head high. 'I didn't think it was as bad as that, Annie, and this Mrs Davies' existence . . . I just cannot take it in.'

Annie sought desperately to find something to say to help, but she too felt like she'd had a body blow. Olivia's father had seemed such an honest and open man. A kind and jolly person who she'd loved in the way one would an uncle. Now, this secret that had devastated Olivia put him in a different light.

'Let's go and have a cup of tea, Olivia. There's a cafe over the road.'

It sounded such an inadequate thing to say, but it was all she could come up with.

'I will go to Wrexham and meet this Mrs Davies . . . Will you come with me, Annie?'

'Of course I will, luv. But how? I mean, you must report to this Baker Street place every day.'

'We could go in your car. We could share the driving. If we go back home now and collect the children, we could get there in five hours, book into a hotel and then find Mrs Davies in the morning. We could be back by tomorrow afternoon in time for my briefing.'

Knowing what this meant to Olivia, Annie agreed. 'But let's have a cuppa first. Everything we've heard today has devastated me.'

As they sat with their tea, Annie got out the letters she hadn't opened from this morning's post. 'Oh, look, judging by the postmark, there's one from your aunt and uncle.'

Olivia's eyes filled with tears. 'I so wanted to go down to Cornwall to see them. It's shocking what's happening . . . I can't get Loes out of my mind . . . Oh, Annie, why?'

Annie knew what Olivia meant. Not one isolated incident, but all of it – the war, their losses, their separations from their beloved husbands, and now Loes, and their lives once more about to be disrupted. She had no answers, but did what she always did and reached for Olivia's hand. Together they were strong. But once more they faced being separated.

Chapter Five

Olivia

Standing in front of the detached house on Kingsmill Road, Olivia felt again the feeling of being betrayed by her beloved father.

How could this have happened without her having an inkling? Why did he keep it a secret? How often over the years she'd wished he'd had someone of his own in his life. But then, she'd never voiced this and maybe her father had thought she wouldn't accept it.

They'd been so close, so protective of each other. Maybe he hadn't wanted to spoil that in any way.

She turned and looked at Annie still sitting in the car with the children, waiting to see what the next stage of the plan was. Trouble was, now that she was here, Olivia didn't know.

During the hours she'd lain awake in the hotel overnight she'd gone from wanting to tear into this woman who'd had such a large part of her father without her knowing and wanting to know her as a friend, as someone who had shared something wonderful in her life – her father.

Olivia had never known her mother. She'd died giving birth to her, but always she'd been looming large in her life and her photo had been the focus of her love for her and her longing to have known her. Copies of that photo had been at the centre of her father's life too, always occupying a prominent place on his desk, in his bedroom and in the lounge of their home in St Peter Port.

A pain sliced through Olivia's soul at the memory. Now she had nothing left of her mother and the only tangible thing of her father's was his clothes – now worn by others in need. But always she would carry them both in her heart.

The curtain of the window Olivia was staring at twitched.

When the door opened, Olivia stared into a face she thought beautiful – that of Rosemary Davies.

'You're Olivia? I would recognize you anywhere . . . But seeing you here can only mean that either your father has at last told you about me . . . or . . . No! Please don't tell me . . .'

The look of pain and utter devastation that crossed Rosemary's face cut into Olivia. Without thinking, she put out her arms. Rosemary almost fell into them. They clung on to one another.

Rosemary was much smaller than Olivia, so Olivia had to bend to enclose Rosemary in her arms.

To Olivia, it was like holding the lovely Cissy, something she could never do again.

She crumpled, as her new-found strength dissolved and her pain sliced her afresh.

'Oh, my dear, come on in.'

Olivia followed Rosemary into a hall she felt held love and comfort for her. The sort she'd never known – that given by a mother. For at this moment, she couldn't say why, but Rosemary seemed to be that to her.

Trying to dismiss the thought, she let Rosemary take her

through to a lounge that she could hardly see through the mist of her tears, but which again uncannily welcomed her.

'Sit on the sofa next to me, my lovely.'

The endearment seemed right, even though they had only just met. As did leaning into this stranger, who didn't feel like a stranger, but a person she knew she would love.

Rosemary held her, gently patting her back.

'I see you have others in the car, my dear. Do you want me to fetch them in?'

Olivia shook her head. 'I – I need to compose myself first . . . I – I have my son with my friend, and two children my friend cares for – her niece . . . she lost her sister, and a little boy who was bombed out and lost his mum.'

'Oh dear. Those poor little mites. I'm sorry . . . but . . . Oh, Olivia, have you come to tell me that my William is . . . Oh, no . . . I – I can't hear it . . . I wrote to him, telling him that I was ready to . . . to let you know about me . . . to become his wife . . . I didn't receive a reply . . . I – I can't bear to lose him.'

Olivia found that none of this hurt her. All she felt was the pity of this lost love that hadn't been allowed to bloom for a reason she couldn't fathom.

It was her turn now to offer comfort. Holding Rosemary to her, she answered her questions, but fell short of telling the truth. She couldn't voice how the rotten Gunter had held a gun to her father's head, but just said that he got caught in crossfire.

'My poor darling. Oh, why didn't I go to him as my heart wanted to?'

Olivia wanted to know the answer to this but didn't ask.

'I was wrong. You see, I wanted William to tell you about me from the start, but he wouldn't unless I agreed to marry him and move to Guernsey with him. We met when you were two. You would have easily accepted me. But William had this notion that unless I agreed to marry him, he couldn't present me to his daughter!' Rosemary gave an exasperated sigh. 'It was all so silly.'

But to Olivia, it was typical of her father. He had principles he wouldn't compromise. Not even for his own happiness. But she wondered at how Rosemary didn't just give in to this simple request if she loved her father.

'I – I was so stupid. I stuck out, wanting you to know me, to love me before I married your father. And so, we forged a relationship that worked. A love that was deep and bound us even though we were miles apart. A spoken love down a telephone line. A love snatched whenever he visited England and could make it here. A love written in beautiful letters. A love that protected me by taking care of me, giving me a home and looking after me financially. A love that was beautiful.'

Olivia held Rosemary even tighter as they both cried together.

It was Rosemary who took control in the end.

'Your friend and those poor children will be freezing out there, Olivia. We must hold our emotions in for their sake and get them into the warmth. But just before we do, may I say that I know I would have loved you and been a good mother to you? I feel that love for you now.'

Once more they hugged. 'I do too, Rosemary. And as best I can, I will look after you . . . You see, Father didn't leave a lot of money or property as he always hoped to.'

Olivia quickly put Rosemary in the picture of how things were.

'Oh, but I am so lonely here!'

This shocked Olivia. 'You mean, you don't want to stay here?'

'I have wanted to move for a long time. I wanted to go to a village where I would be part of a community. My neighbours here are all young. The men have gone to war now, and so have a lot of the women who didn't have children. I help at the local Red Cross centre, and know people there, but I have no one I can have a cuppa with and a natter. I wanted to be part of something that wasn't just providing help in a practical way, but that gave me friends.'

Olivia thought of Annie's home crammed with friendly folk but it was so dangerous to move Rosemary to the heart of the East End with the constant bombing.

The thought came to her that the other way around would be a perfect solution – for Annie and the children to come here! 'How big is this house, Rosemary?'

'Too big. I have four bedrooms. I never wanted anything so big.'

Olivia looked around her for the first time and saw that the room they were in was large too. Her senses came alive as she took in the smell of polish and how the dresser against the wall opposite the roaring fire shone in the light from the large bay window. How the carpet – red and gold – allowed her feet to sink into it. The beautiful three-piece suite, in a deep red, with gold antimacassars matching the gold of the carpet. The lovely china cabinet next to the fire, full of beautiful tea sets, teapots and cake plates, which somehow Olivia knew her father had bought. He always loved nice china. Opposite her were French doors that stood ajar, showing that the room they opened into was a dining room with a highly polished, long dining table and six gold chairs. And through that she could see another set of French doors that led to a long garden, looking beautiful as it was dressed in frosty cobwebs and with the grass of the lawn tinted with white frost too.

'It's lovely here.'

'It is, but this is my best lounge and hardly ever used. I just light the fire and polish it most days. A sign of my lonely hours, my lovely . . . My real sitting room is across the hall. Let's get your friend and the children in and take them in there. I'll make cocoa to warm them up.'

Olivia sat up. A kind of excitement entered her, and she hoped that Annie loved this house as much as she did and that her idea would work. But she would wait and see how they all got on.

'Are you sure you can cope with us all, Rosemary?'

'Cope? I'm loving having you and cannot wait to meet the rest – to fill this empty shell with the sound of children and chattering. Hurry and fetch them in, lovely.'

Olivia gave Rosemary one more hug. To her, it seemed that Annie's future was settled. How safe they all would be here . . . and loved . . . Oh, if only Annie and the powers that be would agree!

Rosemary welcomed Annie and the children with hugs.

Ian looked up at her. 'Yer give cuddles like me . . . me granny used to give me.'

Rosemary bent over him. 'And you give them like I always imagined a grandson would. Though I never had one.'

Ian had tears trickling down his face as he said, 'If Annie don't mind, yer can be me granny, if yer like? Me . . . me granny were killed by the bombs, like me mum.'

Rosemary hugged him to her. 'Oh, my little one, I'd be honoured to be your granny.'

Beth was having none of it. 'Me want a granny!' came out in a determined you're-not-having-anything-without-me voice.

Rosemary laughed. 'Well, now I have two grandchildren when half an hour ago I had none!'

It was then that she was introduced to Karl. Her smile widened. She looked up from him to Olivia. Olivia understood. Karl should have been her step-grandchild.

At that moment Olivia felt cross with her father and his silly principles. He'd denied her years of love from Rosemary, and Karl had missed out on having her in his life too.

Karl, as if sensing Rosemary was special, went into her arms once more. To Olivia, it was as if she could see the bond between them developing and a little part of her heart healed.

If only her plan could come to fruition, her beloved son would be with the woman who she already knew loved him with all her heart.

As Rosemary dabbed at a tear in the corner of her eye, Beth once more stole the show. 'Me granny died and I loved her. You won't die, will you?'

Ian piped up, almost as if it was a competition. 'Me granny died as well, and Karl's Cissy died.'

Rosemary smiled at them. 'Then it sounds like you were all sent to me by your lovely grannies. I'll try not to die. I promise.'

Olivia caught Annie's eye.

Annie winked, telling Olivia that she was glad all was well between her and Rosemary, making Olivia remember that she'd come here spoiling for a fight with an enemy. She had a moment of shame wash over her for that. The fault had been with her father, not Rosemary.

Remembering what he had meant to Rosemary and how she'd only just found out about him having gone, Olivia felt a surge of love for her at how she'd managed to put that aside to welcome them all, especially the children.

A whistling sound brought their chatter to a halt as Rosemary said, 'Whoops, that's the kettle telling me off, as I haven't got the cups ready. Who's for a nice warming cup of cocoa?'

'I'll help,' Annie offered.

'No, my dear, you stay near to the fire and get warmed through. And you're needed to keep my surrogate grand-children from getting under my feet while I deal with hot water!'

She gave a tinkling laugh as she went through a door on the other side of the fireplace.

When she'd gone, Annie said, 'Oh, Olivia, it's just lovely here and Rosemary is a smasher. How did it go?'

'As you can probably see, with floods of tears.' Olivia bent to pick up Karl who was clinging to her legs. It was as if he sensed that she would be leaving again. Her heart dropped at the thought. She hugged him to her. 'Annie . . . well, Rosemary's lonely . . . I was thinking . . .'

'Ha! Olivia! That took yer all of five minutes! But I know what yer mean. It seems as though it would be perfect, but such a lot to put on her. And then would it sit right with them in you know where?'

Olivia grinned. As always, Annie was in tune with her thoughts. She hadn't even had to say what she had in mind.

'We could broach the subject with Rosemary and see what reaction we get.'

Annie grimaced. 'It's a bit soon.'

'I know but we have so little time.'

The door Rosemary had gone through opened, and she put her head through. 'I could do with help to bring them through, or would you like to come into the kitchen to have it? We could all sit around the table then.'

'Ta, Rosemary. I reckon the kitchen is best as the little ones will handle a cup better sitting at the table.'

Olivia agreed with Annie. This room, though not as posh as the other one and much more homely, still had that not-lived-in feel. Nothing was out of place. As with the 'posh' room, it was furnished with a three-piece suite, but this time in brown leather with soft beige cushions that were filled with feathers, so you just sank into them. There was a book-case next to the fireplace on the other side of the kitchen door. The carpet was beige with blue and pink flowers patterning it. The curtains picked up the blue, as did loose cushions arranged on the chairs and sofa.

Apart from this there was a sideboard on the back wall, which Olivia noticed for the first time was covered with framed photos, many of her father and of him and Rosemary together. On the side wall behind her a piano stood covered with a cloth as if hardly used, and on this rested a large framed photo of her father, his smiling face looking at home in this room, and she wondered at the happy times he'd shared here – a part of his life lost to her.

Once again, a feeling of being cross with him hit her.

As if following her gaze, Karl pointed. 'Poppa!'

Always Annie and dear Loes had shown him photos of herself, Hendrick and her father. The latter he called Poppa.

'Yes, Poppa.' Olivia held him closer, but then not letting her threatening tears flow again, she said, 'Let's go and have cocoa with Granny Rosemary, eh?'

The title had slipped so easily from her tongue.

As they chatted about their lives, their losses and the war, finding lots to laugh about in a tragic tale, which surprised Olivia and she could see it did Annie too, Beth piped up.

'Proper Grannies have toys!'

For such a little girl she was endlessly full of sayings and no one knew where they came from.

'Oh, I have a box too!'

To Olivia's and Annie's surprised look, Rosemary explained, 'I collect them for the Red Cross. I've a box full that I have washed ready to take, but I think are more needed here for children who have been traumatized by the war and need to find a replacement for all they have lost.'

Getting up and putting her arm around Ian, she said, 'Will you help me, Ian? They're in a cupboard under the stairs. And I think there's a couple of things you might like. A potato man, a jigsaw that is far too difficult for the little ones, and a football, but it's too cold to go out in the garden with that!'

Ian jumped off his chair, grinned at Annie and followed Rosemary through to the hall.

'Would it be fair to ask her, Olivia?'

'I think so.' Olivia quickly told of Rosemary's loneliness and how she wanted to move. 'She sees children in the street with busy mums who pass by without a glance in her direction.'

'Well, that wouldn't happen in the East End! Toffee-nosed these areas are!'

'Under different circumstances, I'd have said that we should ask her to take your mum's flat, but as you must disappear as much as you can, this would be ideal. A place where the neighbours don't ask questions. Brinston has to agree.'

Once the children were playing happily, Olivia said, 'Rosemary, we need to talk to you. Can we go into your best room for a moment?'

Rosemary looked apprehensive but showed them the way. As they told her all they could, she listened intently, until they got to asking her how she would take it if they asked if Annie, Daphne and the children could move in with her. Then her face lit up.

'Really? You mean, you would move here? Oh, I would love that . . . I know it seems a hasty decision, and things may not work out, but if they don't, we'll sort it out then. But for now, it seems to me that you are heaven sent . . . I was wondering what I would do once you'd gone. I cried in the kitchen while making your cocoa, thinking of my darling William, of how I was to live now. Of what the house would feel like once you'd gone and I had to cry alone.'

'Oh, Rosemary, luv, ta. I mean, there is someone who'll have to agree, and I'd have to be approved for a transfer to the police station here, but I can't see why they shouldn't.'

'I'm proud of you, Annie – a policewoman! My! And what does Daphne do?'

Olivia explained how Daphne had come with her from Guernsey and then continued, 'So, she hasn't had time to sort anything out yet, but she will. Though this may mean you're in charge of the children on your own at times.'

Annie chimed in, 'But Ian's a great help with them. Listen! He's sorting them out now. And he gets their morning milk – if we have any milk. If not, he gets them a glass of water each, and reads them a story when they go to bed.'

'Stop, girls! You don't have to persuade me! I'm loving the idea. William has sent you to me – a few years blooming late, but he has. I need you and your brood, more than you need me, Annie. Come on, I'll show you both around.'

The house was bigger than they thought as besides the huge kitchen, large living room and posh lounge there was a little sitting room in a conservatory on the back.

'This is where I sit quietly and read as I can enjoy the

garden all year around then, or when my gardener comes, Old Colin as he is known, I chat to him from my chair.'

'Well, this should remain your own little sanctuary, Rosemary. You ain't to let anyone come here unless you want them to. The kids'll be taught that. They mustn't bother you while you're in here.'

Rosemary nodded. 'Yes, I think that's sensible. We all need a sanctuary. But the main living room and kitchen will be the hub of the house and family. As you will be my family. My William's and my family.'

Her tears did spill then. Olivia went to her, quickly followed by Annie.

'You cry whenever yer want to, Rosemary. I'll do a good bit of that meself, and Daphne will, but crying alone is an awful thing. Crying together, we can give comfort.'

Rosemary went into Annie's arms.

Watching this, Olivia thought Rosemary, her father's love, wasn't someone to despise, but someone to love. And it gave her comfort to know that she would be with Annie, Daphne and the children while she was away.

For a moment her world rocked at the realization of leaving them all and her heart hurt to have to say goodbye to Karl again. But then she thought of Hendrick and his courage, and of how Karl and all the children deserved to grow up in a peaceful world as she had.

She swallowed hard and knew that whatever the near future held for her, she was ready to take it on. Ready to help in the fight to make this a better world for them all.

Chapter Six

Annie

When Annie arrived home after dropping Olivia off in Baker Street, she found that all her new tenants were happily settling in.

Despite the cold she found Bertie and Ron standing on the front step chatting and smoking their pipes. The sight warmed her heart. As least those two would be all right. Then just down the road she spotted Rita's kids playing with their mates from the street.

Daphne met her and took a sleepy Beth indoors while Annie carried Karl.

'Annie, what's happening? First Loes was taken away, and then with hardly any explanation, you and Olivia grabbed the kids and disappeared. I've been worried sick, as have Rita and the menfolk.'

'Help me get these little ones upstairs, luv, and I'll tell you what I can.'

After the children had been sorted and given a biscuit and a drink of weak tea before the pot had brewed properly, Annie put them down for a nap.

Beth wasn't going that easily and told Daphne all about

the lady who was to be her granny. 'She's nice, Daphy, you'll like her.'

Daphne's eyebrows knitted into a frown.

'Come and sit at the kitchen table and I'll tell you what I can.'

Picking up the brown teapot, Annie poured two mugs of steaming hot tea, each only getting a touch of milk and no sugar. None of them liked the saccharins that were supposed to supplement the sugar, so were weaning themselves off sweet tea.

'Everything has changed, Daphne. Me sarge had to send me mate Betty around to get Loes because . . .'

Annie explained about foreign nationals and how Loes could be conceived as a target for those wanting to use her.

'Oh, Annie, Loes has never known her father . . . Well, she did as a youngster, but she told me when we worked together that her mum said that she had lived in Germany when she married her dad but had fled back to Holland to her own mum because he systematically beat her, and took pleasure in doing so.'

'Poor Loes. I know, luv, that it all seems unfair, but she's safe where she is. The people involved know things. They must know there is a danger to her from her dad. We can do nothing about it.'

'Will I be able to go and see her, or write to her?'

'I'm going to find that out once our other change is in place, luv, but until then, no, we can't.'

Annie could feel the pity of this and could imagine the fear Loes must be feeling. She so wanted to break down over it all, but she denied her tears and put herself in policewoman mode as Daphne asked, 'So, what else is going on? Who is this granny? Where have you been?'

'Daphne, I know you have a lot of questions, but I can't answer them all.' Annie prepared herself to tell Daphne what she and Olivia had rehearsed in the car on the way home.

'Olivia had to go to the War Office yesterday. You already know that she was contacting the mainland and Hendrick too from Guernsey. Well, she had to give information about what was happening on Guernsey, as at some point the island will be liberated.'

'Oh, God, I hope it's soon. Things are getting bad over there . . . So, Olivia will come back here afterwards? She's not going anywhere, is she?'

To this, Annie couldn't touch on the truth. 'She will come back for a couple of days. She's going to Switzerland to be with Hendrick. And you and I are moving too.'

'What? Where to? Why?'

Annie told her about Rosemary, not taking notice of Daphne's gasps of shock at her ex-boss's secret love affair.

'And so, as we no longer have the safe place in Kent for the children that I told you of, I'm going to see the sarge in a few moments and ask to be transferred there and to live with Rosemary. You're very welcome to come too . . . I mean, I so want you to, but of course will let you stay here if you want to.'

'I don't want to stay here, and I wish that Rita wouldn't. Her kids should never have to live through the hell that is happening each night.'

'Some folk just won't budge. They defy Hitler to try to make them. Thousands of kids were evacuated from here, just like in Guernsey, but some mums couldn't stand it and went and brought them back. Rita was one of them.'

'And just look what they've been through, poor little mites.

But in a way, I still think they're better off with their mum. Mums on Guernsey are pining for their kids. They have no idea where they are or if they remember them. It's heart-breaking.'

'It is, luv.' Annie sipped the last of her tea. 'And so, you're coming with me then? I'm so glad. We'll manage the three little ones together. I expect you'll find work easily enough and Rosemary will help all she can with the kids too.'

'Three? Isn't Olivia taking Karl? I never thought she would leave him again!'

'She has no choice. Now, Daphne, I'm going to have to ask you not to ask any more questions, mate. We're at war, remember? Just trust that me and Olivia are doing the right thing.'

'Sorry. I – I . . . well, everything is so . . . Oh, I don't know.' Daphne burst into tears.

Annie put her arm around her. 'I know, luv, we're all going through the same things. We just have to be strong and stand together, eh?'

Being brave was the last thing Annie felt like being, but she dared not give in too often to her heartache and pain.

'Now, watch the kids for me, will yer? I've to go and see me sarge.'

'I'll get a veg pie made for tea while you're gone. There's a few odd ends in the pantry. A carrot, an onion and some beans. I've checked on the flour and marge for the pastry, and we've enough of that and some potatoes. I'll use some of the dried milk to make a sauce. I can flavour it with the cheese rinds you've kept. No one will know once I grate them, and they melt into the sauce.'

'Sounds lovely. Olivia will be here for tea, and Bertie. Do you know if Rita's got organized for food yet?'

'Yes. The Red Cross brought her a bag of stuff – tins of spam, as well as veg and flour. She was planning a hash tonight.'

'That's good as we've not enough to go around them all . . . See you in a while, luv . . . And, ta, Daphne. I know how hard everything is for yer.'

'You're my inspiration, Annie. After what you've been through, mine's nothing, and yet you remain strong. I want to be like that.'

Annie could only smile. If only Daphne knew that all she wanted to do was to find a hole and curl up in it, and cry for the rest of her life.

Skipping down the stairs, she ran past her mum's and Cissy's flat, keeping her eyes on the front door and getting out of it quickly.

Bertie and Ron were still on the step. Bertie was reciting his sea-faring tales and Ron looked fascinated.

'Can't stop, you two. See you later.'

Bertie called after her, 'Annie, I wanted to tell you, I got meself a canal boat. I get it tomorrow. I'll take you all out for a trip, eh?'

Annie grinned with delight at this news. 'So pleased for you, Bertie, but I'll let yer know about a trip out when I get back, luv.'

Bertie nodded his head and gave a gleeful laugh. But then his words didn't match that. 'Aye, and you can tell us what's happened to our Loes!'

Annie ignored this and hurried to the front of her car to crank the engine.

The fuel gauge showed very low, and she'd used up all she'd had in cans as well as her month's ration by going to

Wrexham! Somehow, she had to get more as now she faced moving to another area. *Please, God, let it be to Rosemary.*

'Annie!'

'Well, that's a better greeting than last time, Sarge!'

'I know. I was very upset thinking you'd let the side down. I shouldn't have done, but you women can let your hearts rule your heads at times.'

Annie didn't argue with this, though she felt like doing so. *When will men learn to trust women in the same jobs?* But that was an age-old question, and she hadn't time for such thoughts.

'Have yer heard from anyone, Sarge?'

'No?'

'Can I have a word?'

In his office, Annie told the sergeant all that had happened.

'Oh, Annie, that's a bit harsh on Olivia. Poor girl. Is she up to it?'

'I don't know. She's very fragile and she went through so much. Some of it she hasn't been able to tell me, only to say she was violated.' Annie shivered and her heart felt heavy. She always felt for any woman who had been a victim of rape or violence, but to think it had happened to her lovely Olivia tore at her heart. She didn't need to know the details. She'd dealt with many cases of gangs of men raping a woman so could imagine.

'Oh, Annie, no!'

'And so, I think she may be up to doing anything that helps to beat the bastards.'

The sarge raised his eyebrows but didn't pull her up on her language.

'Well, I can report that Loes is all right. She's been put

71

into a camp not far from here and there are a couple of Jewish families with her.'

Despite the relief Annie felt at hearing this, she couldn't give in to it. 'Any news on whether we can write to her?'

'No, and I wouldn't bank on it . . . Look, Annie, until this war is over, I wouldn't even try to communicate. Loes will be all right, but neither of you will be if your location is compromised.'

'I was thinking of the maid that came over with Olivia. They worked together and were friends.'

'Let's leave it a while. This maid might tell Loes things that it's best that Loes doesn't know . . . Now, about you. So, you have to transfer too? Did they say where?'

'Yes, but I don't want to go. Can yer help me, Sarge?'

'You've got to go, Annie, I'm sorry . . .'

'No, I mean where they plan to send me . . . I have something else to tell yer.'

The sarge listened to the story of Rosemary and her connection to Olivia. 'Please, Sarge, the children will be happy there and they've been through enough.'

'Leave it with me. As it happens, I know the sarge in Wrexham. A good bloke. We trained together after we went through the last lot in the same battalion.'

'But can you get him in the War Office to agree?'

'I don't know who "him" is, and don't want or need to know, but I can get in touch with someone in the same department to give a message to whom it may concern that your transfer is arranged and give the details.'

'Do it quickly, Sarge . . . Oh, I didn't mean to sound like I was giving you an order, but I so want to choose where I go with me family and not be shoved somewhere.'

'I understand . . . Look, go to the canteen and have a

cuppa while I make a couple of calls, though before you do, write down the address of where you'll be living so that it can be checked out . . . And, Annie, I'm sorry you're going. But you are sure you're doing the right thing, aren't yer? From the sound of things, you want to go to this lady because she's lonely. You ain't looked into the area, or thought if you'll be happy there, you just want her life to be made better.'

Annie didn't answer this. She nodded her head and went towards the canteen.

Part of her knew that the sarge was right. She didn't know Rosemary, her ways, her likes and dislikes. She didn't know if she would get fed up with them after just a week, or if she really was happy to have them. But then, that happiness could be driven by the salve it would be to her heart not to be lonely when she was grieving as she was.

Sighing, Annie opened the door to the kitchen and was glad to see her one-time enemy, now her friend, Betty was in there.

'Hi, luv, I saw you arrive and knew you'd come in here for a cuppa. Sit down, I'll pour yer one – and we've got sugar, so it'll be a good 'un.'

Annie looked around the familiar canteen – the place where they went to get a breather, to hear their briefings for their shift, to socialize and to calm down if things were hectic, or the case they were dealing with was traumatic. The place where she and Ricky sneaked to for a quick kiss when they were both on duty.

Tears stung her eyes as her Ricky, always cheerful, always kind, always loving, seemed to be in the fabric of this room. She could see him, wanted to reach out and touch him.

73

Wanted to hold him and never let him go. Would she ever do that again?

Betty sat down next to her. 'How's things? And when yer coming back? The work's piling up around us, mate . . . Annie? Oh, Annie, don't start, you'll 'ave me in buckets . . . Look at me eyes, I cry for me man every night.'

'Oh, Betty, I've got to leave . . . leave everything that's familiar to me.'

'What? Why? Oh, mate, I miss yer when yer off. 'Ow am I to get through it all without yer? Yer keep me going.'

'It's the kids. I can't keep them here, sleeping in the shelter every night, crying with fear . . . And when I'm back here and having to work nights, they'll never cope. I have to get them out of London.'

'It ain't nothing to do with that Loes business, is it? I mean, I know how close yer were to her.'

'No . . . Well, I'm upset, of course. I love Loes, and will miss her, and hate what has happened to her. She was a calming influence on the kids too, and I felt safe leaving them in her care. But everything changed after what happened in Kent. She and the children found the bombing terrifying. And now with Loes gone, I think this move is a good thing for them and for us all.'

'Didn't what happened in Kent show yer that wherever you are, or the kids are, there's danger?'

'More than anything it did. But what happened there, though devastating, was the only time the Kentish people of that village had seen anything of the war up close, and it's the same in Wales where we're going. It's all very unlikely to happen there. But here, the children are subjected to it night after night. I just feel I have to take them away, and

74

now I have been given the chance to. They . . . we've all been through enough.'

Betty's hand reached out to take hers. Annie hated having to lie to her, but she had no choice.

'I'm going to miss yer, Annie . . . Ha! I couldn't stand yer in the beginning! You were teacher's pet for the sarge! Then you won the love of the copper we girls were all in love with – despite his ugly mush!'

Annie grinned. 'My Ricky ain't ugly! Yes, he has scars given to him by a rough diamond of a criminal, but he's got a beautiful heart . . . Oh, Betty, I know the subject's taboo, but I do miss him so much.'

Betty dabbed at her eyes. 'And me my man. But then, we were both only married a couple of days before they had to go.'

'That was our own silly faults. We thought women should have the same rights as men. And we refused to marry the ones we loved because we'd be forced to give up our careers. But now the police force begs us to work, whether we're married or not!'

'Oh, but we had some bleedin' fun, didn't we? . . . Well, me and my bloke did. Ha! We didn't wait for the marriage vows, I can tell yer.'

Annie laughed. 'No, nor did me and Ricky. Though I have nightmares about one time . . . We were in Southend and the urge took us. We nipped into an alley . . . in broad daylight!'

They went into a fit of laughter that suddenly turned to sobs. Annie didn't know how or when it happened that she was in Betty's arms clinging on as if her life depended on it as they both sobbed their hearts out.

They didn't hear the door open. It was the sarge coughing that alerted them to the fact that they were not alone.

They broke apart and turned to see him wiping his eyes on a big hankie.

Annie remembered that he hadn't long lost his beloved wife. On impulse she opened her arms. The sarge came into them and hugged her, but quickly straightened up, coughed again, and said, 'In my office, now, Annie!' and hurried out.

The effect of this was to steady them once more. Betty straightened her uniform, then went to the mirror hanging by the window. 'I look a bleedin' mess now, girl!' She turned. 'But I needed that, Annie. All of it. The laughter and the tears. Ta, girl. Now, get bleedin' gone before I start again . . . And Annie, good luck, in whatever it is you're going to do.'

This told Annie that, like any good cop would do, Betty had seen through her lies. She smiled.

'I feel better for our chat, Betty. Ta, luv, and I'm glad we made friends in the end. When this lot's over, me and my Ricky and you and your bloke will go out and have pie and mash together, a few beers and a good old music hall sing-song like my Ricky loves so much.'

Betty came back with, 'Yes, and a bunk-up in the alley as well!'

Annie burst out laughing as she closed the door. Everyone at their desks looked up and smiled at her. One shouted, 'When are yer coming back to work, Annie?'

She could only smile back, and hurry into the sarge's office.

'Right, Annie. Sorry about that. Are you all right now?'

'Don't be sorry, Sarge, you're only human like the rest of us . . . Yes, I'm all right, ta. Me and Betty finished on a laugh.'

'Good.'

'Right, your request has been accepted. And it's been

sanctioned that you can use your police warrant to get the fuel that you'll need for your car.'

Annie had forgotten mentioning this, but remembered that she had said she didn't know how she was to transport them all.

'Ta, Sarge, that'll be a big help.'

'In the meantime, Ben has filled your car up from one of our cans.'

Ben was one of the coppers brought out of retirement to fill the gap of the younger ones who'd gone to war, two of whom had already lost their lives.

They flashed into Annie's mind now, and she could see their grins, and their anxieties, all played out in the office at various times.

'Annie!'

'Sorry, Sarge.'

'I suggest you walk out of here calling out your goodbyes as usual as if you're going to be returning. I think after that emotional show with Betty, you've had enough for one day . . . Annie, I've felt so sorry for all that happened. I tried to be there for you, but—'

'You were, Sarge. Taking me down to Southampton to pick up Olivia and the rest of them was such a help . . . and it was a comfort to me to have you there. You weren't Sarge then, it was like having me dad there . . . as he would have been if he'd been alive. Ta for that, Sarge. I'll be back, yer know. Yer ain't got rid of me yet!'

The sarge grinned. 'That's the spirit, Annie . . . Annie, you're like a daughter to me . . . I shouldn't say it, but just as Ricky was – is – like a son, I think a lot of you both. Ricky will come home. No German can stop him. And we'll have a celebration then – a good old East End knees-up, eh?'

Annie smiled. 'We will, Sarge, all of us, the returning coppers and the old buggers, as we call them, and the women coppers, who at last have the same standing as the rest of yer.'

'Always did in my eyes, Annie, only rules were rules.'

'I know. It's water under the bridge now . . . Sarge, on your days off, you can always come down to see us . . . Not as a sarge, but as a friend – a father figure.'

Annie saw his Adam's apple move up and down as he swallowed hard. 'I'll do that, Annie. I will . . . Now, get gone!'

Annie laughed. She knew she wasn't being dismissed in the normal sergeant–copper way, but to save his emotions. She was glad to close the door behind her before she did something daft like try to hug him again.

Waving to everyone, she shouted, 'See yer. Be good!' and hurried out of the door.

Once in the fresh air, she took a deep breath. What the future held, or how it would all work out living with Rosemary, she didn't know, only that another era of her life was beginning and for the sake of the loved ones she had left, she had to grasp it with both hands and make it work.

Chapter Seven

Olivia

Laughter rang out, sending clouds of visible breath into the air as they sat on benches fixed to the sides of the boat, at the front – or the 'bow' as Bertie called it – Daphne, herself and Annie, with Karl, Beth and Ian, and Rita and her boys, faces glowing, noses red.

But none of them seemed to mind the cold as the canal boat chugged along sending sparkling, if muddy, water in folds behind them. Trees and bushes hid London's broken East End, giving the impression that they had entered a different world.

Olivia hugged Karl to her and looked back at Bertie as he steered the boat from the stern, his face glowing with happiness. He was in his element to captain a boat once more and was treating Ron as if he was his first mate shipman.

The last time Bertie had sailed a boat had been fraught with danger as he had rescued herself, Daphne and Stefan from certain death on Guernsey – she would be for ever grateful to him.

Now, he didn't mind the bombs, the rationing, the strange land, as London was to him, as long as he had some water to go to and a boat to sail in. Even a canal barge was a good enough substitute for him – not that he was a full-time sailor back home. But the harbour master of St Peter Port had been a very important position, and his boating had been for pleasure only for many years. How easily he had adapted to this chugging vessel – what almost seemed like a floating home, though a smelly one, as he'd only been interested in its ability to float in the first instance. His future plan was for him and Ron to paint it throughout and make it into an attraction, charging for rides along the canal.

Olivia was amazed at how he'd adapted to his new life.

His son Joe came to her mind. A lovely lad, who'd always had his eye out for the main chance. If he could make a penny or two, he was happy, right from being a lad, when he'd board the ships that came into the harbour and carry cases, get taxis for passengers, or even walk them to their hotel carrying their heavy luggage for them.

A smile creased her face with the memory. The sun always seemed to be shining in these snippets of life how it used to be. A carefree, lovely life, which she dared not think too much about as it would break her heart at it all having gone.

Instead, she turned her attention to Karl and his delight in everything he saw as he pointed to the ducks quacking loudly at their intrusion, or maybe in greeting, making him giggle, and how he was mesmerized by the swans gracefully gliding in pairs.

An old saying came to mind. It was said that the swan's grace was propelled by frantic legs keeping them afloat under water, and how people used it as a comparison to themselves when they were coping on the surface of things. She was like that right now – appearing calm, in control, enjoying the moment, but really, she was filled with scurrying panic as to how she was to cope with the future.

Part of her was excited about it, she had to admit. To be given the chance to do something to disrupt the Germans' quest to take over the world, and to be part of the effort to beat them back and conquer them.

But she didn't know how she was to cope with no loved ones by her side, even though she would have Lucy, the girl who'd been Annie's contact here when Hendrick's messages were being sent between herself and Annie.

Olivia remembered the time she'd met Lucy, and how she hadn't liked her at first, but had come to very much, as she'd realized she'd been in the wrong at the time. And Lucy had been right to show concern. It had happened when she'd come back to England, hoping to stay for the duration of the war with Karl and Annie, and had moved back into her father's London apartment, when, to protect Annie, the order was made to not have links between them and her father – links that could have meant them being targeted.

Catching Annie's eye, Olivia could see she was enjoying the boat trip as much as herself.

Dear Annie. If only they could stay together. But Annie would do her duty as a police officer and she must do hers by helping the French Resistance. Always Guernsey islanders had an affinity to France.

These thoughts strengthened her resolve. She straightened her back as if ready for battle, but then giggled as Annie shouted, 'Bridge ahead! Duck, everyone!' And the children ducked their heads as if one and on command!

'Can I go and 'elp Bertie and Ron to steer the boat, Annie?'

'Good idea, Ian, they could do with your help.' Annie turned and yelled, 'Midshipman coming to stern, Captain!'

Bertie shouted back, 'Aye, Aye, Chief Mate! Pub ahoy, we can stop and take midshipman on stern then!'

Everyone went into a fit of giggling. It was the perfect way to spend what would be their last day together for a long time. Olivia only hoped that Karl would remember it.

Looking down at his beaming face, his twinkling eyes were just like Hendrick's. She touched his hair and was given the memory of touching Hendrick's in the same way.

'Karl love Mummy.'

'And Mummy loves Karl . . . I do, my darling, with all my heart . . . One day . . .'

She stopped herself as her tears welled up. Beth changed the mood. 'It's "Mum", not "Mummy"!'

Annie pushed a stray curl off Beth's forehead as she told her, 'Everyone has a pet name for their mum, Beth. Let Karl call Aunty Olivia what he wants to, eh?'

Beth's mouth pouted. But she nodded.

Olivia felt that in telling everyone off, Beth was finding a way to cope with everything she'd been through. She particularly hated anyone having a mum or a gran, but that was understandable. All they could hope was that what she'd been through didn't scar her for life. But being so young, she had every chance, surrounded by love as she was and always would be.

Beth was now staring ahead. What was going through her little mind Olivia couldn't imagine but she was glad of the distraction of the boat docking outside a ramshackle old pub.

'Pie and mash all round, eh, me land lubbers?'

'Ha, Bertie, you've never tasted it yet!'

Bertie grinned at Ron. 'Well, the way you Londoners go on about it, I feel as though I have!'

The two men chuckled as they set about mooring the boat.

It took a while for the pub to organize their meals, so Olivia suggested they go for a walk along the towpath.

Daphne wanted to stay by the warmth of the pub fire. 'I'll keep the kids here while you go. It's freezing out there!'

Karl went willingly into Daphne's arms.

Rita chipped in, 'I'll stay with Daphne, luv. You and Annie enjoy a walk together. I'm hungry and want to nab the first of the pie and mash to come out of the kitchen!'

They all laughed. And Rita, for the first time since losing her home, grinned back at them.

Olivia looked over at Rita's dad, Ron, standing at the bar having a drink with Bertie, and knew their friendship was helping them both, although the local ale they were drinking looked like sludge – another thing Bertie had adapted to after the clear pale ale mostly drunk on the island.

As Annie and Olivia walked with their arms linked, Annie said, 'There's been no time to talk with everyone around. How did it go when you went to Baker Street?'

Despite Olivia being told that all was top secret, she knew she could share with Annie.

'Well, if it wasn't for leaving Karl and you, I'd be fully excited about it all, but as it is, a big part of me is looking forward to doing my bit . . . I know we have already, but this is different. I'll be in the field. I'll be doing something to disrupt the Germans' efforts, and giving information on what is happening on the ground, not what is planned . . . Can you understand that, Annie?'

'I can, luv, more than you can know. I'd love to go with yer and wish I could speak French. If I did, I would volunteer. Anyway, what's yer next step?'

'Training. I leave in a couple of weeks. It takes place up in Scotland. I have to get kitted out before then as I'm joining the army!'

Even though Olivia knew Annie was feeling the same tug on her heart as she was at them being parted again, Annie as always made light of things. 'Right! Stand to attention, Private!'

'Ha, I don't think I'm officially army, more secret army, and I'll expect an officer rank at the very least!'

'Of course, nothing less! But what will you do until you are called to duty – I mean, training?'

'I have asked if I can go to Cornwall to see Aunt Rosina. I think they will allow me to. I'm going to buy a small car . . . I know it will take a lot of my money – not my legacy, but I made enquiries about accessing the money Hendrick and I had saved. You see, I need the car as I still can't travel far by train.'

Annie grabbed her hand and nodded. 'Nor me . . . The memories of the crash fill me with fear.'

'I don't think that will ever go away. Anyway, I'll come to Rosemary's with you for a couple of days and buy a car there . . . You see, I have a plan, Annie. I now know where Hendrick is and I'm thinking about chartering a light aircraft to take me to him.'

'Olivia, no! It's too dangerous. Your new commanders would never allow it!'

'They needn't know . . . It's perfect, Annie. I can do this, love, I can. Please help me. I'll say I am going to my aunt's for two weeks but only stay a couple of days. You and the children can come with me for a couple of days and then go back to Rosemary's.'

'Oh, Olivia, I hate to say no, but I must . . . Not to you

going, but to me and the children going with you. It's too disruptive for them and will mean that I won't have enough time to make sure all is set up properly before I begin work . . . I need to get my idea to make two flats out of the house with a shared kitchen into motion. I – I was going to ask you if you could find the money to make a downstairs bathroom for Rosemary. I want it so that we are living together, but not . . . I mean, well, imagine how it will be for Rosemary with two women and three children suddenly occupying her home. If we have separate living accommodation, it will be so much easier for her.'

'It will, and I agree, love. I'm intending to ask my uncle for a loan. But there's something that is worrying me over how you're going to manage. I mean, with you and Daphne out at work, we can't expect Rosemary to look after the children.'

Annie was quiet for a moment. Then let out a massive sigh.

'I know. I would rather Daphne looked after them, but there is talk of conscription of unmarried women!'

Olivia didn't have an answer. Though she did think she would ring the local council in Wrexham and ask about nurseries in the area, but before she could voice this, Annie was saying, 'Look, if Daphne is conscripted, then I will have to give up work. It's the only solution . . . But to think that I never gave up work to marry my Ricky, and now I may be forced to because of the kids, makes me feel a bit guilty.'

'I'm sorry, Annie. I'll try to find a solution, I promise.'

As if Annie had suddenly realized this was a worthy sacrifice, she smiled. 'Don't worry if there ain't one to be found, luv. I love the kids with all my heart, and they'll be worth it . . . I ain't saying I didn't love Ricky as much, but ha! We found other ways of being married without being so!'

Olivia pushed Annie on her shoulder in jest as they both laughed out loud, then grabbed her as Annie was in danger of going into the canal!

This made them laugh even more and lightened the mood. They ended in a hug.

'Life ain't how we'd like it to be, Olivia, but we've to make the most of it. Come on, let's get back. I'm still starving, you know.'

As they walked back, Olivia asked Annie, 'Have you adopted Beth and Ian yet, Annie? It may be vital if they decide to conscript married women. Surely they wouldn't call up those who have children?'

'I hope the adoption's all going through. Rose's solicitor – the one sorting out the affairs of her estate – is doing it all for me but warned it can take a long time. I've had forms to fill in and such, but I wish they'd hurry up. Though me being conscripted isn't a consideration yet as I'm a serving copper . . . Let's leave worrying about it for now. You go to wherever they are sending you knowing that little Karl will always be safe with me . . . But, Olivia, please take care and come back to me. And please think again about going to Switzerland.'

Olivia's Aunt Rosina greeted her with tears in her eyes, matching those in Olivia's.

'I got your letter, my darling girl. I'm heartbroken. My dear brother . . . Why? What's wrong with the bloody Germans!'

Olivia held her aunt's tiny frame against her. 'The true Nazis among them don't have to have reasons, they're not human enough for those. But not all Germans are Nazis,

Aunt. It's easy to clump them all together and think that. Most are just like us, having to do their duty. But the consequences for them not toeing the line are dire.'

'Oh, I didn't mean Hendrick was one of them!'

'I know. A lot are like him, and though it's hard to keep trying to see the good in a nation who are the cause of so much pain to us all, we must. I'll tell you about another good German later – he's called Stefan – and about the many kindnesses the islanders received from individual German soldiers among the occupiers.'

'But let's get inside, my darling. You're not going to leave here, are you? Your phone call said a visit, but I so want you to stay. I want to take care of you for my lovely William.'

Olivia looked up at the sprawling manor house and remembered such happy times there each time she'd visited. It struck her then that her father had always had to go and leave her here for a few days. Did he go to Rosemary?

As her eyes travelled over the huge building with ivy clinging to its walls, Olivia realized that something looked different about the manor. Part of it didn't look homely. Her gaze took in a man walking up and down the path that encircled the house. He seemed to have a dressing gown on.

'I see you've taken in the changes, my dear. I didn't get the chance to tell you on the phone with the line being so crackly, but we only have the left wing to live in now. The rest of the house was requisitioned for use as a military hospital for officers.'

'Oh? How are you about that?'

'Fine. Glad to do our bit. And glad to have our war heroes here. Uncle loves it. He has chess partners at last and smoking mates. He'd be there with them all the time if he could . . . Anyway, let's get you in. You look tired, my dear.'

'Tired, but so happy to be here. It's as if I do have a place that I can call home.'

'You do, and always will have, and one day this will be yours, my dear Olivia . . . Oh, I so wish you could have brought Karl with you. We are longing to meet him . . . and Annie too. It's such a long time since we saw or heard from her. How is she? We're so proud of her. To think she was our maid, and we hardly knew her, and she is now a police-woman, and we owe her so much for saving your life in that awful train crash, Olivia.'

'She's fine. Adjusting, like us all. Firstly, to being without her Ricky and now having to leave her home.'

'It must be awful. I won't ask why. Though I do want to know about this Rosemary woman. I had no idea!'

Olivia smiled. Aunt Rosina wasn't one to let any gossip pass her by.

'We'll have a chat later and I'll tell you all.'

When they were inside they were in a wing of the house that hadn't been used much in the days when Olivia visited regularly. It housed a library, her Uncle Cyril's office, a small quiet living room and, behind these rooms, the house-keeper's quarters.

As soon as they walked through to the sitting room, Olivia found herself in the arms of her uncle. Something that rarely happened as he was a reserved gentleman, who showed his affection in gestures, such as patting her back or, when she was little, ruffling her hair.

'Good to have you here, my dear Olivia.'

'Oh, Uncle, I can't tell you how good it is to be here and yet sad too.'

'I know, my dear. Our hearts are heavy with the loss of your dear father. Are you all right? Was it his heart?'

Olivia gasped. But then quickly coughed to cover it up. Maybe it was better to not enlighten these two gentle people. And as she thought this, she was glad she hadn't put any details into her letter or told them of the horror of what she had been through when the Germans discovered her radio equipment.

What did it matter? Not telling the truth wouldn't undo it all, so why put her lovely aunt and uncle through it? 'Yes. The way we were forced to live and losing everything – or, at least, knowing that was happening – was too much for him.'

Was it a lie? Didn't everyone die by their heart stopping? What caused her beloved father's heart to stop was too horrendous to share.

After a welcome bath that soothed her aching bones, Olivia sat down with her aunt and uncle to dinner. Only instead of in the huge, beautiful dining room with chandeliers hanging over the table, they sat around a table in the library, a musty room that smelled of old books.

The meal, though, was served as always by their butler, who oversaw a maid bringing out several courses. Olivia noted that they weren't short of food. Their vast estate had always kept them in fresh produce, and there was also plenty of meat from the estate's livestock and fish from its well-stocked lake as their land sprawled away from the clifftop the house stood on and for miles into beautiful rolling hills of meadows and forest, the latter providing plenty of game birds, rabbits and venison.

As if reading her thoughts, her uncle told her, 'We share everything with the hospital next door. Our officers eat well, as the town folk do, as we dig for Britain now!'

Olivia smiled. It all seemed so surreal and, in a way, wrong when she thought of how Annie and all her people made do with spam most nights and how the islanders were almost down to starvation rations. But she knew that life was never fair, and these two shared all they had as far as it would go. They couldn't do any more than that. And she was glad they weren't suffering. Like her own father, Uncle had fought in the last war. They'd done their bit.

When the talk came around to the war, Olivia told them that she was joining the army.

'But your leg, my dear! Have they accepted you, knowing you aren't fit?'

Olivia had been trying not to think about her damaged leg with its ugly scars, a legacy of the train crash.

'Oh, it's a lot better, Aunt. I can run now and hardly feel pain, only when I'm tired, but I will have to undergo a medical before I am finally accepted.'

'That's good – about your leg, I mean. I did notice that you didn't limp when you arrived . . . But the army! Why? What can you do? . . . You won't shoot people, will you?'

Olivia laughed at her aunt's shocked expression.

'Of course she bloody will! She wouldn't be her father's daughter if she didn't. He killed practically an army of Germans in the last lot when they were closing in on his men!'

Aunt Rosina raised her eyebrows and then winked at Olivia. 'It was a small battalion of about a dozen Germans. Oh, and did he suffer for it. He had nightmares when he came home, saying how young they were. We had to keep reminding him that the same number of our young men went home to their families because of his valiant action.'

Olivia knew her father held the Victoria Cross, but he'd never told her why. Pride in him swelled her chest.

Changing the subject, Olivia knew what she said next would shock them, but she needed her uncle's help. He knew everyone and would know if there was an owner of a light aircraft that would help her.

'Talking of young men getting back to their families . . . I know you haven't asked because you're afraid of the answer, but Hendrick is safe.'

Her uncle humphed.

They, like everyone, must believe he'd gone to serve Hitler and betrayed them.

'Uncle, I cannot tell you all, only that Hendrick has been on our side. When I say he is safe, I meant he has escaped being put to death because he was betrayed.'

They both gasped.

'His father and his father's friend have both been executed. They were helping the Jews. So, you see, as I told Aunt when I came, not all Germans are bad. Hendrick has said that very few want what is happening. But they are ruled by a tyrant and the hateful Nazis, but mostly by fear.'

Her uncle cleared his throat. 'So, Hendrick is one of us?'

'He is, but that's all I'm allowed to say. However, he cannot return here. If he did, he would be imprisoned just because he is a German. He is living on a farm in the mountains of Switzerland – a goat farm.' Olivia allowed herself to smile as she thought of her lovely, clever husband, who'd only ever known working in a bank with foreign clients, getting dirty on a farm.

'Uncle, I want your help to get me to him. I only have two weeks' leave before I, too, will be doing things I cannot tell you of. I want to use one of those weeks – the middle days of the fourteen – going to see Hendrick.'

'Good God!'

91

This was uttered by her aunt. Her uncle snorted.

'That's impossible, Olivia! What on earth are you thinking, my dear? Please put such a notion out of your head.'

'Please, Uncle. Please help me. Switzerland is a neutral country. My only danger would be the journey and that is why I need you to find me a pilot who could take me. A pilot who really knows what he's doing.'

Her uncle looked at her for a full minute, then wiped his mouth and moustache with his napkin and said, 'Leave it with me, my dear. I will see what I can do.'

Chapter Eight

Annie

By the time they arrived at Rosemary's the children were tired and fractious. It had been a gruelling five-hour journey, not helped by the signposts having been removed and them having to stop umpteen times to ask the way.

When they knocked on the door Annie bit her lip and closed her eyes. *Please don't let Rosemary regret taking us in.*

But she'd no need to worry. Rosemary was understanding, and set about making cocoa and putting out biscuits, then turning everything into a game.

'When little ones come to see Granny, they get goodies. Granny doesn't mind them being tearful, she understands. So, come on, let me be the granny from the offset. Up to the table, little ones, and drink your cocoa and eat your biscuits, while Aunty Annie and Aunty Daphne prepare your bath for you. I've a big tub so you can all go in together.'

'I'm not going in with the boys, Granny!'

Rosemary laughed at Beth's indignant face. 'No, of course not. You're going to have the first dip as girls are never as dirty as boys. They can go in after you.'

Beth looked suitably appeased as she grinned at the boys. But then she shocked them all by saying, 'I pee in the bath!'

Ian grimaced, but Karl giggled.

'Beth! You're a madam at times! Well, you ain't getting into the bath until you've been on the toilet, I'll see to that!'

Annie couldn't help laughing despite her stern tone. Beth had lightened the moment and all grumpiness had lifted as Ian now saw the funny side of what Beth had said.

As always, Annie wondered about this niece of hers. She wasn't a bit like her timid mum. Janey had been fragile – in mind and body.

A pain jolted Annie's heart on thinking of her sister. As always, she dealt with it by busying herself. 'Right, come on, Daphne. We'll get everything sorted upstairs.'

Once up there, they looked around, taking in the three bedrooms allocated to them. Each was furnished with twin beds.

Annie hoped that the four bedrooms, Rosemary's included, would eventually be for their use and form a separate flat for them to live in.

She remembered how big Rosemary's bedroom was when shown it on her last visit and had thought since of how it would make a nice sitting room for her, Daphne and the kids. If it worked, this would mean their flat would have three good-sized bedrooms, a living room and a bathroom and they could share the kitchen downstairs with Rosemary.

With this in mind, she asked Daphne, 'How would you feel about sharing a bedroom with me, Daphne?'

'I'd love that. We can natter about the day and make plans and have a giggle . . . There's so much I need to talk about, Annie, and I feel ready to do so now. But not where the children are as most of it will make me cry.'

'I know, luv. I'm the same. Some I just keep putting out of me mind but I know that ain't the right thing to do . . . So, that's settled. Let's get all the blackouts in place first, shall we? Then we can get the rest sorted.'

Annie stood a moment looking out of the window of the bedroom she and Daphne were to share. She couldn't see much, just shadowy trees, and marvelled at how different this area was to Bethnal. Not that Bethnal didn't have trees, but here they surrounded the house, giving it privacy from Kingsmill Road that it stood back from. Sighing, she pulled the blackouts and went to join Daphne once more.

As they worked, putting theirs and the children's clothes away in drawers, filling wardrobes that had stood empty for ever and placing boxes of toys in the children's bedroom, Annie outlined her plans to Daphne of how she saw the flat laid out.

They were in the bedroom they were to share. 'This room's big enough to put another bed in if Beth doesn't want to share with Karl, but she often has, so I can't see it will be a problem, and then Ian can have a bedroom to himself. But it will all depend on Rosemary being comfortable with it and on Olivia being able to find the money to have a bathroom put in downstairs. Rosemary already has a lav down there, but it's outside. She'll need one inside as well as a bath.'

'I think it'll all be perfect and will be a lot easier for Rosemary having her own space which she's always been used to. And the good thing is that there is a door leading off the hall to the kitchen so we wouldn't have to go through her room to get there.'

'Yes, and yet we can all be together whenever Rosemary wants to be so that she doesn't still feel lonely in her own house – being lonely in a crowd is possible, you know. I come across it a lot. You wouldn't think anyone would be lonely in a big city, but there are plenty who are.'

With this, Annie sat on the end of the bed she'd chosen as hers, as it suddenly hit her that she'd left home – the big city of London and her end of it, the East End. She'd never thought she would leave the life she'd had. But then, that life had been taken away from her – snatched by a rotten little moustached man, who thought he was God!

'Hey, I can see you've gone down into the dumps. Let's get the bath ready and bring the children up as they always lighten our moments.'

Annie grinned. 'Or drive us mad!'

They both giggled as they went into the bathroom, a square room that held what seemed like an enormous bath, a toilet and a little sink. Its walls were covered in white tiles and the floor with beige linoleum. A rail held fluffy beige towels and another pile of the same colour were neatly folded on a little stool.

'Blimey, there's even a radiator in here! The whole place is as warm as toast. I wonder if Rosemary manages to get enough coal for the boiler. We need to tell her she doesn't have to keep it roaring – we're hardy enough and the kids are too. She'll soon use up her rations this way. We can manage with a fire lit in what is to be our sitting room.'

'Yes, you're right, Daphne, and if we have to light the ones in the children's rooms, it wouldn't take as much as a boiler does. But saying that, I've never yet had to light fires in the bedrooms back home in Bethnal.'

'No, Annie, because being upstairs, your flat pinched warmth from downstairs, as this will, so we must make sure Rosemary has a fire and is warm enough downstairs. She has older bones than us.'

Daphne leaned over the bath as she said this, put the plug in, and turned on the hot water. 'Annie, we must never stop thinking of our homes as our real homes. We have to think we will go back to them. Mine will always be in Guernsey with me mum.'

She straightened then and turned. The look on her face made Annie move towards her and take her in her arms.

'I'm glad I've got you, Daphne. It's down to us now, girl. We'll do all we can to find out where Loes is and see if we can write to her, but we'll not be able to contact Olivia. So, it's up to us to shore everything up that we can, eh?'

'It is, I know that. And Annie, me being with you will make it easier for me . . . I just hope that I can be a good stand-in for Olivia for you.'

'You don't have to be a stand-in, luv. You're you, and I love you for that, not as a substitute for Olivia.'

They hugged, but then Annie winced as Daphne said, 'How can Olivia leave Karl again? I just don't understand it. I know we all have to disappear, I can see that, but she could have gone to stay with her aunt in Cornwall and taken Karl with her.'

All Annie could say was, 'Knowing Olivia as you do, you know she wouldn't choose to leave Karl. That what she is doing is what she must do and that she has no choice. What that is cannot involve her son. It is up to us to care for him and to keep her memory alive for him.'

Daphne shivered. 'You mean . . . She's not going to Switzerland at all, is she . . . ? But then, where?'

'There's a war on, mate, and walls have ears.'

'Oh . . . I'm sorry. I – I . . . oh, Annie, we will pray every night to keep our Olivia safe.'

Annie nodded. 'I'll fetch the kids.'

The next hour was full of giggles. Beth decided she did want to get in with the boys after all and showed no modesty as a coming up for three-year-old shouldn't. Though in her case, it was more like coming up for ten!

Water went everywhere, as she smacked the surface and splashed the boys, but she was the first to yawn as they wrapped her in a warm towel. Annie cuddled her close. Like this, with her eyes half-closed, she looked like an angel, not the little devil she could be. Annie's love for her warmed her whole body.

She could see the same thing happening for Daphne as she dealt with a sleepy Karl.

When these two were tucked up in bed and Ian was drying himself, he yawned as he asked, 'Are there any books to read, Annie? I used to read me comics in bed at night. It made me sleep instead of thinking about things.'

'I haven't any for your age group yet, Ian, but I'll ask Granny Rosemary. Is that what you want to call her, Ian?'

'I do. She's a nice granny. A bit posher than me gran but she gives the same cuddles.'

As he said this, they walked onto the landing to find Rosemary at the top of the stairs smiling. 'I like the sound of your gran, Ian. And I so want to be like her for you . . . And yes, I do have some books in that box I told you about before. You get your pyjamas on, and I'll go and fetch them up and then you can choose.'

To Annie, Rosemary looked the happiest she'd looked since she'd met her. The tension had gone from her, and she wondered if she'd cried all her tears while waiting for them to arrive.

*　　*　　*

98

Ian was soon tucked up with *Tales of Robin Hood* by Enid Blyton, and she and Daphne were enjoying a cup of tea with Rosemary when Annie broached her idea of making the house into two flats.

'That's a good idea, Annie, but how would it work? I mean, well, I shouldn't sound as though it would all be a relief to me, I didn't mean that. Only for the children and all of us, it is better to have our own territory. And to be honest, I do find the stairs a bit much.'

'You won't feel isolated, will you? We wouldn't want that in your own home.'

'No, I'll hear you walking about and hear the laughter of the children and know you'll come down and sit with me in a shot if I need company in the evenings – they are the worst times, when the blackouts are in place. They seem to shut the world out. Well, they can now as I shall have all of you in my world with me.'

Annie couldn't help herself; she got up and went to Rosemary and hugged her. 'You've given us a sanctuary too, Rosemary. The children will be safe here and able to lead a normal life without bombs dropping around them. I can feel that they love it. Ta, luv. I just know this will all work out.'

The next day was busy – visiting the council to see if planning permission was needed for the proposed bathroom but luckily finding it wasn't. Visiting the local school to book Ian in and finding he could start the following week. Shopping for supplies, using her ration coupons, and finally, but with trepidation, calling in at the police station.

Sergeant Green, a portly man, greeted her with a look that said, *I'm the boss*. He twiddled with the end of his long, old-fashioned moustache and eyed her up and down. His cockney accent surprised her as he said, 'I'll tell yer from the offset that I ain't much for women coppers, but yer've come highly recommended by a bloke I respect, so I'll give yer a chance, Stanley!'

Annie was used to being called by her surname, so this didn't bother her, but Sergeant Green's remark about women did.

A warning bell set up in her head. She would have to prove herself, but then, would she be given the chance to? As she looked through the glass of the sarge's office at the many male heads in the main office, some balding, some with greying hair, all looking as though they'd been pulled out of retirement, she wasn't so sure. There wasn't a female head in sight.

'Am I the only woman officer, Sarge?'

'You will be if you fit in, though we could do with someone to make the tea and keep the kitchen clean – the bogs and all – so if you're good at those things, then you'll be accepted.'

Annie bristled. 'I ain't a skivvy, Sarge. I don't make tea and clean, I'm a police officer. I walk the beat and deal with criminals. I keep order on the street, and help those who need helping. I've worked during air raids, rescuing folk from burning buildings and—'

The sergeant let out a bellow of laughter. 'That's what yer did do. 'Ere, we don't need yer to do any of that, ta. One: there ain't any bombs. Two: we take care of crime and 'ave done without your 'elp so far. So, we need to be left to get on with our work – police*men*'s work. But I agreed to yer coming as, like I said, we need a woman's touch around the place.'

Pulling herself up to her full height, Annie looked directly into the sergeant's eyes. She wanted to spit in his face, but instead, and with dignity, she said, 'In that case, I resign from the police force. I'm still on compassionate leave, so I'll serve me notice while that lasts. I'll hand in me letter of resignation tomorrow. Goodbye, Sergeant.' Her salute was an insult, which she hoped he understood. Turning on her heel, she walked out and slammed the heavy door behind her.

Once outside, she hopped down the few steps and out of the gate. But then leaned against the wall that surrounded the building and took several deep breaths to calm herself.

What she was going to do now she didn't know. This would mean she would have to live on the army allowance paid to wives of serving soldiers, when she'd always put that aside for her and Ricky's future . . . Gasping at this last thought, she told herself, *My Ricky will come home, he will. Didn't old Aggie Brown tell me that? Aggie may have sold flowers near to London Bridge, but she could see into the future too.*

Slinging her handbag over her shoulder, Annie dug her hands into her pockets and pulled her arms in as if to hug herself as she walked with her head down against the sting of the bitter wind towards where she could see a shop, hoping it was a grocery shop where she could stock up.

As she opened the door a loud clanging of the shop bell set her fraught nerves on edge. But she was glad to see a sign saying, *Deliveries 1d extra on all orders.*

She'd been wondering how she would carry all she needed to buy.

With her shopping done and a delivery sorted for later that day, Annie looked along the street. Next to where she'd parked her car, she saw the welcome sight of a cafe. She'd go and have a warming cuppa and think through what had just happened.

*   *   *

101

Blowing the steam away and warming her hands at the same time, Annie clasped the mug of tea as if it was a lifesaver as she stared out of the window. Figures walked by, huddled against the cold. The odd car passed, leaving a trail of fumes in its wake, but to Annie, it seemed almost like a ghost town compared to Bethnal Green.

But one thing was the same as back home as the folk stopped to chat despite the cold and she heard many a cheery greeting.

Only she wasn't at home, nor were all her loved ones. Most of them were gone for ever. She didn't have her Ricky, or Olivia either. And now she didn't have a job! She'd always been so proud of being a police officer, something Ricky had made her believe she could do, when all she'd known previously was shop work and being a maid. Ricky had given her confidence; shown her she was a person worthy of something better. Oh, how she missed him. If only she could get news.

Her hand went to the huge locket tucked into her blouse.

As she clutched it she thought of its contents – the only notes she'd received from Ricky since his capture. Written on the back of labels taken from canned food that she guessed had been delivered to his POW camp by the Red Cross, they told of his love, and how she was to believe he would make it home.

As always, Ricky helped her as her strength and determination returned. She would manage easily on Ricky's army allowance. She had no rent to pay. Olivia had scrapped any rent payments, saying it would be her contribution to keeping Karl fed and clothed. And Annie thought how what she had saved already would set her and Ricky up as she'd added it to what he'd left in her safe keeping for her future, should he not return.

Is this me future now? Would Ricky want me to scrimp and

save when I could make me life better? She knew he wouldn't, and knew too that her life would be better if she could stay home and bring up the children. That was a rewarding job and they needed someone constant in their lives.

They'd been pulled from pillar to post, suffered the terror of explosions and fires, and of losing all they had – in Beth's case, her mum and two grans being killed, and her dad being sent to prison for murdering her young baby sister. In Karl's case, he had lost his mum and dad, as they gave their all to fighting the war. And in Ian's case, his mum being killed in an air raid, and then the only person he'd had left, his gran, being killed by a stray bomb at Christmas while at Rose's farm in Kent – the same bomb that had taken Annie's mum, her sister and her mum-in-law.

Despite the agony of revisiting this time, Annie told herself that at least she could replace the children's pain with the love of a mum, just as Rosemary was giving them the love of a gran.

With her pride and determination restored, Annie stood up and walked out of the cafe with a new feeling of gumption in her belly.

As she walked to her car, Annie spotted a sign saying *Plumbers' Merchant* and on impulse she walked through the gate. An old man met her. His eyes were lively and twinkled with his easy smile.

'What can I do for you, miss?'

Annie told him about how she had plans for a bathroom to be fitted and gave him their address. 'Would you call sometime and give me an estimate for the work, please? And can you get me a bath, sink and toilet to fit into it? Oh, and I need a builder too, to section off the space where I want it to go.'

'I can do all of that, missus.' Annie noticed that he'd spotted the ring on her finger and so had addressed her differently this time.

'Ta. When could yer come?'

'Well, I'm not over busy at the moment . . . You're from London, aren't you? I hear that tradesmen like me are all kept busy there. Maybe I should move there.'

'You wouldn't want to do that, believe me. It's like living in hell, and this is heaven.'

'Aye, I've heard it said. So, what part are you from?'

'Bethnal Green. It's in the East End.'

'I've heard of it as it's taking the brunt of the bombs. You'll find life different here.' He looked at the address Annie had handed to him. 'Ah, Rosemary Davies. So, you're living there, are you? I like Rosemary. A lovely quiet lady. Not many of them in Wales. They like a natter, do the ladies of Wrexham.'

Annie laughed. 'Just like back home. Many a doorstep scrubbing takes an hour when it should take five minutes as the women start to gossip – after they've made every effort to be the first with a clean step, that is.'

The plumber, who she knew was called David from his sign, laughed with her. 'Same everywhere. All the women want to be first with their step scrubbing – mind, they get the wrath of the others' tongues if it's not done.'

Annie laughed, knowing that's just how it was in Bethnal Green and feeling strangely comforted and a little more at home here than she had done by hearing this.

'Well now, you'll know I'm David Willian, so what do I call you? Are you a relative of Rosemary's?'

'No, not a relative, but . . . Well, me friend knows her and we're all glad that Rosemary's taken us in.'

'I think I know who your friend might be. We all see him visiting. A nice bloke . . . Though he had a posh accent. He's not from your neck of the woods. Some say he's Rosemary's brother, but others . . . Well, it's none of their or my business.'

Annie coloured. Of course locals would have noticed, and some would have gossiped about Olivia's dad. She felt trapped for a moment, but then decided the best way was to deal with it.

'Oh, you mean Mr Riverstone? My friend is his daughter. Mr Riverstone and Rosemary were cousins.'

As soon as she spoke this lie, Annie knew she'd done wrong. Now she would have to explain to Rosemary. The thought came to her that if she told David that Rosemary was now bereaved, then he may never mention a cousin to her.

But things got worse when she did.

'I'm sorry to hear that Rosemary will miss him. We all knew when he was due to visit as she changed. She became happy again and smiled a lot. She shopped and needed deliveries, instead of just picking up a few bits. I'll bring her some flowers when I come to look at the job.'

Annie shook inside. She just wanted to get away from here. Why had she even said anything?

David picked up a grubby-looking notebook. 'Now then, let's see when I can fit you in . . . Ha, now, or later today, or anytime.'

He showed her the empty pages, his face a picture of amusement. 'You name it, I can make it.'

Annie smiled. She liked David. Maybe she should tell him the truth. But was it her place? Maybe best she confessed to Rosemary so she was ready. She was probably oblivious to

105

the town gossip about her. Deciding on the latter, she said, 'Ta. David. Yer can come when yer like. We're always in – well, one or the other of us is.'

As Annie got into her car, she sat a moment and thought about the hostility she'd been subjected to at the police station, just for being a woman, and how that had resulted in her giving up the job she loved most in the world.

A feeling of being bereft took her, but then the three kids who relied on her came to mind and she determined that she wouldn't dwell on it but would just get on with life as it was and do the best job of being a mum that she could.

When she arrived back at Rosemary's, she opened the door of what she now must look on as home, and all three children rushed at her. Annie hugged them to her and knew she'd made the right choice.

PART TWO

Choices Made

PART TWO

Chapter Nine

Olivia

Olivia couldn't believe that today, 16 March 1941, she was going to fly to the arms of her Hendrick.

In her mind she imagined it would all be so wonderful, but the reality was that her mission was very dangerous as the plane taking her was part of a profitable but illegal trade with the Swiss. Isolated as they were from anyone other than the occupied or aggressive countries surrounding them, her uncle had told her that the Swiss paid good money for goods they could not get access to.

All had been arranged by her uncle, who'd told her that the plane had made a lot of successful runs. But that if they didn't fly too near to where Hendrick was, she would have to make her own way to him and be back within less than a day as the plane had to return to England the same night – once more carrying valuable cargo for markets here.

Olivia began to wonder about her uncle and his dealings. Her father had once told her that he suspected there was more to her uncle's fortune than met the eye. And thinking about it, Uncle Cyril couldn't have possibly made his money from the rents his tenant farmers paid, or from the land that he farmed himself.

Father said that the Cornish coast was ideal for such activities as smuggling. However, no matter how her uncle had made his fortune, Olivia was only glad that he'd moved his assets from her father's bank and wasn't a loser in the collapse.

And she was grateful too that, after hearing of the alterations that needed to be carried out on the house Rosemary lived in, he'd made her a gift to help with the cost. Weirdly, though, he showed no surprise at the existence of Rosemary, whereas Aunt Rosina had been shocked.

'That property will stand you in good stead, Olivia,' Uncle Cyril had said when they'd spoken about it. 'So, make sure the work is done properly and doesn't compromise the structure of the building.' But then he had added, 'But you have no need to worry. It was a tragedy how your father's empire collapsed, but you're our sole heir and that will keep you for the rest of your life.'

Olivia had hugged him. Always she'd loved him, and so she was finding it easy to turn a blind eye to his dealings. And at this moment she could only feel grateful that they had led to the help he was giving her.

She took the wad of Swiss francs he offered her without question but did marvel at how he portrayed this doddery exterior to the world when underneath it all he must be an out and out criminal!

The flight took them north, and then across to the bottom tip of Germany. When she realized this, Olivia's heart was in her mouth.

'Don't worry,' the pilot told her as she sat just behind him. 'The Germans are occupied with bombing England, they won't notice us, and in any case, palms have been crossed with silver, so to speak.'

As they broke through cloud land became visible below, leaving Olivia wondering how this illicit business worked. How contacts were made, and silences and safe passages paid for and guaranteed.

The pilot broke into her thoughts. 'You're best to pay a driver to take you on your onward journey. That way you're sure to get to the farm you're heading for in plenty of time to have a few hours there. We've a few men on the ground who'll be willing to take you, but they'll need paying handsomely. The Swiss make their living by wheeling and dealing. They know that whatever is wanted of them, they can get money for, especially if the request is from a country under threat of occupation. Your man must have had a stash to give them to get a safe house.'

Olivia couldn't think from where. She couldn't imagine that Hendrick had been paid any wages, and what bank accounts he had in Germany would have been frozen, if not closed altogether.

At last, they landed.

'Right, see that truck? That's one of the drivers who offer transport. Ask him how long it takes to get to the address and book him to pick you up so you're back here in time. If you're not, I will leave without you as I only get small pockets of safe flight paths – ha, I call them safe, but they're only as safe as not being spotted makes them. I've been shot at before now and one of my mates was shot down.'

Olivia felt the colour drain from her face, but then she'd be an idiot if she imagined that couldn't happen.

'It was a returning Luftwaffe plane. My mate didn't stand a chance.'

Not answering this, Olivia, with the noise of the aircraft still ringing in her ears, ran to the waiting truck. She greeted the driver in French, but received a German reply, making her aware that she was nearer to the German border than the French one.

The journey was very short, something Olivia was grateful for, and made with full headlights on past houses blaring with light – a sign that these people really were free from the threat of war.

When the truck pulled up outside the farm, another sign of their freedom was that the driver blared his horn, deafening her.

They hadn't conversed much along the way, except for him to ask in German for a lot more money than she had expected him to ask for.

When she questioned whether this was for the return journey too, he scoffed. 'If you want to ride back, you pay twice as much. I know the importance of you getting back and that you've no chance if you miss the plane.'

Olivia didn't argue.

Nothing mattered anyway. Nothing but that she was here!

Running towards the house, she realized that the blast of the horn mustn't have been anything out of the ordinary as no one came rushing out to see what the reason for it was.

Nearer the house, she caught sight of her beloved Hendrick through a window. He had his head thrown back, laughing. A young girl was laughing with him. For a moment Olivia stopped in her tracks as a pang of fear and jealousy attacked her.

Telling herself she was being silly, she hammered on the door.

The girl answered. Speaking in German, she asked, 'Who are you? What do you want?'

'I'm Hendrick's wife.'

The door was snatched out of her hand and held wide. There he stood before her, more beautiful than she remembered. His eyes wide with wonderment as he stepped out and grabbed her, clinging on to her, his sobs wracking his body as he said over and over, 'Olivia, my Olivia . . . How . . . how . . . ?' Then, 'Where's Karl? Is he with you?'

Through her own sobs Olivia garbled out that she only had hours and how she'd got here and how Karl was fine and with Annie and Daphne.

'Oh, my darling.' Hendrick drew her into the room out of the cold. 'I can't believe this! How did you get off Guernsey?'

The woman Olivia had thought was a girl but could now see was in her thirties to forties joined in with the amazement. 'But this is wonderful! We have a job to cheer Hendrick. Always he pines for you and his son.'

Olivia's fear left her as the scene that had shocked her didn't matter any more. She just wanted to be alone with Hendrick for the few hours they had.

She clung on to him, felt how much thinner he was, and now in the light, she could see a gauntness in his face. His beautiful face.

The woman said, 'I will leave you. I must make sure the children are in bed.'

Hendrick paid her no attention but gazed into Olivia's eyes. 'I can't believe this, darling. You've risked your life for me . . . Oh, Olivia, can I fly back with you?'

'No, Hendrick, only certain imprisonment awaits you there, just for being German, despite all you did for Britain.

113

You wouldn't be able to stand that . . . and, well, the War Office has plans for me . . . Is there somewhere we can go?'

'Yes, I have my own place. It's part of a Swiss house that belongs to the farm. It was ramshackle, but I'm doing it up. When I had a communication that I was to stay here, I decided that it wouldn't be right to intrude by living in this house for a long period . . . But, oh, my darling, I have longed to see you . . . Come.'

The room they went into in the house, just a few yards across a cobbled yard, was warm and cosy with a roaring log fire.

'This is all I have, with my bed in the corner, but I am working on the kitchen. I have an oil stove so can put a kettle on and make coffee.'

'All I want is to be held by you. The time is ticking, my darling.'

His arms enfolded her. Their kiss went on and on, deepening to a hunger that consumed them. Soon they were on the rug, the fire warming their naked bodies as they came together as the one being they knew themselves to be.

Olivia cried out her joy at the exquisite sensations taking her body. Hendrick gave of himself to her, as if he would never stop, and she didn't want him to. She wanted to drink him in, devour all he gave to her, and give more back.

At last, they lay next to each other, still as close as it was possible to get without being coupled, still caressing, but spent.

But then realization hit that their time was running out. They dressed quickly, giggling as they hopped about trying to get pants on and then trousers.

Finally, they could sit together and talk.

The talking led to tears as both told of losing their fathers in a brutal manner. They mourned being apart and not being with their son. When Olivia told Hendrick about Gunter raping her, they cried the most.

Hendrick's sobs were gut-wrenching, his anguish and pain wracking his body, his anger coming out in vile threats of what he would do to Gunter, until he came to a place where he could see that she needed him to channel his emotion into comforting and reassuring her. Then they quietly wept together, speaking of their love and how nothing would ever taint it. No animal like Gunter would put a chasm between them – they were one.

It was then that Olivia told Hendrick what was planned for her. How Lucy was working with the Maquis group in Limousin.

'And you will be joining her . . . Don't they think you have done enough?'

'There's something else and it led to this . . . Loes . . .'

Hendrick was as shocked as she had been by what had happened to Loes. 'So, you see, I must disappear as Annie has. They are wanting to use my skills, though of course I'm to go through training. So, it isn't cut and dried that I am going . . . But I want to, Hendrick. I want to do all I can to stop the Gunters of this world – the true Nazis. They must be beaten!'

'Yes.'

Hendrick was quiet for a moment, and then said, 'I will do my bit too. I will find a way to cross into France and to join the Maquis.'

'Hendrick! There is so much danger, please don't. Please stay here.'

'I cannot. I must fight against the Nazis too. I must help to free the good, decent Germans – my true countrymen – from the tyranny they are ruled by. I have to stop their sons dying. But I will have to see many more die, probably by my own actions, before there is an end to this. I can do nothing here, but farm and live well. I don't want that. I will make it to the French border, then find my way down to the Maquis in Limousin. I can fool them that I am a Frenchman who was captured and who has escaped, and they will accept me when they know the languages I speak and how useful to them I can be. I will tell them that I was teaching in Guernsey when I was captured.'

Seeing he was determined, an idea came to her. She told him about Leonard Preesley, the young man who'd taken his place in her father's bank. How he had one useless arm so couldn't join the forces. Of how he'd been shot by Gunter and his men. 'You can make him live again and do great things in his name to honour him. You can take on his identity. It's perfect as he did have a French aunt, Madame Durand. She lived in Paris . . . Wait a moment . . .'

Delving into her memory, Olivia tried to bring to mind where it was Leonard's aunt lived. Suddenly it came to her. 'Rue Montorgueil, that's it. I remember telling him that it meant Mount Pride. And that he had a mountain of that . . . He was a very proud man despite his disability – proud of his achievements and of his singing . . . His aunt lives in an apartment. He'd been hoping to visit her before the invasion and that is why we were talking about her. He never gave up thinking that he would see her again and was constantly worried what her life was like under German occupation.'

'That's perfect. And, yes, I remember Leonard. I was glad when you told me he'd taken my place. I trusted him . . . I'll go to see his aunt. I am sure she will back me up when she hears how we worked with Leonard and grew up knowing

116

him. I can get papers in his name. It will cost me a pretty price, but they will be a help. I still have my German identity papers and can be fitted out with a German uniform.'

'Have you enough money for all of that, Hendrick? Only I thought you would have lost all you had.'

'I stole . . . It was needs must. I knew I would need money to buy help from people . . . There was a safe in a small office near to the one we translators occupied. I knew the combination. It was easy to access it, and I was shocked at how much there was and could only think that it wasn't legally obtained, but the spoils of awful deeds. I prayed for the people who had lost it, and probably their lives too. But I never would have got this far without it and have convinced myself that they would rather that I had it than the Nazis.'

'I know they would, and I thank them for helping you to safety and for now helping you to get to France . . . Oh, Hendrick, it all seems so possible. We have a chance at being together, my darling, but you must be careful, please.'

'I will, and so must you. You have a precarious journey to get back to England.'

The sound of the truck's horn had them scurrying to get her coat on. 'Hurry, I know Michael and he won't wait a minute longer than you are paying him to. Goodbye, my darling.'

They kissed again, and then she left him, taking one more glance back at him standing in the doorway before she jumped into the truck and it sped off.

Chapter Ten

Olivia

When the plane landed back in the long field Uncle had easily lit up as a runway, Olivia decided she was ready. Ready to report for duty in a few days' time. Ready to do all she had to do.

Her aching leg caused a trickle of worry, though. Somehow she must convince those who would oversee her training that she could keep up with others, and not show the pain that overactivity could give her.

But as she snuggled down in bed in the early hours, Olivia knew her bravery and determination to crack and to almost desert her. Fear gave her a sinking feeling in the pit of her stomach.

Her fear was for Hendrick as much as for herself. She would not know if he had made it and was part of the Maquis until she arrived in France.

But suddenly she sat up. Did Lucy know what Hendrick looked like? Would she recognize him? Would she betray him thinking that he was lying and was infiltrating them to pass information to the Germans? Or would she still trust him as she had done all through the time his messages were sent through her to the War Office?

Should she mention Hendrick's plans to Brinston?

Would he allow Hendrick to be part of the Maquis? What if he didn't and . . . Oh, God, he might decide Hendrick wasn't to be trusted and order him to be executed!

Olivia's body broke out in a sweat. The dreams she'd planned she'd dream of her time in front of the fireplace with Hendrick now turned into a nightmare of terrifying scenarios. *What should I do? What?*

After a fitful sleep, Olivia woke and felt sure that the conclusion she'd come to was the right one. She'd decided she should do nothing, only hope that she made it to the Maquis in Limousin, France, before Hendrick did. That way she could pave his way with Lucy's help. She would understand why Olivia hadn't reported Hendrick's plans once she'd explained her fears to her.

The morning brought lovely winter sunshine to Cornwall. The cliffs gave way to the turquoise sea, which sparkled with what looked like a million diamonds. Olivia gazed out at it for a moment, letting the calm waters, with cotton wool surf breaking the small swell, soothe her.

Her goodbyes later to her uncle and aunt were tearful as Aunt Rosina dabbed at her eyes and Uncle Cyril blew his nose loudly.

'My dear, whatever it is you must do, may God be with you. We will be thinking of you all the time, won't we, Rosina?'

Her aunt couldn't speak, only nod. Olivia hurried to her car and started her journey, waving till she was out of sight. Though sad to leave them, she was also filled with joy as she couldn't wait to see Karl. And to be held by Annie.

119

It was late evening when she arrived to find Annie, Daphne and Rosemary enjoying a glass of sherry. This made her smile as she knew how giggly Annie got on half a glass!

They all hugged her, Annie holding on the longest. They both knew they must part again tomorrow, but for tonight, she put that out of her mind as she rushed upstairs to gaze at her sleeping son.

Tears rolled unchecked down her face as she took in his lovely fair hair and cherub-like face. 'I've been to see your daddy, my little one. He told me to tell you that he loves you with all his heart and that one day we will all be together, and nothing will ever part us again.'

Fishing for her hankie, Olivia buried her face in it for a moment and allowed her heart to bleed her pain out.

After a moment, she dried her tears and stroked Karl's hair. He didn't stir. Sighing, she looked over at a sleeping Beth and whispered, 'Take care of him for me.'

This gave her comfort, even though she knew Beth hadn't heard.

With one more peek at Karl, Olivia took a deep breath and made her way to the bathroom.

By the time she came out she felt refreshed once more and ready to face life again.

Downstairs they all fussed over her, and she accepted a plate of stew they'd kept hot for her and a chunk of bread, which they told her had been freshly made that day.

'That'll warm the cockles of yer heart, Olivia, luv. Now tell us all that happened and how Lord and Lady Wallington are?'

'I'll have a glass of that sherry first, Annie. You've all got a head start on me, and I don't have to report until tomorrow afternoon.'

120

As the golden liquid warmed her gullet and then her stomach, Olivia felt she could cope once more.

They were all pleased to hear that her aunt and uncle were well, but then Rosemary shocked Olivia.

'I met your uncle, Olivia. He was at the same function that your father was at when we met.' Rosemary laughed. 'He cornered me and, as if he and your father were still schoolboys, told me that your father was rather taken with me and asked if I would like to join them for a drink. Of course, I couldn't as I was working. But you know the rest.'

Olivia put her hand out and took Rosemary's. 'Yes, and, like you, I wish I'd have known a lot sooner.'

They smiled at each other.

'Rosemary, are you all fine with Annie's plans?'

'Oh, I am, Olivia, my dear. I think that it's right we should all have our own home. And I know there will be many cosy evenings like this together, or I can choose to have a quiet evening. I feel so comfortable having them around and my life has already changed for the better in just this short time.'

Annie told Olivia how the plumber had been and told them that the changes would cost in the region of thirty pounds. 'And that's to include the division of the best room and fitting the bath, sink and toilet. You see, Rosemary has decided to have the hall extended along the front so that her bathroom can be situated at the end of it. Then she doesn't have to go through her bedroom to pay a visit, as she calls it. Ha! We laughed about that. I thought she meant she would have a visitor in there!'

They all giggled.

'Yes,' Rosemary said. 'And it's also because I want to keep the dining room as it is, so that we can have special meals in there together. Christmas and birthdays. I didn't want to lose the view of the garden from there, or the French doors that lead to the garden and my garden room.'

'That all sounds excellent and doable. I'll leave plenty of money with Annie to see to everything. My uncle made sure I had enough.'

'Now, tell us your news, Olivia. Did you make it to see Hendrick?'

Olivia told them all she could, leaving out Hendrick's quest to go to France.

'Well, yer took a massive risk, mate, but I'm pleased for yer. I thought you had a glow about your eyes.'

Olivia blushed and they once more laughed out loud. She laughed with them, but a small part of her heart felt the pain of longing to be back with Hendrick.

Annie continued. 'Well, you've spurred me on. I've made my mind up to go to the Red Cross and try to find out anything about Ricky . . . And I have news of me own.'

Olivia listened with mixed feelings to how Annie had given up her job. She knew how much it would hurt Annie to have done this, and yet she was filled with relief as now with what they had said about Daphne finding work, the children would still be looked after by someone they knew and who loved them. It went a long way towards easing her mind.

The next morning, having not slept much on Rosemary's sofa and eventually creeping upstairs to slip in beside Annie, Olivia woke first.

Looking out of the window gave her the sight of a winter wonderland. It had snowed heavily during the night. The branches of the trees were laden with it and bowed under the weight. But it all looked beautiful as, defiantly, Rosemary's daffodils had kept their heads above the snow and looked like a sea of yellow on a white carpet.

The excitement of childhood clutched her as she remembered snowballing and building a snowman, but with it came sadness, until a picture of her father's laughing face came to her mind, as he lay in the snow behaving like a windmill with his legs and arms and how she'd fallen giggling on top of him. Then her heart felt gladdened that she'd had such a wonderful man as a father – one who'd even given up finding happiness in case it upset her.

He must have thought that him bringing a wife home would have been less painful to her than her getting to know the woman he loved before they were married.

She shook her head as she couldn't see his logic . . . Unless he'd never felt ready to commit again and had used his child to ward off making that final commitment.

Annie woke and stretched her limbs. 'Hey, I'm cold now you're not in with me.'

'It's been snowing, Annie! Hurry up and let's get breakfast . . . Where's Daphne?'

It was then that the delicious aroma of frying drifted up to them.

'I bet she's got those leftover spuds in the pan. I'm starving!'

'Ha, you always are, Annie.'

As she said this, the bedroom door opened, and the children stood there. The little ones had their eyes wide open. Spotting Olivia, Karl ran with his arms up to be lifted by her. This she did willingly, holding him tight, wanting to give him as many hugs as she could before the late afternoon when she would have to say goodbye.

'It's like Christmas pictures, Annie! Come and see!'

Annie jumped out of bed the best she could with Beth tugging one hand.

When they got to the window beside Olivia, Annie gasped. 'Oh, it is, Beth – it's just like the pictures we see of Christmas. How lovely. Come on, let's get yer all dressed, then we can have breakfast and go out and build a snowman, eh?'

The morning was one that Olivia would never forget.

Laughter filled the air. Little red faces glowed with happiness as snow was scraped into a heap then more piled on top of it.

At last, they had a body and Ian was busy rolling a ball of snow, making it bigger and bigger to form a head.

Rosemary called from her viewing point in her garden room, 'I have two lumps of coal here for his eyes, and an old pipe of William's that he left here once, so Mr Snowman can have a smoke . . . Oh, and I have a scarf here to keep him warm.'

'He needs a nose!'

'He does, Beth. I'm racking my brains as we can't waste a carrot on him. That would be very naughty as food is so short.'

Ian piped up, 'What about the potato man in that box you have, Gran? There must be a nose in that.'

'What a good idea! So there must. I'll go and get it.'

When Rosemary came back with the nose from the game, it was magnificent. All the adults agreed that it reminded them of the pictures of General De Gaulle as it looked the same shape as his nose. This caused giggles from the four ladies.

Olivia looked around this family of women and children and felt the sadness of not having their men with them. But then she saw the joy in the faces of the children as their laughter blew out plumes of steamy breath into the cold air and thought to herself that she would hold this picture in her mind and remember her own carefree childhood. This she knew would spur her on to conquer her fears and to do her bit to get them a safe world to live in – a place where peace reigned just as it had when she was a child.

Chapter Eleven

Annie

Waking up the next day to find no Olivia snuggled up to her gave Annie a sense of deep loss. As her eyes got used to the darkness, she looked over to where Daphne was just a mound in her bed.

Their friendship was growing with familiarity and their ways were becoming known to each. Daphne reminded her of Janey, wavering between being strong and needing shoring up.

Before she could go down the path her memories would take her, and then break her, Annie swung her legs out of bed, gathered her clothes from the chair next to her and headed for the bathroom.

The house was quiet and still, though she knew it would soon be a hive of activity and noise.

Stopping to pull the curtain to one side, Annie peered out into the blackness, trying to see if the snow still hung around. But then a light came on downstairs and lit the garden. From the white blanket it had been it was now a patchwork quilt of green and white, but De Gaulle, as they'd named their snowman, still stood strong and proud with his huge nose protruding.

Annie smiled to herself at the lovely memories of yesterday, then sighed. Life was becoming just a bag of memories, but she mustn't let it. If she did, she'd drift into a grief-stricken stupor, functioning as was necessary. But now she must enter a new era. Become a proper mum and guide her family through the horror of war to a better life. Today she would plan for this.

After washing and dressing, Annie thought of how life could be if she had her sitting room to go to now and could sit quietly and think everything through. She made her mind up that the alterations were the first thing to concentrate on. Olivia had left her a huge sum of money, so now she must push David and the builder he'd found for her to start the work. She would give them a deposit and promise them payments as they reached various stages. This, she hoped, would make them work faster.

She blushed as the thought came to her of how Rosemary had been shocked at being the talk of the town and even more shocked at how Annie had handled it. She said that she didn't want to deny her love for William, but after a moment had changed her mind and agreed that to save fuelling any scandal, she would go along with Annie and not deny the story she'd told.

Annie had been left wishing she hadn't said anything, but she'd found the need at the time to defend Rosemary's reputation. Nothing had been said about it since and she hadn't detected an atmosphere. If anything, Rosemary seemed more relaxed about having workmen in and had already begun to cover the furniture in her front room and to sort out what she would like where. 'The suite and furniture in the living room can go upstairs for your use, Annie, as I'd like the furniture from the front room brought in here for my use.'

Annie had liked this idea, feeling that the lived-in feel of this furniture would suit them better and she wouldn't have to treat it with kid gloves. She realized too that the front room furniture was probably more precious to Rosemary as she and Olivia's father may have spent more time together in there – folk always kept their best room for special occasions.

To complete the move, all Rosemary's bedroom furniture would be fitted into the front room.

Annie let out a sigh at these thoughts, and then turned her attention back to her priorities now that was all sorted in her mind.

First on her list was to try to find out information about her Ricky. Was he well? Was he coping? What was his life like in the POW camp? Was he fed well? To this end, she went back into the bedroom to try to find her writing case – a present from Olivia from a long time ago. It was a lovely book-like case covered in flowers, with a tab that press-studded it closed. Inside there was a pocket on each side, one for a writing pad and the other for envelopes and in the middle were loops to hook pens into.

Finding it, Annie clutched it to her heart. Not only did she treasure it because it was from Olivia, but because of the many letters she'd written to Ricky, not knowing if he even received one of them.

Daphne stirred and yawned. 'Good Morning. You're up early.'

'I am, luv. There's a lot to do to get everything sorted. And I need to be doing it.'

'You've done so much already, Annie. The alterations have

been arranged, Ian has a school, you've sorted your job out . . . which I know was a real blow to you.'

'It was, but it may be a blessing in disguise, luv. This conscription thing is all the talk, and once they think we're all used to the idea, it will happen, and if it does and you have to go somewhere, the kids will be looked after and not left to Rosemary to see to.'

'Well, as we've said, I'll sort out a job before it does as I don't want to be sent away. Besides, I need to contribute to our budget, and be of use somewhere, though I haven't got many skills other than household ones as that's all I've known, being a maid.'

'You can learn new ones. I'll ask around and see if there's a typing school, or maybe farm work, or even a factory . . . Though I don't see you cooped up in a factory somehow.'

'No, I can't even imagine it. I've seen pictures and it looks horrid . . . But typing, or farming . . . Yes, I think I'd enjoy either of those, especially farming. I'll ask Rosemary if she knows of anything going . . . Are you writing to Ricky?'

'I am.' This was said on a sigh.

'I wish that I could write to Stefan, but I have no idea where he is.'

Annie was thoughtful, but then mulled over something that had occurred to her. Something that would have been much easier to do when she'd lived in London.

'Daphne . . . I'm thinking of going to the Red Cross HQ in London . . . It'll mean going by train and that's daunting for me, but I've to overcome me fear at some point. Only, going in the car will take too long. If I do get there, I can ask about Stefan for you. I'll need as much information as you have. His full name, date of birth, his regiment and rank.'

'I know all of that.'

This surprised Annie. She hadn't realized the relationship between Daphne and Stefan had gone this far; she'd only thought of it as fledgling love.

'Write it down for me. I'm really going to get the courage up to go . . . Now, I need a few minutes to write this letter . . . It makes me feel close to my Ricky when I do.'

'I'll go and bring you a cuppa up.'

By the time Annie was sipping her tea, she'd written to her beloved Ricky and was delving in an old handbag that she kept for all sorts of oddments – letters, old rent books, old grocery books. Why she kept them she had no idea, but somehow they made up her, Janey's and Mum's past. She found what she was looking for – her birth and marriage certificates, and her collection book for her separation allowance. She wasn't sure she would need this, but it might add weight when she asked the Red Cross for information about Ricky.

Her hands dwelled a moment on the post office book with her and Ricky's savings in as she put the items she wouldn't need back into the bag.

The little buff-coloured book with the red insignia and red words proclaiming 'Post Office Savings Book' represented their future together. *Please, God, let us have one.*

Putting this thought away from her, Annie gathered what she would need and transferred it all to her handbag before checking that she had sufficient money in her purse. This done, she tried to relax as nerves about the journey churned her stomach.

Staring out of the window didn't help. The calmness of the view of the trees didn't stop the screeching noise and the screams in her head, or the terrible crashing sound of the train she and Olivia had been travelling in – or that of bending steel. Neither did it stop the images of the carriage closing in on her. Or of Olivia, trapped and broken. But it was the smell of smoke in her nostrils that had evoked the most fear as she felt again the sting, and the choking that followed, as it had been that moment when she'd realized there was a fire.

Screwing her eyes tight and digging her nails into her hand as she clenched her fist, Annie fought the memory back. *It won't happen again to me! I must go on a train to find out about my Ricky . . . I will do it, I will!*

Saying goodbye to the children, Daphne and Rosemary early the next morning, Annie managed a smile. 'I'll be back tomorrow, I promise.'

Beth clung to her. 'Me come. I want to go with you.'

'I know, but I've to go to places yer can't go in, luv, and there's no one to look after yer while I do.'

Beth began to cry. 'Want Mummy.'

Daphne scooped her up. 'How about we go to the park and play snowballs.'

'What's snowballs?'

Ian didn't mock her by saying they'd only done it a few days ago but answered her by stepping outside. 'Like this, yer remember, don't yer?' He gathered a handful of snow from a patch on the front lawn, shouting, 'Shall I throw it at Annie, eh?'

Annie pretended to scream and run. Beth laughed. 'Yes. Yes!'

Ian missed. Annie knew it was intentional, but now they were all laughing.

'Beth wants to play snowballs.'

'Right, come on then. Let's get your coat and wrap up

warm,' Daphne said as she disappeared into the house with them.

Annie hurried out of the gate feeling once more grateful for Ian. What a lovely lad he was. She recalled the time she was called out to his street and had found him standing alone staring at his bombed-out and blazing home. How she'd taken him to her home, and he'd become part of their family, as had his gran.

For a moment, a sadness enveloped her as her losses crowded her, but she fought the feeling, knowing that if she didn't, it would consume her.

Walking briskly, she made it to the station and checked the trains to Elsmere. Finding there wasn't one until later that evening, she went up to a cab parked outside the station and was soon on her way.

Feeling less exhausted than she had been by the car journey to Wrexham, Annie finally walked down the Old Ford Road in Bethnal Green. She was home and had conquered her fears of travelling by train – even finding she enjoyed the journey, especially through some of the most beautiful scenery she had ever seen before when they travelled through Wales.

When she reached home, Bertie was the first one she spotted. He was standing by the gate, wrapped up against the bitter March wind. Smoke curled up from his pipe.

Catching sight of her, he hurried towards her and took her small case. 'Annie! I was just thinking about you and the day you arrived on the island. I pictured you in the sweet shop lining up the paper cones of sweets you'd filled. I used to love to wave to you.'

There were tears glistening in his eyes. And then, as a father would, he hugged her. 'You must be cold. I left me kettle on the hob for after I had me pipe. Come on into your mum's flat and I'll bring you a cup up.'

He smelled of freshly laundered clothes with whiffs of pipe smoke and at that moment, Annie felt such love for him.

As she sat in her mum's flat, Annie tried to get the scent of her mum, but all she could do was close her eyes and imagine her sitting next to her. This made the image so vivid that she reached out her hand. But there was no one to take it.

Making herself get up off the sofa, Annie made for the lav. It had been a long journey, and her need had suddenly become urgent.

She'd only just come out of the bathroom when Bertie came back in. He was carrying an open letter. 'It's from our Joe to Loes . . . I – I recognized his handwriting, and, well, I so wanted news of him, Annie.'

He looked shame-faced, but Annie understood. Joe was his only son, and he hadn't seen or heard from him since his escape from Guernsey.

'I'd have done the same thing, luv. Joe won't mind, he'd only be elated that you've made it here too.'

Bertie visibly relaxed. 'Well, Joe's all right, thank goodness, and he says Harry is too. But I didn't know he and Loes were in love, did you?'

'No. I could see there was something between them but didn't know it was as deep as that.'

'I didn't even see a spark. I mean, Joe used to chat a lot to her, but then he did to all the women, young and old, whereas I had a need to keep meself to myself, me being in charge of the harbour.'

Annie smiled. She remembered well how most were a little afraid of Bertie as he ruled his patch.

'Anyway,' Bertie continued, 'his flirty ways changed when the Germans arrived. They didn't allow what they called a "gathering" so you daren't chat to folk for long . . . Maybe their love developed when Joe got here?'

Annie grinned. 'Stop fishing. If it did get that far, I didn't know.'

'I opened it, just to get news, but now I know and I'm going to write back and tell him all that's happened, but I wish I could get his letter to Loes.'

'I'll try as I'm going to try to find out where she is.' Annie told him about her other quests.

'Well, I hope your Ricky's all right, Annie. And Stefan, he's a good bloke. He always had a natter with me, and we had a smoke together. He'd give me a fag, which I ain't keen on, but it was hard to get tobacco for me pipe.'

'From what Daphne tells me, and how he rescued Olivia, I love him already . . . Well, I'd better pop upstairs and leave my stuff up there and then make tracks. I promised to be back in Wales by tomorrow night.'

As Annie alighted from a cab at 44 Moorfields, London, just after four o'clock, she was glad to see it was still open. Her heart was in her mouth as she joined the queue but as she, like the others, stamped their feet and hugged themselves to keep warm, she calmed herself.

When she was finally facing a young girl who sat behind a glass partition, she presented her requests and paperwork, expecting rejection, but instead she was given a ticket and asked to wait.

At last, she sat in front of a kindly lady who listened patiently to what she had to say.

After rummaging through a cabinet full of files, she pulled

out one marked *Stalag XX1-D, Poznań, Poland* and searched through the papers.

'Well, now, I can tell you that we do have some information on Sergeant Richard Stanley . . . I'm not sure this is good news, though, but he and a fellow prisoner escaped three weeks ago. They contacted the Red Cross in Poland, and were given money and food, but that's all the help they could offer. There's been no news since. I see I have dictated a letter to you to tell you about it.'

Annie gasped. Her Ricky was free!

'I'm afraid this isn't joyous news. What he has done is extremely dangerous and, if caught, always ends in death.'

'No! Oh, God! What . . . what are his chances?'

'A few have made it, so don't give up hope . . . I'm sorry, I wish that I could tell you more, Mrs Stanley . . . You're a police officer, aren't you?'

Annie explained how she'd taken her adopted children to safety and no longer served. Somehow, as she spoke, she felt as though she'd let the side down. 'But I intend to volunteer to do something of use, just as soon as I can get meself sorted. There's a lot of poverty where I am, and women on their own. I'm going to help them all I can.'

'Good. Help is needed everywhere. Make enquiries to the local Red Cross. They would welcome someone with your experience . . . Now, your query on German officer Stefan Braun. He is in Trent Park House in Cockfosters, north London. He's with fellow German officers and is being well treated.'

'Can me friend write to him?' Focusing on Daphne's problems helped Annie to settle her stomach. The way it was churning over the news of her Ricky was making her want to be sick.

135

'She can try. The officers' letters are sorted by those in charge and are all censored, so tell your friend that hers will be too before they are handed to Stefan. She must take great care in what she writes, nothing that could be misconstrued, or she and him will be in a great deal of trouble. No information about where she lives; she may only say general things such as that she is living in the countryside . . . You say he rescued her?'

'Yes.'

'Well, tell her to write more along the lines of being grateful to him rather than being in love with him, so she wanted him to have letters to look forward to – British girls fraternizing with the enemy might be frowned upon. They were in the last war.'

Annie had wondered about this; she'd guessed letters to the German prisoners would be censored.

'I'll inform the officer in charge that his letters addressed to her can be sent care of our address here. We will see that she gets them . . . Ah, I see you have written your new address here. Thank you.'

'Ta for that. Daphne will be relieved . . . And what about Loes?'

'Loes Bakker, you said?'

Annie nodded, already feeling that she couldn't take any more but wanting to know where poor Loes was.

'Right, I'll need my file on the latest internees and their whereabouts . . . Ah, here it is!' Muttering to herself, she said, 'As . . . Bs . . . Ah, here: Loes Bakker, class "A" detainee. We don't know why this is, we only have notification of where detainees are, and only those who we are likely to have to look after, or help with getting post to and from . . . I understand she is to be shipped to the Isle of Man.'

Annie gasped. 'But that's up north, ain't it?'

'It is. Most women aliens are sent there. She will be safe and cared for, and again, you can write to her, and she can write to you via us. The Red Cross workers on the island visit the camp and give help to the women . . . I'm sorry. Is Loes a special friend?'

Annie told her about Loes and what she meant to them all. 'I've a letter here from her boyfriend, a British serving soldier in the Far East. Can yer get it to her?'

'I will, I promise. Can you write to him and ask him to send letters here?'

'I don't know. His father could just redirect his letter here, that might be easier.'

'Yes. That's a good idea. And rest assured, she will get them, and she will be all right, but I'm sure it will help her greatly to hear from you if you write too. Again, you must not give details of anything to do with your home town, or anything about the war.'

'I understand.'

'Good. And I'll make sure we monitor Ricky's case. Any news – anything at all that comes in – I will see that you get it, Annie. Have you a telephone where you are?'

'Yes. We've everything. It's a big house.'

As she finished writing the number down, the lady said, 'Well, it's nice to have met you, Annie. I'm so sorry about all the troubles you're going through. Keep believing. A lot can happen if we keep our faith.'

As Annie left, she wasn't so sure about this last statement but when she got off the bus in Bethnal and walked past the bombed-out St Matthew's, she had second thoughts and found herself turning into its gates and walking up its long path.

There was a kind of peace here even though the church was a testament to the war with its roof and one wall collapsed. It was as if it had suffered as she had, but it wasn't broken – Annie felt herself gaining strength from that. One day, she was sure, St Matthew's would be rebuilt, and so could she be. She just had to be strong like the front of the church was, still showing its face proudly to the world.

With this, she turned away and headed for the Old Ford Road and what would for ever be her home, even if she couldn't live there for now.

Chapter Twelve

Annie

As if their relationship had taken a new turn, Bertie greeted Annie with a hug when she reached home.

'I've a stew simmering, Annie. Will you join me later for a bite to eat?'

'I'd be glad to, ta, luv. But first, I need a bath to warm me up. Has the boiler been lit today?'

'It has. Ron lights it every day . . . Well, if he can get enough wood from what he collects from the ruins around to get it going with. But the water's hot today, love.'

'Good. Are Ron and Rita and the children all right? I haven't seen them about.'

'Aye. They're out for a while. They left this morning. This is the day that Rita likes to get in the queues for the food stores as soon as she drops the kids at school. They sometimes don't come back until they pick the kids up as they visit Rita's mother-in-law.'

'They've settled in all right, though?'

'Oh, aye. We all have. We all jog along well together, especially me and Ron . . . We mess around on me boat a lot and Ron sleeps in the bigger of the two bedrooms in my flat every night while Rita and the kids sleep in the shelter.'

Annie shuddered. She hadn't been looking forward to a night in the shelter and the horror of hearing bombs dropping around them and wondering if the house had caught one. She'd much preferred being on duty when she lived here. That way she could see what was happening and help folk.

Bathed and dressed and feeling comfortable in a pair of old grey slacks and a pale blue jumper, Annie went downstairs to be met by Rita coming out of what Annie would always think of as Cissy's flat.

'Hello, Annie. Bertie told me yer were back. I've been listening out for yer coming down the stairs. 'Ow are yer, and 'ow's the little ones and Olivia?'

Annie suddenly wanted to break down and cry, but she swallowed hard. 'Everyone's all right and things are working out fine, Rita, ta. Bertie tells me yer settled in.'

'I am. It's the best thing to be so near where I've always lived, despite seeing me lovely 'ouse in ruins every day. But I know where everything is from 'ere and can carry on me life as usual. But, Annie, I want to talk to you about me rent. 'Ow am I to get it to yer? I've got what I owe yer till now. 'Ere yer are, luv.'

Rita handed Annie an envelope. She hadn't thought to charge rent, just have them all pay their own bills, but suddenly the money seemed like a godsend as it would make her income up for her.

'I've reckoned it out at ten bob a week,' Rita was saying, 'as I've asked around and that seems a fair price. I've me other bills sorted as I've changed the electric into me dad's name. He always sees to the bills for heating and lighting.'

'Oh, that's too much, Rita. I know from me own allowance from Ricky that yer ain't getting much to get by on. Let's halve that. I'll be happy with five bob a week, luv.'

'Are yer sure, Annie? Yer've already been an angel to us. I don't want yer going short.'

'I'm sure. Where we're living out in the country, the price of stuff is nowhere near what it is here in Bethnal and there seems a lot more of it.'

'I've 'eard tell that's the case, but it wouldn't do for me. Despite the bombs there's nowhere that I'd rather be.'

Annie knew exactly what she meant.

'Anyway, you keep that pound note that's in that envelope and that'll be four weeks paid. Though I still owe yer more.'

'Ta, that's fair enough, and no, yer don't owe any more. Let's say this has brought us up to date, as yer needed some settling in time. It was costly getting yourselves sorted. I'll ring me solicitor tomorrow before I leave and sort something out with him for the future payments, luv.'

Annie thought it sounded grand, her having a solicitor, but didn't explain about him being Rose's solicitor really, or how he'd come up trumps for her sorting out all of the estate in Kent and how he was working on the adoption of Ian and Beth. But the thought did occur to her that she'd find out how the adoption was getting along too when she rang.

After a fitful night's sleep, Annie had the best news. The adoption was finalized! The papers would soon be with her. She was elated. Her grin was wide as she shouted, 'I'm a mum!'

Rita appeared in the hallway. 'Oh, I am glad, mate, and you'll make the best one ever!'

'Ta, Rita . . . Ooh, I've waited for this moment. I can't

wait to tell the kids. No one can ever take them away from me, and I can take care of them without fear of being conscripted.'

'I'm 'appy for yer, luv. And if it weren't such an hour as half past nine in the morning, I'd say let's have a sherry to celebrate!'

Annie laughed. 'No need, I feel tipsy with happiness!'

Bertie and Ron came upstairs then from the cellar flat. Bertie grinned. 'Well, I was just stirring the porridge when you yelled but that can wait. I could just do a dance as I know how much this means to you, Annie. And to them little ones.'

Ron nodded, a wide grin on his face. 'Good news, Annie. We don't get much of that these days.'

'No, we don't, but we keep plodding on. And I must too. I've a train to catch . . . Oh, and the rent . . . I really hate charging you all rent. I wouldn't but, well, you know I gave me job up . . .'

'We wouldn't 'ave it any different. You should know, Annie, us East Enders 'ave our pride.'

Annie smiled. 'Well, the solicitor said the best way was for you to send me a postal order every week. Will that be all right for you all?'

'It will, Annie. I've never bought one of them in me life, but I can soon learn 'ow it's done.'

'What about you, Bertie? Is that all right for you?'

'More than all right, Annie. But here, I've put mine up to date in this envelope for you. Then we're all square.'

As she thanked Bertie, Annie did worry as to how he was going to manage. In Guernsey, besides his wage, he took cuts of anything the smugglers brought ashore and charged for turning a blind eye, but he had no means of adding to the money he'd brought with him and it must have depleted with what he had paid for the boat.

'You will all tell me if it gets difficult to pay, won't you? I won't mind you staying here rent-free as long as you all keep yourselves going with food and warmth.'

They all agreed they would, and this settled Annie's mind. She would need the money so was grateful for it but not at the expense of them going without.

Saying her goodbyes, Annie wondered when she would see them again, or her beloved house and Bethnal, but she didn't dwell on this and waved cheerily as she set off for the station feeling pleased that everything was settled and with how they'd become a family.

Once home, Annie was greeted by an eager Daphne giving her a hug, telling her the kids were resting and Ian wasn't yet in from school. 'So, is there any news, Annie?'

'Let me say hello to Rosemary, then I'll tell yer all about it, luv.'

Rosemary beamed. 'I can see from your face that something's pleased you, my dear, but that something is hurting you too,' Rosemary said as she hugged Annie.

The feel of the older woman's arms around her gave Annie a jolt as she remembered her mum's and Cissy's cuddles. But she didn't give into the tears that threatened. 'You're right, Rosemary, I've got mixed news.'

As she told of Stefan and Loes's fate, Annie felt the pain of how her Ricky wasn't safe.

The tears pricking her eyes as she told them of his plight almost spilled over, but she wouldn't let the fear of him not making it back to her become a truth in her mind. She would believe that he would.

Moving quickly to the good news helped. 'But it ain't all bad news for me. I'm a mum!'

Their faces were a picture.

'I had the best news ever. Me adoption of Beth and Ian is finalized!!'

'Oh, that's wonderful!' Rosemary beamed.

'It is, Annie. I'm so pleased for you and the children. And thanks for finding out that I can write to Stefan. Just having that link with him and him knowing I'm thinking of him will help.'

'I'm happy for you, luv, and we can both write to Loes too. Now, I've to pop upstairs before I burst!'

After having relieved herself and making her way into her bedroom, Annie took the letter she'd written to Ricky out of her pocket and reached for her old handbag. Finding the post office book with her and Ricky's savings logged, she popped the letter along with the cash she now had inside and returned it to the bag. She would carry on writing to him every day and then tie the letters with ribbon and keep them for when he came home. They would be a history of her life without him and a testament to her love for him. *Ricky will read them one day,* Annie told herself as she clamped her lips in determination that this would happen. And she thought, *I'll hold him in me arms as he does.*

Sinking down onto the bed, Annie felt in limbo. The not knowing was awful. Her imagination had kept her awake most of the night, giving her nightmare scenarios of Ricky running through woodland chased by gun-wielding troops of Germans. She even called out and woke Rita, who'd crept upstairs to see if she was all right and then brewed a pot of tea and sat sharing it with her. This had helped to break the agonizing cycle of horror dreams, as had listening to Rita's hurts and comforting her. Everyone in London had lost so much. Some their lives, some their loved ones, some their homes and all they'd ever had, and yet still they soldiered on.

Could she do that? Hadn't she already?

But then her heart sank as she lost that determination and faith and suddenly couldn't make herself believe that anyone could survive out in the bitter cold. Nothing to eat, no one to turn to. *Oh, Ricky, me Ricky.*

The door burst open and Beth came in, dragging Annie from her morose thoughts.

'There you are! I wanted you, Aunty Annie.'

The moment lightened. Annie held out her arms unable to believe that this was truly her daughter. But she wouldn't say until Ian was home and they were both together.

Beth bounded towards her, followed by a slower and sleepy-looking Karl.

Enclosing them both in her arms, Annie lifted them onto the bed then climbed on herself. They both jumped on top of her.

Giggles filled the space around her as Annie tickled them, and they tried to scramble away. This time with them was a salve to her shattered dreams.

It was the smell of baking drifting up to them and Rosemary's call of, 'Tea and cakes are ready! Come along, let's all have tea together,' that stopped their antics and had them scrambling off the bed.

Annie smiled as she saw the table laden with best china plates and cups and saucers. She was used to this concept of afternoon tea, but still, how Bertie had served tea – much later and as their main meal – seemed more right to her. As did having dinner at what others called lunch. Tonight, though, Daphne and Rosemary would serve dinner up at around sixish.

Annie lived in two different worlds. But she knew that she preferred her East End one any day.

The cakes were delicious. How Rosemary produced them every day with sugar being rationed Annie didn't know, but she tucked in with the rest of them.

As if he'd smelled the baking too, Ian came in from school just as they sat down. He ran straight to Annie and hugged her neck.

'Hey. Are yer all right, luv?'

'I am, Annie. I just missed yer, that's all.'

Annie squeezed him. How quickly this young lad had made his way deep into her heart and now he was officially her son. 'So, how's school been?'

Ian hung his head. A trickle of worry set up in Annie. 'Have yer had problems, Ian?'

'They take the rise out of 'ow I speak – they sort of sing when they speak. A lot don't understand me and keep making me repeat me words and then laughing.'

Annie knew what he meant about how the Welsh spoke. To her, it was a lovely sound and to describe it as 'singing their words' fitted well. 'Don't let it upset yer, Ian. Laugh with them and at yerself, it's the only way.'

'But I'm proud of being an East Ender and me mum and gran were too.'

'Well, East Enders are also proud of how we can laugh at ourselves and make others laugh. It's a long tradition. When you're older and this war is over, I'll take yer to a music hall. Ha, you'll hear then how the cockneys make fun of themselves. You give it a try, eh?'

Ian nodded, though he didn't look too sure.

'Anyway, I have a present for yer that'll help yer to forget all of that.'

Ian looked at her in surprise. Beth's head lifted and her expression said, 'What about me?' but before she could ask, Annie said, 'For both you and Beth.'

'Oh, what is it, Aunty Annie?'

'I am no longer just your aunty, Beth, and no longer a friend who helped you, Ian, but I am mum to you both!'

Ian's face went into a wide grin. 'Really? I can call yer Mum?'

'You can, me darlin'. And you can too, Beth, if you want to. You see, I am officially your mum here on earth. Yer mums in heaven will for ever be your real mums. We'll always think of them, and they'll never leave our hearts. You can still talk to them as you do now. You to your picture of your mum, Beth, and you, Ian, to the picture you have of your mum that we found in your gran's house.'

Ian, looking all knowledgeable, told Beth, 'It's like Rosemary is gran to us on earth, but our real grans are still our grans in heaven.'

Beth looked mystified. 'Aunty Annie, now Mum?'

'Yes, me darlin', that's right.'

There was a silence, then Ian said, 'I'm feeling like a happy bubble is inside me.'

'Me have bubble too. Right here.' Beth tapped her chest. The look that she gave Annie was as if she was battling with a mystery, but as Ian stepped back into the circle of Annie's arms, Beth clambered down from the table and ran round to them.

As Annie held them both to her, Ian said, 'We're a proper family now. Yer ain't ever going to leave us are yer, Aun . . . Mum?'

147

Annie clung on tightly to him. 'Never, me darlin'. And you're to be a good brother to Beth. I know yer will be as you are already.'

Beth frowned. All of this was too much for her. 'Me brother?'

'Aye, I'm yer bruvver for real now, Beth. And I'll look after yer like a bruvver should.'

Beth just giggled.

A little voice said, 'Mum . . . Mummy . . . gone . . . Nanny gone.'

Annie looked at Karl. He was a child of few words, and yet always she understood. 'Come here, me little luv.'

Daphne helped him. As she handed him over, Annie saw the tears running down her face. Her own were so close, but she wanted this to be a happy moment for the children so wouldn't give in to them.

As she gathered Karl to her she told him, 'Your mummy is the bravest person I know, me darlin'. She cannot be with you as she is making the world safe for us all. But she will come home, I promise. Until then, Aunty Annie and Aunty Daphne will look after you like Mummy and Nanny Loes would. And Rosemary is your gran, and you have Beth and Ian. You're going to be all right, as we all love yer.'

'I love you, Karl, even though you're a pest sometimes!'

Karl grinned at Beth. 'Love you, Beth.'

Ian joined in. 'And I love yer both, even though yer a bigger pest than Karl, Beth.'

Beth's face looked like thunder. Annie put in quickly, 'So, we all love each other, and that's what will get us through, eh?'

'Don't love Ian!'

Rosemary intervened. 'There are many kinds of love, Beth,

my dear. And all can be tested. Ian, you should say sorry for your remark. You're much older and these two look up to you. Though we know you were joking, Beth can't distinguish that, and it hurt her to hear you say she was a pest.'

'But she . . . I mean, yes, Gran . . . Sorry, Beth. I didn't mean it. You're not a pest. You make me laugh, and you're all right, really.'

Beth beamed. 'Well, I'll love you then . . . But Karl's still a pest!'

Karl, as if he was years younger than Beth, said, 'Like being a pest.'

This made them all laugh, and the moment lightened again as Daphne lifted her cup. 'A toast to the new mum and sister and brother!'

Rosemary began to applaud and before long they were all clapping and hugging.

Annie felt she would burst with the love she had for these little ones. Pride swelled in her chest. She would be the best mum ever . . . and one day, Ricky would be the best dad.

Annie felt she'd become a real mum the next day as she took Ian to school and asked to speak with the headmaster.

A tall man, whose appearance was stern but who turned out to be a gentleman and kindly, invited her to sit down in a chair on the other side of his desk. 'How can I help you, Mrs Stanley? Is Ian settling in here? He seems to be a bright child according to his teacher.'

'To be honest, Mr Franklin, he ain't too happy.' Annie told him about the mickey taking and what she'd advised him. 'So, I'll see how he is in the next week.'

'Yes, that was good advice, and I'll ask the teachers on

dinner duty to keep an eye out to make sure he's not being picked on.'

'There's something else.' Annie told him with great pride about her new status as Ian's mum.

'That's wonderful news. We all felt so much for him when we heard his story. I'm sure that will help him greatly and you will give him a stable life. I admire you, Mrs Stanley. And all the women of this country. How you're all coping I just don't know . . . Where is it that your husband is serving?'

Annie told him Ricky's story. How she managed to do so without breaking she didn't know, but somehow, she was getting stronger and coping a little better today.

'I'm sorry to hear that. We will keep him in our thoughts and root for him. And for you, of course, as you are now one of our mums.'

Outside the school gates, Annie looked up at the sky and blinked. The April sun was shining brightly, promising that spring was truly here.

When Annie arrived home, the banging and clanging of the alterations had begun in earnest. A section of the front room wall already had a gaping hole in it as the builders had started to demolish it.

She peeked through it to see the dust covers were all in place but sagging with debris.

Mick, the builder, spotted her. 'Morning. Can I have a word, Mrs Stanley?'

He proposed that his men took all the furniture and carpets to his yard where he had a huge garage and could store them until the work was done.

'Ta, Mick, and call me Annie. And that's a good idea to get the furniture out. I've been worried about it.'

Rosemary came through with a tray of mugs steaming with hot tea, smiling widely. 'Annie! I didn't hear you come in. Daphne's just making our tea for our elevenses. You're home just in time.'

Suddenly, Annie knew she could agree. She was home. These people had all made her feel so, and yes, it would never top her home on the Old Ford Road, but here she felt loved and welcomed and her family were too.

William, Olivia's father, came to her mind. He'd always looked out for her, and it seemed he still was by providing this lovely home and bringing Rosemary into their lives.

Chapter Thirteen

Olivia

How Olivia had come through the three-week preliminary stage of her training she didn't know.

They'd been told it was designed to test their mental capacity to take on all they had to as agents.

Her mind wasn't stable – she was veering from being fine to being in the depths of despair – and yet she had given a good account of herself, even though she'd lagged in some of the physical trials of unarmed combat as the weakness in her leg had let her down. What they had put it down to she didn't know. Nor could she fathom why they hadn't been concerned about it. Maybe they didn't care as much about her being able to defend herself. Maybe she was dispensable. Whatever it was, she was through to the next stage of training.

This stage would be her greatest challenge. Not the weapons handling, demolition, map reading, compass work, field craft, elementary Morse or raid tactics, but the physical training. Somehow, she must get through that. She so wanted to be chosen.

Though they had a couple of days off, they weren't allowed to go home. Olivia couldn't wait to gain just a little freedom to give her a chance to contact Annie to ask how Karl was, but she doubted she would be allowed near a telephone. But at least she would have time to write to them. Censored or not, it was a thread of contact with her darling son and Annie.

To get her letter through censorship she wrote some of it in code – the code she and Annie had used during the passing of information from Hendrick. This way she was able to tell Annie how she was really feeling – her hopes, her fears, and her agony of being parted from Karl. Things that would be construed as weakness if understood and may have meant she would fail the course.

It seemed no time at all until she was packing for Inverness, Scotland, and the SOE staff headquarters based at Arisaig House.

When she arrived, Olivia took in the rambling grey-stone building surrounded by trees that sloped down to an ice-blue sea. This would be her base for the next three weeks. It had a haunting beauty that in other days must have made it a stunning family home.

Here she would triumph or be broken. She had to be strong. She had to endure physical pain and come through it. And then, if Hendrick made it through, they would at least be together to soldier on and do all they could.

Feeling exhausted, but showing the world a strong mind and body, Olivia was at last sent to a safe house three weeks later to await instructions. She'd done it! She'd mastered the gruelling mountain climbs, the runs with heavy weights on her back, the simulated torture, designed to see if they would break if captured and betray others to save their own skins.

Now she was equipped with all she would need, and her life would belong to her country. She determined that she would conduct herself with honour.

Within days she found herself sat in a small plane, its droning engines vibrating the cabin. Its destination – deep into France.

Olivia's heart pounded in her chest. She mentally checked that she'd gone through all the necessary procedures and her parachute was correctly fitted.

Sweat dampened her body as she rehearsed in her mind at what point after her jump she should pull the rip cord. She had to time it precisely.

Terror held her limbs stiff. Her weak leg throbbed. Would they make the landing strip? Would they overrun it? Would she get caught up high in a tree and hang there until she starved to death?

'Coming in low. Ready on three.'

The pilot's voice seemed disconnected from the world.

Olivia stood. Then came the command, 'Hatch open . . . JUMP!'

Now she was floating on air, but not in a beautiful way. The land below her spun ever nearer. Panicking, Olivia wanted to open her parachute, but she knew it was too soon. *God help me!*

Now! Please . . . please, let it open!

A violent jolt to her body and then it was as if two strong arms had slowed her descent. She was drifting downwards towards the lit torches below and she guided herself to target her landing.

The jar when she hit the earth sent shockwaves of pain through her leg, but she rolled over as she'd been taught and began to haul in her parachute.

The dark figure of a man came to help her. In French he said, 'We must bury this.'

No other words were spoken as Olivia helped with burying her parachute, and then to his command of, 'Follow,' she gritted her teeth against the burning agony she was experiencing. She asked no questions but determined to keep up with him as he took her deeper and deeper into forested land.

At last, the clinging darkness and dampness of the trees opened to a clearing and a camp, though looking up, Olivia saw that the thickly leaved branches met in such a way above that she couldn't see the starlit sky and knew they were well hidden.

'Come towards the fire and meet everyone. Have you brought us messages? Are we to get weapons?'

'Yes, there is an air drop of all you have requested scheduled for two nights from now, weather permitting.'

This pleased them all and introductions began. Olivia wondered but didn't ask where Lucy was.

She learned that the man who had met her was called Claudius. She guessed that this wasn't his real name and no surname was offered. The others were Frédérique, Julian and Philippe.

Once introductions were done and they sat drinking hot but disgusting tasting coffee, Lucy was mentioned.

'You two will be our only British agents. You are to join her at the *ferme laitière*.'

Olivia knew this meant a dairy farm, but the next part of the information told her the farm was on the outskirts of Paris. From her studies of the map of France during her course she remembered that Paris was at least five hours away from here.

Her heart sank. If Hendrick made it, she wouldn't be near to him!

Claudius continued, 'There, you will work as a dairy maid alongside Lucy. This farm sells milk to cafes the Germans frequent.' Claudius spat on the ground, making his hatred for the Germans a visible action. 'You will be useful in that you will do most of those deliveries and, we hope, overhear their conversations. Lucy's German is very scant, and she hasn't been able to decipher much. What you overhear you will communicate to us through radio contact, as well as back to your HQ in London. We have provisions for this in a loft at the farm. Lucy organizes any raids we may make according to information gained and through her boss. We will take you to her in the morning. Now we have supper and turn in for the night.'

The stew was delicious and it was washed down with a lovely crisp wine. No one made food as tasty as the French, not even when it was rough and ready food from oddments gathered in the forest and wild animals they had killed, and neither did they serve better wine, but even these delights were spoiled by Olivia's anguish. How was she to bear being so far away from Hendrick? And how would she know if his subterfuge worked, and if this band of Resistance workers accepted him as a Frenchman wanting to join them? It was all so risky.

Lucy greeted Olivia with a hug like an old friend would. It felt good to be with her again.

As soon as the men who had brought her left, Lucy said, 'Come into our home – a room above the barn.'

As they entered the brick barn with an arched roof, she continued, 'The farmer would have me living in the house – he is very kindly and so is his wife – but I must not be

156

perceived as anything other than a worker and then they won't be implicated.'

The barn had that lovely smell of dried hay, which was welcoming and comforting to Olivia. Their quarters were reached by climbing a ladder where she was surprised and pleased to see a cosy loft with two beds, a sofa, a desk at one end and a sink and cooker at the other, and a tall cupboard next to the cooker. In the space between the two ends there stood a scrubbed table and two chairs. The one window at the far end was dirty and seemed as though it would be impossible to see out of but it did give some light. Olivia guessed this was to maintain the look that this was just a barn.

Next to this, Olivia could see a trapdoor in the roof and wondered if this led to the roof space that was boarded off and where their radio might be kept.

'Like it?'

'I do. It has a homely feel and yet from the outside you would never guess there was a home up here.'

'I'm so glad and I'm glad too that you're here, Olivia . . . I'm sorry about Hendrick's plight.'

'You know?'

'Yes, I was informed . . . I – I . . . well, I am to look out for him appearing here – not that I know what he looks like, but . . . Oh, this is awful. After everything he has done for us, but the worry is that his escape is a sham. That he has been forced by the Nazis to infiltrate our government, and the Resistance.'

Olivia gasped. 'How can they think that? . . . How? Hendrick's only motive in becoming a German officer was to try to save his father's life. He then used his position, at great risk to his own life, to give useful information to our government.'

'I know. But his father has been executed and the question being asked is did Hendrick betray his father? We cannot know for sure.'

'No! Oh, Lucy, it was Gunter – an SS Officer.' Olivia explained who Gunter was and how he betrayed Hendrick.

'I'm truly sorry, Olivia, but you must see the position it has left "O" in.'

Olivia thought about the mysterious 'O' always referred to by Lucy in communications as the code name for her commander. She guessed it was Brinston.

'Look, Olivia' – Olivia brought her attention back to what Lucy was saying – 'how can we be sure? Well, I shouldn't tell you this, but it is known that Hendrick has crossed into France . . .'

'He is being watched! Why? Hendrick wants to help! Nothing more than that. He has had to pose as a German in the first instance to get over the border safely, but will then pose as a Frenchman . . . Lucy, please believe me . . . Please, help Hendrick. I cannot bear it.'

'All I can tell you is that if he makes it to the Resistance camp, in recognition of what he has done, he is not to be harmed, but detained. Then he will be picked up, flown back to Britain for interrogation and his fate decided. It's the only chance they are prepared to give him. They are in an impossible situation, Olivia, you must see that.'

Olivia's legs went to jelly. Why should anyone trust a German officer who passed secrets that harmed his own country and then escaped when his father was executed? And now, he had gone against orders to stay where he was.

Despair sank into her bones and she only just made it to sit on the sofa. Tears streamed from her eyes. 'Help me . . . Lucy, please help me.'

Lucy was quiet for a moment. When she spoke a little hope entered Olivia.

'If I do, I will go against orders of our country . . . but I haven't passed on to Claudius that he is to detain Hendrick yet.'

Olivia sat up. 'Will you help him?'

'I – I . . . Oh, Olivia, please don't ask me, and yet . . . I believe in him. From all that Annie told me, and all I know for myself, I do trust Hendrick. He has been caught up in the middle of all this and at great danger to himself made the best of it by helping the side he believes in. Now he needs our help, and we are turning on him. But I also believe that it is right for the government to be cautious . . . Oh, I don't know . . .'

'Please, please, Lucy. Hendrick has done nothing wrong and doesn't intend to. He hates the Nazi regime and wants to bring this war to an end for his own countrymen as well as the world.'

'But how can we contact him to warn him?'

'You mean, you will help?' Olivia held her breath, a little of her fear dissipating, though some remained. Should she tell of how they could contact Hendrick or not? Would that save him or betray him?

'I can see you do know a way, and now it is for me to ask you to trust me, Olivia. But you must be asking yourself would you do the same for me? Given all the circumstances and the reason our bosses have given for detaining Hendrick?'

'I know I would. We have worked together for so long, Lucy. I trust you with my Hendrick's life.'

With this, Olivia talked about how Hendrick was going to Madame Durand's apartment in Paris and how he was going to take on the identity of her nephew, Leonard.

'So, he was going to present himself to Claudius as a Frenchman?'

'Yes. He didn't think it likely that the Resistance leader would accept a German. But he had every hope he would take his services as a Frenchman and especially because of his language skills. We both thought, too, that he would gain the help and support of Madame Durand when she knew of our background with Leonard.'

Lucy's eyebrows rose. 'How do you know all of this, Olivia? Have you seen Hendrick?'

The fear Olivia had felt re-entered her. But she decided to be honest and tell of her visit.

'My God, you took a tremendous risk!'

'I love Hendrick with all my heart. When the chance came to be with him, I didn't think twice.'

Lucy bit the side of her lip. Her brows knitted together. After a moment she said, 'It is no more than I would do for my Dan. Do you remember that I told you about him when we were in that cafe alongside the canal, opposite Annie's? How he only wrote to me as a friend in the beginning as he needed someone to write to him to keep him going, and how I loved him before he was called up and how he came to realize that he loved me?'

'Yes, I do remember. I was so happy when Dan declared his love for you.'

'So, you know that I know what drives you, Olivia, and that it would drive me too. I will help you, but I have to think how. It will all need meticulous planning. If caught, we will face dire consequences ourselves.'

Olivia rose. 'Oh, Lucy, thank you. Thank you so much . . . May I hug you now and get us back on our usual footing?'

Lucy nodded and grinned. The grin changed her plain looks and seemed to fade the million freckles covering her face.

As they came out of the hug, Lucy's grin had turned to a beautiful smile. 'I have so needed that. Just someone to hug me. Someone who knows me – well, as best as us agents can know each other.'

Olivia smiled. She knew the feeling. She had known it in the direst of circumstances. 'Well, we can always give each other plenty of hugs. After all, there's only us really. I felt that I wasn't entirely trusted by the Resistance group.'

'No one is. And after all, are we trustworthy? When it comes to the affairs of the heart, I think we are proving we're not . . . I know you don't think it and cannot see a time when you will . . . but just suppose those in London are right about Hendrick. Would you be completely loyal to your country and turn him in?'

Olivia didn't know how to answer. Her heart said no.

'Think about it. I have met your lovely son, Olivia. If the worst happens and we are proven wrong, think of him and his life. Because if Hendrick isn't who we think he is and he is plotting to infiltrate, then it is your son he will put in danger.'

Olivia held her head high. She would never lose her faith in her beloved husband.

'I trust Hendrick with mine and my son's life.'

'That's all I want to hear. We will work out how to do this, Olivia. I never thought I would go against orders, but in this case my judgement is urging me to.'

'Hendrick won't let you down. I promise.'

'Right. We will try to contact this lady he is heading for to give him a warning. But it won't be easy. It helps with you knowing most of her address. There are Resistance groups near to Paris. I will contact them and ask them to get a message to . . . was it Madame Durand?'

'Yes. Oh, I hope your message gets there before Hendrick does as he won't stay long.'

'We can only try. Now, I must introduce you to the farmer, Pierre. But first, I've laid out some overalls – bib 'n' brace they call them. Very handy and make you look the part – oh, and you need to tie a scarf around your hair. Let me show you.'

They giggled as they tried to wrap Olivia's long dark hair in a scarf that was tied into a knot on the forehead.

'There! You only need a yoke with two buckets, and you'll be transformed.'

'I won't have to wear one of those, will I?'

Lucy burst out laughing, 'No, you goose! I was only joking. You carry the milk on a horse and cart in a churn with a tap on and fill jugs to take into the cafes.'

Memories came to Olivia of her home where the milkman was a familiar sight and delivered his milk in just the same way.

'Household customers have their own jugs,' Lucy was saying. 'They will be looking out for you coming and hail you if they need milk and will pay you there and then. You are familiar with the French money and can handle giving change, can't you?'

'Money is the one thing I can handle well, with my father owning a bank. We dealt in many currencies.'

'Of course . . . Olivia, I'm so sorry for all you have been through. I can only imagine some of it, but you deserve a medal. You risked your life for our country and still they ask more of you.'

'And I am glad to give it. I want to do all I can.'

Lucy became the agent she was then as she said, 'That's the spirit! Though remember, if you are caught and found out, you're on your own and the prospect of you living, well . . . Anyway, let's get you started on your next mission.'

'Before we do, Lucy, never fear. If I am caught, I won't betray you. Not even if it would save my life.'

'Oh, Olivia . . . It's all so scary. But we can do it. Thank you. I am the same, I would never betray you.'

They hugged again and Olivia thought that having Lucy with her was going to make it all so much easier to bear.

Farmer Pierre, a tall man in his fifties, had bushy eyebrows and coal-black eyes, which twinkled even when he wasn't smiling. He greeted her in the customary way by kissing both cheeks as they walked out into the farmyard where he'd been spreading hay over the smelly mess near to one of the barns that surrounded them. Beyond these she'd seen fields of many colours stretching as far as the eye could see and marvelled at the peaceful beauty in a country of turmoil.

Pierre's French was not as precise as Claudius's, but peppered with slang words, which Olivia picked up on, knowing French as well as she did, but she could see that Lucy struggled despite having been here longer.

The farmyard was neat and clean now the cows' dung had been dealt with. It was not a bit like those she had seen at home with old broken-down tractors rusting away in one corner, sludge ankle-deep and stinking, and weeds coming through the cobbles.

Olivia felt immediately at home with the friendly Pierre and knew she could grow very fond of him and his wife, Violette, who came out of the house as they chatted, bearing steaming mugs of hot milk – a luxury Olivia had almost forgotten about.

A small woman, almost as round as she was tall, Violette had a beaming smile on her face.

Pierre nodded. 'She's in her element. She feels she is being sent the daughters she never had. We're so missing our son . . . He was killed in the first wave of this lot.'

Olivia gasped. '*Oh, je suis désolée.*'

'*Merci.*'

Just to say she was sorry seemed so inadequate but it was all Olivia could do. Her heart went out to them. She thought then about how she should hate all Germans, as most people seemed to, but knew different to most and realized that German mothers were suffering just as much as British ones. She wanted to tell the world to only look on these horrors as being perpetrated by the Nazis, not all Germans.

In a sweet-sounding tone and yet a shaking voice, Violette said, 'But you will avenge us. You girls will make them pay for the life of my son and that is why the best we have is for you.'

Olivia instinctively put her arm around her as Lucy took the cups. 'We will do our best, madame.'

The lovely smile came back, and Olivia wondered at the resilience of these country folk. Their whole lives had changed and yet they weren't broken. Just like the people on her island and those of the East End – it really would take more than Hitler to break the spirit of ordinary folk.

It was later as she and Lucy were rolling the churns of fresh milk, just extracted from the cows by Pierre, that Lucy said, 'I have a plan.'

Once in the cooling shed, where the milk would be stored

before they took it on their rounds in the morning, she continued. 'Now Hendrick is in France, he cannot be tracked easily by "O". We tell Claudius that we know about Hendrick, only we will give the name Leonard. We will instruct that when he arrives, a note we send is to be handed to him and that no conversation is to pass between them before Leonard reads it. You will write that note in code. Start it by talking of Rupert, the bear you told me you used as an indicator that your message is coded. Then you tell him he came from another posting, which he cannot talk about, and that he is good at . . . What else is he good at other than languages and maths?'

The plan sounded doable and excited her. Olivia didn't hesitate to recite some of Hendrick's many talents – architecture, carpentry, strategic planning, Morse code, radio operating, and . . . She winked. 'And stuff I can't tell you of!'

Lucy burst out laughing.

When they'd calmed, Olivia asked, 'Will that be enough? And if so, what then?'

'Well, hopefully he won't be called upon to use the unmentioned skill, but then we carry on as if this was how it should be. Though you will have to promise me that you and Hendrick will be on your best behaviour . . . I'm not saying we won't find some secret moments for you, but they must be by arrangement of us both and must not be discoverable by anyone else, not Claudius, not Pierre or his wife, no one.'

'I promise. And if it suits you better, I won't ever meet up with Hendrick. I can tell him in my coded message that it must be so. But do you think it will work? Will Hendrick be safe? And how can we ensure that Hendrick can contact the Maquis?'

'It will work if we never reveal that he is here. We will treat it as we would any member of the Resistance that has newly joined, leave it to Claudius to vet him, which he probably won't do as we know of him . . . But getting Hendrick to the right place is tricky.'

'But you will try to contact Madame Durant? Ask her to give a message to Hendrick saying who to ask for?'

Lucy sighed. 'So many risks. But it is the only way . . . Oh, God, Lucy, if ever we're caught, we'll be in so much trouble.'

'Hendrick would never connect us to him if he were caught . . . I mean, not say we helped him. He would deny that we did and say that it was a coincidence that he found me here.'

'But us not reporting him?'

'Did they give a description of Hendrick to you?'

'They said he was tall with fair hair, but that's all.'

'So, if he doesn't look like that, how would you be expected to know that a new member of the Maquis is Hendrick? You could leave instructions for him with Madame Durand to dye his hair, and tell him to grow a moustache – funnily enough, though he is fair, his facial hair does grow through much darker. And I will add in the note that he and I are to have nothing to do with each other.'

'But I cannot put you under the torture of knowing he is just a few miles from here and you cannot see him. We will arrange something, but it won't be often.'

'Oh, Lucy, I could hug you. Thank you. You're a real friend.'

Lucy gave a wry smile. 'Let's hope that trait in me doesn't cause our downfall. I once gave in to Annie and got away with it. It was when Ricky came home unexpectedly. Do you remember?'

'Yes. And nothing happened as a consequence, only that they got to spend a night together. Poor darlings had so few of those after they were married.'

Lucy laughed. 'I know, but they prepared for marriage well. And I'm glad they did. Annie once told me she felt married even though she hadn't said her vows as Ricky was her life and giving herself to him didn't feel wrong, but very, very right . . . If I get the chance to do the same with my Dan, I would like a shot.'

'Oh, I wish that would happen. You deserve some happiness, Lucy. But at least you know that as a war correspondent, Dan is reasonably safe, love.'

'You would think so, but there have been so many reports of them being caught in crossfire. No one is safe, Olivia, no one. What do you think will happen to us if we're discovered by the Germans?'

Olivia shuddered. That part of the course – the torture, the possible execution – had terrified her. She put her hand in her pocket and pulled out the most shocking object she'd been given and told Lucy, 'This is what will happen.' She held aloft the little capsule containing the arsenic pill.

They stared at each other for a moment. Then Olivia said, 'Please God it doesn't ever come to that.'

Lucy nodded. 'I have one of those too – I don't know if I would be able to use it or not.'

As they came out of the barn, Olivia looked heavenward and pressed her hand to her chest.

Please, God, let my Hendrick make it safely to me.

Lucy's hand came into hers. 'Sorry to be the devil's advocate, but we must keep on our toes at all times, Olivia.'

Olivia smiled her forgiveness. Lucy was right. It was time to put love aside and focus on why she was here. She could do that. Somehow, she could do that.

Chapter Fourteen

Ricky

Ricky lay on the damp grass. Gunshots pierced the air; German voices carried to him. He turned his head to look at George, a young cockney recently brought into the stalag in Poznań.

Ricky hadn't wanted to bring him with him when he'd escaped, telling him he wasn't in danger being young and strong as the Germans would want to keep him alive, knowing that he could do twice the work the older among them could. But George had worn him down, saying he'd be better using that energy back with his regiment.

Ricky lifted his head. He could see the woodland they'd been making for.

They'd followed the route given to them by the Red Cross to get this far. One of the farmers along the way had taken them to their base. There they'd given them fresh clothes: a warm pullover, and shirt and trousers each. They'd fed them and sent them on their way with a pack of sandwiches and a little money, telling them the best way to go.

'Ricky, mate, let's make a run for it, eh?'

'No. Stay still and quiet, George, it's our only chance. The

Jerrys were in a convoy when they spotted us. That bloke in the escorted car looked like an important official. 'E ain't going to wait long to get on 'is way and 'e'll soon be pulling 'is troops off our back, you'll see.'

'But if we get to them trees, we'll 'ave somewhere to hide.'

Ricky sighed. George was only twenty and he thought like a lad – in his mind, he could conquer the Jerrys on his own. His attitude had got him on jankers a few times in the camp, although Ricky admired his courage.

However, this time courage wasn't what was needed, but common sense. How can you put that into a young lad's head?

'I'm going. I ain't laying 'ere to be found and shot.'

George got up. His body immediately fell beside Ricky, his eyes staring, his forehead showing a bullet hole burned through it from the back of his head.

Ricky's body shook with terror and his heart felt torn in two. Such a waste of a young life. Lying back, he awaited his fate, but nothing happened. He hoped with everything he was that those hunting them down had thought there was only one of them. When he heard their voices next, they had receded into the distance. As he lay still, Ricky knew he should feel relief, but instead he sobbed with the pain of losing George. They'd travelled miles together, watching each other's backs, and the lad had made his way into his heart.

Finding George's hand, tears of despair stung Ricky's face. The poor lad had a lifetime ahead of him. And what of his girl, Lindsey? George had always talked of her, kissed her photo so often, not taking heed of the jokes of the other prisoners.

Ricky put his hand into George's shirt pocket. Struggling to get under his jumper, he found the photo. A pretty face framed in a mound of curls smiled back at him. Ricky turned it over. On the back it read, *One day, we'll be together again, me darlin'* and it was signed Lindsey, and then simply said, *I love you x.* George had written underneath, *And I love you. You're me girl.*

Thinking it should be given to Lindsey, Ricky put it carefully into his own shirt pocket. Then, with tears running down his face, he found George's dog tag and took it from around his neck. That too went into his shirt pocket.

After what seemed like an age, he slowly got up, kissed George's cool cheek and ran for the cover of the trees.

Weakness overcame him. He hadn't eaten for days. They'd been about to cross a road to get to a farmer's house, who they'd been told would help them, when the convoy had come along. He'd managed to get out of sight, but George had been seen. They'd run like the wind and had put distance between them before the soldiers had time to climb out of their vehicles.

Now, Ricky was exhausted, hungry, and despair was weakening his resolve.

Blinking to take the tears from his eyes, Ricky looked up and saw the pattern of the sunbeams dappling through the leaves of the branches above him. *If this is where I am to die, then it is a pretty place, a peaceful one, but it isn't me choice. Me choice would be to be lying in my Annie's arms.*

Closing his eyes, he tried to bring his lovely Annie to mind. Somehow, he couldn't focus on any one thing. Not even Annie. Her image kept fading from him . . . *Don't desert me, me darlin' Annie. Stay with me and help me.*

The sound of snapping branches and voices froze all thoughts. Fear gripped him, but then a feeling of resignation gave him peace. *If this is to be my death, then so be it.*

His spirit lifted then. It was as if the decision on whether he lived or died was out of his hands. He would just accept.

As a figure came and looked down at him, Ricky thought, *Goodbye, me lovely Annie. I did me best. I tried to get back to yer, me darlin'.*

The cold steel of a gun pressed hard into his forehead. Words were spoken to him in Polish. With the sound of this language, some hope came into Ricky. He opened his eyes and through cracked lips that would hardly move managed to say, 'POW . . . British Army.'

The gun moved away. In English the man said, 'Ah, we have been told to watch out for you . . . You're safe now, English soldier. We'll take care of you.'

Ricky couldn't answer. Stinging tears ran down his face.

'Jakob and Marcin, make a stretcher. Jan, bring water!' With this command given, the man turned back to Ricky. 'I'm Filip.'

When Ricky next woke his body ached with pain. An alien feeling to him as for days, maybe weeks, he'd felt nothing, as if his body had given up warning him of where it hurt.

A hand came under his head. 'Here, drink this, soldier. You'll be all right now.'

An English accent. Ricky tried to ask where he was, but the words wouldn't come. Only one word formed, 'Annie?'

'Is Annie your girl?'

Ricky nodded.

'Look, soldier, you're safe now. What's your name? The Polish officers who found you understood only that you were a soldier and British.'

Ricky swallowed the mouthful of cold water, then found he could speak. 'Sergeant Richard Stanley . . . Ricky. Essex Regiment.'

171

'Well, Ricky, mate, you're in a Resistance camp. I'm Captain Sellers. John. I'm a British agent working with the Resistance. We know about you and your escape; the Red Cross informed us first, but we have since had a communication. There were two of you, weren't there?'

Ricky sobbed his, 'Yes.'

'What happened? And what was his name?'

'George . . . George Makepeace. He was shot . . . Jerrys . . . I have his tag and a photo of his girl.'

'Poor lad. Look, try not to worry, it's over for him now, and we'll take care of you and make sure George's family get this photo.'

'Ta.'

'One of our men is a doctor. He's dressed your wounds. He said to take this, it will help with your pain.'

Ricky opened his mouth and felt the tablet put on his tongue. Another drink and he swallowed it down.

'Get some rest. The doctor has said you're going to be all right. You're suffering from malnutrition and dehydration and have some infections from untreated cuts and scratches. The doctor has cleaned them all and put iodine on them. I think you'll be as right as rain in a couple of days. I'll radio in that you're safe. But when we can get you back to Britain, I don't know. We get supplies dropped in, but not much goes out as it's too dangerous for planes to land.'

'Ta, mate . . . I mean, Captain, sir.' Ricky lifted his hand. John took it and shook it gently. Ricky managed a weak salute.

'No need to stand on ceremony here, Ricky. Now, do as I say, and get some rest.'

When Ricky opened his eyes, he felt almost back to himself, just suffering from a weakness that made it difficult for him to sit up and seemed more to do with hunger than anything else.

When he did manage to, he found he was inside a tent. Through the open flap he could see men working at lighting a fire and preparing food. He looked for John but couldn't see him. Getting up on unsteady legs, he got to the flap and held on to the flag post. Around him were more tents and wooden lean-to shed-like structures.

One man looked up from where he was tending to a cut on someone's leg. He put the plaster in place and then came over. 'You're awake! I'm Doctor Wanski . . . Antoni. How are you feeling?'

Antoni's English was good, very precise, not a bit like a cockney . . . 'A lot better, ta, mate.'

'You will soon be yourself. Nothing a good meal won't mend, but you must take it slowly. I've had the cook prepare you some oats in milk. We eat well here; the local people keep us supplied. We are all amazed that you escaped from Stalag XXI-D. It is one Poznań camp that seemed impregnable. When we heard of you escaping, we all thought you must have been killed trying to get across Poland.'

Ricky's heart felt heavy as he nodded, his memory filled with George. A proper cheeky cockney lad.

'Look, if ever you want to talk . . . I mean, there are obviously things on your mind. I'm here for you. And John has reported you being found, so your Annie, whose name we all know now with you shouting it out most of the night, will soon know you're safe.'

Antoni laughed out loud. Ricky grinned. 'She's the love of me life. We were only married days before I 'ad to leave.'

'It is hard leaving them. Here it is worse as we don't know if they are dead or alive or being mistreated.'

173

'No, mate. Not worse. Me Annie and me family live in the East End of London. We 'eard there's nightly bombing . . . Can yer find out if me Annie's all right?'

'Oh, I'm sorry. Of course. I – I didn't think . . . Here was me offering to help you and making a blunder straight away. Forgive me.'

'It's all right, mate, we've all got our worries. I'm sorry your family ain't safe.'

'Thank you. Oh, and John will find out about Annie for you. I hope she is all right too. They may even allow her to write to you. John gets the odd bit of mail now and then in the parcels that are dropped . . . Now, try to eat something, only take it very slowly. Let your stomach adjust.'

As Ricky ate the delicious-tasting hot oats, his thoughts went to the Old Ford Road. He tried to imagine what life would be like there, if they had a shelter, and if they managed to get Annie's mum down into it. Then he thought, *Vera's me mum-in-law now, I should think of her as Mum.*

His thoughts went to Vera playing the piano and them all singing, and he and Annie dancing, kicking up their legs and laughing as they nearly fell over.

He could see them all. His mum, Lilly, who he grew up knowing as his sister. Janey and her Jimmy, and little baby Beth. Cissy. Ah, lovely Cissy with her northern accent that he loved.

Sighing, he hoped with all his heart that they were safe. That his Annie hadn't been sent out on duty during the Blitz as George had told him it was called. He could only imagine what it was like with bombs dropping every night.

Annie must worry about how I am and if I'm dead or alive. I wonder if she got me little notes. He'd thought himself lucky to get them out to the Red Cross. But whether they were ever delivered, he had no way of knowing.

Well, Annie, now at least I'm safe. But was he? Weren't the Resistance groups in great danger? News of their under-cover fight against the Nazi occupation had come to them in the camp. The farmer whose land they'd been made to work told them all he could, often passing notes, which none of them understood, but when they got back to camp, a Polish guard, reluctantly carrying out his duties, translated for them. His English was good. He'd told them he'd been a scholar when Poland was invaded and had been forced into the role he did. Though he did it vigilantly on the surface, secretly he'd helped them all he could. It had been him who had helped them escape.

The flap opened. John appeared. 'Finished that, mate?'

'Yes, ta, it tasted like nectar. But I'm full after only 'alf of it.'

'Ha, you'll soon pick up, especially with the news I have for you. Annie's safe. She's living in Wales with three children. No other details, but where she is isn't being bombed, and is not likely to be.'

Ricky couldn't speak. He couldn't swallow. His joy was too overwhelming. He just sat there staring, knowing his mouth was wide open, but not able to close it.

John laughed. 'Well, I don't know if that's good or bad news now!'

At last Ricky could react. 'It's the best news ever, ta, John. I can't think who the third kid is, but one will be her sister's and one 'er friend's, and did they say anything about 'er family and me mum?'

'Yes. I'm sorry . . . but the news isn't good. I've no details, but all were lost. A bomb.'

Ricky gasped. 'Me mum . . . Lilly . . . and all of them?'

'All but your Annie and the kids, and someone called Loes.'

Ricky slumped back onto his pillow. 'No! No . . . not all me family . . . no!'

'Look, you still have Annie, Ricky . . . I'm sorry, really sorry, but you've to pick yourself up and get back to fighting this war to make sure Annie's safe and those kids . . . But take a minute and I'll come back in a while. We've a raid planned for later, and I've just had confirmation that it's on. A train coming from Germany, carrying tanks and other ammunition, so I won't be able to stay long, but we want you to join us. Not on this raid, but we need you. I've been told of your experience not only in this war, but the last. You will have knowledge that we need. Explosives and things.'

Though still shivering with shock, this touched the soldier in Ricky and the person that he was – always ready to do his duty, whether it be on his patch as a copper in Stepney or for his country, fighting a war. Sitting up, he straightened his back. 'I'm ready, Captain, sir.'

'Good man. You're far more worthy of being a captain than I am, Ricky. My title is honorary, not earned in the usual way, but by way of giving me rank over who I might work with in the secret service. I will be very glad of the practical knowledge you have, that I couldn't possibly gain during a six-week course in Scotland! I am a linguist and was training to be a lawyer. I went to Sandhurst when war broke out but was commissioned for this role. I have never seen combat warfare, only clandestine warfare. You will be able to help us a great deal.'

'I'll do me best, sir.'

'John. I'm not pulling rank over you, Ricky. And this isn't

the situation that should call for it. Of course, I'll be the leader with the final decisions, but I'm looking on you as a godsend. A right-hand man. Are you up to that?'

'I am, John. I'll do all I can.'

'Good. First thing is to get strong again. You've got a week to do that in, Sergeant.'

With this John left. Ricky smiled to himself. The bloke didn't mind pulling rank when it suited him. But then, he thought, it was an awkward position for him, and he'd be better off just being the captain as captains should be, not trying to make a friend of the ranks. That didn't sit well. But Ricky thought he would respect John, whichever mode he put himself in. And be glad to.

With this settled in his mind, Ricky allowed himself to think about the awful news he'd just had. He swung his feet off the bed and sat with his head in his hands. *Oh my God! All of them! Me poor Annie . . . me poor darlin'. How is she coping?*

Swallowing hard, Ricky stood up. However his Annie was coping, she would be doing it with courage, and he had to do the same. He had to become a soldier again. He'd do all he could to help this band of men to fight their war against the Jerrys.

With this new determination, Ricky slipped on his trousers and went to find where he could wash himself.

The men now sitting around the fire, smoking or drinking tea, greeted him. Filip stood. 'You look better.'

'Ta, mate. Where's the bog?'

'Bog?'

'Sorry, the lavatory . . . ablution tent?'

'Ah . . . It is at the back of the camp. We ask you go into the trees to do your business. Use leaves to clean. We have

177

no sanitation. The tent is for washing and shaving – if we ever get our hands on a razor. Come.'

Filip showed him to a small tent right at the back of all the other structures.

'Here we have a shovel. It is for covering up what you do. Go as far away from the camp as you can.'

Ricky nodded. 'Ta. I just want a swill.'

'A swill? . . . Ta?'

Ricky laughed. 'Ta means thank you. Swill means wash.'

'Oh, these are slang words? We have those too. I will get used to them . . . Ricky, I'm sorry about the news you've received. The Germans, they are bastards.'

'Ta, mate.'

'Now "mate" I know, as John uses that too . . . Anyway, if you need to talk to someone . . .'

All Ricky could do was to thank him again. These men, though rough and ready and no doubt prepared to slit a throat if they were called upon to do so, were good blokes. He liked them. He'd do all he could to help their quest for freedom.

Ricky spent the rest of the day helping around camp where he could, trying to keep his mind busy so as not to think of his lovely mum, Lilly, and all those lost who he considered family. Even Rose, Jimmy's mum, who he didn't know that well. She'd been through a lot in her lifetime with what Jimmy had done.

But above all his grief, one thing kept him going. His Annie was safe, and so was Beth, Janey's little girl, and Karl, Olivia's young one. The third kid Annie had with her he was mystified over, and yet something told him it would be some snotty-nosed little East Ender who'd lost his mum and dad. His Annie was like that. Kind, caring and loving . . . *Oh, Annie, me Annie, I miss you.*

Chapter Fifteen

Annie

Annie sat in her and Daphne's living room and Beth and Karl played on the rug in front of the unlit fire. Coming towards the end of June, it was raining, but humid.

With her housework done, Annie had an attack of boredom hit her. She just didn't feel cut out to be a housewife. But what could she do? There were no nurseries for the little ones, and it wouldn't be fair to leave them with Rosemary for any longer than she did already, just to pop to the shops if it was a wet day.

It felt to Annie that she was being left behind. Daphne was loving her job on the farm on Rossett Road, about half an hour's cycle ride from here. She even loved her journey to and from work – having always cycled around Guernsey, she was thrilled to be finding many similarities with her journey to her home on the island.

'I've made a pot of tea, Annie!'

Annie jumped up at this call from Rosemary. She'd been dying for company but trying not to be under Rosemary's feet.

'Come on, you two. No doubt there'll be juice for you and biscuits as well!'

Beth and Karl scurried past her and were at the top of the stairs before Annie could get there herself.

'Careful! Wait for me!'

Once downstairs in the kitchen, they all sat around the huge wooden table. Annie loved it in here, with its row of gleaming pans hanging over the Aga, its red tiled floor and bright yellow curtains.

'Well, Annie, I'll pour, then I want to talk to you, my dear.'

'Oh, is there anything wrong? Are yer happy with your flat, and all we've done, Rosemary?'

'More than happy. I love it. My work has been cut in half, and no more climbing stairs . . . No, it isn't me, it's you.'

'Me? Am I in your way? Are the children?'

'Far from it, Annie, stop worrying. Everything is wonderful. I love my flat, I love that you all live above me, separately and yet in the same house. I love hearing you pottering in the kitchen, though you clean it till it sparkles and then clean it again . . . You're fed up, aren't you, Annie?'

Annie nodded. 'I try not to be. I love looking after the kids and keeping the flat nice, the washing done and the ironing, but . . . well, after the life of being a London cop out every night with bombs dropping, helping folk out of burning buildings and keeping order so that looters didn't get away with anything . . . it's . . . well, yes, I'm bored. I don't feel I am doing anything to help me fellow countrymen.'

'I understand. Here, we hardly know there is a war on. Well, we did when Liverpool caught it last year. The top of that mountain was alight, and the town was bathed in smoke for days because of a stray bomb. And we lost a few from the village outside the town as they took a direct hit, but nothing more than that.'

'The thing is, I can't even volunteer for the Red Cross because of the children needing me.'

'Is it me making you bored, Mum?'

Annie stood and went around the table to Beth. It pleased her so much how she'd dropped into calling her 'Mum', just as Ian had, and sometimes Karl did, though she always corrected him and told him she was his Aunty Annie.

When she was next to Beth, she held her in her arms. 'No, no, it ain't you, luv. Nor Karl, nor Ian. You're the highlight of me life. You and Rosemary and Daphne are all I have in me life, but Mum's been used to working, and now I miss it, that's all.'

'Well, Annie, I have a solution,' Rosemary cut in. 'I've been out to the shop this morning, as you know, and there's a card in the window saying that a young girl of sixteen is looking for work. She has put down housework as one of her options besides shop work, and she has put that she's used to being around children and would consider taking babies for walks. Her name's Bryony.'

'You mean, I should hire her? But what would I pay her with? I manage well, especially having the rent from the flats coming in every month, and what Daphne can contribute, but I don't know that I could run to a wage for anyone.'

'I could help. I could well afford to buy groceries for us all, and there was a lot left of Olivia's money, you could use that too . . . I think you should consider this, Annie. With your skills, you're needed.'

A trickle of excitement gripped Annie's stomach muscles. Ideas of what she could do came to her. Not paid work, but volunteering at the hospital where they were very short of staff with a lot of nurses leaving to go to overseas field hospitals, or hospital ships. And some she'd heard had

181

volunteered to work in hospitals that took the influx of the wounded on the coast of England, or in London.

Or she could become a Red Cross worker . . .

'I'll do it. Ta, Rosemary. I'll get the kids wrapped up and walk to the shop.'

'Oh, no, leave them here with me, dear. You can take your car and be back in no time.'

'Ha, if Loes was here, she would take them. "They must be getting fresh air," she would say. Poor Loes. I keep writing to her but have heard nothing back. I hope at least that she's getting letters from Joe. I'll ring Rita later and ask if any have arrived for her and if Bertie managed to send them to the Red Cross.'

'All these people you speak of, Annie . . . I've never met them, and yet I feel I know them. And I feel the same relief that you feel now they are safe, and the bombing has stopped.'

'Yes, but that goes along with this longing in me to do something. I rang me sarge the other day and he said how they miss me and that he never accepted my resignation but left me on compassionate leave.'

'That's what you really want, isn't it, Annie? To go back home.'

Annie bent her head. Then turned to the children. 'Have you finished your biscuits, you two?'

'Yes. Can we go back to our game, Mum?'

'You can, Beth. But no falling out. Let Karl have a say in things too!'

'But he's useless! He makes it all go wrong!'

'Beth! I never want to hear you call Karl names again! Karl having different ideas to you is a good thing, and you should listen to him sometimes and do things his way!'

Beth's bottom lip came out.

'I built the tower, Beth, and mine didn't fall.'

'Sorry, Karl.'

Karl put a chubby arm around Beth's shoulders.

But Beth didn't give in altogether. 'Well, I build the houses better than he does.' But she did grin at Karl, and he was happy with that.

Glad they had sorted themselves now, Annie said, 'Off you go then. And play nicely together. When I come up, I want to see you've built a village out of those bricks for me . . . Oh, and make sure there's a cafe so that I can have another tea and biscuits.'

Annie grinned at Rosemary as the children left and ran back up the stairs.

But Rosemary wasn't going to let go of the subject. 'So, Annie, it is that, isn't it? You want to go home?'

Tears welled up in Annie's eyes. She put out her hand and laid it over Rosemary's. 'I couldn't leave you, Rosemary, and so I'm torn, but me sarge did say that I could come back at any time.'

She didn't say that the sarge had made enquiries and that there was no longer thought to be a threat of any German spy getting at her, but said instead, 'And that has left me feeling torn as, yes, I admit, I do want to go home, but I don't want to leave you, and wouldn't.'

'Look, Annie, you never intended on staying here for ever, did you? Anyway, I have been doing some thinking too. You said you had empty flats in your house in London, didn't you?'

This surprised Annie. 'Yes. Me mum's is empty, and what I always look on as me sister Janey's, but I live in that.'

'And would you consider me renting your mum's? I know you've always told me you hadn't wanted to let it, but I would take great care of it.'

Annie couldn't believe what she was hearing.

'It's safe in London now and I do have many friends there from when I worked there. We still write to each other . . . To tell the truth, now there are no visits from my William to look forward to, I cannot think why I wanted to come back to Wales. When I was a young woman, I couldn't wait to escape. I needed excitement . . . And, well, because of my situation – being a mistress – I didn't want to live near to my family, who have all since passed away. And I've kept myself to myself, ending up friendless and lonely here.'

'Oh, Rosemary, really? . . . Oh, but there's Daphne. She's so happy here. To her, it's as if she's back home – except for missing her mum, of course. But now she has received a letter from Stefan, she's really settled.'

'Oh dear. We couldn't leave her, she would rattle around in this house as I have done for many years between William's visits . . . I – I do miss him, Annie.'

'I know, luv, you're bound to. He was a lovely man. Oh, why was he so stubborn? It makes me cross when I think of all the years you've missed out on.'

'Me too. But I do balance that with thinking how he left me well cared for, and in the end sent Olivia to me, with the bonus of all of you . . . So, what do you think?'

'My heart's pounding at the thought of going home, and yes, me mum's flat is yours to have. I know she would welcome you, and I don't need any rent. I know yer ain't got a big income, only yer savings. William didn't intend that, but he never asked for a war, nor could he plan for it . . . Though, Olivia's solicitor was going to look at assets he may have in a personal account in Switzerland.'

'I don't doubt there is Olivia's inheritance and mine too locked safely away, though until the world gets back right again, there won't be anything the solicitor can do . . . But, Annie, are you sure about the rent?'

'I am.'

'You see, I can sell the furniture I don't want to take, if Daphne comes with us. And then we can rent this place out as two flats. Which will help to get Olivia set up when she returns. We can bank it for her. I don't think we'd have trouble finding tenants. There are a lot of homeless from the bombing of Liverpool moving in around here. The shop-keeper was telling me that the menfolk are getting digs for the week while they work in their banks and offices and coming home here at weekends to their families.'

'Yes, I heard that too at the school gate. So, that's a good idea you've had. And second-hand furniture is selling well . . . But, well, if it's to be two flats, we'll need a kitchen upstairs. I think we could do that. We still have some funds left.'

'How?'

'Your old bedroom is huge. The furniture we took from down here is lost in it. I've been thinking of buying a table and chairs to fill it, but I think we could partition part of it off and make a small kitchen. We could do that between the two windows so that each room has a window.'

'Do you know, I think that will work. Ooh, I'm getting all excited now and cannot wait to write to Doris and May, my friends. It's ages since I saw them. They used to come here for a break every couple of years. Both are widowed now and seem to have hordes of grandchildren, some of whom are away fighting. It'll be good to be together again.'

Annie sighed. 'It all depends on Daphne . . . I know she wouldn't stop us, but I'd feel awful leaving her.'

'Let's not pre-empt her decision. But in any case, dear,

we still must think carefully about shelving our plans for one person – plans that will be the best for us all. I did that once for William's ideas and it left me lonely and heartbroken. Don't let that happen to you. I know now that I should have married William. My life would have been so different, and I would have been able to help Olivia over the shock of meeting me as a new wife to her father.'

This made Annie's mind up. She wanted to think of Daphne, but her own well-being was important too, as was that of the children. Yes, life was good here, and they would grow into it, but in London they would have so many more chances in the future. It was this thought that made her mind up. 'I'll ring Dave and tell him and his builder to come as soon as they can and look at me plan . . . Oh, Rosemary, I'm so excited and happy. Thank you.'

Rosemary stood and held out her arms. As Annie went into them, the telephone rang.

'I'll get it.'

On her way to the hall, Annie couldn't think who would be ringing and hoped everything was all right back at the flats in Bethnal . . . *Bethnal, I'm really going back there . . . really and truly . . . If only Ricky was there waiting for me!*

As she picked up the phone, her sergeant's voice came to her, sounding full of joy. 'He's been found, luv! Our Ricky's been found!'

'Wh-what? Ricky! Oh, Sarge, is he all right? Where is he? Can I go to him?'

Annie's heart was singing. She heard Rosemary come into the hall. And now she was standing by her side.

'No, you can't go to him, Annie, but he's safe.'

Annie listened to how the Polish Resistance had found him and how he had joined their ranks.

This last made her heart sink. 'So, he isn't safe, yet . . . Oh, Sarge!'

'Annie, he's a lot safer than he was, and no doubt a lot happier. He's well and not hurt badly, just exhausted, and cut and bruised. They have a doctor in camp so he's being looked after. That's all I know . . . and, Annie, that's a lot more than I ever hoped for. Let's rejoice, eh?'

'Ta, Sarge, I am, me heart's doing cartwheels. I just wanted him out of danger.'

'Ricky wouldn't want that. Not while all his mates are still facing the front line. He'll be happy to be able to do his bit, luv.'

'I know . . . and, Sarge. I'm coming home.'

'Oh, Annie, that's good news, luv! The best. We need you. The bombing has stopped, but there's so much to do to keep people safe. And policing too, as looting still goes on. I can't blame those who are desperate and bombed out of house and home. We help them, just as you'd want us to, but the criminals trying to make some quick money . . . well, we have to clamp down on them . . . And so much work is needed to be done by us . . . When can you come?'

'I'll let yer know. We've only just decided, but I can't wait. It's just that there's a lot to put in place.'

They said their goodbyes. As Annie put the phone down, she shouted, 'He's safe!'

Two little bodies appeared at the top of the stairs, eyes wide with fear.

Annie ran up to them and hugged them. 'It's all right. Everything's all right, me little darlin's. Ricky's safe!'

Both frowned. Annie realized with a jolt that they couldn't remember Ricky. 'You know, we kiss his picture every night along with your mums' and gran's?'

Beth beamed. 'Ricky? Singing Ricky?'

Annie marvelled at this child. How she'd remembered that she didn't know. Beth had only been nineteen months old when Ricky had left!

'Yes, singing Ricky! Well, he's all safe and with nice people.'

'Was he lost?'

'Yes, Karl, luv. He was.'

Karl still looked puzzled. 'Anyway, no need to worry yerself any longer, mate. Ricky's safe now and we have to pray it ain't too long before he and all the daddies and mummies come home.'

'I told you, you have to say your prayers at night, Karl. I do. And you should!'

Karl grinned. He seemed to love being bossed about by Beth. Annie wasn't sure this was a good thing and yet, it meant a peaceful life because if he objected, all hell would let loose!

'Go and play a little while longer. I'll be up soon.'

Rosemary voiced what Annie was thinking. 'You know, Annie, I don't want to interfere, but we'll have to get Karl to assert himself a little more. It's not good for him to kowtow constantly. Nor for Beth to feel she can make him bend to her will, which is happening all the time.'

'I know. I've too much on me mind just now, Rosemary, but I will address it . . . even though I can see our peace shattered if it happens!'

They both grinned, then what Rosemary said next confirmed for Annie that she really did want the move to London and wasn't just trying to appease her.

'Now, ring David. I want to know the work can be done, and then I want to start packing!'

Annie laughed out loud. All of that had gone out of her

head as her dream of her Ricky being safe had become a truth . . . at least partly. He would be in danger, as the whole world was. But he'd come through the biggest danger of all.

By the time Daphne came home, David had been and had confirmed that their design plans were doable. Especially so as where Annie proposed the kitchen should go was next to the bathroom, making access to water and drainage simple. 'As for putting a wall up and fitting some cupboards, that'll be a doddle. My, you're making changes to this old place, Annie, but good ones. Flats are getting more and more popular. It means these big old houses can house two families and how the country's situated, with so many homes lost, that's a good thing.'

Daphne seemed to know something was afoot. 'It isn't just Ricky being found, is it, Annie? Something else is putting that smile on your face, but at the same time, you seem worried, love.'

Annie told her what they planned.

Daphne's mouth dropped open. 'But . . . Oh, Annie! Where did all of that come from? I never dreamed.'

'Sit down, luv. Rosemary's making tea. We knew this would be a shock to you, but, well, I have to go, Daphne. I've been so unhappy here. I've done everything I could to make meself settle, but I can't . . . I need to do me job . . . I need to be with me own folk.'

'But what about Rosemary?'

'She wants to come with me as much as I want to go . . . Well, I mean, I say me but I ain't excluding you, luv. We both agree that it's your choice. Yer can stay here and have which of the flats yer want for yourself, or yer can come with us.'

Daphne looked uncertain. 'And you'll let the other flat out?'

'Yes, but if yer stay, yer can choose the tenant. We wouldn't want to impose someone on yer . . . Oh, Daphne, I so want yer to come back with me, but I know it's not me decision, you've got to do what will be best for you.'

Daphne's expression softened. She must have thought they were just discarding her. 'I don't know, Annie. I – I'm so taken aback. My heart wants to go with you, and yet I'm so happy here. It's like home to me. I know St Peter Port is all buildings, but I only had to get on my bike as I do now, and I was in the countryside. I think that's where I was meant to be. I always went as often as I could. And Farmer Dai is so good to me, as is his wife. And we're to take in some Land Girls soon as more of our land is to be given over to growing food . . .'

'Daphne, you just said "our land", not theirs. This is your home, isn't it?'

Daphne nodded. 'But so is anywhere you are, Annie . . . Oh, I don't know.'

'Do as Rosemary told me to do – go with your heart, mate. Me and you can meet up, or I can come for a break from the city and me job. We can telephone all the time. But whatever yer decide, decide it to fit in with your needs. It's the only way to find happiness, luv. Rosemary's made me realize that. She put Olivia's possible needs before William's and never got to marry him and now she regrets that.'

'You're right. And thinking about it, I could offer a flat to a couple of Land Girls, couldn't I? I'd like that rather than a family . . . I mean, I love our family, but I have to get up early and suppose I get two or three howling kids up there?'

Annie laughed. 'Good thinking, and yes, that would work as no doubt the government will pay their accommodation for them. After all, they'll be army personnel as I understand it.'

'That's settled then. I'm sorry, Annie, but I don't see me living back in London . . . and I can't see Stefan wanting to.'

Annie went to her and hugged her. 'I'll miss yer, Daphne, but I know you've made the right decision for you, luv. And hang on to that thought, that Stefan would be happy living around here with yer. One day, I know he will.'

Rosemary came in then. 'I've been earwigging. I'm so glad for you, Daphne. It means upheaval again, as you'll have builders upstairs, because I'm sure you'll want this flat for yourself. I hope so. I'd love to think of you here.'

'Less upheaval really, Rosemary,' Annie told her. 'The Land Girls will need furniture, so we can leave it all as it is and you can use Mum's furniture in London.'

'Oh, yes. Apart from the building work, you're all set to go, Daphne . . . But, oh, I will miss you.'

Daphne's eyes filled with tears at Rosemary's words. 'And me you. All of you. But I understand your decision and know this is the right one for me.'

As Annie got into bed that night, it felt to her that so much was coming right for her – not totally; that could never happen until she was in her Ricky's arms. But mostly. And she decided that 'mostly' would do for now. She wouldn't dwell on how she wanted everything right. She would get on with making the best life she could for herself and the kids and others that she'd now be able to help.

'Night, Daphne. I'm putting me light off now.'

'Night, love. No prize for guessing what you're going to be dreaming of.'

Annie giggled. 'None at all.'

She heard Daphne giggle, then closed her eyes. Ricky's lovely face came to her. He was singing 'Knees up Mother Brown' and she saw them dancing together and Ricky playing the fool as he kicked his legs up high, and then she joined in with him as they'd sung their heart out. A happy memory, with Mum playing the piano and all the family gathered. She hoped Ricky held the same memory.

But she didn't let the utter devastation of the bad side of the memory creep into her. She held on to the image of Ricky's laughing face and knew that one day, she would see it again.

Chapter Sixteen

Olivia

As Lucy watched Olivia trying to manoeuvre Nelly, the cart horse, around the yard, she was in tucks of laughter.

'She just keeps going around in circles!' Olivia wailed.

Pierre, always patient, shouted to her to rein Nelly in. When she had, he jumped up beside her and took the reins. 'Like this!'

He turned the horse expertly around to face the gate. Olivia tried and Nelly obeyed, then turned and looked at her as if to say, 'Just tell me what you want me to do, for goodness' sake!'

Laughing, she told Nelly, 'You should know by now, you do it every day!'

This made Pierre and Lucy laugh even more.

Deciding she had to be more in command, Olivia geed Nelly on by flapping the reins, and then brought her to a halt just before the gate. Pleased with herself but still nervous about going through the gate and onto the road, and even worse, taking Nelly through the streets of Paris, her stomach wobbled with nerves!

But a week later, having done the trip with Lucy every

day and taken the reins on three of them, Olivia began to feel confident.

Though wondering what Farmer Fallom back in Guernsey would have thought, to see the bank owner's daughter delivering milk in the same way that he did, gave her a pang of homesickness. *Will I ever go back to my beloved island?*

Sadness made her heart feel heavy as at this moment it seemed impossible that she ever would. Nor could she ever envisage getting back to being the person she had been, newly married, and looking forward to the future with Hendrick. She couldn't believe either that they would ever be able to complete their dream of building the house that they'd planned and marked out with stones in the field they owned. This was scheduled to happen once their language school, which would take the whole of the downstairs of the farmhouse, had become successful. Then after that, they'd planned to make the upstairs into a boarding house for foreign students . . . All an impossible dream now.

She and Hendrick hadn't even been together when little Karl had been born because of this war. Annie had been with her, though, and that had helped.

'You've gone quiet. Not a good occupation, thinking about what might have been, love.'

'I know, Lucy, but sometimes, something triggers a memory, and you find yourself back in a good time and longing for it.' Olivia sighed. 'If only we could hear something about Hendrick.'

They were quiet for a moment. Olivia could feel Lucy's sadness and felt sorry that she'd instigated it.

They pulled up outside Café le Patissier and Olivia, glad to be doing something, jumped down to fill the jugs and take the owner's order inside. The mundane task helped to distract her from her sorrow, as the sound of children playing in the street came to her. Life went on, children still played with a ball in the street. Housewives still washed their clothes and hung them from one window to the next to dry, and people still scurried from A to B.

Véronique, as Lucy had told her the owner was called, greeted her, and took the jugs from her. 'Would you like a coffee, madame? And your friend? I have a moment as so little custom today.'

Olivia looked around. Two Germans sat in one corner talking earnestly. Neither had seemed to see her.

'I'd love that. I will fetch my friend.'

Strange, she thought, how no one asked you your name.

They sat near to the Germans in order to hear their conversation. This attracted a glance from one of them, and a '*Guten Morgen*'.

Olivia nodded. She imagined that most French people would by now understand a simple phrase like 'Good morning' in German, so to acknowledge him wouldn't give him a hint that she spoke German.

Keeping his eye on her, she heard him say, 'Pretty woman. I could go for that one.'

His friend laughed. 'They don't have to be pretty for you to go for them.'

Olivia's mouth dried as the words provoked a terrifying and horrific memory.

'Olivia?'

Lucy's voice brought her back from the depth of the depravity that she'd conjured up.

'Drink your coffee, love, and let's get out. But take your time, don't hurry and show the fear you just did again.'

She laughed then, as if she'd made a joke. Olivia laughed

with her, keeping her eyes on her and not looking over at the two men.

As she sipped the coffee, enjoying the flavour, her nerves calmed. Lucy helped by chatting about everyday things – their next call, the weather being dry for them – but though she interacted, Olivia did as she should and listened to the German officers' conversation.

The one who'd passed the remark about fancying her was saying, 'I hear there's another trainload of Mischlinge and Zigeunerinnen passing through.'

These she knew were half-castes and gypsies. She wanted to scream out that all people had a right to live, and it wasn't for them to decide who peopled this earth! But she just listened and learned that this was to happen the next morning as the conversation went on and further sickened her.

'Tell me about it, I have to supervise its passage . . . Ha, I find it great sport to turn the hose on them and make their ugly faces disappear from the slats they poke their hands through.'

Finishing her coffee and wanting to escape, Olivia stood, smiled at the cafe owner, and said, 'Merci, madame. Bon café.'

She received a smile for her compliment of 'good coffee' and turned, hoping Lucy would follow even though she hadn't quite finished hers.

Grateful for the Germans being deep in conversation, Olivia left the cafe without any comment from them.

'I never want to sit in the same room as them again, Lucy!'

'But you must! How will you be able to hear conversations if you don't? Did you catch that? I understood train; did you get the rest of it?'

'Yes, a train carrying half-castes and gypsies. My heart goes out to them. Is there anything we can do?'

'Did they say where it was coming from and heading?'

'Only where it's heading. It's going to Avrillé-les-Ponceaux.'

'We'll radio it through to Claudius. Hopefully he can get men on the train's route to disrupt and free the people on it.'

'Will we know the outcome?'

'Maybe . . . Olivia, you will hear many things that will upset you. Just think how you are in a privileged position to be able to help some of the people involved. We are doing what we can.'

'I know. I just don't want any of it to be happening, I want all people to be free to live their lives as they please. Why? Why do these Nazis think themselves superior? How can they still go to church and think that God is pleased with them? God made this world and gave people a free will to live how they choose in it. Who are these people to say that others haven't a right to live?'

Lucy didn't answer. Shame washed over Olivia as she realized how the lack of control she'd displayed by her outburst must have increased Lucy's fear. Lucy was doing her best. Like herself, she was away from the man she loved and coping with knowing of horrors that were unimaginable. They were both in a very dangerous situation, facing certain death if discovered.

'I'm sorry, Lucy. I shouldn't have reacted like that. I won't do it again. Please don't worry. I promise I will act as if I haven't understood a word in future.'

'Are you sure, Olivia? I mean, everything you say is true, but if we ever react to what we hear, we will be putting our lives in extreme danger. We must not come under any suspicion. If we did, the farm would be raided, our radio found, and . . .'

Olivia gasped. The pain of what would follow 'and' she'd already experienced because of her radio in Guernsey being discovered. She'd only escaped execution because of Stefan.

'I promise. I'll never let my emotions get the better of me again. I'll remember at all times that I have your life and my own in my hands. Please forgive me, Lucy.'

Lucy stretched out her hand. Olivia took hold of it, causing Nelly to veer to the right. Lucy laughed out loud. 'You're determined to kill us one way or the other!'

Olivia laughed with her. The tension in her released. She had to do this. From now on, she would try to be who she was meant to be: a French girl doing a job as a milkmaid.

She imagined they were carefree. Their job was physically hard at times but had its moments. They were fed well by the farmer and took money home to their family. Many must have dreams of a better life, but they were more than likely accepting of their situation. She would be like them and not draw suspicion to herself, and most of all not to Lucy.

With this new resolve, Olivia found herself feeling more settled in her role each day. Especially as they heard that the train she'd overheard of had been successfully derailed and many of its occupants released, though sadly many had been killed too – shot by those Germans who'd made it into hiding.

These she would pray for, but for those freed she would rejoice, and also rejoice in the part she had played in their freedom.

As the days went on and Olivia became more proficient at driving Nelly, she most often went alone into the suburbs of Paris, where her customers were. Lucy only came if there were groceries or other shopping to pick up.

On one of her trips earlier in the week, Violette went with

her. This helped her to get on real friendly terms with her and it marked Olivia as a local. She could even gossip about a few of her customers such as Madame Fernand, and her many children with different fathers, and show sympathy over Josephina, the wife of the local butcher, who often appeared covered in bruises.

Véronique's cafe was Olivia's main source of picking up information as here she could linger and not seem suspicious, especially now it could be seen they were friends.

Nothing much had been overheard for over a week, but on this, a hot day in the beginning of July, Olivia found the cafe packed with soldiers.

The chatter around her told her that a lot of activity was happening in Palmyra where Olivia knew that the Vichy had allowed the Germans to use their airbases to attack the Syrians. From the talk, it seemed that most of the soldiers were being posted to Palmyra very soon.

As soon as she arrived back at the farm, Olivia ran around all the barns looking for Lucy. She found her in the attic of the barn where the radio was.

Taking the wind from Olivia's sails, Lucy told her that Hendrick had arrived in the camp. It seemed Madame Durand had a few contacts and had been able to link him up with a member of the Maquis.

'Oh, that's wonderful news! Is he all right? Was my note passed to him?'

'I didn't ask. I didn't want to seem as though I knew him as anything other than a Frenchman who was known to "O", which of course he isn't . . . or is . . . Anyway, I told them that Leonard's presence is to be as secret as possible. His role is to be an interpreter only.'

'Oh, Lucy! He's safe . . . Well, at least he has arrived. I feel so much better. It's a relief to know he made it. But Leonard – the real one – didn't ever mention his aunt being involved in any way with the Resistance.'

'He probably didn't know. It's not something you even tell family . . . Yes, we can breathe a sigh of relief that Hendrick has made it to the camp. It appears he has a car. Madame Durand is no longer driving and was saving her car for her nephew Leonard.'

'Poor lady, she must have been devastated by the news of his death. He once told me that they were the only family left. Now there is just her.'

They were quiet for a moment, then Lucy said, 'Anyway, why were you dashing all over the place looking for me? I saw you from the window . . . At least, I assume it was me you were looking for. Nelly's all right, isn't she?'

'Yes, it was you I was looking for, and Nelly is fine. But I have a snippet of information that you might like to pass on to "O".'

Olivia told of what she'd heard.

'Mmm, reinforcements . . . I wonder if they are party to information about what the British army is doing. Not that I know what is planned by our forces, but we are fighting out there, and if the Germans have wind of an operation and are reinforcing troops, it could mean they get an upper hand. I'll let "O" know at once.'

It seemed 'O' was most impressed by Olivia's picking up on the information on Palmyra, saying it was vital information and asking Lucy to congratulate her and tell her that it was exactly the kind of talk they needed her to pass on – anything, whether it seemed significant or not.

Olivia's confidence soared. She could do this job and be of use to her own government as well as cause disruption to rail lines when needed to save hundreds of people who the Germans looked on as 'dispensable'.

Pleased with this, but more than pleased to hear of Hendrick's new position, she hoped her private note added in code to the message she wrote to him – *I love you and will do all I can to see you* – helped him.

The next message that came through told of him working in a bar in Montoir as it was known to the Maquis that German command posts had been established at Saint-Rimay – the place where Pétain met Hitler to agree on his collaboration.

It seemed that the Maquis had thought that he too could collect information given his language skills.

This terrified Olivia. What if he was recognized? After all, he had been high ranking in the German army.

Lucy too was distressed about it. 'I thought they would keep him in camp to use for their own purposes. Often they get crossed wires because of language difficulties. I am so angry with Claudius. He should have consulted me as I was the one to tell him to expect Hendrick!'

'I must go to Hendrick, Lucy. How far is it?'

Consulting the map which Lucy used to locate incidents they heard about and needed to act on, she discovered Saint-Rimay would be less than a two-hour train journey.

'But any contact would be very dangerous, Olivia . . . Though I know how you feel. I would be the same . . . Oh, I don't know. Let's think about it for a while.'

Olivia thought of nothing else when, after a lunch of bread and cheese washed down with a glass of milk, they lay on their beds resting, before helping with the milking later.

Usually, she enjoyed this hour each afternoon, and either read, or closed her eyes and dreamed of how things used to be, but today her thoughts were in turmoil.

It was the unusual sound of a vehicle pulling into the farmyard below that took them away and alerted her to danger.

In unison she and Lucy sat bolt upright, before Lucy jumped off the bed and ran to the window. 'Germans!'

'Oh, God, Lucy, what can they want?'

'Hopefully just produce. Quick, go downstairs to the milk barn and distract them while I make sure everything is safe up here.'

Olivia scurried down the ladder and through the back entrance of the barn to the dairy, thankful that she hadn't taken her overall off as this would help to make everything look normal as she began to move the churns of milk from the bay into the cool of the barn.

After ten minutes passed without any interruptions. she began to relax, thinking that whatever the soldiers had come for had been dealt with, when a shadow splashed across the floor in front of her. Olivia knew without looking that it belonged to a German. His jodhpur-shaped trousers outlined in the shadow gave it away. Halting in her progress, she wiped her brow on her forearm and turned to look at him. His frame seemed to fill the doorway. Olivia recognized him as the officer who'd made the remark about fancying her.

Her heart pounded.

'Monsieur?'

The officer clicked his heels. 'Mademoiselle, I have been looking for you.'

This title for unmarried women was what Olivia expected as she had removed her wedding ring and left it in a safe place by her bed. At night she could kiss it and think she was kissing Hendrick.

In her panic, Olivia almost slipped up by answering him in German, showing that she understood. Instead, in French, she said, 'I do not understand.'

He surprised her then by speaking in English as he came towards her. 'I need you to be my mistress.'

Shocked, Olivia gave an involuntary gasp. 'Ah, you understand English then?'

Olivia collected herself once more and said in French that she didn't understand. That she was afraid.

He seemed to know what she said as he came nearer, put out his hands and grabbed her arms. In German, he said, 'You will understand this.'

His face came near to hers. *Oh, God, help me! Not again, please, not again!*

When his lips landed on hers, she pulled away. Her scream came from her soul as the horrors of last time revisited her. Then the sound of a shot turned her to stone. The officer slunk down, landing at her feet.

Olivia stared at Pierre. Her head shook from side to side. 'Non! Oh, Pierre . . .'

Another shot and then another followed by more. Pierre's body did a hideous dance before he hit the ground with a thud. His staring eyes held shock as blood seeped onto the concrete floor.

Olivia's knees gave way. Just before darkness descended on her she saw the unseeing eyes of the officer.

The shock of the cold water brought Olivia back to consciousness, only then to experience extreme pain as she was dragged by her hair out of the barn.

Outside against the cowshed wall, Lucy stood next to a shivering, sobbing Violette. With her skin scratched in patches revealing her flesh, the heat of the sun increased Olivia's agony as she was lifted roughly and shoved to stand next to them.

The hollow sound of another German officer's boots as he marched up and down in front of them increased Olivia's fear.

Speaking excellent French, he ground out, 'You'll pay for this. And you . . .' He stopped in front of Olivia. 'If one of my comrades wants you, you are to submit to them! You are our property!'

Olivia, though smarting from her scalp to her toes, just stared at him.

A stinging blow sent her head reeling as the gloves he held struck her face. 'You don't look me in the eyes!'

Again, he marched up and down. When he next stopped, he spoke in a low voice. 'You will not refuse a German officer again. If you do, you will all be shot! I will personally shoot you.'

He drew his gun and pressed it into Olivia's forehead. She closed her eyes and prayed.

'Ha! You will learn that we are the superior race – superior to you and to the world!'

At that moment, Olivia knew she was dealing with a true Nazi and the thought terrified her.

Suddenly he turned and shouted in German to his driver to collect the officer's body. 'Let us get out of this stinking hole, where whores abide . . . But' – he once more spoke in French – 'I will be back, then you will be my whore!'

He spat at Olivia's feet.

They stood unmoving as the body of the dead officer was

carried past them and loaded into the truck and didn't move for a time after they left.

It was Violette's sobbing that broke the spell holding them still.

Olivia took the broken woman into her arms.

She stared at the dust kicked up by the receding car as it sped down the lane and the thought came to her that she would be armed with a knife if ever the officer came anywhere near her again.

Together, she and Lucy helped Violette into the farmhouse. There they went through the motions of comforting her.

With so very little time to follow convention, they buried the lovely Pierre the next day.

Many came from the village to help. Most were crying, even the men.

Olivia looked around at them all. Innocent, hardworking folk whose lives had been turned upside down. She looked up at the sky. *Help us, please, God, help us.*

PART THREE

Chances Taken

Chapter Seventeen

Annie

Saying goodbye to Daphne had been a wrench, but as Annie sat with Rita on the steps of her flat's fire escape, she beamed with happiness. This was where she was meant to be.

The sun shone down on her, and the squeals of delight echoed from Beth and Karl as they played together on the lawn below her.

Everything seemed to be right in her world, and her mind was at rest as Rosemary too was settled in Mum's flat and loved it.

Annie sighed happily as she said, 'Oh, Rita, it's so good to be home. And your Freddie, Mike and Philip all get along well with Ian. I can hear them now, just like before that bomb struck yours, playing footie in the street.'

Rita sighed. 'When I look over at the ruin of me 'ouse, I wonder if it'll ever be rebuilt.'

'Everything'll come right one day, luv. Keep on keeping on . . . But in the meantime, I've been meaning to ask yer—'

'If I can I watch yer kids?'

'Ha, how did yer know?'

'Well, yer going to need someone and I'm the obvious

person! And yes, I can and will be glad to pay yer back in some way for all you've done for me and me family in giving us a home. When do yer start back at work, WPC Stanley?'

Annie laughed. It felt good to hear her title. It cemented that she truly was home. 'Sarge wants me in the office for briefings on Monday. He said there's mostly day work for me as Betty, me mate, is settled into the night shifts.'

'Well, Beth and Karl'll be fine with me and Ian and me boys are at school in the week. Will yer work weekends?'

'Ta for that, luv. And yes, I'll have some shifts at weekends, but only once a month. And they mean I have a couple of days off in the week, so it should all work out.'

'It will, luv.'

'Oh, Rita, it means such a lot to me to be able to do me bit again, though it's good not to have to face tackling fires and dodging bombs while doing it.'

'I still feel nervous and can't believe the Blitz has really ended. I'm not sleeping well. It's as if me body's on alert all the time.'

'I was the same when I first got to Wrexham, but oh, the peace there! I can't describe it.'

'Will Daphne be all right?'

'She will. She's carved a life out for herself and loves farming. She'll have mates when the Land Girls arrive. And no doubt a devil of a job to teach them the work!'

They both smiled then Rita said, 'When yer went to the countryside, it made me feel guilty at putting my kids through all they went through during the bombing. I just couldn't live without them. But I break out in a sweat when I think of it all and the danger I put them in.'

'It's done now. But I ain't going to lie, I did think you'd done wrong when I was a copper around here, and it was

210

talked of that we may forcefully take such kids from those parents who did this and evacuate them again. But that didn't materialize, thank goodness. I couldn't have enforced it.'

Rita looked shocked. 'You'd have come across and warned me, wouldn't yer, Annie?'

'Rita, one thing yer got to get clear, I am a cop. I must obey rules.'

Rita's face dropped.

Annie giggled. 'Course I would've. I wouldn't care if I lost me job, I'd have given yer the chance to get away with the kids.'

Rita laughed a relieved laugh. 'You 'ad me going there, Annie!'

'I knew why you did it as Beth, Karl and Ian were in the countryside with Rose and we missed them. And as it turned out they weren't safe . . . Anyway, we won't talk about that.'

Rita's hand found Annie's. The gesture nearly undid her but an argument breaking out between Beth and Karl distracted her and for once she was glad of it.

Annie was ready early on Monday morning. She'd pressed her uniform over the weekend, even though it hadn't needed it as it had hung in the wardrobe ever since she'd left. And now the time was on her, and she felt pulled both ways as Beth and Karl crying tugged at her heart.

It was a blessing to her when Rita promised to take them for a walk to the park and they calmed. But then with Bertie chipping in with a promise of a ride on his boat, and Rosemary saying she would go to the park with them so that she could push one on the swing while Rita pushed the other, it seemed to Annie that she was forgotten as they talked excitedly about these treats, leaving her free to slip out of the door.

A cheer went up as Annie entered the station. Betty came forward and hugged her, knocking her hat off in the process. 'Well, luv, it'll save yer taking it off . . . But, oh, Annie, I'm so pleased you're back. We've missed yer.'

One of the older men chipped in, 'I've heard she makes a better cuppa than you, Betty, as well!'

Annie bristled. 'I'll taste yours first, Wilf, then I might consider making yer one in return.'

'Uh-oh, touchy subject, Annie, luv. Sorry, I was pulling your leg because of what happened in Wrexham. The sarge told us about it.'

Annie coloured. 'Sorry, but yes, it is a sore point.'

'Yer didn't think I'd let them get away with that, did yer, Annie?'

Betty was smiling as she said this and Annie thought to herself that she needed to polish up on their kind of humour, or she'd be wrong-footed a few times.

She smiled at them all. 'I've been knocked for six with the attitude of the sergeant at Wrexham, that's all. I'll soon cotton back on to our way of rigging each other.'

'You're back, that's all we care about, Annie,' Wilf said. 'And we're so pleased that we won't mind treading carefully for a couple of weeks. That's all, though. After that, you take the rigging like the rest of us!'

The sarge rescued her. 'Go on through to my office, Annie. Yer know where to go, girl.'

Once there and with the door shut, the sarge briefed her on the current cases and what she was to keep an eye out for.

'Well, now, Annie, it's good to have you back. How are you?'

'I'm all right, Sarge. I've found a way of coping with everything. And knowing Ricky has been found has helped.'

'It's the best news ever.'

'And I'll sort meself out. I made a bit of a blunder, didn't I? But it's good to be back here. I was going out of me mind doing nothing.'

'Good. Let's put it behind us, eh? Now, Betty's only here today, then she has a day off and goes back on night duty. So, I've assigned her to the beat with you. She can bring yer up to speed better than all of us as she sees everything from the same point of view as you do. We're still handling most things with kid gloves on. Folk around here have had enough. A lot have been left with nothing and that turns a saint into a crook when it comes to feeding the family. There's still the odd skirmish at the food shops, and the incidents of shop-lifting have risen. The culprits will surprise yer. But as I say, gently does it. We're trying not to convict them all but to give them help where we can.'

'I'm glad to hear it, Sarge.'

'Yes, you were always an advocate of that approach. Well, it works for most. But some . . . well, they're out and out rogues. I'll leave that to your judgement.'

Once on the beat with Betty, Annie asked, 'Betty, luv, do yer mind if we go along Westbury Terrace? It's where me Ian used to live. I just want to check up on the residents there. His mum, Peggy Bates, was known to us – that weren't her real name, and she were only prostituting to look after her kids. She had three, but only Ian survived the incendiary that hit his house. He'd come down from his bed and gone outside to the lav.'

'Dear God! The stories we hear, eh? But yes, I remember that night, luv.'

'Yes. We never get used to it, do we? But the reason I

213

want to go there is that Ian never mentions having any friends and I thought I might find some in his old street and see if I can get him together with them again . . . He worries me. He only ever talks of his mum and gran. Nothing of his life, or his brothers. Not after the first time we came across him on the night it happened. I think he's suffering internally, but he's such a good lad, he probably doesn't want to upset me.'

'Peggy was a nice woman, and we all knew what she did was through desperation. If ever she was picked up, we used to give her a cuppa and send her on her way with a few bob.'

Annie marvelled at how Betty had changed from the sour-faced cop who'd always had a downer on everyone to this understanding person who Annie liked and respected a lot. But she didn't remark on this, and just said, 'I know. There was a lot of that – women left to cope with a kid, and then another bloke coming along and promising the earth till more kids were born.'

'Anyway, Annie, we could analyse it till we're blue in the face, but of course we can go down Westbury Terrace. It's a good starting point as there's a lot around that area that might need help. They're a proud lot, and wouldn't ask for anything, but I've had to have a word with a couple of them for nicking stuff.'

They walked along Westbury Terrace – a sorry sight of rows of terraced houses, some still standing proudly as if defying Hitler, with their freshly laundered curtains and well-scrubbed steps – but at the end of the road, several of the houses were just heaps of rubble. This was where Ian's mum would have scrubbed her step and got what she could for his dinner. Annie's heart became heavy as she looked at it. But then a figure darting out of sight caught her eye.

214

'God, Betty, I think I just saw Ian. I thought he was in school!'

'Yes, I saw a lad scarper. Are yer sure it were your Ian?'

'Yes. I have to speak to him; he must be feeling low.'

'Right, you keep going, and I'll nip down Green Street and see if I can head him off.'

'Ta, Betty, but tell him he ain't in trouble. I don't want him scared.'

Betty put her hand up as she ran forward and disappeared down Green Street.

Suddenly, Ian appeared, running hell for leather away from Annie.

'IAN! It's all right, luv, I only want to talk to yer!'

Thankfully, Ian stopped and turned to face her. 'I – I'm sorry, Mum. I don't bunk off school often, but me 'eart were sad today as it's me gran's birthday.'

Annie put her arms out to him. Ian ran into them. His sobs tore at Annie. She didn't stop him crying, but cried with him as she held him close.

As she glanced up, Annie saw Betty sitting on some rubble blowing plumes of smoke from her fag – always she took to having a smoke if she wasn't sure of how to react.

Annie felt glad that she didn't try to stop them sobbing.

'We'll have a little service for your gran, and your mum and brothers, Ian. How would that be, eh? We'll get some flowers for them. We've done nothing with the garden since we came back from Kent. We'll make a special garden for all those we lost, eh? It can be your patch to tend to.'

Warming to her idea, Annie expanded on it. 'We'll see if Ron or Bertie are any good at carpentry and get them to knock a bench up that faces the garden, then we can sit there when we want to think about them all.'

Ian lifted his face. His tears had washed streaks through the dirt on his cheeks. 'I can hold me picture of me gran and me mum and do something special on their birthdays and that.'

'You can, luv. We can't bring them back, but we can keep them in our hearts and talk to them.'

'Will they hear me?'

'Yes, but they won't answer you . . . Only, I was once told that they will try to leave a sign so that they can let you know they are still with you. I had one from Janey the other day. I was sorting out the wash basket and there was one of her blouses that I loved and had kept, knowing she would like me to wear it. When I picked it up, I held it to me face and something fluttered to the ground. It was a white feather, which Aggie – I told yer about Aggie, the flower seller, didn't I? Well, she said white feathers were a sign that loved ones who had passed were near.'

Ian grinned.

Betty piped up. 'Ha, Annie, I knew her! She worked near London Bridge, didn't she? Well, she would see white feathers every day dropping from the seagulls! Blimey, she must have thought her lot who'd passed were proper bothering her!'

They all laughed out loud.

But then Ian said, 'But if it was true, then that would be Janey as we don't have seagulls in our 'ouse, do we?'

'Exactly, so there you go!'

'I'm going to look out for them when I think of me mum and me gran and me bruvvers, and everyone.'

Annie hugged him to her as she changed the subject. 'Ian, did yer have many friends around here, mate?'

'I did. And I was 'oping I'd see some. I do sometimes when I come along this way.'

Annie picked up on the reference to Ian having bunked off school before but thought to tackle that on a different day. She'd talk to his teacher and see how often it was first.

'Right, give me their names and I can see if we can invite them to tea when I'm off duty, eh?'

'I don't know, Mum . . . Beth might be a pest.'

Annie smiled to herself. She knew it was a true statement. 'Well, I'm sure you and your mates can handle that, only it must be done in a kind way. And I'll keep me eye on her. Besides, yer can take yer friends to the park for a kickabout.'

'Some ain't around any more; they were evacuated. There's only Billy and Den. They'll be at school.'

'Right, we'll come back tonight and see them. Now, Ian, I think it best you go back to school. The only way we get through all of this is to carry on our lives. We have to live for them that have gone and make them proud of us.'

'All right. I promise I'll go back.'

Betty put her hand on Ian's shoulder. 'You're a good lad. Yer mum tells me so, and you've come a long way since we found yer that night. You just need to learn to talk to her, and . . .' She looked up at Annie and cocked her head towards her. 'And she needs to learn to talk to you as well. A few minutes each night will do it when she tucks yer up in bed. How does that sound to yer both?'

Ian nodded. An obvious shyness had come over him.

'That's a good idea, Ian. We can help each other then,' Annie told him. 'Now, we'll walk with yer, only we won't come to the school gates as the others'll rib yer, but I will write a note to give to your teacher so that she understands. How's that sound?'

'Ta, Mum . . . You're the best of mums . . . Well, after me real mum . . .'

'I'll never take her place in your heart, Ian. I want a different place to snuggle into. In the corner of your heart, just there.' Annie grinned down at him as she tapped his chest.

Ian laughed out loud.

This was the sound she loved most to hear. His resilience was strong, but the strongest of them could fall. It was getting back up that counted, and Annie felt that Ian had done that.

Wiping his face by spitting on her hankie, which he hated and which had them giggling even more with his squirming, Annie took a minute to write the note and then sent him on his way. He waved when he got to the end of the road. She waved back. Then when he'd gone, she wiped a stray tear from her face.

'Here, luv, you'd better use mine. Yours looks like you've cleaned the windows with it.'

This made Annie smile as she took the hankie Betty offered. 'Ta. I feel like I've been put through the ringer and hung out to dry. When you grieve, it can make you feel lonely at times, and it's true what they say: "weep, and you weep alone".'

'I know where that comes from. I too have felt like that. It's the loneliest feeling I know. I got curious about it and popped into the library one day and asked the librarian. He told me it was from a poem by . . . Oh, crikey, what were her name . . . Ah, Ella Wheeler Wilcox. She wrote it a long time ago, back when me dad were born.'

'Hark at you, coming all knowledgeable on me! Though I wonder what prompted her to write such a thing?'

'He told me that as well. I can tell yer, I began to regret calling in! But it seems Ella came across a grieving woman and tried to console her. When she couldn't she looked at

218

her own lonely face and wrote the poem. It's called "Solitude".'

'Ha! I bet yer won't get curious about anything ever again! But yer know, I think it's good to learn things. When I was taking me exams to be accepted into the police force, I really enjoyed the experience of learning so much.'

'Didn't yer pass yer school certificate then?'

'I didn't even take it! I had to get a job as soon as I reached fourteen! Me lovely dad had passed away and me mum were crippled with arthritis, so someone had to keep a roof over her and our Janey's heads.'

'No one can truly understand. But yer did a good job there and Ian went off a happy chappy . . . But we'd better get on or Sarge will have our guts for garters!'

'Now, where did that saying "Have yer guts for garters" come from, Betty?'

Betty playfully hit out at her, and both ended up laughing.

The morning passed and it seemed no time till Annie sat with Betty in Florrie's cafe just along from the station, eating a stale sandwich and sipping thick brown tea that tasted stewed.

Florrie, with the usual fag hanging from her mouth and squinting against the smoke swirling up and into her eyes, came over to them. 'You girls 'ad a good morning then? Caught any of them bleeding looters? They did a right job on the shop next door.'

'We know, Florrie, but they don't do it in broad daylight. We mostly catch them at night. But most just need help.'

'Huh! That lot who did Manny's shop next door don't. He only stocked pots and pans and the like, and I saw them.'

Against all she wanted to do, Annie said, 'Have yer a

minute to sit down with us, Florrie, and tell us what yer know, eh?'

When Florrie sat down, Annie did her best not to wriggle her nose against the smell of stale body odour as she tried to avoid the smoke curling perilously close to her. Florrie's long ash falling off the end of her cigarette and landing in her cup gave Annie the relief of not having to drink it.

'I'll get yer another one, mate, sorry.'

'No, don't worry, just tell us what yer know before yer have to get back to the counter.'

'I saw that Arthur Kingly from me window upstairs. I'd know him anywhere, and I heard him say, "Let's get this stuff to the market afore we're caught." He does the market on a Wednesday.'

Annie knew which market this was. 'Ta, Florrie. Will yer be willing to be a witness to seeing him if yer called to court?'

'I would. All the bleeders should be locked up. It's hard keeping a business going, and it's broke old Manny 'aving his shop done over. 'E's enough to contend with 'earing that 'is family were caught up in the invasion of Poland. Poor bloke can only imagine what's 'appened to them – well, yer know, with 'ow that Hitler bloke is with the Jews.'

Annie nodded. It seemed folk had heard rumours about how the Jews were being treated, and she couldn't deny them.

Betty was busy taking notes so didn't react either but looked up from her notebook. 'Well, we'll see yer later, Florrie. We'd better report this in.'

'Yer will catch him, won't yer, Annie?'

'We'll do our best.'

As they got up, Florrie said, 'I ain't asked the pair of yer if you've 'eard from Ricky, and your man too, Betty.'

Annie told her that Ricky was safe, but then lied and said, 'That's all I know. But I have to keep faith that he'll remain so.'

'And me Jack last wrote a week back, but so far, fingers crossed, he's still fighting on.'

'Good. I always think of them.'

They said their goodbyes and left. Despite Florrie's un-hygienic ways, they all loved to go into her cafe. They gave her custom, but not many ate what she served up, though they all drank her tea out of politeness!

Reporting back at the station, the sarge was pleased with their progress. 'We had an inkling it was that lot. I'll send Brian and Jeff to pick him up. Good work, girls. Now, one of you type up what Florrie told you and then take it back to her and get her to sign it. Let's get her statement in a file at least.'

'I'll type it, Betty. As much as I wanted us to have the same duties as the men, I used to love typing their notes up. There's something soothing about the tip-tapping of the keyboard.'

'Blimey, Annie, you've some weird ways, girl! I loathe typing!'

Annie giggled. She no longer took offence at Betty's outspokenness but had come to like it. She'd found that she hadn't meant most of it and was only pulling people's legs.

For a minute she thought, *Now, where did that saying come from? I'll have to ask Betty.* But then she giggled as she made her way to her desk.

Typing away, Annie began to relax. All in all, it had been a good morning. It wasn't good to find Ian was skipping school, but the outcome – him talking to her, and her coming up with a plan to help him and herself – felt good. It was as if a curtain that she hadn't realized had been between them had fallen, and now she thought, *I needn't tread on eggshells when dealing with Ian. I can be open with him as we work together on our remembrance garden. I'll think of little Amy too and include her. Though I could never talk to Ian about what happened to her at Jimmy's hands. That will always be a pain in me heart and, yes, the times I bring Amy to mind and all that happened will always be when I weep alone.*

Chapter Eighteen

Olivia

Olivia sat on the cart, trying to jolly Nelly along. Ever since the incident four weeks ago, she hadn't seen the German officer who'd threatened her.

Talk among the German soldiers gave nothing away, and none of them acted as if they knew about what had happened.

This had given Olivia confidence again and so, when she pulled Nelly up outside Véronique's cafe, her last port of call, she didn't feel fear until she opened the door and a silence fell. Olivia stared at the man she'd dreaded seeing again.

When he stood, she jumped, wanting to run. Her heart raced.

'Ah, the whore! I haven't dealt with you yet! Pity, but I haven't time now, though it would be good to take you down in public so all can see you for what you are! I will . . . Very soon I will!'

His laughter brought bile to Olivia's throat. Putting the milk jug on the nearest table, she didn't wait to collect the empty one, but turned and ran outside.

'Please, Nelly, please, get me home.'

As if she knew the urgency, Nelly started off at a good pace, trotting, not ambling.

Every few yards, Olivia turned, fearful that she was being followed.

When at last she reached the farm, her anxiety made her screech, 'Lucy! Lucy!'

Both Lucy and Violette came running out, Lucy from the milking shed and Violette from the house.

'He's coming . . . Oh, Lucy, he's coming!'

'The German officer?'

'Yes. Help me, Lucy . . . help me.'

'It's all right, love, we're moving – all of us.'

'Violette as well? . . . Why, what has happened?'

Violette dabbed at her eyes. 'I tell Lucy today that I am going to my sister's. She lives in Vichy. I have arranged with solicitor to sell everything. There is nothing now. My Pierre gone, and I cannot live here any longer.'

'Oh, Violette, I am so pleased. I didn't want to leave you, but I cannot stay.'

'I have it all arranged, Olivia. We leave tonight for Limousin,' Lucy told her.

Olivia looked from one to the other. 'But this is so sudden . . . I'm glad, so very glad, but no mention was made of this when I left this morning!'

'It is sudden, and I will explain later. But once it was decided and I told Violette that we had to leave, she then told me she wanted to too. That she'd been praying to have the responsibility of us off her shoulders so that she could bring an end to her agony of being here without Pierre.'

Relief flooded Olivia. 'I'm so sorry, Violette. I hope you find peace with your sister.'

Forgetting her own fears, Olivia hugged the little woman who had come to mean so much to her and Lucy.

Violette's hand patted her back. 'One day, when this is all over, you will both come and see me, yes?'

'We will. I promise.'

Remembering the urgency of her own plight, Olivia uttered, 'We must hurry and pack. We have to go quickly!'

'I've done everything, Olivia. A farmer nearby is coming for Nelly and will take over the care of the animals until all is settled. He said he will be glad to look after them for his friend, Pierre.'

Olivia sat down heavily on a bale of straw. Every limb in her body trembled.

'Olivia, love, you're all right. We will be gone from here to the station within half an hour. I've found out that Violette's train will go first so we will be able to see her safely on her way.' Turning to Violette, Lucy asked, 'Have you all your papers in order now, Violette? Did you find everything and put them in one place in your handbag?'

Violette nodded. She looked so vulnerable. Olivia wished they could go all the way with her as she had a long journey in front of her, and they had learned that she hadn't left the farm in forty years and had never been on a train as she only came from the next village.

The thought of the train sent fresh shivers through Olivia, but she knew she much preferred facing that fear than having to stand the rape of her body again.

In English, Lucy said, 'Olivia, it's going to be all right, I promise you, love. And something to cheer you on the way – our train's first stop and where we must change trains is Saint-Rimay.'

Olivia looked up. Hope had entered her heart. 'Will we be able to stay there a while?'

'I've planned that we stay overnight but "O" must never find out.'

'Oh, Lucy!'

Suddenly, nothing mattered to Olivia any more, only the thought of seeing her beloved Hendrick.

'Ha, that put a smile on your face and goes to show that good does come from bad . . . Now, as soon as the farmer arrives to take charge of the animals, we are leaving. His son is bringing him, and he will ride Nelly and the cart home. Violette has arranged for his son to take us to the station, so get Nelly settled in her stable and give her some food and water as you usually do. She deserves this last act from you.'

Olivia jumped up. Lucy was right, and it was the push she needed to snap out of the feelings she was experiencing and do something practical.

Once unbridled and led to her stable, Nelly went straight to the trough as usual. 'Nothing phases you, old girl.' Olivia patted Nelly then stroked her mane. 'I'm going to miss you. You've been a good companion. Though very naughty at times.' Olivia giggled. It felt lovely to be laughing and not crying now she had a chance to see Hendrick and escape an awful fate. A bubble of happiness had replaced the fear and disgust in her.

'Look at the time you stopped suddenly as we went over that bridge! You nearly had me fall off the cart, Nelly! But I forgive you. Have a happy life, my dear Nelly.'

With this, Olivia left the stables and hurried to where Lucy was stacking cases and boxes, most of which were going on the pile belonging to Violette.

'Let me help you. Though I hope Violette is being met at the station the other end! She'll never manage this lot.'

'Her brother-in-law has a truck and will meet her. Everything has been arranged. Though it did worry me at one stage as she began to tell her sister more than she should over the telephone. I had to interrupt as we never know if the Germans are monitoring all calls made.'

'Oh dear. It's sad she has been sworn to secrecy. It has meant that she couldn't even have the relief of unburdening herself to her friends.'

'Yes, there are many unsung heroes. Ordinary people who have given up their peace of mind to help those of us trying to make a difference.'

When they reached the station, they were stopped for their papers to be checked.

The guard who checked Olivia's took what seemed an age. Beads of sweat formed on her brow, and though she tried to look as if she had nothing to hide, it proved difficult for her. *Please, please just hand my papers back to me!*

At last, he did, but not before he repeated the surname she'd been given.

'Allard? Is this correct?'

His French sounded very accented.

'*Oui, monsieur.*'

He stared at her. Olivia bit her lip. Then he grinned as if he enjoyed the experience of frightening people to death. 'There is a queue, move on!'

This sounded like a reprimand, as if she had been the one at fault for the delay in moving forward the passengers. But she put this out of her mind as she hurried through the barrier and joined the others.

Lucy's anxious expression turned to one of relief. 'Olivia, try not to look like a frightened rabbit. Look, watch the French. They are resigned to this; they don't even treat it as an irritation . . . Look, love, I know you're on edge and I understand why, but you must not show that.' Suddenly, as if she hadn't spoken the words, Lucy turned and waved. Olivia looked in the same direction but could see no one. Under her breath Lucy hissed, 'Laugh and wave too. The guard is still glancing over at you between checking. You must have spooked him with the fear you showed.'

Olivia did as asked, and let out a laugh. Lucy shoved her in a playful way and giggled, turning her head towards the gate.

'He's not watching now.'

Olivia relaxed. But told herself that she must be more of an actress and show the world a different face to what she was feeling.

It was a sad moment saying goodbye to Violette. They hugged her and wished her happiness with her sister, promising that one day when the war was over, they would visit her.

Violette dabbed at her eyes. For all the world, Olivia could have gone with her to make sure she was all right.

The whole thing – being torn away from the only home Violette had known for so many years, the grief she was still experiencing, and facing a new life – must have been so daunting for her, but she smiled a brave, if tearful smile when she was seated and gazing out of the window at them.

When her train moved off, they waved till it disappeared, leaving them in a cloud of smoke.

Neither of them said a word as they walked over the

bridge to their own platform. They were to head west to Saint-Rimay, and once they left there, they would travel south to Limousin in the Vichy area. The last part of their journey would be fraught with danger as they could not travel by train but would be picked up and taken on a route across the fields in a tractor and trailer and through forests on foot. A test of endurance for Olivia's painful leg.

Once in Saint-Rimay, they found the bar where Hendrick was working – the Bar Le Paris. It looked so unlike a Parisian bar it made them smile. The straw veranda to provide shade hung in parts as if it would collapse, and the exterior was anything but inviting. Neither of them thought it a place where ladies went and so decided to find digs and then waylay Hendrick when he came out of work.

Olivia couldn't believe that Lucy was prepared to take such risks for her.

As they walked along a street they were eyed by many more Germans than Olivia had expected to see. But then they had heard that Hitler did order that those who had been engaged in battle, or were about to be, should have rest periods. This, she imagined, was a good place for that, not being as prominent as Paris. But still, she felt conscious of the radio in the heavy case they shared the carrying of. However, she decided to copy Lucy and look nonchalant.

They found digs a short walk away – a grimy-looking building on the outside, but lovely and clean inside.

Deciding to go for a stroll together, Olivia was unnerved again as two German soldiers leaning on a wall nearby seemed to be watching them. One spoke French and asked what their business was.

Olivia answered causally, telling him that they had come

to visit her aunt who lived outside of the town, but couldn't put them up.

With nothing in place to cover such a story, fear kicked in, but now committed, Olivia embroidered her story, saying she hadn't been since she was a child.

'Show me your papers.'

Once again, Olivia thought that the risk involved in them stopping in Saint-Rimay was a greater one than they should have taken, and at this moment, wished Lucy didn't let her heart rule some of her decisions.

This was underpinned when their papers were handed back and the soldier said, 'A few of us drink in the bar over there. We would enjoy your company this evening. Please attend.'

As he walked away, Olivia knew she had to step up and take charge. 'Lucy, we must go back inside, wait for the moment we think it is safe to leave, then go straight back to the station and get a train out of here. I don't care where it goes!'

'I – I'm sorry, Olivia, I just wanted to—'

'I know, but we're putting the whole operation in extreme danger. Just carrying that case containing the radio was fraught with danger! This was a ridiculous, if a very kind notion. From now on, our heads rule, not our hearts.'

Lucy looked forlorn for a moment, but then lifted her head.

'You're right, we must get out quickly. We will ask for a taxi and tell the owner of the hotel that we're going to visit our aunt. That we will leave our luggage in the room but must take one case as it contains a present for her.'

'Brilliant, now we are thinking like the special agents that we are!'

It was as they were getting into the taxi that Olivia spotted

Hendrick leaving the cafe. He looked so different disguised as he was – his hair dyed black and wearing rimless glasses.

She knew he had seen her. But as she shook her head, he turned the other way. She closed her eyes against the force of the pain as the driver sped off.

It was a relief when the train finally chugged out of the station. They were headed for Tours, which was at least in the right direction.

Both were exhausted and the carriage was hot and stuffy, making Olivia feel sticky and grubby. She could have ripped her clothes off, but decided the best thing was to try to relax.

Her thoughts went to the glimpse of Hendrick. How painful that had been. Her only consolation was that he looked well. What he must think, she couldn't imagine.

Lucy broke into these thoughts. 'Olivia, will we be far away from Limousin when we get to Tours? I didn't look at that when we mapped our journey.'

'Yes, from memory of the map training we did, it's about five hours by road . . . I just don't think I could travel much further. I'm hot, starving and so upset after my glimpse of Hendrick. It would have been better not to have gone there.'

'I thought I was helping you. You've been through so much and then after the terror of it possibly happening again, which was a real threat, I thought it would do you good to see Hendrick and to hear from him how things are. We've had no news apart from snippets.'

'I understand, and I'm grateful to you. But from now on remember, Lucy, love, that I have been trained. I know the importance of not taking any risks that we don't have to take. I feel I am at fault for putting my love for Hendrick above your safety. Yes, you offered me the chance, but I should have said no – what if it had been a test that you were putting me

231

through to check my commitment and loyalty to the cause above my personal life? I would have failed.'

Lucy grinned. 'Well, that made me feel better, and yes, you did fail!'

This lightened the moment, making Olivia realize that she had laboured the point a bit and that Lucy felt bad enough as it was. She giggled with her and said in a mocking tone, 'So, you know now to never test me like that. What if I had reported you?'

'Oh, don't. I can't take any more.'

They were both laughing now. Both knew the seriousness of what they'd done and that it was time to learn from it and never to make such a mistake again.

After a gruelling journey on yet another train that took them within fifty kilometres of their destination, they made it to a field that had an empty barn and prepared to spend the night.

Though almost derelict, the barn held a trailer and had dry hay scattered over the floor. This they gathered and piled into the trailer to make a bed. Luckily it was a warm night.

Shattered as they were, neither could sleep. Their tummies rumbled, and both complained of being thirsty.

Just before darkness fell, Lucy contacted Claudius on her radio. She told him their location and lied about getting onto the wrong train.

Claudius told them that they were near one of the farms that offered shelter to Resistance members and that arrangements would be made to pick them up the next day.

Olivia let go of the breath she'd been holding and finally began to feel safe. As she did, she was filled with renewed energy. 'The farmhouse Claudius mentioned will be the one we saw lit up, just as we came off the lane, Lucy.'

'Yes, it will. It must be, as there are no others in the near vicinity. Are you up to trekking to it?'

'My stomach is. It's begging me to.'

Pulling the bits of straw from her clothes and hair, Olivia felt that she could walk a mile if she was fed at the end of it. As it happened it was only a short walk away along a dusty track.

The next morning, after going to bed with full stomachs, having been offered thick crusts of homemade bread laced with ham and spending the night in the cellar, which housed one bed and a bucket for them to relieve themselves in, Olivia felt much better. She could tell that Lucy did too as she hummed a tune while getting ready for the day ahead.

Upstairs the breakfast table was a sight they had thought they would never see again: fresh loaves, cheeses, fruit. But it was the abundance of everything that they were so unused to.

'*Servez-vous, mes chéries.*'

They didn't need inviting twice to tuck in, but thanked the lovely, rounded farmer's wife, who looked to Olivia as if she'd spent her life outside burning her skin to the hard crepe surface it appeared to be. Though that didn't detract from her lovely smile and kindly ways.

No introductions had been made, only assumptions that the lady's status was wife to the farmer.

It was better not to know names, then there was less chance of slipping up if questioned.

It was late that evening when they arrived at the camp.

Claudius greeted them in a professional way, as he had done when Olivia had first met him, but what he told her made her blood run cold.

'You have come at a very dangerous time. Your transmitted messages to us have increased the danger we are in. Since the first of the month, the Vichy government have allowed the Germans free access to hunt for transmitters.'

Lucy's glance told of her fear.

'And that is not all. Leonard has contacted too. I have ordered radio silence because of this. He has said that the Germans there are searching for two girls. These girls left their luggage behind in the hotel they had booked into and vanished. A German soldier had challenged them, but then invited them to join him. When they didn't turn up for what he thought was a date, he discovered they had left, and in a hurry . . . All of this Leonard overheard as the soldier concerned went back to the bar and told the others, who seemed to be waiting for the girls.'

Olivia knew that Hendrick would be at his wits' end worrying if she was safe as he had no knowledge that they were back in the camp and must fear they would be caught.

'You two have arrived with no luggage, and you told me that you had got on the wrong train – did you end up in Saint-Rimay?'

Olivia decided that they should own up. 'We did. We were exhausted and had intended to spend the night. But we were challenged and propositioned, so changed our minds as we didn't want to be in the company of Germans – they would ask too many questions. We decided to get out of there.'

'This is all bad thinking. You knew the place where Leonard was working undercover for us. When you found yourselves there, you should have stayed on the station and caught another train out of there.'

Olivia hung her head. She willed Lucy not to try to make anything up but to leave it to her.

Claudius was now saying, 'Leonard's last message told of him seeing the Germans questioning the taxi driver. Then he heard you being discussed in the bar. He is an asset as his German is so good. The driver will have told the Germans where he took you. It is an easy matter to find out which train you caught. This will lead them to Tours. We had to risk life and limb to collect you!'

Olivia stared at Claudius, her mind frantically trying to process all of this. What had they done? Shame washed over her.

'Are we able to tell Leonard we are safe?'

'No! It is impossible. Besides, we have found him to be professional and he won't think it important, only that you don't compromise operations here.'

A voice of reason spoke then. Frédérique, one of the Resistance members Olivia met when she was dropped off at this camp.

'Claudius, it is unlikely that they will be traced here. How are the Germans to find out if they haven't been seen? Even the checkpoint at the station gate is overwhelmed by the number of people coming through. I asked when I collected them if they were checked, and they weren't. I think mistakes have been made, but they're not a disaster. We should carry on with our plan.'

Claudius shrugged then explained, 'Frédérique has a plan. He thinks you would be best posing as farm workers again. That you can be in an area where there is no suspicion of radios. That you can cycle to a butcher's we know and give him messages and we will pass messages through him. He delivers meat to a safe house – a cafe that is easy for us to access.'

Olivia looked at Lucy and saw her nod her agreement.

Her expression was one of shame. Olivia understood this. Taking charge again, she said, 'Once we are in this safe area, we will message "O" to inform him. If he agrees with the plan, then we will stay where we are, but it depends upon his decision.'

All agreed with this.

Olivia couldn't sleep much for thinking about Hendrick – his worry over her might make him act differently to his instincts. He might put himself in danger to find out how she is, imagining her captured, tortured, and maybe shot. The thought came to her that she must find his radio frequency and contact him! When she'd arrived here from England, she'd seen Claudius use a list to find the frequency he needed.

She remembered he'd not taken well to her saying that was a dangerous thing to do. That her instructions were to never write things down, but if she had to, then she'd destroy it immediately, even eating it if that was the only way. But Claudius had grunted and shoved his list into his pocket.

Now, she thanked God that Claudius had a bad memory and had to deal with this by writing things down. She had to find that list!

Waiting until all was quiet and then another hour, Olivia crept out of her and Lucy's tent and made her way to Claudius's, taking with her the small pen torch she always carried in her pocket which was part of the equipment she'd been supplied with – ordinary everyday things that easily turned into something useful.

The eeriness of the camp unnerved her. A loud snore froze her to the spot, but logic told her that if her torchlight was spotted, it would be assumed that someone was going to the bushes to relieve themselves.

Carrying on with her mission and with her eyes getting used to the dark, she saw Claudius's jacket still hung on the branch where she'd seen it before.

Hope urged her forward. Feeling in the pockets, she found a folded note. Shining her torch on it showed her that her luck was in. It was a list of the frequencies!

Hurrying into the woods, she made her way to the place Frédérique had told Lucy to store her radio, retrieved it and opened the case. Inside she found the notebook and pen they used to write down their deciphered messages before destroying them. Quickly writing down the frequency listed as Leonard's, she stuffed the paper into her knicker elastic and replaced the radio, shuffling the leaves over it to make it look as though it hadn't been disturbed.

Retracing her steps, she just managed to stuff the list back into Claudius's coat and step away towards her own tent when she saw a figure . . . Frédérique! Had he seen her?

Her already heightened nerves intensified, making her feel sick. But he turned from her and went back into his tent without acknowledging her.

They didn't make it to the farm the next day. Following instructions given by Claudius to contact 'O' once they were in the town of Saint-Germain-des-Fossés in Auvergne, Rhône, nestled in the French Alps and out of the zone thought to be too dangerous to use the radio, they found a guest house to board in.

The proprietor signed them in and took them to a small room with twin beds. It smelled fusty and unused. Olivia opened the tiny window to let in the fresh air sweeping down from the mountains in the far distance.

Contacting from here took some time, but at last they got through.

'O's anger at them compromising themselves seemed to vibrate through the Morse code of his message.

'I've blown it, Olivia!' Lucy plonked down onto the bed. The creak this made almost had Olivia giggle. But her anguish was too high to release in this way.

'We both have, Lucy. But seeing as though we have, we can't make things worse by contacting Hendrick and letting him know that I'm safe.'

It was a relief to Olivia when Lucy agreed, though Lucy was shocked to hear how it had been possible to come by the frequency. 'We'll have to report that, Olivia. That list could jeopardize everyone who Claudius has to contact!'

'I should have told you before, but . . . well . . . Oh, Lucy, I don't think I am cut out for this work. I've let my feelings rule me again!'

'Me too, but after this, I think we could be called back home.'

For Olivia, this became a hope. She'd do anything to be back in London with Karl, Annie and everyone. She dared not hope for more than that. The hopelessness of such a dream hurt too much.

Chapter Nineteen

Hendrick

Hendrick stretched his aching body. Tiredness dogged him. He hadn't slept a wink worrying about Olivia.

How did she come to be in Saint-Rimay?

He didn't have to ask himself why. Her love for him had made her reckless.

Where was she now? Contacting Claudius hadn't helped. Not only didn't he know but now he couldn't contact again for fear of disclosing the Maquis' position.

Fraught with worry, he went to the window to look outside. Across the road, the bar he worked at looked busy. He'd had a quiet lunchtime session there and now had to go back for the evening shift – the time he hated the most as the Germans got drunker and drunker and molested young French girls in public view, even having full sex with them in the booths that could be curtained off or paying a fee and taking them upstairs.

Hendrick felt his stomach churn. It took all his willpower not to intervene when it was obvious the girl was there under duress and didn't want what she had to give. Those times sickened him.

He no longer felt as though he was an honourable man even though he knew he could do nothing.

If he did, he would be shot instantly, and the act would still take place. He'd seen it happen when a young husband had come into the bar and tried to take his distraught wife away.

Not only did they shoot him but they flung his wife on top of his body and raped her in that position!

Later, she was found hanging from a window of an apartment. Her children were collected by grandparents. Hendrick had joined the small crowd saying their goodbyes and had cried with them, telling them he felt so helpless as even if he gave his life, he wouldn't be able to save the girls this was happening to.

They understood. But their forgiveness didn't appease him. He would remember the things he'd seen for the rest of his life. His only solace was the useful information he picked up. But now, with radio silence, who would he be able to pass it on to?

But worse than that, how would he find out how his beautiful Olivia was?

A German jeep came into focus. Already the men looked drunk as they called out and waved at passers-by. Hendrick's heart dropped as one grabbed a young girl who looked no older that twelve and dragged her into the bar with them.

Stepping back, Hendrick sank back down onto his bed. His head dropped into his hands. His body shook with his sobs.

It had been a long time since he'd prayed, but now he begged of God to end this war, to bring peace to their lives, to give him strength to continue to do his work, but above all of these, he implored God to keep his Olivia and his little son safe.

Composing himself after a few moments, Hendrick swilled his face in cold water and began to shave. The light above the mirror showed that his hair dye was fading. An inch of his natural blond hair showed through at the roots. His moustache was dark, which helped, and maybe with that and wearing his beret in the way the French did he could manage until he could buy some henna again. He'd used the last of the bottle he'd bought in Paris.

Once he had his beret at a jaunty angle, he felt more confident.

Staring into the mirror, Hendrick hardly recognized himself, and yet Olivia had known him. Once again, he asked himself why she'd come to Saint-Rimay. It could only be to see him, but she'd placed herself in so much danger.

Tears pricked his eyes once more, but he swallowed hard. He had to carry on. His heart wanted him to run. To make it back to the camp in Limousin and find out for himself where Olivia was. But if he was caught, so much would be ruined – the Resistance might even be exposed and that would be disastrous.

His heart felt like a ton of lead as he walked across the road.

Pushing the swing doors open revealed a quiet and orderly scene with two farmers drinking in the corner and a couple of Germans stood at the bar ordering their drinks. There was no sign of the rowdy gang and yet their jeep stood outside.

Suddenly, the swing doors opened again and a farmer stood there holding a shotgun, his face red with rage. In French he shouted, 'Where is my daughter?'

At the sound of the scraping of chairs on the floor, Hendrick turned his head, saw the two Germans stand. In an instant shock zinged through him as the room vibrated with the sound of a gun being fired twice. Both Germans slumped to the floor. Blood flooded from their wounds.

Hendrick could only stare. Fear vied with a small rejoicing for this lone father who would defend the honour of his child when no one else dared to.

Shame washed over Hendrick, but he reminded himself that stepping forward would have achieved nothing. So much suffering and he could only help by disrupting the Germans' war efforts. Nothing else would accomplish anything.

The door to Hendrick's left, which led to the stairs, banged as it hit the wall with force. Hendrick froze. Gunter came through, his hair dishevelled, his shirt open and hanging out of his trousers.

With one precise movement, Gunter aimed his gun at the farmer.

Hendrick wanted to run – not as a cowardly act, but out of fear of Gunter recognizing him. But his legs wouldn't work, and then a shot rang out and seemed to take the space around him.

The clatter of the farmer's gun as it dropped to the floor brought reality back.

Blood reddened the farmer's shirt sleeve, but he stood defiant and asked, 'Where is my daughter?' This time in German, which shocked Hendrick.

Screams told where his daughter was. Gunter turned towards the hysterical sound and beckoned. A soldier brought the naked girl to the door, dragging her by her hair.

Gunter indicated that she should be brought further into the bar.

Her screams had quietened, but her almost whispered, 'Papa,' sliced Hendrick's heart. In that moment, he didn't care what happened to him. His mind could only see the broken girl.

The image conjured up his lovely Olivia going through the same ordeal. In one swift movement, he stretched out his hand and retrieved the loaded gun his boss kept under the bar.

Gunter was the first to fall, one shot to his forehead. Next the man who held the girl. Hendrick shouted at her, '*Cours vite, mademoiselle! Vite! Vite!*'

The girl obeyed and ran to her father. Clutching his good hand, she dragged him outside.

As Hendrick held the gun on the other two men who hadn't yet drawn a weapon, he heard a car speed away.

Knowing he had no choice, Hendrick pulled the trigger twice more.

Almost instantly more Germans appeared at the door, their guns pointed at Hendrick.

'Don't shoot! It isn't what you think! This man stopped the shooting by hitting the farmer in the arm and making him drop his gun – look! On the floor!'

The Germans seemed to understand Hendrick's fellow barman as they looked down at the gun that lay at their feet in a pool of blood. They kicked it aside and walked forward, still pointing their pistols at Hendrick.

'*Identifikation!*'

The word was easily understood in any language, so responding to it didn't compromise Hendrick. He lay his gun down and reached into his trouser pocket for his papers.

The German soldier read his name slowly. 'Leonard Durant.' Then looked up and shouted in French, 'Remove your beret when talking to a German officer!'

A sick feeling gripped Hendrick's stomach as he obeyed.

The German came closer. He stared at the roots of Hendrick's hair, then back at the picture on his papers.

'*Verhaften Sie diesen Mann!*'

Hendrick stood stock still. If he resisted the arrest the officer had commanded, not only would he show he understood German, but he would be shot immediately. Being arrested gave him time to plan. Yes, they were suspicious because of his hair, but that didn't mean they suspected him of anything else. The officer would naturally want questions answered.

Stepping over Gunter, the soldiers came forward. Hendrick pretended to shake, protesting that he hadn't done anything, letting the dribble run from his mouth and proclaiming, '*Je suis innocent!*'

The German caught hold of Hendrick's arm and twisted it painfully up his back. Hendrick went with him as he pushed him from behind the bar but purposely stepped on Gunter's body and ground his foot, wanting to spit into the staring eyes and kick the gaping face.

Sitting in the back of an open jeep with a gun pointing at him, Hendrick focused on Olivia's face and that of his little son, seeing Karl running towards him when he'd managed to get to Sark to see them both and hearing his voice say, 'Dada!'

A tear seeped out of his eye. His German captor laughed. '*Dieser ist wie ein Baby! Er weint!*'

The officer and the other soldier laughed with him.

At this moment, Hendrick did feel like a baby – a friendless baby. But he'd saved the girl, hadn't he? He only hoped it was before she was raped. And he'd rid this world of the vermin that was Gunter. If he died today, Hendrick would feel that his life was worth having had the chance to do that.

* * *

They pulled up outside the police station where the German administration for the area was housed on the top floor. Handling him roughly, they propelled him inside and down the stairs to the cells.

A stench of urine met him as he hit the floor. Lying still, Hendrick waited. The gated door clanged shut. A key clunked the lock into place.

As the sound of footsteps receded, Hendrick gave way to his heartache and fear. Huge sobs wracked his body.

'*Monsieur, quel est votre nom?*'

Hendrick lifted his head and turned. Opposite him, caged just as he was, an old man sat on a bench.

'Leonard Durant . . . *Et vous?*'

'Jacques.'

Jacques went on to explain that he'd been caught stealing food. And that it was the French police who had detained him. He called them bastards who licked the arses of the Germans.

His French was that of a peasant.

Hendrick told him what had happened at the bar – the version he wanted the Germans to believe. 'But then they saw the roots of my hair.'

'I can see from here. How are you going to explain dyeing your hair?'

'My father was albino, I inherited some of his genes. I—'

'You will need a better story than that. Try saying that your mother was raped by a German during the last war. They will like that . . . But I don't. I suspect the truth is more sinister. You had better pray that the Germans believe your story . . . Have you got a weapon?'

'No.'

'You look strong, so your hands are your weapon, as is your wit. Use your wit and then your hands. You can grasp a chair, or a vase – anything. If not, it is certain you will be shot. Me? I will probably be shot too, but I look on that as a release. I am dying. I am not as old as I look. I can no longer plough the field to provide for my children. They would be better off without me – already my wife is sleeping with my neighbour. He is welcome to her. He is a good man at heart, and he likes my kids.'

Hendrick didn't know what to say to this and didn't have a chance to answer as the man went into a fit of coughing.

Shivering from the cold dankness of the cell, Hendrick sat up. He removed the plain-glass rimless spectacles from his nose and rubbed his eyes.

The man was right, he needed to use his wits. The story of his mother being raped had a ring of truth about it. He could embellish it by saying he'd been called names all his life for his fair hair and for his poor eyesight. He had decided to dye his hair to protect himself from some of the constant rigging he had to endure – the colour of his eyes being blue he could get away with, as he could say he believed his father was a true Aryan.

Now he needed to think of a story for the rest of his background. For this, he could partly tell the truth – his mother had died, and an aunt had collected him and took him to Guernsey. He spoke English as a result. He had worked in a bank. When his aunt passed, he came back to his native France hoping to fight for his country. But because of his eye defect he was rejected by the forces. He hadn't had much education and so found a job working in the bar.

Feeling it was all feasible, Hendrick relaxed.

Days of questioning followed. During it he was asked to

read passages in English. He was asked how he viewed the Germans, knowing he was half-German.

Playing his cards as he thought he should, he told them he felt an affiliation to them and that was why he shot the farmer. He wished he'd killed him and not let him get away. He told them he'd picked up a little German from the soldiers who used the bar and that they had liked to teach him words, telling him that one day France would speak German as its first language.

All the time he felt like a traitor, but his own survival instinct drove him forward.

The worst part of the whole ordeal was when the torture began. The pain of his fingers being bent back and then one of his nails being pulled out was excruciating, but still he stuck to his story.

Always he kept his mind on Olivia and Karl and his desire to get back to them. But always, in his heart, he didn't think he would.

Nothing prepared him for the day they took him from the cells, and he was confronted, for the first time, by the officer who'd had him arrested.

Speaking in French, the officer asked him to repeat what he'd just said in English. This was a different tactic, and Hendrick knew a moment of uncertainty. But he decided that as he'd said he'd been brought up in Guernsey – a story that he thought would not make it easy to trace his history – he could do no other.

Translating it perfectly, the officer then spoke to him in English. 'How much do you hate the English?'

'I want to see them defeated. I know people of Guernsey. Why? Why didn't they protect that country? . . . I'm not saying that it shouldn't be in German hands. Germany would have conquered there as they have done here, driving them out. But they left Guernsey to their fate . . . A fate that to me is better than being governed by the British.'

To emphasize this, Hendrick spat on the ground.

The officer rested his chin on the tower he'd made with his joined hands and stared at him.

When he spoke, he said, 'You may be useful. You haven't changed your story no matter what our methods. You will be tested further. Your intelligence. You say you have picked up some of the German language while working and you speak good English. You will be sent to learn more German and other skills. You have already been tested for endurance by withstanding interrogation – most, although telling the truth, change their story many times in the hope of receiving mercy.

'If you pass the mathematical test, we will put you through as it will prove your story of being a banker, then you will begin this further training – I am sorry for what you will be put through next, but we will need a story. A story that will stand up to why you are not in the British army, for if you pass all we test you on, you will be sent to England to work as an agent for us. You will become accepted in circles of people who are privy to information.'

Not believing his luck, Hendrick made a snap decision to tell more of the truth.

'I already know many of them. I made trips with the boss of the bank I worked for to attend meetings. The British like to spend the money of their clients – money they haven't earned but they take. I attended many functions and was accepted in their society.'

For a moment Hendrick thought he'd gone too far as a frown crossed the officer's face. 'So, why did you drift to France and become nothing more than a bartender?'

Hendrick thought quickly. 'I was grieving the loss of my aunt who had been like a mother to me and was the only family I had. I just didn't want to be in Guernsey any more, nor did I want the responsibility and stress of the banking world. When I became stronger, I was enjoying bar work. I drifted from one job to the next and had no responsibility.'

'You do not like responsibility?'

'I didn't, but recently I have thought back to those days and thought that I would go back into banking if the opportunity came.'

The officer again leaned his chin on his hands and studied Hendrick. The scrutiny was unnerving.

'Give me the name of the bank you speak of in Guernsey.'

Hendrick's stomach turned over. Once more, he decided on the truth as he knew that William's bank was no more and it would be difficult to trace former workers. And though he had Leonard's first name, he didn't have his last, but that of his French aunt.

The officer got up and walked out of the office.

For a long moment, nothing happened. Hendrick could feel the beating of his own heart. What was it the officer had apologized for? What was going to happen?

He looked around the room, bare but for the desk in front of him. It wasn't like an office at all.

Patches that looked like blood stains darkened parts of the wooden floor. Hendrick swallowed. Sweat beads stood out on his forehead.

With the click of the door handle, he jumped.

The man Hendrick had called 'the Torturer' came in carrying bolt croppers.

Hendrick's screams as one of his fingers was severed went with him into a deep faint.

Chapter Twenty

Annie

Life had settled into a pattern over the past few months, and now here they were in late autumn.

Annie stood on the top step of the stairs leading down to the garden and admired how the remembrance patch still showed colour, with the geraniums at the back blooming as if it was still summertime.

She loved gardening and had encouraged her fellow officers to help to cultivate the overgrown square of land behind the station.

Before the war it had been planted with flowers and she and Ricky had often sat on the bench having their sandwiches or just chatting.

She'd made sure they kept a tub of flowers next to the bench, but in the rest of it they already had spuds doing well – the only crop advised for their first year by Brian, another keen gardener, to see if the land was fertile enough for vegetables.

Annie couldn't wait to dig them up and to share them out among all the staff – it would feel as though she'd truly fulfilled the 'Dig for Britain' remit asked for by the government.

Sighing, she thought of the bliss she felt to have respite from the constant dropping of bombs and hoped they would never experience that horror again. But the war still raged, and still she missed Olivia, and most of all her darling Ricky and all those she'd lost.

Her hand went to the locket that held Ricky's messages. As always this brought him closer to her. She couldn't imagine what he was doing, nor what Olivia and Lucy were engaged in. No one ever mentioned the work carried out undercover. Most didn't know of their existence.

Annie smiled at this thought. As if they would! Her mind gave her the headline 'Special agent in France helps to blow up the Germans'. She laughed out loud at the ridiculousness of it.

But then she stopped abruptly as a voice behind her took her by surprise. For a moment she felt as if she'd gone mad and was imagining things, but then it came again. 'Annie! Annie, I'm home!'

Annie swung round. 'Olivia!'

How it could happen Annie didn't know but suddenly, she was in Olivia's arms, something she hadn't dreamed would be possible in a million years – at least until the war ended.

With tears streaming down her face, she asked, 'Are yer home? Really home? No more going away?'

'I am. Oh, Annie, I'm so happy to be here! Where's Karl? And what are you doing here? Is Rosemary all right? I let myself in and managed to get up the stairs without seeing a soul. I thought to move into this flat but wanted to check it was empty and you hadn't let it. The last thing I expected to see was you up here. What's been happening? Have you still got lodgers?'

'Hey, slow down . . . Karl's out at the park with Rita and Beth, Ian's at school, and I've just come in from working the early shift and found a note saying where the little ones were. Rosemary now lives in Mum's old flat and is probably taking a nap. Bertie still lives in the basement. He and Ron will be mucking about on the boat. They're getting it ready to do trips up and down the canal . . . But why are you here?'

'Oh, Annie, Lucy and I were compromised at the end of July. We had to lie low until we could be flown out, and then had to go through debriefing. It's been awful.'

Annie could see Olivia was on the verge of breaking down.

'Well, you're here now, love. We're together again.'

They hugged once more. Olivia sobbed. Annie held her, letting her get to a place of peace. Her own throat tightened, but she didn't let go herself. Olivia needed her to be strong.

When she calmed, Annie asked, 'Is there anything on your mind, Olivia? You know I'll always be here for yer.'

'It's everything. It just gets you down at times. I'm on leave now, but not discharged. I've been told there will be an assignment for me, but it's still being decided . . . Oh, Annie, I've had enough. I don't want to fight any more, I just want to be with my Hendrick and little Karl, and . . . Oh, I don't know . . .'

'Well, I do know, luv. You can add make babies to that!'

Olivia looked up at her. Her face held shocked surprise, but then she smiled, then giggled, and before long they were both laughing hysterically.

When they controlled themselves, Olivia said, 'Exactly that – get our lives back, our normal lives. Were they ever that, Annie? Were we ever just young women with hopes and dreams?'

'We were, though mine were misguided, luv. I dreamed of making something of meself, of becoming a cop. I should have married Ricky, but I denied us that because married women couldn't be part of the police force. That soon changed once they needed us, didn't it?'

'It did. Oh, Annie. I so want you to have a family and for us all to have a life of happiness . . . but what if—'

'No what ifs! If we go down that road, we'll fall into a deep pit of misery. We must keep faith that we will win this war and that all we dream of will happen . . . Now, I've a bottle of sherry left from last Christmas. I know it's early afternoon, but I think we should celebrate your home-coming.'

A knock on the door and Rosemary putting her head around it surprised them both.

'Olivia! Oh, Olivia, you're home!'

Olivia got up and ran to her. 'I am, Rosemary. It's good to be back, and to see you. I can't take in that you're all here yet, I still have no idea why, and whether Daphne's with you or not. You haven't mentioned Daphne, Annie!'

Annie didn't answer, but said, 'Rosemary, you must have heard me say sherry!'

Rosemary giggled. 'I did hear the word just before I knocked and opened. And yes, I'll join you.'

They all laughed.

As they sat around Annie's table sipping their sherry, Annie told Olivia how they came to be here and where Daphne was and how she was getting on. She couldn't believe she was sitting with Olivia sipping the delicious, warming sherry at three thirty on a normal day! But doing so filled her with happiness. It was as if she could get through anything with Olivia by her side.

'I'll go and see Daphne while I'm still on leave,' Olivia was saying. 'You say she has two Land Girls living with her? That all sounds intriguing. I'd love to see how the flats have been configured but more than anything to catch up with Daphne.'

'Yer should do that. I have to work solidly for another four days, then I have three off. I might come with yer.'

'What about you, Rosemary?'

Rosemary shook her head. 'I'm happy here, Olivia, my dear. I see my friends a lot and help Bertie do up his boat – mainly cleaning up after them and making tea, but I love it. I always get taken on a trip up the canal as a reward. I find there I can forget the sad things in life.'

Annie caught Olivia's eye and winked. Olivia smiled but didn't ask questions. Though Annie guessed she might be wondering if there was more to Rosemary not wanting to leave. For herself, Annie wondered how Olivia would take the deduction she'd made that Rosemary was getting close to Bertie. It wasn't a year since Rosemary had heard that William had been killed. But then, they hadn't seen each other much over the years before that. It wouldn't be surprising if Rosemary could give her love to another.

They chatted on – some of it about happy memories, some of it sad. When Loes was mentioned, Annie couldn't give much news. 'She's on the Isle of Man. But we can send letters to her, and Joe's letters are sent there. It worries me, though, that we never hear back. I hope she doesn't think we betrayed her, but—'

'Joe? Joe from Guernsey?'

'Yes. It seems they are in love.' Annie told of the letter that had arrived here and how Bertie had opened it.

'Oh, Annie, have you told Loes how it all happened that she was taken from us?'

'I can't. Letters are censored. I just told her how the children are. It's all so very sad.' Thinking to bring this conversation to an end as they'd caught up on everyone, although they hadn't been able to ask Olivia anything, Annie had the notion that it would help to get Olivia sorted and to settle in rather than to become sad over things they couldn't change.

As they did this, Annie asked after Lucy.

'Lucy has gone back to her flat. She said she'll contact soon.'

From this Annie deduced that whatever had happened to compromise them both in France had very much affected Lucy, otherwise she would have come straight here to see her as Olivia had. She hoped it wasn't anything bad but accepted that she might never know.

'And Hendrick, have you any news?'

'Yes. So far, he's all right but he is in danger. That's all I can say, Annie.'

Annie wished she hadn't said that much as now a niggling feeling of fear for Hendrick trickled into her mind.

The reunion between Olivia and Karl was tear-jerking. It happened in the hallway downstairs. She and Olivia had been looking out for them coming back and as soon they spotted them, ran down to meet them.

Not a dry eye could be found among them all as Karl lifted Olivia's hair and let it run between his fingers. His speech had come on in leaps and bounds from being with all the other children and he said, 'Are you home now, Mummy?' Though where he got his posh voice from with how he mixed with the cockney boys – Ian and Rita's three, not to mention Beth, whose every word he hung on to – Annie didn't know. But it pleased her as she wouldn't want Olivia coming home to hear him using slang words.

'Yes, Mummy is home. And I hear you've been a good boy.'

Olivia held him close to her. Annie wiped her tears. Then noticed even Beth – always in charge and poopooing any sentiment – had a tear running down her face.

The reason became clear when in a wobbly voice she said, 'I wish my mum would come home.' Then, regaining her normal spirit, she came out with, 'You're a lucky bleeder, Karl.'

Shock held them all silent for a moment. Then Karl giggled, unhooked himself from Olivia and went up to her. Looking into her face, in a gentle voice he said, 'Your mummy is home. You have Aunty Annie.'

Annie held her breath. Beth looked up at her. Thinking the best thing was to just offer a hug, she opened her arms. Beth ran to her. It was lovely to hold her, but as she did, Annie looked up and silently said, 'We miss you, my lovely sister Janey.'

A head leaning on her waist gave Annie the knowledge that Ian had sidled up to her too. She snuggled him to her. 'I know I ain't a real mum, but I love yer both as if I was. Yer me world.'

When she looked up, Rita was hugging her boys too. It was a moment of knowing that in the midst of all they were going through, their children felt loved.

It was Karl who broke it up. Having gone back to Olivia, he said, 'No one told Beth off for swearing!'

This made them all laugh. For all the love between him and Beth, if they could score off one another, they didn't miss a chance.

'Karl! That wasn't nice. I could see you wanted to get

Beth into trouble. We had all excused her this time as she was so very sad.'

Karl hung his head. It must have been devastating for him to receive a telling off from his mum when they'd only just got together. But he lifted his head and said, 'Sorry, Beth. You can say "bleeding" whenever you're sad. But no other time!'

Annie could see this had left Olivia dumbfounded. She took charge. 'Right, with that settled and two of yer having said a naughty word, I think we'd better get your coats off and get yer all warmed up.'

'I'll make cocoa, Annie.'

Annie nodded at Rosemary. She could see she was dying to laugh.

With Annie's days off falling in half-term for Ian, there was nothing to stop them all from going to Wrexham to see Daphne. And now here they were on their way.

Olivia sat very close to Annie when they got into the carriage, and she understood completely when Olivia said, 'I never thought we'd sit together on a train again, Annie.'

'Me neither, luv, but how things are and what has happened hardens yer to most things.'

'It does, though I never get over seeing London so broken.'

'Only the buildings, luv. And even many of them didn't give in altogether and still have walls proudly proclaiming they're there ready to be put back together. The people will never be broken.'

Even as Annie said this, she thought that many were. But as a city of folk, they weren't broken. Their spirit was strong.

'Only this morning,' Annie continued, 'it was cold and still dark, and I had an hour to finishing me shift at six a.m.

So, I made me way to the WVS truck not far from the station.' She couldn't help adding, 'I much prefer their tea to Florrie's.' Olivia would know what she meant. 'Anyway, there was a lady serving, and I know she lost her home and that she and her kids live with her mum in a two up, two down terraced, and her man is still away fighting, and yet there she was, helping others.'

'I agree, you see it all the time. Look at Rita. How heart-breaking it must be to see her home in ruins every day, as well as, like us, not knowing if her husband will come back or not.'

Annie's heart felt heavy thinking of these poor women and how brave they were, but then she had the bravest of all sitting with her. The thought made her put out her hand and take Olivia's. 'One day, we'll know happiness again, luv. But for now, let's cheer up. We're going on our holidays!'

Olivia laughed her lovely laugh. To Annie, it almost completed her world having her back with her.

After checking in to a guest house, they hurried over to Rosemary's old home. Daphne greeted them with as much happiness at seeing them as they felt seeing her. The children were overjoyed too. Beth and Karl wouldn't leave Daphne's side, plying her with questions until they had to be checked as they were driving them all mad.

As they dutifully sat down, Daphne told them, 'I've arranged a surprise for you all. I hope you've brought warm clothes.'

'Oh, Aunty Daphne, what is it?'

Karl looked at Beth. 'It's a surprise. You don't know what surprises are.'

'But I want to.'

'Well, the surprise will happen when I tell you about it, as you'll never guess . . . I've arranged for us all to go to the seaside! Prestatyn!'

The children cheered though Ian turned it to belly laughing as he pressed Karl's belly button. 'Press that in!'

When they'd calmed, Olivia asked, 'How are we all to get there, Daphne?'

'Well, I haven't got a limo, but I have got the use of a truck. That's why we all need to wrap up warm, as only two can sit in with me. The rest will be on straw bales in the back, holding on for dear life!'

'I'll go in the back, Mum. The nippers 'ad better go in the warm.'

'Ta, Ian. That would be best.'

Beth protested. 'Not a nipper. I want to go in the back!'

'Well, in this case, Mum's ruling. You and Karl will go in the front, and you'll have the responsibility of watching the road with Daphne, to keep us all safe. I know I can trust you to do that for me, Beth.'

'Well, I am the best at that.'

Luckily, Karl didn't take the bait, and the children settled down and were happily wondering what the seaside would be like. Even Ian joined in, saying he'd heard that waves crashed onto the beach and you could collect seashells and paddle.

The journey to the seaside the next day had them giggling one minute and then clinging on for dear life the next. It seemed endless as Daphne negotiated lanes, bends and hills until finally coming to a clearing where they could see the sea sparkling like a blue carpet of stars. The children's excited screams came to her. Looking over the side, Annie could see them hanging out of the window. Her heart leapt to her throat. But Daphne shouted through her own open window that they were safe, she had hold of the harness – a contraption she'd brought with her from the farm that was used for the horses but worked very well when fixed around them both.

Annie relaxed and joined Ian and Olivia on her knees to gaze in wonderment at the coastline.

As soon as they unloaded, Beth ran towards the water. Annie couldn't swallow for fear. The wind took away her voice as she called after Beth to stop.

Ian saved the day. He sprinted and caught her, just as she reached the water's edge. But to save being the brunt of her indignation, he sat her down and took his shoes off and made sure she did too.

To see them running in and out of the freezing water, trying to avoid the splash of the waves, their voices high with sheer delight, made Annie beam. Karl was hesitant, hanging back.

'How they can stand it I don't know,' Annie said.

'Ha, Annie, we used to swim in the sea at St Peter Port, summer and winter! Come on, Daphne, race you!'

With this, Olivia sat and took off her stockings, tied her skirt around her waist and ran to join the children. Daphne was hot on her heels. Annie reluctantly sat down to take her time with her stockings, and Karl came up to her. 'If you're brave, I will be, Aunty Annie.'

This spurred her on and soon she and Karl were holding hands and running towards the sea.

As they sat drinking cold tea out of a bottle later, and eating jam sandwiches with no butter on, Annie looked at her family.

'These are the days we will all remember. Let's make many more of them, Annie.' Olivia's arm came around her.

'We will. Other days, not so good, will always be with us, but like the cockneys always do, we Guernsey Girls will make the most of the best days.'

Chapter Twenty-One

Olivia

Brinston's face glowed red with anger.

Olivia sat across from him, afraid of what he would say, and of what her fate would be. She'd been summoned to his office after reporting back in for duty this morning – a cold first day of November.

'I have never been so disappointed in my choice of agents as I am with you and Lucy. I had so much faith in you both. Compromising yourselves as you did was bad enough, but something has come to light which informs me of why you did it.'

The blood drained from Olivia's face as he turned his glare on her.

'Your husband, Hendrick Klaus, is in Saint-Rimay! You and Agent Lucy helped him to get there. You told him the name of where the Resistance was based!'

His thunderous thump on his desk increased the terror already holding Olivia as if she was made of stone.

'How could you give this information to a German?! Yes, you trusted him, but though we were willing to allow him to live out the war in a place where he could do no harm, we did not trust him. We worried that he could be working for the Germans! If we are right, you have compromised our whole operation in Limousin. You enabled him to work for the Resistance, giving him access to so much that could damage them and us!'

Olivia felt her bottom lip quiver. Her fear for Hendrick tore at her, knotting her stomach and leaving her mute as Brinston went on: 'You then deliberately went to Saint-Rimay to rendezvous with him. You are no better than a traitor!'

Olivia collapsed inwardly at this but didn't show Brinston she had. Instead, she lifted her head. 'Never! Never that! And Hendrick is an honourable man who hates the Nazis and what they have done to his country and now have done to his father. He was forced to work for them, and at great danger to himself, and to me after the invasion of Guernsey. He passed information to you that saved many lives. Now, because of his birthplace – which you know wasn't where he was brought up – you class him as the enemy! You should go down on your knees to thank him for all he did and beg his forgiveness!'

Brinston's mouth dropped open. When he closed it, his manner was not humble, but his rage had gone.

'Of course I know all that, but Lucy would have told you our stance – we had to assume the worst, for the safety of our country. Hendrick could easily have given in to threats by the Germans. Threats on your life, his son's life – any man would!'

Olivia could see this and understood for the first time why Hendrick was mistrusted.

'But he has proven himself! He's passed information to the Resistance.' Even as she said this, she knew it didn't demonstrate Hendrick's innocence. They would see this as a cover – as him passing information that he was given by his fellow countrymen. But nothing would make her believe this. 'What will happen now?'

She asked this calmly, but wanted to scream it out, to tell them that if they harmed her Hendrick, she would personally kill every one of them! But knew she was beaten.

'He is to be picked up at great danger to the team of men sent in to do this, including the agent who has replaced you and Agent Lucy. If he comes quietly, he will be brought back here, but if he tries to alert anyone to get help, he will be shot.'

Olivia stood. 'No!'

'I – I'm so sorry, Olivia, but we are at war. I have no choice.'

Sitting down once more, it came to Olivia that Hendrick wouldn't call for help if they identified themselves, but if they didn't . . .

'Hendrick will know who his abductors are, won't he? If he doesn't, he won't stand a chance. Anyone would call for help if waylaid and they saw the intention. This could be misconstrued as him calling on who you think are his comrades, but aren't – German soldiers!'

'I will make that one concession. I'll instruct that it is explained to him that he is compromised and that they have come to take him out of danger. He will be held captive after that and then brought back here for interrogation. But that is all I can do.'

Although giving Hendrick a chance, this appalled Olivia. She knew what interrogation meant – torture! It was unbearable.

'Now, I need to discuss your position.'

264

Olivia stared at him. How could he be so cold-hearted? But she had to accept that to do his job, he had to be.

'You made a mistake, Olivia. A huge one. I hope you have learned from it and can give of your talents and conquer your emotions. You must leave to one side your personal feelings and your personal life. We expect nothing less from our agents.'

Olivia didn't speak. Her mind was taken up with praying – her prayers were for Hendrick's safety, and for herself to find the strength to carry on.

That strength ebbed away when a knock at the door heralded a woman entering and passing a note to Brinston.

Olivia's gut told her that the note concerned her.

What happened next – Brinston dropping the hand that had held the note, and his expression showing a flash of defeat before he composed himself – sent Olivia's heart plummeting.

Brinston's head shook from side to side. 'I – I'm sorry, Olivia, truly sorry, but your husband has been captured – not by our men, but by the Germans. It seems our men went into the bar and asked after him. They were told of how Hendrick – or Leonard, as they knew him – shot some German customers who had abducted a young girl . . . I'm truly sorry. But there is nothing I can do.'

Olivia's world seemed to come to an end. She couldn't think, react, or move a limb.

'Olivia . . . Olivia . . .' Her name was all she heard before she sank into the oblivion of darkness.

When she woke – for the first time to a world she knew, not a swirling, frightening one – Olivia could hear a loved and familiar voice. 'Olivia, it's me, Annie.'

Forcing her eyes open, she looked up at Annie as if she was her saviour. Only one word came from her. 'Hendrick?'

'I'm sorry, but there's no news, luv.'

'Oh, Annie, how am I to bear it?'

'You can, for Karl's sake, Olivia. I know it can be done and I'll help yer. Don't let go again, me darlin'. If yer do, you'll be lost.'

'Oh, Annie. Help me.'

Annie's hand tightened around hers. 'I've got yer, me darlin'.'

'Where am I?'

'You're in hospital . . . One . . . well, you've been unwell in your mind . . . but you'll get better now. This is the first time you've recognized me.'

'How long . . .'

'A month. They say yer suffered a breakdown caused by hysteria. But as you've been calm for a week now, they've reduced your treatment . . . Olivia, me darlin', don't slip back. Please! Be strong, I beg of you. We need yer, we love yer . . . Karl needs yer. He has been broken-hearted at losing you again . . . Please, Olivia, try to hang on to the good things in your life and get well.'

This answer shocked Olivia. She could remember nothing since being told . . . 'Oh, God! Hendrick . . . my Hendrick!'

But then little snippets entered her mind of her being restrained, of needles injecting her, of screams that had hurt her throat and then more needles.

'I know. It's devastating for yer, Olivia, but this is the last thing Hendrick would want for you and for his son – you being incapable of functioning, and not caring for, or standing by, your child.'

'Annie?' Annie had never spoken to her like this before . . . but then, a whole month!

'I fought, Annie. I did.'

'Yes, me darlin', everyone who tried to help you, and that didn't help your cause, nor bring Karl's mummy back to him. But only you can help yerself, Olivia . . . Please! Yer know I love yer with all me heart. I'm just trying to help. To snap you out of the hysteria. Somehow yer must cope, yer must! No one knows more than me how difficult that is, luv.'

'Oh, Annie. I've let you all down, but I didn't know. I thought it was only yesterday I heard about Hendrick. A month! I can't take that in.'

Annie bent her head. When she lifted it, she said, 'I'm sorry. Oh, Olivia, how could I speak to you like that? I've been so angry. I thought I was losing you. I couldn't take any more, so I blamed yer, when you've been suffering so much . . . Please forgive me.'

Olivia, though feeling weak, managed to sit up and hold out her arms. 'I should have fought against the overwhelming feeling of sinking. I will now. I promise. Help me to, Annie.'

Annie hugged her gently. 'Always, me darlin'. Always.'

With Annie's help, Olivia laid back down. It was then that she noticed the skin hanging on her arms and realized that she'd lost weight. And her mind registered how weak she was. 'Can you help me out of bed, Annie?'

'I will but be careful.'

When she was sat on the side of the bed, Olivia looked around her. 'Where are the other patients, Annie? This doesn't look like a hospital.'

'No. Your uncle has paid to have you looked after in a private hospital – the same one you and I were in after the train crash, only this is a separate wing for illnesses of the mind.'

'Am I losing my mind, Annie?'

'You were, but not now.'

Olivia looked down at her legs, dangling like sticks. How could this have happened? She'd always thought herself strong and able to cope.

'I'm so glad you're back, luv. I've been so afraid. I had memories of me Janey and her illness. But then, knowing she got better gave me hope as she didn't have the expert treatment you have, so I know you can do it.'

'I will. My body feels very weak, though.'

'You've refused food for most of the time. They've had to force-feed yer . . . It's been awful, Olivia . . . I – I thought I'd lost yer for ever.'

'Don't cry, dear Annie . . . I promise you, I'll work hard to get better. Will they let Karl come to see me?'

'Not yet. And when yer see yourself in the mirror, yer won't want him too, luv. Get a bit better first. Start to accept food and get your body strong again.'

Olivia found herself going over it all in her mind. She could see this cat-like creature clawing at nurses; see food flying through the air; remember the dark despair that had driven her to do these things.

The horror of it shook her to the core . . . *How? How did that happen to me?* Then Hendrick came into her mind. Beautiful Hendrick. And for a moment she felt herself slipping back. *No! Annie is right. Hendrick wouldn't want that for me. He wouldn't want that for his son. I've let you down, my darling. But not any longer. I'll be the woman you would want me to be.*

'Take me to the mirror, Annie.'

'There's one in your bathroom. Are yer able to make it that far?'

'With your help.'

Making an extreme effort, Olivia stood. She leaned heavily on Annie's arm and made it to the bathroom. Shock held her rigid at the face that stared back at her – eyes sunken into dark sockets, sagging cheekbones, hair hanging in lank strands. 'Oh, God, Annie!'

'Look, luv. I know I was angry at yer, but you've been ill. Yer can get better and when that happens, when you've put weight back on and are stronger in your mind, I'll bring Karl in to see yer, I promise.'

'Hold me, Annie.'

With Annie's arms around her, Olivia felt new strength come into her. She could do this, for Hendrick, Karl and Annie, and for all her loved ones. She could.

It was three weeks later that Annie came into the ward holding Karl's hand. His little face lit with joy as he ran towards where she sat in an armchair. But then he became cross. 'You said you wouldn't leave me again, Mummy.'

'I didn't leave you, darling. I've been very poorly, and you couldn't come to see me. But I'm better now . . . I can never promise that I won't leave you. But always you'll have Annie with you. And if I have to go, it won't be because I want to.'

'I don't want you to go. I want you to stay with me.'

It occurred to Olivia that this poor little son of theirs had spent so little of his life with her, and even less with Hendrick. Did he even remember Hendrick? And yet, still she couldn't promise. What if when she got better Brinston sent her elsewhere? She'd have to go.

Holding Karl close, she told him, 'Wherever I am, you're

right here. Snuggled into my heart and nothing, or no one, can take you away from me.'

Karl just snuggled in closer to her. In doing so she felt him bring Hendrick nearer to her. Karl was a part of them both. They'd made him – their love had made him. He was so precious. For him, she would be well.

'Annie, I want to come home. I'll discharge myself if they don't agree. I know I'm well enough. I'll pack what things I have and come with you now.'

'Oh, Olivia, really? That's brilliant news, luv. And if they try to stop yer, I'll arrest the lot of them!'

This made them laugh out loud. Karl joined in, though Olivia knew he didn't know what they were talking about. It just felt so lovely to be laughing and to really feel happiness nudging away the deep pit of sadness that had consumed her. She mustn't give up hope again. At the end of the day, it was all any of them had. Her Hendrick would escape. Something would happen to help him. That's what she had to believe. And would believe. With this thought, she said to Karl, 'Get down a moment, darling, while Mummy gets ready. I'm coming home.'

Karl clapped his hands. 'You are ready, Mummy, you just need your coat as it's very cold out there . . . Oh, and you'll love home. It has tinsel and a Christmas tree . . . And Santa will soon come. And Granny Rosemary is baking for the day . . . It's all so pretty, Mummy!'

Olivia's heart warmed to hear how eloquently her son had described everything that would be good for her, and yet it saddened her too, as none of it had been taught by her. She'd played such a small part in his life from when he was born. How he loved her like he did she didn't know. But she felt his love. And now it was time to show him hers.

'That all sounds wonderful! And I know Santa will bring you a lovely present, and Beth and Ian and Aunty Rita's boys too.'

Karl looked up at her and with the innocence of childhood said, 'Well, we must deserve it first, and Freddie may not! He kicked his ball so hard it broke one of Aunty Annie's windows!'

Olivia wanted to laugh out loud. How had her son grown up to be this normal?

'Well, I'm sure Aunty Annie will forgive him and tell Santa he has been a good boy all year.'

'Aunty Rita won't. She smacked his bum, and made him stay in.'

Olivia bit her tongue to stop herself laughing.

Then Karl said, 'But I think if Aunty Annie forgives him, then Aunty Rita should. I like Freddie and I want him to have something from Santa. If he doesn't, I'll give him mine.'

'Ah, that's a nice thing to say, Karl. Now, hop it, young man, Mummy needs to get into the bathroom.'

As Karl left holding Annie's hand, Olivia held on to her newfound strength. She was going home, and she was going to face everything she had to. She was a Guernsey Girl. Yes, she'd been knocked off her axle for a while, but she was back and was ready to face whatever life threw at her.

Chapter Twenty-Two

Annie

Christmas Eve magic didn't completely lift them all. Everyone's emotions were heightened. Olivia, Rita, Bertie, Rosemary, Ron and herself – all of them had memories of happier Christmases with those now no longer with them, due to either fighting a war, death or imprisonment.

But each one of their faces as they toasted the statue of the new baby in the crib showed they also held hope within them.

Bertie helped this as he looked a picture in the Santa costume Rosemary had made for him and his 'Ho, Ho, Ho!' was perfect, making even Annie believe for a moment that he was the real Santa, though she laughed at herself for thinking this . . . But then, in a way, he was. He'd brought happiness into her home and been a father figure to them all. He'd given them exciting trips on his boat and helped Ron by being a good mate to him. The children adored him.

'Well, time I took their stockings to them all,' Bertie now said.

The stockings, also made by Rosemary, who'd been in her element as she'd been busy knitting, sewing and cooking, were filled with little goodies – each one contained an apple, a tiny cone of sweets, for which they'd all pooled their sweet coupons, and a homemade biscuit in the shape of Santa.

Annie felt as excited as the children as they all followed 'Santa' on his rounds.

Rita's boys were the first port of call. As the light splashed onto their bed, Annie swore she saw Freddie peep, and then close his eyes tightly. She wanted to giggle but kept it in.

Upstairs in her flat, it was Ian who was first. At the sight of his screwed-up body with his covers looking like he'd been wrestling, and his thumb stuck in his mouth, Annie's heart went out to him. He too must have thought of all he'd lost as he'd tried to get to sleep. She wanted to wake him and comfort him. She didn't want him suffering alone. They'd shared many moments together, but this being Christmas, he probably hadn't wanted to upset her.

Then came the little ones – Beth, looking the little angel that she wasn't, lying flat on her back with her hands above her. And Karl, on his tummy with his knees tucked under him – both oblivious to Santa. Annie almost wanted them to wake up.

They did – very early the next morning as the whole household was rudely awakened by shouts of glee. A sound Annie wanted to hold on to for as long as she could. Not that there was much time to store it in her memory as three bouncing children slammed into the room, making both her and Olivia jump.

Annie sat up, realizing for the first time that Olivia was in her bed, her own now being one of the two in the room Daphne and Loes used to occupy. Memory of the dream she'd had seeped into her. She'd been cuddled by Ricky, felt his warm body snuggling up to her. Now she knew it had been Olivia, but that didn't spoil the wonderful feeling of Ricky being near. She swallowed hard, not wanting to give in to the tears that painfully pricked the back of her eyes.

Beth soon sent these morose thoughts packing by making Annie laugh. She stood in her indignant pose, with her hands on her hips. 'I didn't see Santa, Mum! I stayed awake for ages!'

'That's good, me darlin'. You're not supposed to see him in the night. But he might be back this morning.'

'Will he bring more presents?'

'He will, but you should be happy with those yer have already.'

Ian, who'd shown less patience with the little ones lately, piped up, 'Yes, many kids don't get that!'

Karl looked astonished. 'Some kids get no presents?'

'No, they don't. It'll be them left in me old street that won't. I were lucky, me . . . Me gran always made me a stocking.'

The wise head of Beth calmed this. 'Well, we'll tell Santa he shouldn't leave out any kids! And we'll tell him about your street, Ian.'

Ian looked taken aback. Annie wasn't sure he still believed in Santa. She remembered the feeling. How it was to get nothing but a toffee and seeing other kids with rag dolls, and wondering why Santa didn't love her as much as he did them. She wished she could make it that all kids got the same.

'Right, that's settled. How about me Christmas kiss?'

Karl was already in Olivia's arms, but Annie had to wait for her two warring angels. She didn't have to wait long as they both ran at her and Ian climbed on the bed, helping Beth up.

Olivia turned this into fun, making them all forget the confrontation that began their day, as she sang, 'We Wish You a Merry Christmas'.

They all joined in. Annie managed to get out of bed. 'Right, follow me!'

Following her lead, they all marched downstairs singing the carol at the top of their voices. Before they reached the bottom, all the flat dwellers were in the hall, and all except Rita's three looked bleary-eyed. Rita and Rosemary still had their curlers in, Rita's covered by a headscarf tied back to front, and Rosemary's held by a pretty mobcap that really suited her.

Annie didn't miss the appreciative glance Bertie gave to Rosemary. She was sure it held love, but then she'd always been an old romantic.

Bertie winked in her direction before he said, 'Well, I have to make sure my boat's safe and sound before I can start to enjoy Christmas. Be back soon.'

This was the cue to get the children settled. Christmas was going to be held in her mum's flat, and there were plans for Olivia to play the piano later.

This thought brought her mum to her. *I ain't put yer out of me home, me darlin' mum, but I know you'd love Rosemary, and better if I call it her flat now. In me head it will always be yours, but I know that you have yours in heaven with our Janey. I love you both and miss yer.*

Turning her face from view, Annie wiped a tear away. Olivia's hand found hers. 'Remember your words, Annie. We can do this. It's a day when we must follow that maxim, love.'

Annie nodded. 'Right, kids, all get into Granny Rosemary's flat and let's get Christmas started, shall we?' Saying it out loud made Annie accept a little and she felt sure it was easier for everyone.

The flat felt warm and cosy with a fire blaring up the chimney, and it smelled of porridge cooking, making Annie feel hungry, but breakfast was scheduled for after Santa's visit. 'Come on, you lot, sit around the Christmas tree!' she called out to the children.

They didn't have long to wait before six little faces with sticky sweet residue around their mouth turned, astonished, towards the door as a hearty, 'Ho, Ho, Ho!' could be heard.

Bertie looked magnificent! He'd borrowed Rosemary's rouge and had red cheeks and a red nose, and his cotton wool beard was as white as snow. His sack was bulging.

He was in his element as he slowly pulled out parcel after parcel and distributed them – all gifts made by one or the other of them. The wooden toys had been made by Bertie and Ron. Those knitted or sewn had been made by all four of the womenfolk as Rosemary had guided them through the skills needed. There was a rag doll, warm mittens, a pretty winter bonnet, scarves, wooden trains, a box of bricks all painted different colours. There were jumpers, and then some shop-bought toys – slates, and boxes of chalk, a spinning top, yo-yos for each of them, and a cricket ball. The stumps and bats to complete the cricket set had been made by the men. All were received with glee, especially the football, and the hoops and stick, the latter of varying sizes also shop bought.

It didn't take long to serve breakfast and for them all to be dressed, wrapped in their warm scarves and mittens and out on the street playing.

'Peace at last! I'll put the kettle on. Who's for a fresh cuppa?'

'No, Rosemary, you sit down. I'll get it, and then we'll all help to get the dinner ready,' Olivia insisted.

'The pud will have to go on to steam first, Olivia, my dear. So, while you make the tea, I'll get that on the go. Rita's going to put it on her stove. Already, the cockerel's cooking in her oven – not that we know where if came from, but Bertie acquired it . . .' She glanced at Bertie as if he was a naughty boy, which they all knew he was as he'd poached the bird when on one of his trips down the canal!

Bertie beamed, as he did whenever he got any attention from Rosemary.

Rosemary giggled. 'Right, come on, Rita. I expect that "acquired bird" is sizzling away so we need to check on that too.'

'It is, mate, and it smells delicious. I'll help yer take the pudding over and get it on the go.'

Once again, they'd pooled what they had to make the pud, and in this, Annie's mum had come into her own as they'd found dried fruit in her cupboard. Goodness knew how long she'd had it, but it was still moist as she'd kept it in a tin with a tight lid. Annie had remembered the tin from her childhood but was sure her mum had refilled it many times. Sherry provided the sweetness, and malt the sticky texture. They'd all had a lot of fun stirring it over the weeks and making wishes – none of which had come true for Annie, but she soldiered on hoping that one day they would.

The spuds Annie had proudly presented from the police station garden, and they were to be peeled and chopped by Bertie and Ron, the sprouts had come from a local market, at an extortionate price, and the stuffing Rosemary had made from breadcrumbs from stale bread, and she'd then added herbs before leaving it to soak. Once it had reached the right consistency, she'd stuffed it into the cockerel's neck.

Everyone was looking forward to their dinner.

After listening to King George's speech, Beth said, 'My brother is too heavy for me to carry.'

For a moment, none of them knew why she'd said it, but then the penny dropped as the King was relating a tale told by a former president of America:

'*A boy was seen carrying another on his back. He was asked, "Isn't that burden too heavy for you?"*

The boy replied, "He isn't a burden, he is my brother."'

The adults had understood this as the King telling them that they should all carry their fellow man on their shoulders as they get through this war, but for Beth it had been taken literally.

'Well, you can carry your new rag doll on your shoulders, little one,' Bertie told her. Happy with this, Beth went off to wash her hands for dinner as all the children were told to do.

But the observation had fuelled a conversation as they set about sorting out putting two tables together and how to arrange the chairs.

'From what the King said, all our nations are being looked after,' Bertie said.

'Yes, and with the Americans now on our side, we've a much better chance,' Rosemary put in.

Annie nodded but couldn't help thinking that the 'Yanks' as they were commonly known had left it late to become their brothers.

Around sixish that night, with everyone having spent the afternoon snoozing, Olivia sat at the piano. This was a moment for Annie when she knew she would need the most control and to call on her strength. She wouldn't allow memories in of past wonderful times with Mum playing the piano and them all singing their hearts out. Instead, she kicked off the singing with a carol for the children: 'Away in a Manger'.

They'd practised this and it was lovely as she sat on the floor with Beth and Karl squatting between her legs, Ian with his head on her shoulder and Rita's three kneeling around her, all singing the chorus with her, their sweet voices filling the room.

It was a moment when the grown-ups allowed a tear to fall but excused themselves to the children, saying that their voices being so beautiful had brought tears to their eyes.

It was when the exhausted children were tucked up in bed that they all allowed themselves to reminisce. A time when they told of happy and sad stories and cried together.

But their stories were put into perspective when Rosemary said, 'For me, this is the best Christmas for a long, long time. Ever since my husband died, I have spent every Christmas alone. On most, I haven't even cooked a special dinner. Though lavished with presents from William, I could never have his presence, and didn't want to pull him away from you, Olivia.'

Olivia put her arm around her. 'It's all so sad to think of you both longing to be with each other and me being the obstacle.'

'No. You were never that, my dear. William and I were that. Our stubbornness. I was trying to remember when I last saw him. I believe it was when you went to your aunt's for Christmas, and then again a couple of times while you were in hospital after your accident, dear. I can hardly recall.'

'But that was nineteen thirty-six! Six years ago!'

'Yes. There was a time we were meant to meet up in thirty-eight, but he rushed home for the birth of Karl and didn't have time to come my way.'

'You never said . . . Oh, Rosemary.'

'I have something to say on that.' Bertie cleared his throat. 'Olivia, I know your father hasn't been gone long and I liked and respected him immensely, but would you feel that Rosemary is tainting his memory if we told you that we are in love?'

Olivia giggled. 'No, of course not, and we all know anyway! We just wanted to be sure our assumptions were right.'

Rosemary beamed.

Bertie laughed, and then said, 'In that case, if I can still get down.' He creakily went down on his knees. 'Rosemary, my dear, will you honour me by marrying me?'

To Rosemary's 'yes', they all clapped their hands, but then were in fits of laughter as they tried to help Bertie to his feet again.

Olivia took the moment to start to play once more, and this time it was a gentle melody. Bertie took Rosemary in his arms, and they began to waltz. The linoleum made a superb dance surface. A loud knocking on the door stopped them all in their tracks.

Ron got up. 'I'll go.'

As soon as he opened the door and she heard 'Good King Wenceslas' blaring out, Annie's nerves settled – a bang on the door these days could, and often did, bring bad news.

But this seemed the perfect end to a lovely day, tinged with sadness as it had been at times. To sing along with and donate to the Salvation Army made them all feel good.

'Well, that put the wind back in our sails. Now we need to talk weddings!'

Rosemary laughed. Her happiness radiated around them all. 'The "when" is all in hand. I was only waiting for the official asking, but I want a spring wedding. So, we can spend the winter planning and dreaming about it.'

This set off a conversation between the women about clothes, the reception and the honeymoon, while the men poured themselves some of Bertie's whisky and chatted about boats.

When they finally went to bed, Annie felt content that what could have been a very sad occasion had turned out to be a lovely day. Yes, their loved ones were in their minds and hearts, but they'd got through by keeping the mood jolly and with the bonus of Bertie's proposal.

'I feel so happy for Bertie and Rosemary, Annie.' Olivia was pulling on her pyjama bottoms – a must on a cold winter night.

'I'm glad, luv. I think they both worried about how it would affect you.'

'Yes, I gathered that, and it did, but not how they may have thought. But . . . well . . .'

'I know, luv . . . Everything that happens makes you feel your own loss.'

'If only I knew what was happening . . . Oh, and I wish I never had to report back for duty ever again. I'm tired, Annie. Weary of fear. Weary of trying to stay alive while doing my bit. And so, so weary of not being with Karl and my Hendrick and not knowing if Hendrick is alive or dead but fearing the worst.'

'I can relate to all of that. Though I feel as though I am doing me bit with looking after folk on me beat and keeping what order I can. I love me job, so that makes it easier. But I loved me life before all of this and I want it back.'

'Can I get in with you, Annie?'

When they snuggled in together, they both shed tears. They lay on their backs holding hands, allowing each one their moment. Trying not to let that moment descend into despair, but failing miserably, until they were exhausted.

The fifth day of the new year made part of Olivia's wishes come true for her – she received a communication saying that she was discharged through ill health. Her cheer brought everyone running into the hall where she'd opened her mail.

'Oh, I'm so happy for yer, luv. Now we need never be parted again.'

'Oh, Annie, and I don't have to leave Karl ever again either . . . It's so wonderful to be relieved of duties.'

Everyone hugged Olivia. Annie couldn't remember feeling this happy for a long time – not even Bertie's marriage proposal and Rosemary accepting topped this feeling. 'Now yer can concentrate on just being a mum, luv,' she told Olivia. Though she doubted that would happen and thought it more likely that Olivia would volunteer in some capacity. She hoped so. And as they often did, Olivia's old housekeeper's words came into her mind: *Busy hands and busy minds don't leave time to pine.*

PART FOUR

Reunions

Chapter Twenty-Three

Olivia

Though every day Olivia yearned for Hendrick, part of her had accepted that he had been executed.

She'd tried to hope, and hated giving up on him, but it seemed impossible for him to have survived.

The agent who had been sent from Limousin to have him transported back there had now informed Brinston of the full facts of Hendrick's arrest. He'd witnessed some of it from across the street, and the barman had filled in the rest, and told how Hendrick had killed three German soldiers to save a young girl from the clutches of the Germans.

Olivia understood Hendrick's motive. Although he was disciplined to turn a blind eye, she knew he couldn't do so in the circumstances as she felt certain he'd be thinking that though he couldn't do anything about what happened to her at Gunter's hands, he could stop it happening again to this young girl and avenge her at the same time.

Pulling her car up outside her solicitor's office, Olivia jumped out and looked around her. The sunshine of late March promised that spring was on its way.

This part of London in the West End had survived extensive bombing, but everywhere showed weary signs of the Blitz. Olivia thanked God that at least the plight of the people of London seemed to be over.

As she turned from getting her handbag out of the front seat, she saw the back of a figure she recognized. *Hendrick?*

Running after him, she overtook and looked back at him. 'My God! Hendrick!'

'Darling, keep walking, pretend you dropped something. I'll get in touch . . . I love you.'

Olivia obeyed though her legs didn't want to carry her away from her beloved Hendrick.

He'd escaped, that was obvious, but why hadn't he contacted her? And why did he all but deny her?

These questions were answered when she sat opposite her solicitor.

'Yes, Hendrick has been in to see me, my dear. He asked me to send you a letter. I have it here.'

'I bumped into him outside, but he seemed as though he couldn't have contact with me.'

'No personal contact, but he will keep in touch through me . . . Look, I cannot tell you much more, but just to say he is still Leonard and will be seeing "O".'

'My God! You know about "O"? And Hendrick, is he involved with the secret service?'

'That is all I am prepared to say.'

Olivia understood his silence. But how? How did Hendrick get from being arrested by the Germans to working for 'O'?

Then it dawned on her. Hendrick must have traded his life for his freedom. He must be a double agent! But then, she knew without doubt where his loyalties would be. If they weren't, he wouldn't have consented to spy for Germany, he'd have died first. But he must have seen a chance, not only to live, but to help Britain once more.

Such was her faith in Hendrick doing this that relief mixed with fear at this conclusion as double agents were in twice the danger.

Olivia bit her lip. She wanted to ask dozens of questions, but knew she wouldn't get answers.

As if nothing had been said, the solicitor cleared his throat.

'Now, my dear, I sent for you as I have some conclusions to your father's business – not all, as the Swiss accounts cannot be accessed until the war is over, and then that depends on which side wins. Pray to God it is ours. I have every faith it will be, especially now that the Americans have put their might behind us.'

'So, how bad are things?'

'Very. There is nothing other than what you have already received or may receive in the future from the aforementioned Swiss accounts.'

'And there isn't to be any comeback on me?'

'No. Your father's property portfolio has covered everything as I thought it would. He didn't add the house where Mrs Davies lived, he kept it as a personal asset, so that part of your inheritance is safe. Nor did he include his house in Guernsey, but whether that will ever be reclaimable, we do not know.'

After many more explanations of how her father's estate had been distributed among his creditors, Olivia left the solicitor's office feeling low.

This changed as soon as she got into her car and ripped open Hendrick's letter.

My darling,

When you read this, you will already know that I am in England. Your solicitor will have given you this note, and I have asked him to pass on any messages from me. Please don't question him about anything, just be content to know that I am near, and I will find a way that we can be together. It may just be a phone call from a phone box as I am sure I am being watched, and you, as a former agent, may be too.

Please do not mention to a living soul – not even your most trusted and dearest – that you have heard from me, or know where I am. I cannot stress how important this is to my safety and to yours and Karl's – I am living under the threat of something bad happening to you if I don't toe the line.

I so want to be with you and our little Karl and one day that will happen, I promise. In the meantime, it will help me greatly just to see you both – to be sitting on a park bench when you are there, playing together. Anything of this nature would be wonderful. I will arrange it with you.

I love you with all my heart. No two people should be asked to do what we have had to do, but one day it will lead to peace and when that day comes, nothing will ever part us again. Hug my little Karl for me.

Until we are in contact again, my darling, stay strong. Your loving Hendrick x

Olivia put her head on her steering wheel and allowed the tears to flow. *What kind of people are these Nazis?*

But there was hope. Hope of just seeing Hendrick from a distance. Hope because he was also under 'O's care and observation. She would do nothing to jeopardize that.

These thoughts brought her to a calm place. Lifting her head, Olivia was shocked to see Hendrick standing at a bus stop looking her way. He seemed to be willing her to get hold of herself and she knew why. If she showed she was coping, he could.

She lifted her hankie and waved it, but in such a way as if it would look as though she was straightening it out as she then wiped her face and put it away.

As she drove past him, she allowed herself to look in his direction and smile. There were many passers-by. Any onlooker wouldn't know what she was smiling at, or who. But Hendrick did. She saw a small lift of his eyebrows – an acknowledgement.

As soon as she spotted a telephone box, Olivia pulled up. Taking her pocket book out of her handbag, she found Lucy's number.

It took a few minutes to get through, but when she heard Lucy's voice, Olivia had to swallow hard. 'Lucy, it's Olivia. Are you feeling all right now, love?'

'Oh, Olivia, I am. I'd so love to see you.'

'I'm in the West End. I've been to my solicitor's. But I need to go back to Annie's as she's going on duty this afternoon.'

'I can come to Gill's Canalside Cafe. Be good to be there and not to have clandestine work to do. Will Annie have time to join us, do you think?'

'I'm sure she will. She'll be over the moon.'

'Oh, Olivia, it'll be so nice just to meet as friends. See you in about an hour.'

Olivia wondered what had cheered Lucy. She'd been so down in the dumps since they'd been recalled to London and hadn't wanted to see anyone.

As they sat together in Gill's, an old haunt, after hugging for what seemed an eternity, Lucy said, 'I've news, and I'm sure you two have as well. So, you're back and on your old beat, Annie?'

'I am. It takes a bit of juggling with my children – I'm a mum now, you know.'

Lucy's mouth dropped open.

Both Olivia and Annie laughed.

'How?'

'Ha, it weren't anything to do with the birds and the bees – they ain't visited for a long time!'

Olivia burst out laughing. Annie could get away with these one-liners, no matter how crude. She just had that way about her.

They explained to Lucy how Annie had become a parent and told her about Rita and how she looked after the children.

'They were just going for their walk with Ruffles, our dog, when I left. Though poor little mites will be dragged to the shops and then to Rita's mum-in-law's, so I won't see them until after my shift. Rita's a godsend, as is Rosemary.'

After they had caught Lucy up with all of their news, though Olivia could only tell how she'd been released from service because of ill health, Lucy then told them that she had been reassigned.

'I was surprised not to be released, I acted so very stupidly, but they think I could still be of use and have done something that I'm ecstatic about. They're sending me to work as a war correspondent! My cover job is to be my real job! I will still be undercover as such, as I'm needed to go to places under the protection of my press badge. And I am going out to Dan who will guide me – I can't believe he is working for "O"!'

'Oh, that's amazing – on both counts!'

'It is, Olivia. I'm so happy . . . I know it's dangerous, but we'll be together . . .' Her face broke into a mischievous grin. 'I might just be like you and Ricky were, Annie, and be married without being so.'

Annie beamed. 'Happy memories, girl. Get out there and make some of your own. The ring can come later – that's what Ricky always said. He said, "You're mine, luv, and me and you know it and that's all that matters."'

There was a moment they'd all tried to avoid when the sadness of their situation overwhelmed them, but Annie cheered them. 'Anyway, me memories will be for real one day, and then you'd better watch out as you'll both be aunties to a huge brood!'

They were giggling again.

When this came to an end, Olivia asked, 'When do you go, Lucy?'

'Sometime in the next couple of weeks. I don't know when. I will get a call and that will be it, I'll be on a flight . . . I am to put coded messages into my articles and BBC snippets I send. So, you will know I am okay, just by seeing my communications . . . If I'm not, you will know as it is always reported if a war correspondent is killed . . . So, what about you, Olivia? Is your discharge your only news? How do you spend your days?'

A feeling of being a no one came over Olivia. It hurt to say she was just a mum. As important as that was, she felt as though all her dreams – ambitious dreams, like owning her own language school – had gone, as had her part in helping the war effort. It took her a moment to think of any aspirations she had that she could tell them about. But then admitted, 'To tell the truth, I'm at a loose end most of the time.'

'Look, "O" was asking about you. I think he will find you

291

something if you feel completely recovered – well, I did hear you'd suffered a breakdown. I can guess why. I did myself but not one that hospitalized me. But you look so well now.'

Olivia so wanted to confide in Lucy. She glanced at Annie. Annie looked quizzically back, obviously wondering at the reason for her not saying anything. But to tell an out and out lie about her thinking Hendrick was dead, when she knew different, was something she couldn't do.

'I'm all right now, thanks, Lucy, I've come to terms with everything.'

'Then why don't you approach "O"?'

'No. I'd rather not have anything to do with any of that again, but I will look to volunteer. I need something that will challenge me, but not take me away too often from Karl. We have Rita and Rosemary, but he's been through so much, he needs to know I will be there for him.'

'I've had an idea . . . It's a long shot, but we were working on a story the other day about the wounded prisoners and prisoners of war in general. It threw up all sorts of things they may suffer from – being afraid as they might expect to be treated how their country treats our POWs, and difficulties with communication – and this is where I think you could help. The hospitals and camps where they are do have interpreters and some of the prisoners themselves can speak other languages, but there must be a place for a linguist such as yourself.'

Olivia's interest was piqued. 'How can I find out?'

'You could try the Red Cross. They seem to organize most things, so I'm sure it's something they would know about.'

Olivia could feel her spirits lifting. 'Thanks, I will. It sounds like something I can fit around Karl . . . I may even take him with me sometimes . . . You see, as we know, not all

Germans are Nazis at heart, and I don't want him growing up hating his grandfather's countrymen – well, his father's too. But we'll see. I wouldn't do that on a first visit, not until I could be sure that who I am dealing with is of the same mind as Stefan and Hendrick.'

'You surprise me, Olivia. You seem able to talk about Hendrick as if everything is all right with him . . . I mean, well, I hope it is, but . . .'

Olivia thought quickly. She had to answer Lucy in such a way that she didn't guess. 'I've made myself do that . . . I . . . It isn't easy, but I've taken a leaf from Annie's book. I – I couldn't see a way that Hendrick could be alive but seeing that Annie refuses to give up, I have decided that I won't. Talking about Hendrick as if I know he is all right keeps that hope alive in me.'

Both Lucy and Annie put out their hands and took hers. No one spoke for a few minutes, and Olivia sighed inwardly as she released her tension. She must be more careful, she told herself.

'It's the only way in the end,' Annie told them. 'If I didn't, I'd go mad – probably will if it proves not to be so. But yer have to keep going and keeping hope alive is how I do it.'

'Oh, Annie, you're an inspiration . . . Look, I haven't said, but some reporting will be in Poland. The Red Cross arrange it. If I get a snippet of information about Ricky, I'll make sure you know it. I promise.' Lucy turned her attention back to Olivia. 'I won't be in France, I'm afraid. Germany, yes, and all those European countries. We're allowed to film so much and report back on what we see – though it's all heavily censored and is why we use code.'

Olivia smiled. 'I understand. Don't worry. I am strong now, in mind, and getting there in body. And I have Annie.'

She so wanted to tell these two dear friends, who'd been through so much and such a lot of it with her, standing firmly by her side, but she couldn't put Hendrick in any danger.

It was a week before Olivia received any communication from Hendrick. And it was as promised: a rendezvous without any contact. The problem was he chose Hyde Park, but then he wouldn't know of ones in Bethnal, not ever having visited there.

As she got Karl ready, she so wanted to tell him he would be seeing Daddy. Instead, she said, 'We're not going to our normal park today, darling. Mummy's going to take you to the one near to where Poppa had his apartment. It's lovely.'

'Can Beth come?'

Olivia didn't know how to answer this. To refuse might upset them both and yet she would hate one of their arguments to break out while in the park and spoil the gem of a moment for Hendrick.

But then, he would see Karl with his very best friend and that would please him.

'Yes, if her mum says it's all right.'

'And Ruffles?'

'No. Mummy has to say no to that. He won't sit down in the car and might cause us to have an accident.'

There were a few protests at this, but Olivia won the day and set out having avoided questions from Annie. It felt terrible just saying she wanted to be near to where her father had been. She was sure Annie could see right through the necessary white lies, but she didn't question it.

The park showed signs of welcoming spring as some daffodils had poked their heads through the grass, and along the edge.

The part of the park that Hendrick knew didn't have much of a play area, but Olivia allowed the children to bring the ball with them.

Her heart stopped when she arrived and walked through the ornate gates. There he was sitting on a bench near to the entrance. How she wanted to run to him and to be held by him. But she walked by without looking.

The trilby he wore, and the scarf tied high over his chin, made him unrecognizable to Karl, who skipped past him holding Beth's hand, listening carefully to her instructions on which game they were going to play.

A slight movement of Hendrick's head and his gloved hand going to one of his eyes, told her that the glimpse of Karl and hearing his chatter had greatly affected him. As it must do seeing her and not being able to hold her.

Olivia thought her own heart would burst with the joy drumming around her body at just being in such close proximity to him.

'Give me the ball now, Karl!'

This command brought Olivia's attention back to the children. She was amazed to see Karl stand firm. 'No. I want to hold the ball, Beth. You can't have your own way every time!'

This was the last thing Olivia wanted to happen. She'd so wanted Hendrick to see the love these two had between them.

Beth's hands went to her hips. 'Well, I'm the eldest!'

Olivia heard what sounded somewhere between a cough and a laugh. She looked over at Hendrick. He had his head down, but she knew he was enjoying the scene played out in front of him, and especially so as his son was standing up for himself.

'That doesn't mean we can't take turns, Beth . . . But if you really want to carry the ball, you can.'

Olivia's mouth dropped open. When did this son of hers become so diplomatic? He had always given in to Beth, but this was different. He was standing up for his rights but making a concession for the sake of peace.

Beth took the ball, but then dropped it, almost as if it had been an accident, but it obviously wasn't. It bounced towards Hendrick.

Karl set off in pursuit. Olivia held her breath. But then Beth set off too and overtook Karl. She retrieved the ball without even glancing at the man on the bench and ran back with it.

Handing it to Karl, she said, 'You have it then, mate.'

Olivia had to smile. She'd won the day in her own way, even if Karl didn't realize it.

Once more, the cough to cover a laugh could be heard as the children went off chasing the ball in the opposite direction.

Olivia looked around her. The park was deserted. She glanced at Hendrick. This was torture and yet exquisite torture as he was there – alive, and not feet from her. She smiled. Hendrick stood and came towards her. Her breath caught in her lungs.

'I believe this is yours, madam? You dropped it on the path.'

He handed her a gleaming white hankie scrunched up in a ball. When she took it, she could feel something solid wrapped inside it.

A whispered, 'I love you, Olivia,' and Hendrick turned and left without a backward glance.

Olivia shoved the hankie into her coat pocket and turned towards the children.

It wasn't until they were back in the car that she opened the hankie – after she had sniffed it to savour the scent of Hendrick.

There, shining against the white of the cotton, lay a wedding ring. Not the one she'd been given on her wedding day – that one was long lost back in Guernsey, taken from her finger by one of the Germans after her capture – but a beautiful band. On the inside was engraved *Olivia and Hendrick for ever*.

Olivia held it to her breast before slipping it onto her finger and staring at it in wonderment.

'Tired, Mummy.'

This plea brought Olivia back to her senses. She quickly took the ring off her finger and slipped it into her handbag. She couldn't share it with anyone – that would expose Hendrick – but she would find a way of wearing it that didn't reveal that they had met.

'Lie down on the back seat, darling. You can sleep as Mummy drives back to Aunty Annie's.'

Beth's determined voice said, 'I don't want to sleep. I'll sit in the front with you, Aunty Olivee.'

'All right, Beth, you can show me the way.'

Not many minutes later, Olivia smiled to herself as her navigator let out a snore to rival any she'd ever heard.

Her love for Beth swelled. At the heart of it, she was just a little girl battling in a man's world – as they all were.

Glancing in the mirror, she saw that Karl was fast asleep too.

Grinning at the thought of them both and their love for each other tangled with rivalry, Olivia let her mind drift to what might have been this afternoon.

One day, it would be again. The ring told her that.

Chapter Twenty-Four

Annie

March 1943

It seemed to Annie that Christmas – their second here in her home in the Old Ford Road since leaving Wales – had come and gone like lightning. And here they were in late March having been faced with air-raid sirens once more. These were due to anticipated reprisals by the Germans to the heavy bombing of Berlin.

The expected wedding day had been delayed due to Bertie falling and hurting his back and his long recovery taking them into the winter. Now plans seemed to be afoot once more, but no date was set.

The air raid had rendered Annie a bag of nerves. Her inner battle to stay calm and get through it all had often deserted her. And the recent tragedy in Bethnal tube station had left her traumatized.

Over one hundred and seventy civilians had been crushed to death in what was thought to be a panic-stricken mass of people trying to get down to the Underground to be safe from the bombs that the piercing sound of the sirens threatened.

The screams, and the agonizing moans, lived with her. As

did her feeling of helplessness as she'd helped to clear the bodies of so many men, women and – what tore at her heart – children.

It had felt she was pulled from pillar to post as voices shouted for her – the ambulance crews needing a hand; the fire service wanting her to calm someone as they rescued them. And worst of all, trying to comfort the bereaved as she sobbed with them, feeling their pain mingle with her own.

Now, as she walked along by the peaceful, rippling Thames with it all revisiting her, Annie had the overwhelming feeling of being exhausted. She'd been stretched to her limits over the past three years but somehow she was managing to stay sane – being needed by her own people helped.

Not a shift went by that she didn't have her arms around someone or found herself helping to talk a distraught woman away from the brink of committing suicide. Then there were the times she coaxed children, who sat around looking gloomy, to play a game, joining in with them until they were laughing and happy in the knowledge that it was all right to just be kids.

Having gone through the worst thing that could happen to anyone, she understood the problems, fear and heartache of her fellow East Enders. And she had come to realize that what they suffered wasn't just for those who had little to start with. War was a great leveller, and the rich and famous needed just as much help.

As she and Olivia did too.

Olivia still wandered into Annie's bedroom and she would wake to find her snuggled up with her, her muffled sobs sounding loud in the dead of night.

Often too they talked of loved ones missed, and this

included Loes. It hurt deeply that she didn't answer any of their letters. Bertie had said that Joe received letters from her, so they knew she was all right. Did she blame them? Did she think they'd shopped her to Annie's sergeant?

Deciding to think of the good things that had happened for them, Annie pondered on how everything was better for Olivia now as her work with the Red Cross occupied a lot of her time. She translated for wounded prisoners in hospitals and those in prisoner of war camps.

When attending a recent assignment, she'd seen, and been able to chat to, Stefan. She'd said how happy he was to see her looking so well. And she said how he was coping, and sent a little message for Daphne.

Being preoccupied with her thoughts, Annie hadn't noticed how far she'd walked and suddenly found she was alongside her and Ricky's bench. Always, this place lifted her. Sitting down and leaning back as she always did, she tried to experience once more the feeling of Ricky's arms around her just after he'd pulled her back from the edge of the water.

Such a long time ago, and yet, as memories go, such a short time, as there'd been so few moments together to crowd it out.

Lucy came to her mind. She hoped with all her heart that she and her Dan were finding those moments too. Yes, they'd all been taught that it was wrong to come together as one before marriage, but it hadn't felt wrong to give herself to her Ricky before they had tied the knot. Ricky was the love of her life – her soulmate.

Annie closed her eyes, then opened them as shock zinged through her with the sound of Ricky's voice. 'Skiving again, eh?'

Annie shot up. 'Ricky! Oh, me darlin', where did yer come from?' She shook her head. 'Is it really you? I ain't asleep, am I?'

Ricky hurried towards her and held her. Annie braced herself for his usual greeting to lift her in the air and swing her around, but that didn't happen. He clung to her. 'It is, me darlin'. I've come 'ome!'

'How? When? I – I . . . Oh, Ricky!'

As his lips came towards her Annie thought that the whys and wherefores could wait. She was in Ricky's arms!

Clinging to him, she sobbed tears of joy and felt the release of so many emotions that had overwhelmed her.

Ricky guided her to the bench and sat down with her. He gently pulled her head to rest on his shoulder and then lay his head on hers. She could feel his tears wetting her hair.

'I'm home, me darlin'. I ain't whole . . . I've been injured and 'ave lost me sight in one eye but I can see yer clearly. Oh, Annie, me Annie.'

Annie pulled back and lifted her head to look at him – saw him close up for the first time. His poor face: scarred down one side, and his nose broken from being attacked by a criminal he'd apprehended in his police officer days, and now one of his eyes had a light blue cast in it.

She put a hand on each of his cheeks. 'Me Ricky, yer beautiful.'

His kiss lingered longer this time, disturbing long-sleeping yearnings. Annie clung to him, trying to make herself believe he was really here.

When they parted, she shivered.

'You're cold! It is a bit nippy, but where I've been the winters are so severe that this feels mild. Where can we go where we can talk, eh, Annie, luv? I – I know what happened

. . . A message was got to me about me mum . . . and all . . . Oh, Annie, it's unbearable.'

'Let's go to the station. I'll radio in to the sarge and ask him if we can go into the canteen. I'll ask him to let us in the side door, so we needn't see anyone.'

'I've already seen them. I called there to see if yer were on duty and was told yer were on this beat.'

'Well, they'll understand then. We just need to be alone and to talk, luv.'

'We do, luv.'

As they began to walk back to the station, Ricky became unsteady on his legs.

'Ricky! Are yer sure yer all right?'

'I ain't, Annie . . . I need to sit down.'

The weight of his body as he leaned heavily on her almost made Annie buckle at the knees. 'Ricky! Oh, Ricky, me darlin'.' Annie looked around her. 'Just a few more steps and we'll be near to that low wall. Hang on, me darlin'.'

''Ere, officer, are yer 'aving trouble with that bloke? Is 'e drunk?'

A cab had pulled up alongside them. 'No, he's a police officer returned injured from the war. Help me get him into your car, will yer, mate?'

'Be an 'onour. Me lad's a pilot taking risks every day in the air raids. I just 'ope if he needs it, someone's around to 'elp him.'

By the time they reached the police station, Ricky had recovered a little. The taxi driver wouldn't hear of them paying their fare but helped Ricky inside.

Everyone crowded around.

'I'm all right now. It 'appens . . . It's been a long day.'

'And you made it worse, Ricky, absconding from the 'ospital!'

'Oh, Ricky, luv, you didn't?'

'I just couldn't wait to see yer, Annie.'

'I'd have come to yer . . . Oh, Ricky, let's get yer back there, eh?'

'No, please, Annie. Just let them know I'm 'ome. Let me stay with yer, luv. I can't be parted from yer again.'

Annie looked at the sarge. He nodded. 'I had a call from the local police in Portsmouth. They said that they thought Ricky may make for here, but he'd already gone to find you then, Annie. I was just going to radio yer to warn yer when you turned up.'

'I were going to radio you, Sarge, but then Ricky collapsed. Can we go into the canteen for a while?'

'Yer can. I'll ring the police in Portsmouth and let them know he's safe, then we'll see what's to be done . . . But whatever it is, Ricky, as your sergeant, I'll order yer to do it.' The sarge winked then and Ricky smiled.

'Try to persuade them to let me stay 'ome, Sarge. I can't take any more.'

'All right, mate. I'll do me best.'

When they sat together in the canteen with steaming hot mugs of tea in front of them, Ricky told her that his injury had been caused by a twig.

'We were leaving camp in the pitch black when suddenly I 'ad a pain in me eye. It became infected. They got me out to the Red Cross, and they cared for me, but then the Russians were closing in and the camp disbanded. That began a journey from 'ell for me. Me infection worsened and I ended up with pneumonia. Somehow, I landed in Spain and were picked up and brought 'ome on a hospital ship. When I got a bit better, I was told they weren't able to save me sight in the infected eye.'

'How long have yer been in England, Ricky?'

'I don't know. I couldn't even tell them who I was, I was so ill. But as I improved, I told them everything. It was then they told me I was in Portsmouth . . . I didn't think it through, Annie. I knew they wouldn't release me, so I sneaked out in the night. I knew where they kept all our clothes, so I dressed and started me journey 'ere. It's all a haze. I just 'ad one focus: to get to Stepney. I hitched lifts and . . . well, I slept a lot – in the back of lorries and vans, and even on a horse and cart at one stage . . . I must 'ave been out of me 'ead. But when I reached 'ere, I went to one of them slipper baths. I just 'ad enough money to do that. Then when I were cleaned up, I landed 'ere. Just the thought of seeing you spurred me on. The sarge believed me story that I'd been medically discharged and had come to find yer, Annie. He assigned one of the officers – Ben Wright, an old colleague of mine – to drop me off near to yer . . . And 'ere I am.'

Annie looked at his pale face. Saw for the first time his sunken eyes, and just how sore his left eye was.

'I love yer, Ricky . . . I can't believe yer here . . . but you've got to promise me that if you need to, you'll go into a local hospital.'

'I will. I could bear that, Annie, knowing you'll come to see me every day.'

'I'll go and see if the police doctor is due. If not, Sarge will call him, and then we'll see what he says . . . Oh, Ricky, I can't believe yer here!' It was as if, if she said it enough times, it would come real to Annie, but as yet, she couldn't believe it.

304

When she got to the sarge's office, he told her that he'd already rung the doctor. 'But, Annie, whatever the doc says, we do . . . Are yer with me on that?'

'I am. But he won't send Ricky back to Portsmouth, will he?'

'Very unlikely. He'll send him local, I'm sure.'

When Annie went back to Ricky, he had his arms folded on the table and his head resting on them.

As she left him undisturbed and sat down next to him, she thought how there was so much he didn't know about – the children, Olivia's time in Guernsey, all she'd lost, the bomb that had destroyed Rita's home. How she now owned Janey's house. How she'd cared for his mum's house – now his.

This thought suddenly struck her and she realized that she and Ricky did have a home of their own when she'd always thought she needed to save hard towards one. She'd never seen them living together in her flat. Always she thought of a little terraced house somewhere where she could put flower pots on the windowsill and scrub her step every morning, and with a yard for the kids – Ricky's mum's had all of that.

'What're yer dreaming of, luv? Yer looked lovely then, as if your thoughts were of something really good. Is it what I dream of every day?'

His mischievous look made her laugh. 'No! You cannot think how different to your thoughts mine were. But I'm feeling the same as you, Ricky.'

He took her hand. 'Things'll get back to normal, you'll see, luv. We'll 'ave a family, and a home of our own. I'll find work of some such.' His face clouded then. 'I won't be accepted back in the police, Annie, not with me eye.'

'We'll think about all of that later, eh? But I do have something to tell yer. Well, loads of stuff, but at this moment I need yer to know . . . We do have a family – kids.'

Ricky's face was a picture as he processed this and came up with the wrong end of the stick. 'You mean . . . I left yer pregnant?'

Annie couldn't help giggling.

As she enlightened him, his face creased into a lovely smile. 'We have two kids! Oh, Annie, mate, I'm so 'appy to hear you adopted little Beth, and this Ian chappie sounds a lovely lad . . . So many have been left alone. I might have known my Annie would rescue someone. I'm surprised yer 'aven't got twenty or more of them!'

They laughed together and Annie saw a glimpse of the old Ricky. She knew he would bounce back, and this filled her with happiness and hope.

When the doctor arrived, he didn't find anything other than physical exhaustion affecting Ricky's health and recommended rest and good food, interspersed with gentle exercise.

The sarge immediately gave Annie leave to care for him for a week, then said, 'Ricky, you and I 'ave always been mates. I could do with a good station cop – it's a position I've long advocated shouldn't be a shared duty, but one that has a permanent face the public can deal with and get to know and trust. With many a good cop returning with injuries, I think me idea may be accepted. If it is, you're the man I would choose.'

This brought tears to Ricky's eyes and highlighted how fragile his mental state was.

'Ta, Sarge, that would suit me to the ground. Though I'd miss me beat and helping folk on the street, but they'll always know they can come into the station and get help from me.'

306

The sarge didn't speak. Annie could see he had filled up too. She didn't cry; she was emotionally drained for now and her instincts to care for Ricky had taken over. 'Right, you two, let's make a start on Ricky's recovery. I've me car outside, so I'll get yer back to Janey's, luv.'

Ricky looked surprised at her saying this.

'I'll always think of the house on the Old Ford Road as Janey's, luv, even though I am the sole owner of it now.'

'What? How did that come about, Annie?'

Annie told him of how Jimmy had signed it over to Janey when he left to go to war. 'That was the good Jimmy we knew. He thought that if he didn't come back from the war, she wouldn't have any legal entanglement, or claims on the property from distant relatives. The Jimmy that returned is behind bars for ever . . . A casualty of war that no one will revere, as his actions were those of a monster. That wasn't truly the Jimmy we knew.'

'Oh, Annie, only you can think that way, but it's a good way. A loving, forgiving way. And we'll be called on to do a lot of that as more return damaged in mind and body just as Jimmy did.'

Home was quiet when they opened the door.

'It feels deserted, luv.'

'It is. Olivia will be doing her Red Cross work. Rita . . . I need to tell you about Rita from over the road . . . She will have taken Beth and maybe Karl too with her to visit her mum-in-law, and Bertie and Ron will be on Bertie's boat . . . Oh, Ricky, I can see from your face that I've lost yer along the way. I've so much to tell you. And I will, but first, I'm going to need to do some shuffling about with who sleeps where, as I ain't having anyone but you in me bed!'

'Oh? Who do yer 'ave now then?'

Ricky was smiling a half-cocked smile.

'Olivia! She has her own room but often snuggles in with me. It's a long story, luv. Let's get you up to my flat and start organizing the space we have.'

This posed Annie so many problems as Annie told Ricky the situation of each of her tenants. There was just nowhere to put Olivia other than where she was. The house was bursting at the seams.

'Ricky, what about your mum's house, luv? I'd like to make that our home . . . The problem is that it would be too much for the children to be suddenly dragged away from all they've known so it will need to be a slow process over time . . . Maybe we could approach one of the others to move into it . . . if yer agree, of course.'

'It sounds to me that the best thing would be if Olivia got used to staying in her own room – did you say it used to be Daphne's and Loes's? Anyway, that way me and you have the double room to ourselves.'

Annie had thought he wouldn't want to share the flat, but she didn't interrupt.

'In the meantime, we take the kids over to me mum's now and again to get them used to the idea that it will be their home as I'm all for that idea, Annie, me darlin'. Our very own 'ome. Me mum would love to think of us living there.'

To reassure herself, Annie asked, 'You don't mind living with Olivia and Karl then, luv?'

'Not at all, as long as I 'ave you to meself at night.'

'Only, well, Olivia's still very . . . well, sort of fragile inside. You see, Hendrick . . .' Annie told of Hendrick's plight.

'Hendrick captured! And after being thought to be a traitor by the Germans! God, Annie, he must be dead!'

'We don't know for sure . . . and to tell the truth, I think Olivia knows he isn't . . . Oh, I don't know. But she often refers to him in the present tense as if . . . I'm being silly. Surely she wouldn't still cry so much if she thought he was alive?'

'That's not always so. I cried buckets at night knowing that you were in danger, and knowing what yer'd been through and how I weren't with yer. I'd imagine Olivia does the same . . . Well, if she knows something she can't talk about. For her, that would be added pressure as she's always confided everything in you, Annie.'

Annie couldn't see a way that Hendrick could be alive, or that if he was, Olivia would know . . . but then it occurred to her. 'Ricky, you don't think . . . ? Well, when I were working with Lucy, who I've told you about . . . I learned things that most don't know. She told me that there are those who are double agents . . . I mean, well, the Germans know about Olivia, how she escaped and . . . My God, what if they threatened Hendrick with hers and Karl's life?'

Ricky stared at her. He probably hadn't a clue what she was talking about. But then what he said showed that he did. 'That's very possible. We had a bloke in camp who was caught. He came back to us in a state, said he'd escaped, but later we found out he was betraying us. When . . . Oh, Annie, such terrible things have happened and at me own hands too . . . I – I had to interrogate him . . . He broke and told me his family would be shot if he didn't do what he did. We lost good blokes because of him giving informa-tion. The others wanted to shoot him, but I persuaded them to use him instead. We fed him false information. But the poor bloke was sussed, and the Germans shot him.'

Ricky hung his head. Annie stood and went to him. She

stroked his black curly hair as he continued: 'Hendrick would be in so much danger if that's what he's doing. Even if he knows the information for the Germans is false. Both sides will be watching him, and his life could be taken just like that if he's found out by the Germans.'

'Oh, Ricky. Oh, luv, if what we're speculating is true, no wonder Olivia cries so much. She must imagine the worst . . . She must fear for Karl too . . . But how would she know if Hendrick is doing that?'

'If I'd had a chance to be 'ere in this country, I'd 'ave taken it, and wild 'orses wouldn't 'ave stopped me contacting yer, me darling.'

Annie cradled Ricky's head. Her heart ached for Olivia, and yet her fear for her deepened too. She hoped to God that if what she and Ricky thought was true, neither Hendrick nor Olivia were taking any chances.

She shuddered as she changed the subject. 'Anyway, back to our situation. So, we'll manage with having Olivia and Karl in our home then? I know it ain't ideal. We've had such little time to be with each other since we married, we haven't built a life of our own yet.'

'I'm fine as long as I 'ave you, luv . . . Oh, and me kids that I didn't know I had!' Ricky laughed. Annie relaxed at the sound. She so wanted them to have their own home, but at least now the dream was going to be a reality one day.

Rita calling from the bottom of the stairs had Annie rushing to the door of her flat.

'I thought I 'eard someone. I didn't expect yer to be home yet, Annie. Is Olivia with yer?'

Annie's 'No, it's Ricky!' came out on a giggle.

'What? Oh, Annie, he's 'ome! Is he all right, luv?'

'He is.' Annie was descending the stairs. 'Well, he is injured, but he's fine, or will be after I've nursed him back to full health.'

Beth ran at her. 'We've been to the park . . . Who's Ricky?' she asked. Then, as if something clicked into place, she said, 'Ricky from the war? Ricky that you miss and cry over?'

This surprised Annie. She thought she'd kept her tears to herself, or at least only shared them with Olivia. Ignoring it, she said, 'Yes! My Ricky and your dad! And Ian's too . . . Only he's not well at the moment so we've all to take care of him.'

'I want Daddy!'

'Oh, Karl, yer will have your daddy, mate. I'm sure that he'll come home one day. But be happy for Beth and Ian, eh?'

Karl smiled. 'I am, Aunty Annie.' He turned to Beth. 'Can I share your daddy till mine comes home, Beth?'

'You can, but you remember whose daddy he is . . . Well . . . you don't have to, only when your own dad comes home.'

Karl grinned.

'But you ain't to call him Daddy. You can call him Uncle Ricky.' Turning her face up to Annie, she said, 'What does me dad look like?'

'You've seen his photo. The one we kiss every night.'

'Has he got a policeman's uniform on and a crooked nose, with a line down here?' She drew her finger down her cheek.

'Yes, those lovely features are his . . . and now because of his bravery in trying to stop the bombs dropping, he has a poorly eye. But folk ain't what they look like, it's their heart that matters.'

'Mummy said Uncle Ricky in the photo is a good man and I would love him as she does.'

Karl saying this warmed Annie's heart.

Then Rita piped up, 'Everyone loves Ricky. I didn't know him that well, but me hubby did. He worked over on the docks in Stepney and used to tell me 'ow Ricky were a diamond geezer. A good cop and a good laugh as well . . . Annie, I'll meet him later. You get the kids settled with him first. I've seen him from across the road when he's been 'ere, but I ain't never spoken to him.'

'I know, luv. And he is what your hubby said, a diamond geezer . . . Oh, Rita, I'm so happy that he's home.'

Rita winked at her. 'I doubt we'll see much of yer for a week, luv. Wish it were me welcoming me man home.'

'You will. I'm sure of that. Me mum always said he had nine lives. Remember when there was that accident at the docks and some crates fell within an inch of him? She said it then as he'd not long fallen off his bike on a busy road and escaped with just bruising!'

'Ha, I remember. She was sat outside one day, and I had a chat with her, and she said it then . . . I 'ope to God she were right, luv. Anyway, I'll look out for the lads coming in from school. Should I say anything to Ian?'

'Just say there's a lovely surprise for him when he gets home . . . The best ever.'

Annie giggled as she hurried the little ones upstairs, her heart rapidly beating with trepidation. *Please let them love me Ricky.*

She needn't have worried. Beth went up to him and said, 'You're me dad, ain't you?'

Ricky answered, 'And proud to be, but my, you've grown since I last saw yer.'

Beth put her head on one side. 'Course I have, I were only a nipper then. I start school soon!'

Ricky laughed out loud. 'And who's this? Not Karl! Well, look what a strapping young man you are!'

Karl grinned. Then ran up to Ricky. 'You look nice. Better than your photo. You're not smiling. I like your smile.'

Beth looked worried. 'I like MY daddy's smile as well!'

Ricky looked up at Annie. She could see he was dying to laugh, but instead he put his arms out and both children went into them. As they hugged, Annie couldn't stop the tear that had pricked her eye from falling gently down her face.

Chapter Twenty-Five

Olivia

Olivia had mixed emotions as they walked towards the school gates, she, Rita and Annie, with Karl and Beth holding their hands and letting out joyful squeals as they lifted them into the air and swung them over the puddles.

Ian and Rita's lads, Freddie, Mike and Philip, jumped in and out of them, earning them the wrath of Rita's and Annie's tongues every time they did.

'Ian, I mean it now. If you jump into another puddle, yer won't 'ave your football to play with for a week!'

'Sorry, Mum, but it's good fun . . .'

'You can do it tonight with your wellies on, eh? But you're all smart for the first day back at school and yer should be setting a good example to Beth and Karl as this is their first ever day!'

Olivia felt a pang of sadness as this drove it home that she truly was going to leave Karl inside the imposing-looking gates and a new era would begin for them both. How she wished Hendrick could have been here to see this momentous day and to hold her and help her through it.

She and Annie had chatted about this day for a while – their trepidations, their sorrow, as it was like they were sending their children on a journey that would take them onwards to something that didn't involve their mums. Olivia didn't feel at all ready for this.

As she hugged Karl at the school gates, he grinned up at her. 'I'm going to be braver than Beth as I'm a boy!'

Part of her wanted to chastise him and tell him that girls could be just as brave as boys, but she knew this was his way of telling himself that he could do this, so she smiled down at him and told him, 'Mummy's very proud of you, and I know Daddy would be too, darling.'

Karl beamed. 'And Uncle Ricky said he was proud of me too. He wants to see my work when I come home as he said I will draw pictures and write my name.'

'Oh, you will. And Mummy will treasure them and keep them safe for Daddy to see.'

Beth piped up, 'My daddy can see mine tonight!'

Annie looked mortified. 'Beth, that was nasty. Say sorry.'

Beth's lip quivered. 'I didn't mean it, Karl.'

With wisdom far above his years, Karl said, 'I _know_ you only said it to help you be brave.'

Beth grinned. But for once she didn't retort.

'Well, off you go, now.'

Ian stood just inside the gate. 'Come on, you two. You have to line up to go into class. I'll take yer to where yer 'ave to be, eh?'

Once again, Beth surprised them and showed just how scared she was really feeling, as without any protest or retort, she grasped Ian's outstretched hand. 'You'll be all right, mate. I'll see yer at playtime and sort anything out if it's not right for yer.'

'Ta, Ian. I like having a big brother.'

Ian beamed. 'Right, come on then. You as well, Karl.'

Karl ran to him. Olivia felt tears prick her eyes. 'Bye, darling. Be good and enjoy.'

But Karl was already out of earshot and didn't give a backward glance. Beth took a sneaky peak back and responded to Annie blowing her a kiss.

'Well, the pair of yer, I know exactly 'ow yer feel. I've been through it three times. But you wait until the school holidays – you'll be dying to bring them back 'ere.'

Rita laughed, but neither Olivia nor Annie joined in.

The feeling Olivia had wasn't sadness – that was a feeling she knew inside out – but a strange kind of having to let go when she didn't feel ready. She looked over at Annie and could see the same turmoil affecting her, though she knew she must be thinking of Janey and how it should have been her standing waving to Beth.

'I could do with a cuppa. How about you two? Shall we go to Gill's Cafe on the canal?'

Both agreed with Olivia. She'd thought that Annie would say she wanted to get back to Ricky, but she seemed as eager as Olivia to delay going back to the house without the little ones.

It was as she followed Rita and Annie into the cafe that Olivia spotted a figure. Hendrick! She hadn't seen or heard from him in two weeks.

Thinking quickly, she said, 'Get mine in for me, I'm dying for a pee.'

Annie looked back and laughed, then said under her breath, 'Enough to use Gill's bog? Ugh, yer must be desperate.'

'I am. I'll hold my nose.'

Rita and Annie laughed at this but they didn't question her further and went inside.

The offending lav was at the side of the cafe building and if you walked by the cafe on the towpath, you always got a whiff of it. Not going into it but waiting by the wall, Olivia's heart thumped. She willed Hendrick to follow her. No one was around. Not even Bertie and Ron had come down to tinker on their boat yet . . . *Oh, my God!* A sudden thought had occurred to Olivia. *Bertie's boat! The perfect place!* Bertie rarely came down to it before ten. And he never locked the cabin. If she could get Hendrick to follow her there, they could hold each other . . . *Oh, God, please let this work!*

Stepping from around the side of the lav, Olivia saw Hendrick approaching her.

The last time she'd seen him had been in Hyde Park, as most of the other times had been. She'd dropped a piece of paper near to him and walked on. On it she'd told him of Karl starting school today and where, but she hadn't expected him to come. She gestured now to him to hurry.

Then he was by her side, holding her, kissing her, touching her face, kissing her eyes.

'My darling, I dare not stay too long, but I had to see you today. I saw our brave little soldier march into school without a care. I'm so proud of him, but oh, my heart hurt. I had to see you, I followed you . . . I love you. I love you with all my heart.'

'Oh, Hendrick. I – I can't stay long as Annie will come and look for me. I'm supposed to be relieving myself but there might be a way we can have a little time together.' She quickly told him of the boat.

'It's perfect. It's almost deserted here. But Bertie won't find out, will he?'

'I could come out early and tell Annie that I've to meet someone from the Red Cross. I'll do it on a day that I normally work, as we've arranged that either she or Rita take the little ones to school on that day. My next workday is Wednesday.'

'Oh, Olivia, in just two days we will be together. I'll be here as six when no one is about. You come just as soon as it seems practical that you can.'

His kiss then held a promise. Olivia's yearnings overwhelmed her as she clung to him. She felt his need of her wrapped in his love. 'Soon, my darling, soon.'

'Wednesday?' His voice was deep and croaky.

As she went to leave, she turned and clasped his hand. A shock zinged through her. 'Hendrick . . . Your finger!'

'I'll tell you about it sometime, darling. Don't worry. I forget I ever had it now.'

Sensing that he'd endured something too terrible to talk about, she lifted his hand and kissed it.

'Nothing matters now, darling. You have healed it with that kiss.'

When Olivia walked into the cafe, she was met by Annie.

'You look flushed, luv. Are yer all right?'

Making herself grin despite the shock, and her imagination running riot as to how Hendrick's finger was severed, she said, 'I've been retching. God! Why doesn't Gill clean that lav!'

'I don't suppose she can stand the smell either. All the boat people use it to empty their week's waste into. And these days, the cart doesn't come round that often. Next time, 'ave a good pee before yer leave!'

They giggled at this reprimand from Annie, and the

moment became normal. Though to Olivia, no moment would be normal until she was in Hendrick's arms again. Could she wait two days till Wednesday? She knew every minute of that time would be agony.

The children coming home in the late afternoon provided some distraction as their excited chatter and reciting every minute of the day they had loved lifted them all.

And to see Beth clinging to Ricky and kissing his cheek was something Olivia loved. Though it did make her long to see Karl do the same to Hendrick.

He wasn't left out as his turn came to hug this new-found uncle and relate all he had done.

Scribbled drawings were cooed over and praised and squiggly attempts to write names were given a round of applause, leaving Beth and Karl preening themselves and grinning from ear to ear.

It wasn't long, though, before both were curled up asleep on the sofa leaning on Ricky's lap. Annie winked at Olivia and nodded. When she turned her head, Olivia saw that Ricky too had closed his eyes.

It was then that Annie scared Olivia a little as she seemed to be digging for information. 'Yer haven't been so down lately, especially today, luv. Have yer come to terms with things?'

'A little. I have to. And my work has helped.'

'Good . . . Only, well, if ever yer are having a bad patch and yer need me in the night, you only have to come and tap on me door and I'll come in to be with yer for a while.'

It was as if Annie knew that hadn't happened lately. The regular sightings of Hendrick and passing notes had helped her. He'd instilled confidence into her that he was safe. And now, she'd once again known his kisses and . . . Her mind skipped ahead . . . Would she know more on Wednesday?

'Olivia?'

'Oh, sorry, I lost concentration for a moment.'

Annie put her knife down on the draining board. 'Olivia, luv, yer will tell me if anything is troubling yer, won't yer? Having Ricky home hasn't changed how I care for yer.'

Almost blurting everything out, Olivia thought quickly and turned it into a joke.

'Well, it has to, love. Your cheeks are always glowing, especially in the morning!'

Annie burst out laughing. 'Ha, you've noticed!'

'I have and I'm very jealous and yet so happy for you, Annie.'

'I'm always here for yer, Olivia. Yer can share everything with me, luv.'

'There's something I can't, Annie. So, please believe me when I say that I'm all right.'

Annie pulled away from her and stared into her face. 'Oh, me darlin', be careful.'

Nodding her head, not trusting herself to speak, Olivia said, 'Anyway, I won't get much chance to do any other on Wednesday. I'll have to leave early as I'm going to a prison camp that's a good few miles away. So don't worry if you hear me sneaking out early.'

Annie's, 'Oh?' spoke volumes but she didn't say any more other than that she was on a late shift so would take the little ones to school. 'Rita will bring them home if you're still not back, and Ricky will be here to watch over them.'

When Wednesday dawned, it was easy for Olivia to get ready and slip out. She hated lying, especially to Annie, but she had no choice.

The cold early April air made her cheeks tingle, and the

blackness of the early morning gave her the fear of something horrible lurking ready to jump out at her. But her mission spurred her along as she ran across the road and felt her way down the steps, clinging to the cold iron rail to guide her and save her from tripping.

Eerie sounds of the first awakening crows cawing and the creak of boats swaying on the water spooked Olivia.

Daring to use her pen torch found in the lining of a coat gave her a beam to light her way.

When she reached Bertie's boat she climbed aboard, not knowing if Hendrick had arrived or not, but then two arms grabbed her, and her name sounded over and over as his lips kissed her hair.

'Hendrick! Oh, my Hendrick!'

They didn't speak but clung on to one another, kissing and touching, their breath coming in heavy gasps until Hendrick guided her further inside. 'There's only a hard bench, my darling, but to me it will be like a soft feather bed.'

Olivia couldn't answer him as his lips once more opened and covered hers. She just allowed the exquisite sensations that quivered through her and went willingly with him between the benches until he gently lowered her.

Her hunger for him consumed her. Her love burst out of every part of her body. At this moment, she wouldn't have cared if the world came to an end, as they tugged each other's clothes off and lay down.

It was then that all she'd dreamed of happened. She was one with her Hendrick. Her darling, her soulmate. Her body took over and she gripped him with her legs, accepting his every thrust and crying out with ecstasy as he took her to heights she could hardly bear and yet welcomed and begged for.

At last, they lay panting, clinging to each other, telling of their undying love, until Hendrick's tears wet her naked body and brought her back to reality.

They sobbed as they held on to each other. And then Hendrick pulled back from her and looked into her eyes. She could feel his breath on her as he said, 'My darling, this will be the first and last time.'

'No! No, Hendrick I cannot bear it! Why?'

'I – I think I've been exposed. I've taken too many risks in trying to see you, my darling. My German contact got in touch late last night and told me that I'm to be pulled out. He gave me instructions to make my way north . . . I should have gone straight to "O" but I just needed to be with you for the last time for God knows how long. But now I must report to him . . . and he will have no choice but to imprison me. He and I have already discussed this scenario.'

'No!'

'I will be safe, darling. And you will too. "O" told me that if ever this happens, they will leak it out that I was caught giving information to the Germans and imprisoned. This way the Germans will have no need to harm you or me as it will serve them no purpose.'

'Oh, Hendrick, is there no other way?'

'No, darling. But you and I will get through this, I promise. There are things afoot. I cannot tell you of them, but they could mean an end to this war. Then we will be together. We will go home.'

Getting up, Hendrick dressed quickly. Olivia could only stare at the shadowy figure he made. Then he was saying, 'Goodbye, my love,' and he scrambled away from her, leaving her lying in a sobbing heap.

After a while, Olivia calmed as it came to her that if

Hendrick could do this, she could too. There would be a day when they would be together. Hendrick had promised her that.

A sudden shiver made her realize how cold she was. Dressing quickly, she climbed the steps and took a deep breath of the crisp air.

When she got to the steps that would take her off the towpath and onto the road, it was light enough to see Annie's house. The blackout windows made it look dismal, but it wasn't. It was a place of love and safety for her and for Karl.

Making up her mind that she wanted to be within its walls, and back with Annie, she decided to return and say her mission had been cancelled.

Taking a minute to compose herself, she took her scarf from her pocket and tied it around her dishevelled hair, then took out her hankie and spat on it and used it to wipe under her eyes, hoping to remove any mascara from beneath them.

But as it happened there was no one about when she re-entered the house and she was able to creep back upstairs into Annie's flat and get to her room without being detected.

The sounds of the household waking and getting ready for the day ahead woke Olivia. She glanced at the clock. A quarter to eight! She'd slept for an hour, and yet she couldn't remember falling asleep.

Annie jumped when Olivia opened her bedroom door.

'Oh, Olivia! I thought you'd left!'

'I did, but my assignment was cancelled so I crept back in.'

'Are you all right, luv? Yer don't look it.'

'No. I've a thumping headache. I'll ring and cry off today. I'm just not feeling up to it. I felt a bit under the weather when I left this morning so was really glad when they said I couldn't go today – something about a breach of security at the prison . . . Oh, I don't know, I – I . . .'

'Oh, Olivia, luv, what's wrong? Why are yer crying? Come here. Let me give yer a hug.'

'I need more than a hug . . . Oh, Annie, I have to tell someone . . . Have you got time? I need . . .' Olivia could say no more. Her sobs took over her willpower. It felt to her that her world had come to an end.

As Annie guided her back into her room and they sat down on her bed, Olivia said, 'I have to tell someone, Annie. And you're the only one in the world that I trust to understand and to keep everything I tell you a secret.'

'Is it Hendrick, luv? Is he working as a double agent?'

Olivia could only stare at Annie. How did she know?

'Look, I had an inkling that yer knew Hendrick was alive and safe. Me and Ricky talked about it, and we came up with this theory that Hendrick had somehow traded his life by saying he would spy for the Germans, but we knew he wouldn't do that, so deduced that maybe he was a double agent – Lucy told me about them and their work.'

Olivia nodded. 'But there's more. Hendrick will now be a prisoner of war for his own safety. He's been recalled to Germany and that can only mean one thing – that they've discovered what he's been up to. I – I met him this morning . . . Oh, Annie, I may not see him again for a long time . . .'

'Well, this may sound harsh, but I'm glad. He was at risk doing that work, and even more so meeting up with you! If he's a prisoner, he'll be safe and looked after. And who knows, he may be allowed visitors, eh?'

Olivia shook her head. 'No. That would put him in even

324

more danger as it would show his imprisonment for what it is – a sham to keep him safe . . . But you know, it isn't all about that. The powers that be in the clandestine world are ruthless. They know that if Hendrick went back or was got at, he would be tortured and the threat the Germans put on my life and Karl's would be increased to make him talk.'

Feeling she would break in two as the reality of Hendrick's situation was truly hitting home, Olivia paused.

'Oh, God, Olivia, will he really be safe?'

'They will make sure he is – not because they care about him, but because he knows things that could really jeopardize Britain's war effort if our enemies knew. They cannot take the chance that anyone can have access to him, which still could happen in an open prison . . . I know them and how they work. And so, Hendrick will be put into a secure prison and won't be allowed any contact with me or the outside world.'

'That's a good thing, isn't it? I mean, if no one can get at him, he'll live out the war, and then you'll be together again, eh?'

Olivia's head dropped.

Annie's arm came around her. Leaning her head on Annie's shoulder, Olivia didn't cry. She felt drained of tears. Besides, what Annie had said was true. There might be months, years even, of loneliness for her, but in the end, she could be certain she would be with her Hendrick. She lifted her head and smiled at Annie.

Annie visibly relaxed.

They were silent for a moment and then Annie said, 'I've got news too, Olivia . . . Only mine's happy news . . . I wish yours was, luv.'

Olivia decided that she must face the world as it was and

not make the life of everyone around her a misery too. 'Well, tell me your news and maybe it'll make me happy too.'

'I'm leaving the police force. And me and Ricky are going to make a new life in his mum's, Lilly's, house . . . Well, Ricky's house now. We're going to do it gradually, taking the kids there after school for a bit while we're doing it up – painting it and that . . . So they get used to it. And you and Karl can have this flat all to yourselves. Yer can make it a proper home, luv.'

'Oh, Annie, I'm glad for you . . . But I'll miss you so much.'

'I'll not be far away, luv, just a short car ride, me darlin', and you're welcome whenever yer want to come around. You can even stay the night if yer like. It'll have to be on the sofa, but I will have a second bed put in Ian's room so Karl has a bed and can come and stay over whenever he wants too.'

Though it didn't feel like it, Olivia said, 'It's perfect! I'm so happy for you, love. At last. You and Ricky, making a proper home for yourselves.'

'Yes, and not just that . . . Well, there's no way of being certain, but me monthly didn't appear last week . . . I might just be late, I have been before, but something feels different inside me.'

'Annie! Really? Oh, Annie!' Despite her own sadness, Olivia clapped her hands and then grabbed Annie and hugged her as she swallowed down her own conflicting emotions and thought, *Please, God, let it be so.*

Chapter Twenty-Six

Olivia

Two days later Olivia was sent for by Brinston. As she sat opposite him, she waited. Her hands clenched tightly in her lap; her body stiffened as if bracing herself against an attack.

After asking how she was, Brinston cleared his throat. 'I've brought you in to tell you good news, Olivia. Hendrick has been found alive. He made it to this country and is now a prisoner of war.'

Shock zinged through Olivia. They had no idea that she and Hendrick had met! Or was she being tested?

To make sure, she gasped. 'He's safe? How? Can I see him?'

Brinston stared at her for what seemed like an age.

Olivia knew then that yes, she was being tested. 'Please tell me he's not hurt!' she begged.

As if he decided she was genuine, Brinston shook his head. 'No, he isn't hurt. It seems that he broke away from his captors and made it back to the Resistance group. They transported him back here.'

Olivia relaxed. She wasn't under suspicion.

But she did wonder if this was how it had really happened.

She'd never asked Hendrick how he got here, but if the Germans wanted him here, they wouldn't transport him but let him escape and find his own way.

'So, can I see him?'

'No. I'm sorry. He is to be kept away from anyone for his own safety and yours.'

Still acting the innocent, Olivia asked, 'But how can he not be safe? Why shouldn't he be?'

'I think you know better than to ask questions, but anyone escaping from the Germans is, as I have told you before, a potential threat to security here.'

Olivia decided to accept this. She'd convinced Brinston that she hadn't known Hendrick was here. This left her safe from anything he may have planned for her. But what he was saying now made her heart heavy.

'Now, we need to talk about your war work. It must cease immediately. Any one of our German prisoners may have ulterior motives and you are now at risk of them taking advantage of Hendrick's position and getting at you to get at him.'

'But how? They won't know about Hendrick, will they?'

'The world of espionage isn't just for us British, you know. The Germans know quite a lot. Some we have deliberately fed to them, and some their agents here have given them. So we cannot take chances. You won't be allowed to help the prisoners of war any longer, Olivia. The Red Cross already know this.'

When Olivia left Brinston's office, she felt as if her world had done another somersault. All at once, she had no Hendrick, maybe for years, Annie was moving into her own home and wouldn't be on hand in the next room, and she had no war work to do either. But she took a deep breath.

This wasn't going to beat her. She'd take a trip to see Daphne, and then go to her aunt's for a while. She'd school Karl herself during these trips. Yes, he would miss Beth, but her plans would also give Annie a chance to get herself and the children settled into her new home. And then when they came back to the flat Annie was letting her have, Karl would be used to being away from Beth. And Annie . . . *Well, I hope she looks like a pudding by then!*

This thought made Olivia giggle – something she thought never to do again. But now she realized it was something she must do often, and could do, safe in the knowledge that Hendrick wouldn't be hurt by anyone, and as Annie had said, one day she, Hendrick and Karl would be together again.

It was the end of May before Olivia finally thought she could make the trip to Wales and Cornwall.

Karl was tearful when they said their goodbyes, but Rosemary helped to cheer him by telling him how much fun he was going to have. He hugged her and said, 'But I'll miss you, Gran, and everyone.'

'Ah, but you will see Daphne! How lucky are you? None of us have seen her for a long time, have we? And when you come home, you'll have my wedding and you'll be a page boy!'

They were all so happy about this that they hugged and kissed and giggled, and then asked a million questions.

Bertie said, 'Yes, it's happening at last! I've been trying to get her to tie the knot with me, but she wanted me to be totally well first, and I am now.'

Olivia thought this so sweet, and yet could see that Rosemary had more of a determined streak in her than they realized, and stood her ground over issues she felt strongly about, as her father had done too. It wasn't a wonder to Olivia now that they never married.

Karl asking what a page boy did had them laughing at his very worried expression.

'Oh, it won't hurt. You'll have to take care that all is right for me on my day and look after Beth, who is going to be asked to be a bridesmaid!'

Olivia had never been more thankful that Beth wasn't there but had already left for school. Otherwise no doubt there would be something to be said about Karl looking after her!

Daphne welcomed them with such joy it made Olivia realize how much she had missed her, but in all the worry, trying to find a direction, and then becoming needed and busy, not to mention all that had happened with Hendrick, the time just seemed to have flown since their last visit.

After hugging for what felt like an age, Daphne said, 'You've come at a busy time, I'm afraid. It's lambing season and the time for planting the crops too! So I won't be available much, unless you wouldn't mind coming to work with me? There's plenty you could turn your hand to – driving the tractor, fetching bags of hay for us from the barn on the trailer and mucking out the pigs . . .'

'Oh, stop! It all sounds wonderful, except the mucking out. Karl can do that!'

Karl pulled a face, but then giggled. 'I will if you like. I like pigs.'

'Good. You'll be up to your knees in muck, love, but it won't do you any harm.'

Karl did look a little apprehensive then, but grinned up

at Daphne, who bent down and said, 'Ooh, I could just squeeze you, but you're such a big boy now, it might embarrass you, love.'

True to Olivia's last thought, Karl said, 'I like squeezes,' and he ended up in Daphne's arms.

To have the rest of that day with Daphne was a tonic as they gossiped about anything and everything. Especially about Olivia having seen Stefan. Daphne wanted to know every detail and Olivia shared how Ricky had come home. She was dying to tell Annie's other possible news, but stopped herself as she thought it best to leave that to Annie. She did tell her about Annie's move, but couldn't say a word about Hendrick, just to tell Daphne that she was worried sick about him, which was true, but adding the lie that she didn't know anything and was just keeping her fingers crossed.

Best of all was Daphne's news that she'd heard from Loes.

'Oh, Daphne, is she all right? Does she think we betrayed her? It made it look awful with Annie's sergeant not letting us see her. I couldn't blame her if she thought bad of us.'

'Yes, she did have those thoughts. But it seems Joe wrote to Bertie about it, and Bertie told Joe in a letter what really happened. Joe then wrote to Loes – all this takes around six months or more to happen as letters to and from soldiers take ages to be delivered. Anyway, it seems that Bertie had the foresight to ask Joe to tell Loes that I was in Wales. He gave the address, and Loes wrote to me through the Red Cross. I was so surprised when her letter came. I was going to telephone you about it, but like I say, I've been so busy, and it was only a few days ago.'

'Have you answered it yet, Daphne? Only if not, can I write one and put it in with yours?'

'I don't think that's a good idea . . . It's just that Loes is very bitter and doesn't believe Bertie. At least, her wording sounds that way. I'm sorry, love . . . But, look, let me build bridges for you. I know the truth and Loes knows that I wouldn't pull the wool over her eyes.'

Olivia agreed, though was saddened that Loes thought as she did. But she didn't blame her.

'So, how is she other than this?'

'She sounds quite happy. She said they are treated well, despite them being looked on as the enemy. She's allowed to come and go and is free to shop, and to swim in the sea, as well as attend classes. She says that she is allowed to write four letters a month. What she didn't say was that the letters are censored, but I know they are as the one she sent me has parts that are blanked out with a heavy black pen.'

'That's worrying. If they don't know this, they could unwittingly write something that could make them suspect.'

'Yes. She wouldn't to Joe, as she knows his letters are censored by the army, but to me she might, and then get herself into trouble. The bit that is cut is partly about you and Annie. So I only got the gist that she thinks you betrayed her.'

'Maybe don't talk about it to her. When the war is over, we can explain – better that than get her into trouble or leave her not being allowed to write to you. I'd just put something like, "I'm so sorry you are there, but glad you're all right and have loved hearing from you and about your life. Please write as often as you can." That way, she will carry on thinking badly of us, but she won't jeopardize her future there.'

Daphne sighed. 'I agree but will feel awful not defending

you. We'll have to leave it that Joe has told her and hope she will conclude that's she's mistaken. If not, as you say, we can put it right when she's released.'

They dropped this subject at that and went on to chat about days gone by.

'Will you ever get your dad's house and your farmhouse back, Olivia?'

'I don't know. Father's solicitor is looking into everything, but he's struggling with it all. He does know that father's house wasn't part of the collateral to try to save the bank. So, if the Germans are beaten and leave our homeland, then he sees no reason why it shouldn't revert to me. As for mine and Hendrick's farm . . . well, it depends whether it's still standing and if our solicitor in Guernsey has a copy of our deeds to the farm. As you know, I had to leave everything there.'

'Oh, I hope that one day we get back all we had. And I so wish I knew if my mum was all right. I've asked the Red Cross – well, I wrote to them – but I've heard nothing.'

'I'm sorry. It's all so sad and frustrating. But I ask myself time and again what we would do without the Red Cross. I've been working for them as you know, and they're wonderful. They look after all people, no matter what nationality, creed or political alliance. If they need help, they get it.'

Karl, who'd sat quietly listening, now asked, 'Can we go for a walk, Mummy? I'm bored.'

This was so unlike him, but then he was usually at school and with Beth, so he must be feeling at odds with the world.

'We can go to the farm if you like? I can show you around and you can see the pigs. You might change your mind about mucking them out then!'

'Yes, please, Aunty Daphy! I'd love that. Will I see cows and horses? Will it smell bad?'

'All of those, young man, including the stench!'

Karl giggled. 'Will I need wellies?'

When he was all kitted out – luckily Olivia had anticipated this happening and had packed his gumboots and waterproof – they set out on what to Karl seemed a huge adventure.

To Olivia, it was a revelation seeing him with the animals. He seemed to have an affinity with them, and he watched fascinated as the vet arrived to help to bring a lamb into the world.

It was as if he was where he should be, and this made Olivia think of her farmhouse and the land they had with it. If ever they did get back to it, she made her mind up that they would have as many animals as they could for him . . .

The farm, though it was all of the things Daphne had said – smelly and muddy – was also in a beautiful setting, with rolling hills in the distance. Green fields made a patchwork with those that were ploughed. Sheep grazed, bleating every now and again as if saying all was well. And cows bellowed.

'They're ready for milking,' Daphne told them. 'They always remind us. The farmer will open the gate and they'll all come down to the shed and get into the stalls that they always use. They're amazing.'

Karl showed his first sign of fear when the herd approached pushing and shoving each other. But Olivia understood this as it unnerved her too.

But Karl soon forgot them as the vet called to him, giving him instructions.

Olivia was amazed to see him tugging the half-born lamb's feet with the vet.

'Good lad, that's the way . . . Here it comes. Careful!'

Too late, Karl landed on his bottom with the lamb on top of him. Never had she seen such joy in his face, or heard his squeals so full of delight.

'It's a ram! Well done, Karl.' The vet removed the lamb and helped Karl up.

The farmer, who stood nearby, said, 'We'll call it Karl after you, young man.'

Karl beamed as he helped to rub the lamb down to get it breathing. Then he loved having a cup of tea with the farmer and the vet out of a huge enamel mug.

'So, are you going to be a farmer, Karl?'

Karl looked up at the farmer and shook his head. 'No, I want to be a vet and help the animals . . . Is it hard to be a vet?'

As they went into a deep conversation about this, Daphne took Olivia away. 'Let's walk, love. I can see a lot is on your mind. Can you talk about any of it?'

Olivia sighed. 'I can't. But you're right. I'm feeling very depressed over everything. I just want to go home – back to how we were.'

'We all do, Olivia, though out here and working on the farm, I'm as happy as it's possible to be with missing Mum and Stefan. I love it.'

'That's good as Stefan is from a farming family, isn't he? He might want to return to it.'

'He is, but he was more of a manager, not so much of a hands-on farmer. His family are very rich, and he is highly educated – as befits an officer. It's the mucking in that I love – all of it from planting to reaping the harvest, the animals, and the dairy side. It's as if I was born to it. And I think Karl has that same instinct.'

'I think that too. While I was watching him, I dreamed of not building our house on our land but of giving it over to animals for Karl, but then I fell into this despair. Like we were saying earlier, we don't know if we'll ever return, let alone own what we did before all of this.'

They stood a moment gazing over the fields, when what her uncle had told her occurred to Olivia. He was going to leave his estate in Cornwall to her! Suddenly, she cheered. She didn't want anything to happen to her aunt and uncle – that would devastate her – but what he'd done was try to give her hope, only she hadn't latched on to it.

Now she could see that it was ideal and especially for Karl – the future did hold a promise.

Just three weeks into June they were in Cornwall. To Olivia, it was as if God was unfolding all the beauty of the British mainland to her. Yes, Guernsey was wonderful and would always be her home, but she'd let that longing overshadow all she should have seen and made dreams over.

Both Wales and Cornwall were so beautiful and rugged, and both had wrapped her in a kind of welcoming comfort blanket, almost saying to her that if her beloved Guernsey was never open to her again, they would embrace her and give her beauty and peace for her family.

This thought had brought tears to her eyes as she stood with Karl on the clifftop looking out to sea.

'So, darling, you loved the farm that Daphne works on, didn't you?'

'I did, Mummy. I didn't want to leave, and the farmer said I can visit whenever I like.'

'That's nice of him.'

'Yes, and he said you are good at driving the tractor. I had a feeling as if my heart had swelled when he said that.'

Olivia laughed but felt pleased herself at such an accolade and the pride her son was trying to convey. To her, his words were poetic and not for the first time, she thought how special he was.

'Well, none of us know how the future will turn out, but I think you will get your dream to be a vet, as long as you work hard at school.'

'I do. I love school. And I show my friends how to do the work so they will love it too.'

Olivia hugged him to her. Some of her longing for home left her then as she knew that wherever she was, as long as she had Karl and her Hendrick, she would be happy.

It was a few weeks later when they had returned to their flat in Annie's house, to a much quieter home, that Olivia realized that maybe it wouldn't be just her, Karl and Hendrick.

This morning, she'd got out of bed and only just made it to the bathroom before she was leaning over the toilet heaving her heart out.

'Mummy! Are you all right? Mummeee!'

As soon as she could, Olivia wiped her mouth, then swilled out in the sink. She turned and smiled. 'Yes, Karl. More than all right . . . Very happy.'

Karl looked at her as if she was mad. 'Ugh . . . I wouldn't be, not if I was sick!'

'Well, darling, you'll come to learn that there are different reasons for being so. My reason may be a very happy one, but that's all I can tell you for now! So, be a good boy and let's get you to Annie's, eh? Mummy has to help to pack a lot of boxes for the soldiers for Christmas.'

'Christmas! But it's only August!'

'I know, but by the time they're packed and sent on their way on a long, long journey, it will be Christmas. Now, hurry!'

Olivia felt blessed to have found new work with the Red Cross that she liked, though still it seemed strange to not have Annie, Beth, Ian, Ricky and Ruffles to come home to when she'd done a hard day of collecting items, sorting them and packing them.

But gradually she and Karl had settled into this new life.

Annie met her on the doorstep, looking rounded and glowing with health. As she greeted them, her hands were protectively holding her bump.

'You look beautiful, Annie, love.'

Ricky appeared at the door behind her, dressed in uniform. 'And what about me, mate? I reckon I cut a fine figure in me working gear.'

'Ricky! You're starting back already?'

'Can't wait, me darlin'. So I'll leave yer with Annie . . . But will yer talk to 'er and tell 'er to stop doing so much?'

'You're not a king, Dad! Besides, you have me and Ian!'

'Oh, me Beth. Always telling me off! Yes, I have yer both, me darlin', and no one better. You're me angel and Ian's me best lad, so I've room for a princess or prince as me heart's big and can swell with love for yer all.'

Beth smiled up at him and put her arms up to him. He scooped her up and kissed her cheek. 'No one can replace you in me heart, luv, but we can squeeze another in for yer to look after and keep warm, can't we?'

Beth nodded. 'Yes, Dad, I'll look after our new baby. And I'll love it too.' She kissed him and clung on to his neck.

Olivia thought the best thing to happen to Beth was Ricky and it was lovely to see the love between them.

Stepping inside, she called to Ian to ask if he was ready for school.

He put his head around the door and grinned. 'Ready, but I'm going with me mate this morning, Aunty Olivia, so can yer drop me off at me old street?'

'All right, love.' Olivia turned her attention to Karl and Beth. 'Well, you and Beth had better shake yourselves up, Karl.'

When Olivia returned from dropping the children Annie said, 'I've the kettle boiling, luv. Won't be a minute.'

Olivia looked around her and thought how Annie had soon made this little house her home. Never having visited when Lilly was alive, Olivia didn't have anything to compare it with, but gradually Annie had furnished the little house from the money she and Ricky had saved and from the sale of Lilly's old but good stuff.

The front room that led straight from the street housed a ruby-red, comfy three-piece suite, and the rag rug Annie had told her Lilly had made had been given a spruce and looked as good as new as it covered a good piece of the floor in front of the hearth. Under the window stood a table and chairs, with what Olivia recognized as Annie's mum's table-cloth draped over it.

Annie looked around the door Olivia knew led to the kitchen. 'Let's go and sit in the garden – well, the backyard, Olivia. It's a real suntrap.'

Olivia followed Annie through the kitchen – a bright, sunny room with a pot sink, a dresser, a coal-fed Rayburn, with doors leading off to the pantry as well as to the yard, the last of which they went through.

Outside was a walled-in square with a small building containing the lav. Annie had always had pots of flowers dotted around and a shelf with some trailing plants on too.

As they sat on the bench that Ricky had built long ago for his mum, and Annie put the mugs down on the little table he'd also made, Olivia linked in with Annie and told her, 'I've only gone and joined you in what they call "the pudding club" around here – at least, I think having had morning sickness a few times and missing a monthly qualifies me to join?'

Annie stared at her . . . 'What? How? Oh, Olivia . . . You and Hendrick . . . Well, I know when, but where? I can't get me head around it!'

'Ha! Bertie's boat!'

Annie squealed – a sort of cross between sheer delight and absolute incredulousness. But it didn't stop her from hugging Olivia to her, and then standing and doing a funny wobbly jig that had them both laughing out loud.

When they calmed, Olivia held Annie's hand and said, 'There will be a new dawn tomorrow, Annie, and for all our tomorrows as you and Ricky and me and Hendrick are making sure that our children will see a better world.'

'They will . . . Oh, Olivia, I just wish that it was today.'

Olivia understood. Her own longings were for that too. But bringing new life into the world held hope for them all.

Chapter Twenty-Seven

Annie

At last, it was the day of the wedding – Saturday 4 December. Umpteen things had delayed this day coming around, from difficulties with filing the banns as neither had registered as residents, to papers having to be changed and waited for, to trying to get enough food stored for the breakfast.

But here they were.

Rosemary looked lovely in her pink costume with matching hat, which had taken all of their clothing coupons but was so worth it. The fitted jacket and pleated skirt enhanced her tiny figure. None of her elegance was reduced by the addition of a fox-fur to keep her warm.

Bertie looked dapper in one of William's dinner suits, as did Ron, his best man, though one suit was grey and the other black!

Beth was a picture in the same pink as Rosemary and was kept warm by the addition of a thick knitted cardigan of the same pink, with Karl dressed in short grey trousers, long socks and a little black blazer made of pure wool. Annie had found it at a jumble sale. It had obviously belonged to someone rich, as it was the winter attire of a child who had attended a posh school. It fitted Karl to a tee.

Olivia, having had her pregnancy confirmed, wore a dark

blue suit – one that Annie hadn't seen her in before. It had an elasticated waist to the semi-flared skirt and a longer-than-usual box jacket which almost hid her bump. Daphne wore a woollen navy suit from Olivia's trunk and Rita a lovely lemon frock under a navy shawl, which she held around herself to stave off the cold, but for herself Annie proudly wore her mum's best soft cotton frock, altered a little at the waist to accommodate her bulk. Green and printed with little rosebuds, it was loose-fitting and had suited Mum being in the wheelchair. And, to keep her warm, a beautiful cream woollen shawl that her mum had kept wrapped in tissue paper. It felt to Annie as though her mum was holding her as she wrapped this around her, giving her strength that her baby was draining from her. Not that she minded. She'd give her life for the little footballer in her tummy – she was sure he would play for England with how he kicked. She'd long thought of her baby as being a boy. But really she didn't mind which sex it was. Only that it was born healthy. And that it wasn't born today!

Though a worrying niggle of pain had started in her back earlier in the day, and had her thinking – well, panicking really, as she didn't want to take the limelight by giving birth! But thankfully it had disappeared.

Carrying on as normal, Annie soon forgot it had happened as the happy service unfolded and then came to an end, and they were all heading back to what Annie still thought of as her mum's flat, but was now used to calling Rosemary's.

There waiting for them was a wonderful spread – the result of all the baking and pooling of resources the four women had done, with Annie and Ricky turning a blind eye to the black-market contribution of sugar from Olivia. Annie had guessed these were from her old boss, Olivia's Uncle Cyril.

To add to this, Daphne had brought eggs, milk and butter from the farm and Rosemary's friends had provided the flour.

Both Rosemary's kitchen table and her dresser were laden with sandwiches made from homemade bread, cakes and a mound of sausage rolls. The sausage meat they'd bought with their meat coupons.

There was even a wedding cake made by the local bakery. It was round, dusted with icing sugar and decorated with the rosebuds that Rosemary had carefully pressed over several weeks.

As they sipped sherry, ate the wedding breakfast and chatted away, Annie suddenly felt a sharp, gripping pain. She turned to Ricky, grasping his arm for support.

'Annie? Annie, luv . . . Ron, Bertie, help me with Annie. She ain't feeling good.'

There seemed to Annie to be a sea of faces around her and many arms supporting her and steering her through to her mum's bedroom.

When she lay on what used to be her mum's bed, Annie closed her eyes. *Be with me, Mum, and you, Janey, luv. I ain't ever done this before, but I can with your help.*

With this, Annie felt sure they were there, and it was them undressing her and getting her into bed. That it was them ordering that the kids be wrapped up warm and taken to the park, the kettle be boiled and clean towels be fetched, and them gently rubbing her back and holding her hand tightly.

By the time the midwife arrived, Annie was wanting to push. Then it was as if Cissy had returned as the midwife who attended had the same lovely northern accent.

'By, lass, you're doing well. It can take up to two days to really get going for a first but, eeh, you're well on your way.'

'Where's Ricky? I want me Ricky!'

'Naw, it's naw place for menfolk, lass. They've done their bit. This is women's work. Now, come on, you've more than most here to help you.'

'Ricky's gone to get some stuff from your house, Annie, love. But we're all here with you – Daphne, me, Rosemary and Rita.'

'Ooooh!' was all the answer Annie could give to Olivia.

'Push, lass . . . Good girl, that's the way!'

'Come on, Annie, love. Remember when I had Karl and you encouraged me on? Do all of that yourself, Annie, and get your baby into the world.'

As the pain subsided Annie lay back. 'I'm sorry, Rosemary, so sorry.'

'No, Annie. This is the best wedding present you can give to me – another little one to call me Granny. I can't wait . . . That's it, push, my lovely.'

'I've got its head! One more, Annie . . . Aw, there you go.'

A cry to rival any Annie had heard sent a surge of love through her. 'What is it? . . . Ooh! I – I . . . aghhh!'

'Eeh, good Lord, there's another coming! Olivia, is it? You say you've had a babby?'

'Yes . . . Do you mean there are twins?'

'There are. Now take this one and clean its eyes and then wash it.'

'I'll help Olivia. I'm practically a midwife with all the lambs and calves I've delivered,' Annie heard Daphne say.

And then Rita's voice came to her. 'And I'll help yer with this second birth, Nurse. Rosemary, yer'd be best getting a cold flannel and wiping Annie's brow.'

Annie couldn't take in all this activity, or that there was a second baby coming as her pain now consumed her. She

344

grabbed the bedstead and screamed out, 'Help me, Mum, help me!'

And then it happened, a second cry which seemed to startle the first baby, who joined in in unison.

'Have you any sugar in the house, lass?'

Olivia answered, 'Yes, a little.'

'Well, one of you make a strong cuppa with plenty of sugar in for Mum. By, she's had a shock and her energy's drained.'

Annie lay back. She couldn't ask what her children were, boy or girl. She was filled with a mixture of elation, incredulousness and exhaustion. And yes, fear, as when she glanced over, the nurse seemed to be shaking one of the babies.

But then Olivia was by her side smiling down at her. 'They're all right. Your little girls are fine . . . Oh, Annie, twins!'

'Bring them to me, Olivia, I want to see them.'

It was the nurse who answered as she came back to be beside her. 'That will happen soon, lass. We've the afterbirth to see to first. Have a couple of sips of your hot tea, and then lie back again.'

A few massages by this kindly nurse and it was all over apart from Rita and Olivia washing her.

'Ricky's back. He's brought you a nightie, and now he's having a drop of whisky for the shock!' Olivia laughed her lovely laugh. 'Let's get you all cleaned up, love, and then you can hold your babies and Ricky can come in . . . Your little girls are beautiful, Annie, just like you, though they have Ricky's curly hair.'

'Oh, Olivia . . . twins.'

Olivia hugged her. 'We'll all help you, love. They'll bring joy to us all.'

Annie glanced over and saw Rosemary and Daphne holding a child each. Her heart longed to hold them herself but knew she must be cleaned and have a clean nightie on first.

As soon as she held her girls in her arms, the love she had for them overwhelmed her. Tears streamed down her face as she watched their expressions change from kissing movements with their lips to eyes staring up at her.

All the women around her cooed over them.

'Have you any names for them, Annie, dear?'

'Well, I did have a dilemma, as I had so many lovely women to honour. But with having two of them, I can honour them all!'

She took a deep breath and nodded at the tiny form in her right arm. 'You will each have four names to honour all the women who I love and loved with all me heart . . . You, little one, will be christened Janey Vera Rose Rita. And your sister will be called Lilly Olivia Rosemary Daphne.'

'Eeh, I don't knaw who all these women are, but I hope you can get all of that on the babbies' birth certificates! By, I've never heard the like!'

'Ha, it's common in me family to have four names. I'm Annie Vera Dorothy Jane. And me sister, she . . . she was Jane Vera Annie Dorothy!'

Annie marvelled how she could say her mum's name Vera and her sister's name Janey without feeling the same dragging grief she'd always had. She held her girls tighter. *You've given me their love in two little bundles. They'll always be with us, little ones, and you honour them with your names. But now I can let them rest in peace.*

The nurse shook her head and giggled a girlie giggle. 'Well, it's time their da came in and met all eight of them!'

They all laughed at this.

When Ricky came in, he was smiling wider than Annie had seen him do for a long time. But at the same time, tears were glistening in his eyes. 'The nurse said I had eight little girls, Annie!'

Annie laughed as she explained.

'That's lovely! All lovely names of lovely ladies. Let me look at them, but first let me kiss me beautiful wife.'

Suddenly they were alone.

'Ricky, me darlin', meet Lilly and Janey. I'll tell yer the rest of it later!'

'I can't believe there's two! Blimey, I'm the dad of four kids, when I just had two this morning . . . Oh, Annie, Annie, they're beautiful. I love them with all me heart.'

His lips on hers completed her world.

It was the nurse coming back into the room who parted them. 'By, we'll have none of that in front of the kids!'

They laughed again.

'It's time to put them to your breast, Annie. The sooner it's done, the better, lass. It'll be like nowt you've ever experienced.'

'In a nice way, I hope!'

'Aye, in a beautiful way as you'll be nurturing your own flesh and blood . . . Now, Da, you've to help with this. I ain't one for thinking this part is only the ma's job . . . Now, we'll start by getting out your milk jugs, Annie, lass.'

Ricky howled with laughter and Annie joined him. Neither had heard this expression before!

Soon Janey and Lilly were sucking at Annie's breasts as if they'd always been doing it. Annie marvelled at this and loved how they each had a little hand on the breast they fed from.

Once the feeding was over, Nurse showed them how to burp the little ones – Ricky held one over his shoulder, and Annie the other.

When the door opened and Ian and Beth came running in, both scrambled onto the bed. Beth was speechless for the first time in her life, but Ian was full of questions. 'What are their names?' How was he to remember all of that?! And then, 'I love them, Mum.'

Ricky sat down on the edge of the bed and with his free arm hugged him to him. 'And they will love their big brother and sister.'

This broke Beth's silence. 'I ain't big yet, Dad!'

'No, you're still me little girl. Let me put your sister down and give yer a cuddle, eh?'

Beth scrambled down the bed and clung to Ricky's neck.

Pandemonium broke out then as the room filled with everyone, all cooing over her adorable twins. When she yawned, the nurse asked for a drawer to be made into a bed for the twins and then ordered them all out, only allowing Ricky to stay. She darkened the room by closing the curtains just before she crept out.

Ricky pulled Mum's chair up and leaned over, resting his head on the pillow next to Annie. 'I love you more than all the world, Annie, me darlin'.'

When Annie woke, she was on her own, but she could hear merriment coming through the door. She willed it to open, and then as if she'd made it happen, it did!

'She's awake! Our new mum's awake!'

This from Rita made her smile. Though she wanted to say she wasn't a new mum.

What followed was a hive of activity after the women had

helped Annie to use the commode, brushed her hair and Olivia had put a small amount of rouge on her cheeks and some bright lipstick on her lips, before the men came in and wheeled her bed into the living room.

They left Janey and Lilly in the bedroom with the curtains drawn and the door ajar so they could be heard. Not that they were on their own for long as one of the others constantly went in to peep at them.

Neither woke, not even when Olivia began to play the piano and a good old London sing-song began.

Then it was time to cut the cake. Rosemary, looking flushed and beautiful, said, 'I just want to say a few words. Olivia, you are like a daughter to me, and with Annie, brought three little ones to me who all call me Granny. And now, Annie, you and Ricky have given me an extra gift – little twins who I already look on as grandchildren! Thank you. This has been the best of days.' She turned to Bertie then, and with her words, there wasn't a dry eye in the room as she said, 'And you, my darling Bertie, have made me so happy.'

Everyone clapped as Rosemary and Bertie cut the cake, and Bertie bent his head and gave Rosemary a quick kiss on the lips.

The babies woke with the noise, and this had the women all rushing in to fetch them to Annie.

As Annie held them, she looked down at them and told them, 'Welcome to the bestest of families, made up of old friends and new, and the most wonderful daddy, sister and brother you could wish to have.'

As if acknowledging this, they each curled a hand around one of Annie's fingers. And to Annie it was as if her world had been made whole again.

EPILOGUE

Finding Peace

Chapter Twenty-Eight

Olivia

1945

Olivia stood with Daphne outside Trent Park House in Cockfosters, north London.

As if to crown an already wonderful day, the sun beamed down on them on this late June day, as she clutched the hands of seven-year-old Karl and eighteen-month-old William, named after her father. Though following Annie's example, Olivia had given him four names at his birth – William Hendrick Klaus Bertram, Klaus being Hendrick's courageous father's name and Bertram her beloved Bertie's full name.

All deserved the honour of naming her son.

In the past month she'd been able to write to Hendrick. She'd told him about William – the son he never knew he had – and had filled the envelopes with pages of love, in letters from herself and Karl, and photos of the three of them together.

And she'd sent news, bringing him up to date with all that had happened. She told him about Annie and Ricky's family – the twins, Janey and Lilly, and Ian and Beth and how they now lived in Stepney in Lilly's old house, reminding him that Lilly was the late mum of Ricky.

She'd written too about how Bertie had married Rosemary, how happy they were and how they were looking forward to going to Guernsey the next week.

Bertie is hoping to get his old job back and has heard that his old home is fine and that the islanders have cleaned it up for him. It appears it had been used by a couple of German soldiers as their home. Oh, and he cannot wait for Joe to arrive home – he's on his way by ship. Henry is with him, she'd told him. Both had survived.

Then she'd written about Rita, her boys and her father, Ron. How Rita's husband had also survived. And the best bit of news, that Loes was on her way back to them.

She hadn't mentioned her trepidation over how Loes would be with them. Or how she lay awake at night anguished about how she and Loes would ever get back to being the friends they had been.

Their friendship had started in 1938 when Loes had become nanny to Karl – how simple life had been then. How full of dreams they had all been, and how happy.

Would they recapture all of that?'

Some news she hadn't yet written about, as she'd only just heard, was that all property in Guernsey was to be returned to its rightful owners. Olivia's solicitor was in the throes of filing papers for her to reclaim her father's house and was in touch with Hendrick's solicitor in Guernsey, who assured him that the process of her and Hendrick's farmhouse being reclaimed was well advanced.

Her father's house, she had learned, was in pristine condition. A German officer had taken it over, had it repaired, and used it as his own residence. Hendrick's solicitor had written to hers, saying: *Tell Olivia that there is much that she will remember, as many of the family's possessions had been very carefully used or stored. The officer had been respectful of her home.*

The farmhouse hadn't fared so well, he'd told them. Not being in a convenient place to be taken as a residence, it had stood empty. Sadly, tiles had fallen from the roof and rain had leaked in.

But all that mattered to Olivia was that she and Hendrick would still own it and that she hoped he, like her, would like to rebuild their dream and fulfil it – only with a difference. She hoped with all her heart that Hendrick would agree to the plan she'd formed in her mind – to eventually use her father's house for the purpose of a language school and boarding house for foreign students and convert the farmhouse back to a family home. Then she could do as she'd promised herself and turn the field they owned behind the farmhouse into a small animal farm, with chickens, pigs and even a couple of sheep as it was big enough for them to have plenty of grazing. Oh, and she wanted domestic pets for her boys too – especially Karl, whose love of animals had grown to be a passion. They could have a dog as Karl and William loved Ruffles. Karl had lovingly cleaned and dressed a small wound Ruffles had sustained on his leg and tended to it until it had healed.

Her thoughts had run on to them also having a cat, and rabbits . . . Whatever Karl wanted as Olivia felt a deep need in her to make up for all he'd missed in his young life and for the fact that, though he'd had a good substitute, he'd never known family life how it should be with Mummy and Daddy and a home that was theirs and his to grow up in. Nor had he ever had a chance to know his daddy – just a few snatched days on the Isle of Sark at the beginning of the war.

Olivia hoped with all her heart that building the animal farm together would bond Karl and Hendrick as father and son, as Hendrick helped to nurture the dream Karl still held of one day becoming a vet.

Daphne moving closer to her and linking arms with her brought Olivia back to the present. 'They're coming!'

Olivia followed Daphne's finger as she pointed towards the long drive leading to the castle-like building of Trent Park House. And there he was! Her Hendrick, looking beautiful in a navy pinstriped suit. And walking beside him was Stefan. They were both the first to be released as a concession for the work done to help the British.

Olivia gasped as the sun caught Hendrick's fair hair, now back to his own colour. She saw him smiling. Saw how he looked as he had done before all of this had begun – her beloved Hendrick, tall and handsome, loving and kind. Her man.

Then she was in his arms, held tightly, with whispers of love in her ears and tears of joy wetting her cheeks as her skirt was tugged by two anxious little boys.

Drawing away, she said, 'My darling, meet your sons – one much grown since you last saw him and one you have never met, but born out of our love when we were last together.'

Two little boys looked up. Hendrick put out his arms. Karl didn't hesitate to go into them, his voice hardly more than a whisper. 'Daddy . . . are you really coming home?'

'I am. And I'm never going away again, my darling boy.'

William wasn't so sure. He clung not only to Olivia's skirt but her leg too.

'Karl, my beloved son, we have a lot of ground to make up for, but we will,' Hendrick told him.

'Yes, we can now you've stopped the bombs, Daddy, and made VE Day.'

Hendrick looked at Olivia. His love for her burned into her soul. This pleased him as it showed him how she'd portrayed him to his son.

'Well now, Karl. You have a little brother to present to me. How lucky am I? Will you do the honours and introduce me to William?'

Karl bent over William. 'Will, this is our daddy. He's been very brave. He couldn't be with us as he was making the world safe.'

Olivia smiled as her words, said many times, were repeated.

'But now, we're going to be a proper family and Daddy will look after us and Mummy. Say hello.'

William looked up at Hendrick. Hendrick squatted in front of him and said gently, 'Hello, son. I'm your daddy.' Then he opened his arms.

'Dada?'

'Yes, Dada!'

William went tentatively forward, then melted Olivia's heart as he put out a finger and touched Hendrick's face. Hendrick waited as slowly William took stock of him, and then went willingly into his arms.

Scooping Karl up too, Hendrick stood holding both boys as if they were a precious bundle. Though Olivia knew by how he swallowed hard that he wanted to cry, he smiled and said, 'Never has a daddy had two such brave boys. I'm proud of you both. Especially you, Karl. You have been through so much, and yet here you are ready to help Daddy get accustomed to the outside world and family life. I love you both with all my heart.'

'And I love you, Daddy. I kiss your photo every night to say goodnight to you.'

Hendrick held them closer and in a way that they were facing over his shoulder. His eyes met Olivia's and his lips outlined the words, 'Thank you. I love you.' His tears had free rein as they tumbled down his cheeks.

Olivia thought that there was much they would need to do to become the family they should have been from the start, but they would do it together. She and Hendrick and their sons would grow up in a peaceful world surrounded by love.

Turning then, Olivia saw Stefan and Daphne locked in each other's arms and marvelled at how two warring nations could come together in the love of two men, one born in Germany but brought up on British soil and one born and bred in Germany, for two British girls.

Daphne laughed as she caught Olivia's glance. 'At last, Olivia, at last.'

Olivia smiled. 'Yes. Our life can begin again, love.'

Back at what Olivia would always think of as Annie's home, everyone was there to greet them on their return.

Hugs and introductions followed as they all laughed and chatted.

It was Bertie who brought a more sombre note. 'We've poured the last of the sherry that each of us had kept for this day. Take a glass, everyone, as I want to propose a toast.'

When this was done, Bertie said, 'To two very brave men, who I love and respect as if they were my sons. Stefan, you and I forged a friendship during the occupation of Guernsey that kept me going and kept my faith strong in true human nature. I will be for ever grateful to you for saving Olivia and helping me to get her and Daphne safely to the mainland.

I'm sorry that in doing that you were detained for so long but I trust you have been well cared for.'

Stefan nodded. 'Excellently so, and with this man' – he patted Hendrick's back – 'who is now my best friend and who helped me, I have come through it all. I – I mean, best friend after you of course, Bertie!'

This made them laugh.

Bertie continued, 'And to Hendrick. One of our own islanders, who put himself in the gravest of danger for us and all British people . . .'

After they had all raised their glasses and taken a sip, Hendrick said, 'Thank you, Bertie. You helped me to maintain my subterfuge, and kept me safe in doing so, until Gunter betrayed me. But I had my ultimate revenge on him for all he—'

'Well, I think you both deserve a medal, my darling, and I want you to know that the past is in the past and will stay there. Whatever happened during the awful years we have been through, our losses and our heartache, our loved ones will never be forgotten, but all else will be buried from this moment on.'

There was a silence following Olivia's words. Maybe they hadn't understood and found her abrupt, but to her, she had to establish that Gunter, what happened to her at his hands, and how he met his end, must never be spoken of again. She looked around her. 'The bad things done and the evil people we came across do not deserve a place in our memories.'

Glancing at Hendrick, feeling fear that she may have embarrassed him, she saw his face crease into a smile – the beloved smile that had been etched in her heart.

'I agree, my darling. The future is ours and it will be a happy one.'

He reached out for her, and she went into his arms, to cheers and everyone hugging everyone else, as Ricky proposed another toast. 'To the new future we are going to build for our children! To peace in the world and in our minds, and a 'appy life ahead.'

They drank to this, and then as food was prepared, Olivia took Hendrick up to the flat that had been her home. Karl wanted to come too, but Annie rescued her. 'Come on, Karl, mate, yer ain't getting out of helping like that. Let Mummy and Daddy have a minute, eh?'

Karl grinned a mischievous, all-knowing grin. 'I bet they'll have a kiss and cuddle.'

Olivia blushed, but then Rosemary said, 'They better had. That's all I'd want to do if it was my Bertie returning.'

This relaxed Olivia but made Hendrick laugh out loud. 'Rosemary, I may have just met you, but I love you already. And thank you for making Bertie a happy fellow – he's not the same grumpy man who kept us all in check in Guernsey!'

Bertie's laugh filled the room, but then he said, 'You blooming kids needed keeping in check! Gave me a right runaround you did!'

Once more the laughter broke out and it was music to Olivia's ears as she and Hendrick ran upstairs.

Once there, they held each other and kissed, spoke of promises for later when they would snuggle up in bed, and swayed together in happiness.

'I can't believe all that has happened, Olivia. It's like a bad dream. I – I'm sorry that I brought up—'

Olivia put her finger on Hendrick's lips. 'Let's start afresh from this moment. We won't ever forget, I know that, and we will talk to each other whenever we need to, but we won't let the past encroach on our future.'

'You are amazing, my darling. If you're able to live with it all, then I can too. Now, show me around where I am to live until we can go home . . . If we still have one to go to.'

'We do! Oh, Hendrick, I have some wonderful news and so much to tell you of plans I have in my head. But just to say for now that Father's and our houses are safe.'

He hugged her again. 'So, all can come right for us?'

'It can and it will, my darling.'

Downstairs, Annie was waiting for her, her smile confirming that all was going to be fine. 'Oh, Annie, I'm so happy.'

'I am too, me darlin'. It's hard to believe, but we are going to be all right at last. I'm that happy for yer, Olivia, I could do a jig.'

'Ha, don't do that, love, you'll start everyone off!'

Daphne had come up to them and she was laughing, but then became serious. 'Can I have a word with you both?'

'Of course. What is it? Is something troubling you, Daphne?'

'A little. I'm worried that Stefan will have to go home soon, and well, I . . . we can't bear to be apart again.'

'Are you going with him?'

'I can't . . . well, I mean, I have my commitments at the farm. I promised to stay until the menfolk came home and took up their jobs again. That could be an absolute age . . . I don't know what to do.'

Hendrick leaned forward. 'Stefan can elect to stay. We were all told that. Most of the generals, of which there were many, did so. I'm sure it's not too late, and then Stefan can go home when his country is sorted out. I mean, things won't get back to normal anywhere for a while, but in

Germany, my guess is there will have to be a lot of conferences between the allies to find a path they all agree on as this time the Germans must never be allowed to revolt against other countries again.'

'What are Stefan's plans, Daphne?' Olivia asked.

'He does want to go home. He so wants to see his mother and father and find out how everyone is – his family, but also all the workers who worked his father's farm. Though he isn't expecting much of what they owned to be left . . . He wants me to go with him.'

'Oh dear, you have got a problem. For me, I would say follow your heart, not your loyalty. But you must make your own mind up, Daphne,' Olivia told her.

Stefan came over then. 'You look upset, Daphne. What is it?'

'I – I . . . well, I don't want you to go. I have commitments that I can't leave easily . . . Oh, I don't know. The most important thing to me is to be with you, Stefan, but how can I leave the farmer in the lurch?'

Stefan smiled. 'Then I will apply to stay, though ultimately I must go home to my parents. I have responsibilities.'

Olivia smiled as Daphne's face lit up. 'And you'll come to Wales? . . . I mean, well, there are many bedrooms in Olivia's house where I live!'

Everyone giggled. Daphne coloured but grinned too.

'Well, I will only want to use one – the same one as you.' With this, Stefan went down on one knee. The room hushed. 'Daphne, my one love, will you marry me?'

Daphne gasped, then said, 'Yes! Yes! Yes!' before hugging his neck, leaving Stefan begging to be allowed to stand up amid cheers from everyone.

When he did, he said, 'I cannot believe how well you are

all treating me. Thank you. I – I apologize for what my country has done to you and to your country.'

It was Hendrick who answered. 'You have no need, Stefan. You and I may have been born in Germany but we're not Nazis. Anything we did was forced upon us, but both of us did what we could in the circumstances . . . I know that I am a British citizen so in a little different position than yourself, but my father wasn't. He was a good man, as you are. I hope the British always welcome you and don't paint us all with the same brush.'

Stefan shook Hendrick's hand. 'Thank you. I don't know what I will find when I eventually get home, but until I left Guernsey, I did have regular communication with my parents.'

'We'll help you to find out. We'll try the Red Cross and a solicitor. Olivia has one. He's been engaged in finding out how our lives stand back in Guernsey, so has contacts.'

Stefan smiled a watery smile. Daphne took his hand. 'Whatever we have to face, we'll face it together, Stefan, but first of all you have to make me your bride.'

'Can that be done here in England?'

Again, Hendrick answered. 'I'm sure it can, but that's another question for our solicitor. In the meantime, the children are looking a little downcast, so let's liven things up, shall we?'

'I think we should take them to the park and let them 'ave a run around and then call at the pie and mash shop and all 'ave a taste of the real London. What does everyone think?'

Olivia smiled at Ricky. 'I for one think it a brilliant idea, Ricky. Hendrick loved pie and mash when I took him once but that was in the West End. There's nothing like pie, mash and liquor, cockney style.'

* * *

With glowing faces from the exercise of playing football, they all ended up in a cafe and ordered their meal.

As they ate the delicious dish, Olivia thought, *It doesn't matter where you come from, this dish and fish and chips – the good old British staples – are a treat for everyone.* She watched as Hendrick fed William some of his, and her heart swelled. Already they were bonding as William looked up at him with adoring eyes.

At that moment, she knew she was right to put the past in the past and look ahead. To her, they had a wonderful future ahead of them.

Chapter Twenty-Nine

Annie & Olivia

'It'll be fine, Ricky, luv. The people of Guernsey are lovely. You'll love it, me darlin'.'

They were all together on the dockside waiting to board the ferry.

For Rosemary, this was a new lifetime adventure as she and Bertie were going to live on the island in Bertie's cottage.

For Stefan too it was a life-changing moment. Sadly, he'd found out that his house had been hit by a stray British bomb and his parents had died. He'd been able to access funds and was determined to make a new life on Sark where Daphne's mum had settled back with her family. He and Daphne were to begin negotiations to buy a run-down farm and Daphne couldn't be happier.

For herself and Ricky, it was to be a long holiday but a working one as they were to help Olivia and Hendrick to settle back in – the truth being that she and Olivia couldn't part yet. They knew they had to, but they weren't ready. This was going to lead them up to the time when they must live miles apart once more and talk on the telephone or make visits, but they needed easing into that.

Olivia came over to her, holding the hands of the two-and-a-half-year-old twins. 'Here's Mummy. Now be good.' Olivia giggled. 'They're so excited – made so by the boys and Beth – that they keep running towards the gangplank. I'm scared they'll fall in.'

'You monkeys! I said you could stand with Aunty Olivee.' Annie loved how this name had stuck from the time Beth had christened Olivia with it. 'But you must be good!'

They turned huge dark eyes on her and looked suitably sorry. Annie wanted to laugh out loud at them but kept a straight face. She looked over to where Beth stood with Karl and Ian, holding the hand of William. It was going to be a huge wrench for them when they finally parted but she was glad they would see Karl on his home ground as for them to see where he was going to live and how happy she was sure he was going to be would enable them to imagine him in his settings, and give them some things to ask him about when they wrote to him.

'It's the excitement. I wish they'd board us all. Though Daphne's nervous for Stefan as they're both worried how he will be received, both on the boat and in Guernsey.'

'I can understand that, Olivia. But we'll all stand firm by Stefan's side. I'm sure it'll be all right. Hasn't Bertie spoken to a few folk, and told them what Stefan did?'

'Yes, and he made sure they knew what Hendrick did too, and how he spent such a long time imprisoned despite it all.'

'Well then, there you go, luv. It'll all be fine.'

'It will. Though I can't get Loes out of my mind. Bertie said that Joe has managed to get her back to Guernsey. He and Henry both went to the Isle of Man and were able to take her out of there . . . She didn't want to come to London, but said she needed time.'

Lucy, there to see them off with her lovely Dan, told them, 'Everything works out. We three know that better than most.'

Annie sighed. Their continued estrangement from Loes hurt both her and Olivia, though Daphne was certain that she'd been able to build bridges in her many letters.

Lucy was right, though. Everything worked out in the end.

At last, the barrier was moved. She, Olivia and Lucy went into a hug.

'You and Dan will come out to see us, won't you, Lucy?'

'We will. Once Annie comes back, she and I will start to plan it and save up for it. Maybe next summer . . . If . . . Well, if my baby is able to travel then!'

'Lucy!' This was said in unison by Annie and Olivia.

Lucy laughed. Dan hugged her to him. 'Right, darling, let Olivia and Annie go now. Time for *au revoir*. Their ferry's boarding.'

As they filed onto the ferry, Annie couldn't keep the excitement out of her voice as she turned to Ricky. 'Oh, me darlin', our first holiday together as a family!'

Ricky's expression told her that at last he was excited and looking forward to it. He hugged her body into his until their hips clashed. 'And yer say we're to be in a big 'ouse?'

'Yes, wait until yer see it, luv. It's lovely. And Olivia has said that we will have a sea-facing bedroom with an adjoining one for the twins and Beth. And Ian will be in the one the other side of the landing to us. It'll be on the top floor. And Olivia and Hendrick are having what was her father's suite. So, she'll need our support, luv. It ain't going to be easy for her.'

'She'll have us by her side, as well as Hendrick, and by the sounds of things, she'll very busy sorting her farmhouse out and filling the field with animals.'

367

'We all will be. But there'll be plenty of time to show yer the island . . . I need this time, Ricky, luv.'

'I know yer do, me Annie. And me trepidations are leaving me, and excitement is taking over. It's going to be smashing.'

Annie cheered then as she knew Ricky meant it. Whatever his misgivings had been, he'd sorted himself out about them and now she could relax and enjoy herself.

And it all became real to her as they stood waving to Lucy and Dan until they were a little dot in the distance. And Annie thought she'd be all right when she returned as she would have Lucy and Rita still.

She looked upwards. *And I know you'll always be with me, Mum and Janey, Lilly and Rose.*

'You all right, luv?'

'I am, Ricky. I was thinking about when we come home, how different it's all going to be, but how it will still be lovely as we've so many folk we love that will surround us.'

Ricky just hugged her to him. He didn't speak, but then, there was no longer a need for words. Life was coming right again.

They all stood on deck as the ferry approached Guernsey. It looked beautiful, as if the buildings and church spire were saying, 'Welcome home, Olivia.'

For she was home . . . At last, she was home!

As they neared the jetty, she was amazed to see a sea of faces, and hands waving.

Hendrick squeezed her. 'This is it, my darling.'

Annie came and stood on the other side of her and held her hand. Neither of them noticed Hendrick step back.

'We did it, Annie.'

'We did, luv. And yer really are home. Will yer be all right?'

'I will. I'm me now, not the me of then.'

'I know. We're different and yet the same.'

'Oh, Annie. I'm going to miss you when your holiday is over, love.'

'I know. I'm dreading it, but we've this time together to get used to it. And we will see each other every year, we've made that promise.'

Olivia leaned her head on Annie's shoulder. It all seemed like a bad dream now. But one thing that wasn't and would always be one of the best things to happen to her was the day that Annie had come into her life.

As the boat docked a cheer went up. It was deafening and yet uplifting. Olivia turned to see that Hendrick had hold of William and Karl and Ricky had the twins, one in each arm, though how he managed that she didn't know. Stefan held the hands of Ian and Beth.

They were a family, bound together by war, but having a lasting love for one another and for their children. The children too thought of the adults that weren't their parents as aunties and uncles. At this, Olivia thought of how much good had come out of the past few years. It was a thought that filled her with a sense that evil would never win.

The crowd cheered them as they went up the steps that led them through and around the rocks. And then it happened. They were being hugged and tears were being shed. And the hugs weren't just for her, Annie and Daphne, Bertie and Rosemary, but for Hendrick and Ricky, and, yes, for Stefan. Then the crowd parted and there was Loes, clinging on to Joe's hand, and behind them Henry.

Olivia forgot all else and with Annie ran forward. 'Loes . . . Oh, Loes!'

As Loes ran towards them too, they collided in the middle. No explanations, just hugs and tears and sheer joy.

The cheers began again but were silenced when the vicar of the town church of St Peter Port spoke.

'We welcome you home with open arms. And we thank you all, Olivia, Annie, Hendrick and Stefan, as we have all our returning young men, for all you have done for the war effort that eventually led to our freedom.'

Olivia looked around at Annie, saw her wipe a tear from her eye, and found her hand once more.

'It's truly over, Annie.' They hugged and then turned to see the people of Guernsey shaking the hands of Hendrick and Stefan – two German men by birth. Two honourable men, who had stood for what was right, against the fear of what might have happened to themselves, and she felt a great pride swell in her chest.

'I'm home, Annie. I'm home.'

'Yes, luv. Now we can truly know what peace feels like as we both have such a lot to look forward to.'

'Peace. What a beautiful word. Yes, the Guernsey Girls have at last found peace, Annie.'

Acknowledgements

My thanks to all the wonderful team at Pan Macmillan for all the attention they give to my books. My commissioning editor, Katie Loughnane; new to me, but it's as if we have worked together for ever. Thank you, Katie, for all your efforts in making the transition to your team so seamless. To Rosa Watmough, whose desk editing brings out the very best of my story to make it shine. And, as always, thanks to Victoria Hughes-Williams, who is responsible for the structural edit and makes sure the story flows. To my publicist, Philippa McEwan, and her team, who seek out many opportunities for me to showcase my work. And to the cover designer and the sales team, who make sure my book stands out on the shelf. My heartfelt thanks go to you all.

And a special thank you to:

My son, James Wood, who reads so many versions of my work to help and advise me, and works alongside me on the edits that come in. I love you so very much.

My readers, who encourage me as they await another book, supporting me every step of the way, and who warm my heart with praise in their reviews.

Paul Falla, the Guernsey taxi driver, who helped me so much with my research when I visited the island. Thank you, you made my day perfect.

But no one person stands alone. My family are amazing. They give me an abundance of love and support, and when one of them says they are proud of me, my world is complete. My special thanks to you all. You are all my rock and help me to climb my mountain. I love you with all my heart.

Letter to Readers

Dear reader,

Hi. So, we have finally come to the end of Annie and Olivia's journey.

Like me, I expect you have shed tears, laughed and had moments of tension, anger and fear. Yes, I feel all those emotions as I write. And when I come to 'The End', I feel bereft. Even more so when it is the end of a series, and I have to say goodbye to the characters who have lived inside my head and in my heart for eighteen months or so – it is a wrench.

If you have picked up this third book of the trilogy before reading the others, don't worry. Each book is a complete story, and you can go back and read the others to find out how the girls got to this point and still enjoy the series.

And if you have enjoyed reading it, as your first or as a conclusion to the series, may I ask you to show your appreciation in the very best way you can: by leaving me a review? Reviews are like hugs to an author.

And now for the question I am always asked: What comes next?

In the spring, the first of my stand-alone novels will be published – *Mia's Promise*. I had so looked forward to completing my characters' stories in one book, and I wasn't disappointed. It made such a pleasant change not to have to set up storylines that were threads for the next in the series. To have a beginning, a middle and no asking, 'What happens next?' when you come to the end. I hope you enjoy it too.

As I write this, the book is approaching the structural editing stage, and I'll be working on that next. But by the time you read this book, *Mia's Promise* will almost be at the fourth stage – proofreading – and may even have had a cover designed too.

If you have any comments you would like to share with me personally, I love interacting with readers and will always personally reply to emails and messages. You can see my contact details below.

Don't forget that I am also available for talks to any groups, and in libraries. Here are my contact details to chat, or for bookings:

My Facebook page, where you can 'like' and 'follow' me: www.facebook.com/MaryWoodAuthor
My Instagram: www.instagram.com/mary.wood.7796420
My TikTok: www.tiktok.com/@marywood616
My X: www.twitter.com/Authormary

And for news and email contact, my website: www.author-marywood.com/contact-subscribe

Take care of yourselves and others.
Much love,
Mary x

If you enjoyed
The Guernsey Girls Find Peace
then you'll love
The Jam Factory Girls

**Whatever life throws at them,
they will face it together**

Life for Elsie is difficult as she struggles to cope with her alcoholic mother. Caring for her siblings and working long hours at Swift's Jam Factory in London's Bermondsey is exhausting. Thankfully her lifelong friendship with Dot helps to smooth over life's rough edges.

When Elsie and Dot meet Millie Hawkesfield, the boss's daughter, they are nervous to be in her presence. Over time, they are surprised to feel so drawn to her, but should two cockney girls be socializing in such circles?

When disaster strikes, it binds the women in ways they could never have imagined. And long-held secrets are revealed that will change all their lives . . .

The Jam Factory Girls series continues with
Secrets of the Jam Factory Girls and *The Jam Factory Girls
Fight Back*, all available to read now.

The Forgotten Daughter

**Book One in
The Girls Who Went to War series**

From a tender age, Flora felt unloved and unwanted by her parents, but she finds safety in the arms of caring Nanny Pru. But when Pru is cast out of the family home, under a shadow of secrets and with a baby boy of her own on the way, it shatters little Flora.

Over the years, however, Flora and Pru meet in secret – unbeknown to Flora's parents. Pru becomes the mother she never had, and Flora grows into a fine young woman. When she signs up as a volunteer with St John Ambulance, she begins to shape her life. But the drum of war beats loudly and her world is turned upside down when she receives a letter asking her to join the Red Cross in Belgium.

With the fate of the country in the balance, it is a time for bravery. Flora's determined to be the strong woman she was destined to be. But with horror, loss and heartache on her horizon, there's a lot for young Flora to learn . . .

The Girls Who Went to War series continues with
The Abandoned Daughter, *The Wronged Daughter* and
The Brave Daughters, all available to read now.

The Orphanage Girls

Children deserve a family to call their own

Ruth dares to dream of another life – far away from the horrors within the walls of Bethnal Green's infamous orphanage. Luckily she has her friends, Amy and Ellen, but she can't keep them safe, and the suffering is only getting worse. Surely there must be a way out?

But when Ruth breaks free from the shackles of confinement and sets out into East London, hoping to make a new life for herself, she finds that, for a girl with nowhere to turn, life can be just as tough on the outside.

Bett keeps order in this unruly part of the East End and she takes Ruth under her wing alongside fellow orphanage escapee Robbie. But it is Rebekah, a kindly woman, who offers Ruth and Robbie a home – something neither has ever known. Yet even these two stalwart women cannot protect them when the police learn of an orphan on the run. It is then that Ruth must do everything in her power to hide. Her life – and those of the friends she left behind at the orphanage – depend on it.

The Orphanage Girls series continues with *The Orphanage Girls Reunited* and *The Orphanage Girls Come Home*, all available to read now.